FIRST NIGHT
BY
DEBRA WEBB

AND

CHRISTMAS GUARDIAN
BY
DELORES FOSSEN

MILLS & BOON

Cool fingers touched her shoulder.

Merri's eyelids opened and she sat up from the tub, crossing her arms to cover herself.

Brandon Thomas stood next to the tub. His bare chest immediately captured Merri's attention. Wide shoulders, lean waist and lots of muscled terrain in between. The jeans hung low on his hips, giving just a glimpse of the dark, silky hair that vee'd down to off-limits territory.

"Is something wrong?" She really didn't know what else to say.

"The house phone is ringing off the hook." He planted his hands on those lean hips. "Didn't you hear it?"

She twisted the faucet knobs to the off position then flashed him a proper glare. "I guess not." Her chin shot up a little as defiance arrowed through her. "The water was running and the door was closed."

"What do you want me to do?"

Climb in here with me crossed her mind. But this was definitely not the time, much less the place.

His dark, dark eyes connected with hers then and what she saw startled her. Approval. He liked what he saw.

FIRST NIGHT

BY
DEBRA WEBB

All the characters in this book have no existence outside the imagination of the author, and have no relation whatsoever to anyone bearing the same name or names. They are not even distantly inspired by any individual known or unknown to the author, and all the incidents are pure invention.

First published in Great Britain 2010
Harlequin Mills & Boon Limited,
Eton House, 18-24 Paradise Road, Richmond, Surrey TW9 1SR

© Debra Webb 2009

ISBN: 978 0 263 88278 0

46-1210

Harlequin Mills & Boon policy is to use papers that are natural, renewable and recyclable products and made from wood grown in sustainable forests. The logging and manufacturing processes conform to the legal environmental regulations of the country of origin.

Printed and bound in Spain
by Litografia Rosés S.A., Barcelona

Debra Webb was born in Scottsboro, Alabama, to parents who taught her that anything is possible if you want it badly enough. She began writing at age nine. Eventually, she met and married the man of her dreams, and tried some other occupations, including selling vacuum cleaners, working in a factory, a day-care center, a hospital and a department store. When her husband joined the military, they moved to Berlin and Debra became a secretary in the commanding general's office. By 1985 they were back in the States, and finally moved to Tennessee, to a small town where everyone knows everyone else. With the support of her husband and two beautiful daughters, Debra took up writing again, looking to mysteries and movies for inspiration. In 1998, her dream of writing for Mills & Boon came true. You can write to Debra with your comments at PO Box 64, Huntland, Tennessee 37345, USA, or visit her website at www.debrawebb.com to find out exciting news about her next book.

This story is dedicated to all the loyal fans who couldn't wait to read the next story featuring Merrilee Walters.

Chapter One

Merrilee Walters shut down her computer and sighed. Her first report as an assistant field investigator was complete. She smiled. She was a full-fledged Colby Agency investigator now.

Merri slid back her chair and stood. She'd proven to Ian Michaels, the second-in-command here at the Colby Agency, that she could pull her weight despite her disability. Ian was still dubious, hence the continued insistence that for a time Merri would be teamed with another investigator on a case. Getting past that final test would be a breeze.

Pulling on her coat, she considered the seven years that had passed since she'd lost her ability to hear. Life had been tough at first. Being a grown woman and an elementary schoolteacher at the time, she'd had to work particularly hard to regain her bearings. She'd taken a year off from work to adjust to this new soundless world of hers and during that time she'd realized that returning to the world of teaching wasn't possible.

Not for her, anyway.

She'd also realized during that time that she had not lived up to her expectations—expectations she hadn't even realized she'd had at the time.

Merri grabbed her purse and shook her head as she recalled those confusing months. She'd lacked the confidence necessary to have a classroom full of elementary students depending upon her when she couldn't hear a single word or sound. Anything could have happened when she had her back turned, to write on the blackboard for instance. But there had been *more* missing.

Her family had been worried. Her country singer fiancé had broken off their engagement.

Life had pretty much sucked.

Until she'd realized, sort of by trial and error, her true calling. Another smile tugged at her lips. She'd come a long way since then.

Merri turned off the light and stepped out of her office. A stint with Nashville's Metro Police

Department had provided the challenge she'd needed and the opportunity to prove she was still a viable member of society. Not to mention she'd had a hell of an adventure.

Four years as a detective back in Nashville had been good, but she'd needed a change. She'd needed to do something more, something much more personal. Victoria Colby-Camp had been willing to take her on and Merri had made a move north, leaving behind the two men who'd turned her world upside down—Detective Steven Barlow and former Mob wiseguy Mason Conrad.

Talk about covering both ends of the spectrum.

Merri had needed a change, professionally and personally. No offense to her colleagues, and certainly not to her family.

She paused in the lobby to peer out the window at the falling snow. She liked Chicago. It was a lot colder than in Nashville and her folks were seriously missing her, but the change had been a good one. One she'd needed on every level.

The rest of the agency staff had gone home for the day. There were last-minute Christmas shopping and holiday parties. But Merri had already done her shopping. Presents to her family had gone into the mail last week. She didn't know enough folks to be invited to any parties, except for the Colby Agency New Year's party. But that was okay. Merri was still getting her Yankee legs under her. And she felt comfortable with being all by herself on Christmas.

If she had gone home, her family would have spent the entire holiday explaining how she needed to come back home to them. One or more of her former colleagues would have dropped by to say how sorely she was missed.

Maybe next year. Right now, she needed distance…distance and time.

She pressed the call button for the elevator and considered what she should have for dinner on the way home. It was actually cheaper for one to eat out and the restaurant crowd prevented her from eating alone, which was something she, as much as she hated to admit it, missed about being back home. Her close-knit family liked nothing better than to get together over a big meal—no special occasion needed.

The elevator light for her floor blinked and the doors prepared to glide open.

"Finally." One would think that with most everyone in the building gone for the day that the elevators would be ready instantly. Never happened. The elegant cars had one speed—*slow*.

The doors slid apart and Merri prepared to move forward.

A blur of movement had her stumbling back several steps.

"You have to…me."

Merri blinked, stared at the man's face. He'd said something but, distracted by his unexpected burst from the car, she'd missed part of it.

"Excuse me?" She kept her attention fully on the man's face this time.

"I need help."

His frantic expression and the fear in his eyes told her he was in trouble. "What's wrong?" She should have just told him they were closed, but she couldn't bring herself to ignore a person in need and this gentleman was definitely in serious need.

The question of how he got past security briefly crossed her mind. But it was the night before Christmas Eve, and it was only minutes before six. Security was likely on rounds. All entrances were secured at six o'clock. A lapse in vigilance could be expected under the circumstances.

The man in front of her shook his head. "I am… my roommate was murdered and…" His head started that fierce wagging again that prevented her from a descent view of his lips.

It was then that Merri noticed the blood-splattered on his T-shirt and the fact that he wasn't wearing a coat. It was freezing outside. Snowing! He had to be nuts! Or drug-crazed.

Merri's instincts shot into survival mode. Her right hand slid into her purse, her fingers going automatically around the canister of pepper spray. "Let's start with what happened." She gestured to his blood-splattered T-shirt with her free hand.

He looked down at himself, shuddered and then shook his head a third time. "My roommate was… back at my…"

This simply wasn't going to work. Merri waved a hand in front of his face to get his full attention. "Look at me when you speak, please."

A frown furrowed his brow. Dark brown tendrils of hair fell around his face. His hair was a little long and unkempt, as if he hadn't combed it today. And his eyes—they were so dark brown they were almost black. She blinked, surprised that she'd gotten that hung up that quickly with his eyes.

"What?" he asked, the demand etched in frustration across his brow.

"Why is there blood on your shirt and where's your coat?" She wasn't going to mention her inability to hear until absolutely necessary. This man had apparently come to the Colby Agency looking for help. She was the only one here, that left determining a course of action up to her. She consciously steadied her breathing in order to slow her heart and to keep the panic in check. She was a professional. A full-fledged investigator. She could handle this. Whatever *this* was.

As requested, he directed his full attention to her face and said, "My roommate was murdered early this morning. I evidently slept through whatever happened. When I woke up and discovered his… him, I called 911. The police hauled me in. I didn't get a chance to get my coat." He shrugged as if he didn't know what else she wanted him to say.

He was wearing lounge pants, she realized. And flip-flops. Damn. His feet had to be freezing. It was a long walk from the nearest precinct to here. And since she didn't see a pocket for his wallet, he'd likely been without the funds for a cab. "So," she surmised, "you've just come from the police?"

He nodded. "They didn't arrest me, but they said I was a person of interest or—" he looked at the floor, shook his head again "—is crazy. I didn't do anything. I wouldn't kill anyone. Not even my roommate who was a complete jerk most of the time, but he was my best friend." Those dark eyebrows drew together. "He's dead."

Though she'd missed part of his words, she got the point. She considered taking him to her office, but that probably wasn't such a good idea since she was here alone. She should call Ian or Simon. Simon Ruhl was another of Victoria's seconds-in-command. He'd been really nice to Merri from the beginning. He believed in her and she appreciated that more than words could say.

Okay. Do this right, Merri.

First step, get the client at ease.

"I'm Merri Walters," she said, "What's your name?"

"Brandon Thomas."

"Well—" she gestured to a chair with her free hand "—Brandon, have a seat." Her fingers released the canister and she dragged a notepad and pen from her purse. She crossed to the receptionist's desk and leaned a hip against it, then prepared to take notes. "Let's start back at the beginning and you tell me exactly what happened. Every detail."

She had to remind him a time or two to look at her when he spoke. Most folks believed she was measuring whether they were telling the truth when she did this. Since he didn't ask why, she supposed he assumed the same. According to his statement, he'd awakened at six and discovered his roommate dead in the living room. After determining that he could not help his friend, he'd called the police. But they weren't buying his story, particularly since some of the neighbors had reported that he and his roommate, Kick Randolph, had an intensely volatile relationship. The roommate apparently owed Brandon a considerable sum of money. All in all, there was plenty of motive and no other suspects. The police had every reason to treat him as a person of interest.

Brandon threaded his fingers through his thick, dark hair. "Look, I don't know who killed him, but—" he looked straight into Merri's eyes "—Kick was into something. He was scared the last couple of days. The police won't believe me, but I'm telling you it had something to do with this CIA-type guy he'd covertly met with on several occasions."

"Can you be more specific about the man?" A CIA-type guy was a pretty broad description. Probably an analogy he made from the movies he'd seen. "Do you know the man's name or where he works?"

Brandon gave another of those adamant shakes

of his head. "I only saw him once, and that was at night from across the street. Dark hair." He shrugged. "Medium height and build."

"What gave you the impression he worked for the CIA?" Merri understood the stereotype he meant, but she needed his interpretation.

"You know. Trench coat. Fedora. Starched trousers. The whole federal agent style. Like you see in the movies."

That was what she'd thought. She inclined her head and considered what he'd told her. "You said the man had dark hair. Did he have dark hair or did he wear a dark hat?" From a distance it would be difficult to distinguish one from the other, particularly at night.

Brandon blinked as if he didn't understand the question. "I…I think it was his hair. Maybe he wasn't wearing a hat."

"But you're sure you saw him at night…from across the street?" They needed to get the facts straight. No guessing.

"Definitely at night." Brandon nodded. "I was going into the building. We live in one of the old duplexes off the South Loop. The front stoop is fairly close to the street. He and Kick were having an argument outside his car. I heard their raised voices, but I can't remember precisely what they were talking about."

"What did his car look like?" A tag number would be good.

"Dark. Blue or black. Four doors…I think. Not American, I don't believe."

If this was any indication of the kind of information he gave the police, it was no wonder they considered him a suspect. He contradicted himself almost as often as he concluded with any certainty.

"You didn't see the license plate? Illinois tag or another state?"

He moved his head side to side. "The car was parallel parked. All I saw was Kick arguing with him next to the passenger side of the car."

"You weren't close enough to make an estimation of the man's age?"

"No."

"To some degree, your roommate confided in you as to his dealings with this man. You said the meetings were covert."

Brandon nodded. "Kick said the meetings were very secretive."

"Was he working for this man? Running errands? Can you give me an idea on the nature of the business? Was your roommate gainfully employed?"

"Kick is…was a junior reporter over at the *Trib*. But he said he had the proof he needed to write the kind of story that would put him on top in the investigative journalist field. He wanted his own byline. Problem was, the other guy—the one he argued with—wanted the proof, too. He said it was Kick's civic duty to turn the evidence over to him. Kick refused."

"You don't have any idea what this evidence was or against whom it proved significant?"

"I know it was some kind of video…but I don't know what it was about or who it involved."

"Did he talk to anyone at work regarding this big story he was working?" Perhaps one of his co-workers wanted this big story badly enough to kill for it.

"No way." Brandon finally reclined in his chair, as if he'd relaxed to some degree. "Kick said he couldn't risk telling a soul or they would steal it. He couldn't tell anyone exactly what was going on. Not even me."

Merri could understand the dead man's doggedness and uncertainty about sharing. She'd been digging around in a cold case for days before anyone found out. Been there, done that. Problem was, she could have gotten herself killed…just like this potential client's roommate had quite possibly done.

She summoned her determination. The Colby Agency prided itself on solving the most puzzling cases. If Brandon was being straight with her, then he had plenty of reason to worry and very few pieces of what could only be called a bizarre puzzle. "All right, then." Merri closed her notepad, shoved it and the pen into her purse. "We'll just have to determine the nature of the story your roommate was working on and uncover the identity of this man with whom he exchanged heated words."

The fear and frustration laid claim to Brandon's face once more. "Kick kept his files hidden. What he was working on, the notes, the video, all of it could be anywhere. That man could have the story by now, for all I know. He may have killed my roommate for the information he needed." He blinked. "But what if we can't find him?"

"That's a strong possibility." Merri couldn't speculate just yet exactly what steps they would take if the only other known suspect was beyond their reach. "But," she went on, "whether we find him or not, our top priority will be proving your innocence. It's possible that the forensic evidence will do that for us. It's too early to know that yet. If the police had solid evidence linking you to the murder, you would have remained in custody. Cutting you loose means they aren't sure just how you fit into the equation yet."

There was one other thing he needed to be made aware of. "There is a possibility that if this man is concerned that you saw him, even from across the street, he may consider you a threat. If he, in fact, killed your roommate, he may decide it's in his best interests to tie up any loose ends."

"That's what I tried to tell the police." Brandon rocketed to his feet. "They questioned me for hours." His jaw hardened visibly. "I think they wanted me to confess or something. But I didn't do it."

Merri felt for the guy. "Since you don't have an alibi, we'll need to find someone who can vouch for your character enough to convince the police that you wouldn't commit such a heinous crime. Or," she offered, "we'll have to find evidence that proves, in addition to having had access to your roommate, someone, like the man you saw, had an equally strong motive for wanting to kill him. Before we can do that, we have to determine what your roommate was working on."

Brandon looked at her as if he'd just experienced an epiphany. "If the evidence hasn't been taken, I have the means to locate it."

Hold on. "You have proof of what you're saying? Then why didn't you give this proof to the police?" That would have made his life immensely less complicated the last several hours. He wouldn't have had to come here. She would already be having dinner at a fine restaurant.

Brandon bit the inside of his jaw as if he were considering a logical response. "I can't remember the riddle…the clues." He closed his eyes and shook his head. "I did tell the police but when I couldn't produce the proof, they assumed I was lying."

His face said that he desperately wished he hadn't had to tell her that last part. For the first time in a very long time, Merri wished she could hear the inflection in his voice. The little nuances that gave meaning to one's words. But she couldn't. So she had no choice but to rely on her instincts. And her instincts were screaming at her that something was very wrong with this guy and/or his story.

Maybe not with him personally, but with the sequence of events or with his reasoning. She couldn't quite put her finger on the problem, but the teacher side of her—the one that sized up kids in a heartbeat—was sounding that too familiar alarm.

"What do you mean, you don't remember the riddle or clues?" The first stirrings of fear awakened in her belly. She was well aware that drug addiction created memory lapses. She surveyed her would-be client once more. To say he fit the profile would be an understatement. But she knew from experience that first impressions were not always fair. She needed more.

"I told you that Kick kept everything hidden so no one could steal his work?"

She nodded, though she wasn't sure where he was headed with this or why he felt compelled to ask the question. Could he not remember what he'd said to her two minutes ago? Her right hand slid automatically back to her purse.

"He didn't trust a safe or jump drive or any damn thing." Brandon's forehead lined with his determined concentration. "Once when he was drunk he gave me this ridiculous riddle and explained that he kept the important stuff hidden that way. The riddle had clues to the location. I couldn't get it right for the police. They had cops checking all the wrong places." His chest heaved with a big breath. "I ended up looking like a fool and as guilty as hell."

Merri had an idea. She had used it with her students all the time. Maybe she was crazy, but she had nothing more exciting to do tonight. Her appetite had vanished in the wake of the adrenaline coursing through her veins. Truth be told, she wasn't afraid of this guy, despite the blood on his clothes.

"Do you recall how long ago it was that Kick told you this riddle?"

Another of those halfhearted male shrugs. "Couple months ago, maybe. Not all that long ago."

"Where were you when the two of you had this conversation?"

"The apartment. Drinking cold ones. Watching a game." Another shrug. "That's what we did most of the time since he was always broke. His need to sink all his earnings into the tools of his trade was an ever-present sore spot between us. I didn't like paying his share of the rent along with mine."

Merri made up her mind. "Let's take a look at your apartment."

Yeah, she probably was crazy.

But this was her case.

And she might be deaf, but she wasn't blind. If this guy made one wrong move, he would be begging for the police to pick him up again. She was well-trained and knew how to protect herself.

If her plan didn't work, she would call Simon for backup. She headed for the elevators, her client followed. When she turned back to him, he stabbed the call button for the elevator and said, "Thank you."

As the doors glided open behind him, Merri searched his eyes. "For what?"

"For taking a chance on a guy like me. That doesn't happen real often."

Chapter Two

The apartment was in an old building off the South Loop that lacked the care and restoration of some in the neighborhood. There was no elevator, so that meant climbing the stairs to the third floor. Ancient graffiti covered the stairwell walls. The tile floors were worn. The doors looked secure, but the place smelled of neglect. If Brandon had said anything to Merri on the way up the stairs, she missed it. Since he didn't look back at her in question, she assumed he hadn't.

She'd noticed him shiver once or twice. He had to be freezing, especially his feet in those flip-flops.

Brandon paused at the door marked 11 and looked at her for advice on proceeding. Two strips of official yellow crime scene tape had been placed

across the center of the door, along with a procla-
mation declaring the premises off limits to anyone
but official police personnel.

If, as he'd said, Brandon had been questioned
for hours, chances were the forensics techs had
come and gone already. The scene wouldn't likely
be released until the detective in charge determined that there was nothing else to be gained by
maintaining the off-limits edict. All that meant, in
her opinion, was that they shouldn't touch anything that might be evidence.

Been there, done that, too. Merri wasn't exactly
concerned about bending that particular rule. She
knew her way around a crime scene. Holding out
her hand, Brandon placed the key there. She
unlocked and opened the door, then ducked beneath
the warning tape. If Simon had been here he would
have called someone, a Colby connection with
Chicago PD, to get permission. But Simon wasn't
here. As long as Merri was careful and didn't
prompt any serious repercussions for the agency,
all would be okay.

She could do this.

After closing the door behind Brandon, she locked
it to be sure no one else was tempted to try the
same approach.

"Don't touch anything unless it's absolutely essential. And watch your step." She glanced pointedly at the bloodstained carpet and official signs of where the body had been discovered.

He nodded, his attention lingering on the place where he'd found his roommate early that morning.

With a long, slow perusal around the room, Merri decided the apartment was the typical bachelor pad. Not neat by any stretch of the imagination, particularly after the tossing the forensics techs had done in their search for evidence. The signs that prints had been lifted dusted most surfaces—not that there were that many pieces of furniture. A futon for a sofa, a television and a long, narrow coffee table were the only furnishings aside from a desk with its mountains of computer equipment and a drawing desk with much the same. The roommate clearly had had a serious compulsion when it came to technology. Merri hadn't once seen a setup like this outside a major tech center.

"Wow."

Brandon said, "Yeah I know. Kick didn't take any shortcuts when it came to having the latest and greatest in hardware and software. It was just his share of the rent and basic essentials for survival that he had trouble coughing up."

Merri considered the statement. "Is that why the two of you had what your neighbors termed a *volatile* relationship?"

"Mostly." Brandon glanced around his disheveled living space. "Kick didn't see this environment as permanent. He was a dreamer. Had big plans."

Whereas Brandon was a realist. That part she got. "Let's talk about the proof you mentioned." The fact that he couldn't remember exactly where that proof was didn't offer much security in the way of proving his innocence. Seemed to her that the police, given enough digging, would find some trace on the two or three hard drives of what the victim had been up to. The Feds certainly knew how to discover the unfindable when it came to digital footprints. The Colby Agency too had analysts for just that sort of investigation.

"No one will find anything related to the big story on his computer," Brandon observed when her gaze settled on his face once more.

"How can you be so sure?" No matter that his roommate obviously had bragged about maintaining a high level of security, new ways to find digital traces were discovered every day. Few could proclaim exception to that ever-changing investigative technology. But many tried. "If he worked on his equipment in any capacity, a digital trail was left behind. Even if he meticulously wiped his hard drive. There are those who know how to resurrect the smallest detail."

"No one was more aware of that vulnerability," Brandon explained. "Kick did his secret work someplace else." Brandon walked over to the desk with its mountain of hardware and monitors. The dramatic waving of his arms told her he'd said something about all the stuff there but he hadn't been looking at her so she had no idea what came out of his mouth.

When he turned to her in question, she asked, "What do you mean?" That prompt usually worked at garnering a repeat of a statement.

Brandon plopped down in the swivel chair next to the desk. "He did everything right here as long as it wasn't related to *the* story. *That* he did someplace else. The police won't find what they're looking for here."

And that was what he'd tried to explain when questioned. Merri risked turning her back on him—which meant she wouldn't know if he said anything—and wandered through the rest of the two-bedroom, one-bath apartment. The two bedrooms were furnished in an equally Spartan manner.

A bed, nightstand and dresser stood in each. No curtains, just the blinds that had likely been there a few decades. The closets had been ransacked for evidence. Mounds of clothes and other stuff had been piled on the bed.

The kitchen was tiny, with only the essentials. Two days' worth of eating utensils cluttered the sink.

When she returned to the living room, Brandon still sat in the chair at the computer desk. The telephone nearby served as the base, with two satellite handsets, one in each bedroom. The red light that indicated the answering machine was set to record incoming calls wasn't blinking. No messages. If there had been anything relevant on the phone, the police would have taken it.

Her new client hadn't attempted to follow her around the apartment and simply stared at her in question when she returned. That assured her that he hadn't asked or said anything she had missed.

"How long have you lived here?" Surely a man who put down roots for an extended period would have decorated to some degree. The quilt with all the little flowers that covered the bed in Brandon's room didn't count. A mother or grandmother had likely given that to him in an effort to ensure he didn't freeze. Either one would likely be mortified by his leaving home this close to Christmas wearing nothing but flip-flops. Not to mention the blood-splattered T-shirt.

"Three years." Brandon braced his forearms on his spread knees. "Kick moved in about six months after me. He responded to an ad for a roommate I placed in the classifieds. We became close friends over the past two and a half years."

The idea of just how much time the two had spent here gave new meaning to living sparsely. "Okay." Deciding not to shrug off her coat, Merri took a seat on the futon-style sofa facing her client. "Let's talk about the time when Kick told you about how he hid his big story."

Brandon straightened from his relaxed position immediately. He sat up straight and blinked. Merri gave him sufficient time to think about her prompt. Still, he hesitated, allowing the minutes to drag by. The confusion in his gaze and the lined expression of concentration on his face told her he was struggling with a response. The suggestion hadn't been that complicated.

She'd watched the kids in her class do this plenty of times. But Brandon Thomas was no kid. That he took so long to finally attempt an answer had dread trickling through her. If he had planned to lie, he'd have come up with something to say a lot faster. The truth should have come nearly as quickly as a manufactured statement.

Delayed reaction. That could point to a number of problems. She needed more insight into this guy.

"Was it nighttime or daytime?" she prompted.

He blinked. "Night."

Good. "You said he was drinking? Were you drinking?" That could very well be the underlying problem with his slow responses to her questions.

He started to nod, but then shook his head. "I don't really drink. Not…" His shoulders rose and fell in one of those shrugs that typically indicated indifference, but she had a feeling the action was more about hesitation for him. He was filling the time until he decided what to say next. "Not really."

She rephrased the question. "So you weren't drinking that night?"

"Maybe a beer or two." He searched her eyes a moment then dropped his head.

"Brandon."

He lifted his gaze back to hers.

"A beer or two is all?" She'd learned numerous techniques for getting around the warning that he must look at her when he spoke. She'd said that a couple of times already. Restating the warning would only raise his suspicions.

"I mostly nurse a drink. Just…to fit in. You know, socially."

That she understood. She did it too often to admit. Most folks, especially Merri, resented admitting his or her challenges. "Then you clearly recall that he specifically mentioned keeping this story—the one the man you can't identify was interested in preventing him from pursuing—hidden where no one could possibly find it."

"Yes."

"What portion of the riddle do you remember?"

"On the range." He concentrated long and hard. Several seconds. "Nothing can change. My space and no place. Invisible."

"You're sure that's exactly what he said and how he said it?" Merri pulled her notepad and pen from her purse and wrote down the words. Range could mean stove or cook top. His space could mean where he lives or works. No place? Nothing came to mind…except that she could see why the police had no idea what the hell any of it meant. She guessed Brandon's statement regarding the so-called puzzle was being run through the Bureau's ciphers to determine if it was some sort of code.

Then again, perhaps she was reading far too much into this case. Kick Randolph wasn't a high-level reporter. He was just a junior wannabe. Did the police really have any reason to extend any extra effort to solve his homicide? As much as she despised the idea, the wealthier or more high-profile the victim, the more time spent on the investigation. Considering the deceased was basically a nobody, chances were this case would end up one of two places—closed, with charges pressed against Brandon, or shoved into a cold case file.

"Maybe. I might not be remembering it correctly."

Those big dark eyes were filled with frustration and defeat. "Brandon, are you on any medication?" A guy who hadn't been drinking and wasn't on any sort of medication shouldn't act so frustrated if he simply couldn't recall the statements made by someone else. Distraction, a busy schedule, any number of excuses could explain his inability to recall the details of that night. Why not say as much rather than becoming more frustrated?

Extreme frustration. Another indicator of an underlying problem.

"No." He looked put out that she'd asked.

"Let's try something else." Another tactic she'd used with her students. "We'll try writing down the dialogue. Sometimes when you look at the written words you remember something you otherwise wouldn't."

He twisted in the chair and picked up a spiral notebook from the desk along with a pen.

"Write what you remember about that evening. Anything at all. Take your time," she assured him when uncertainty claimed his face.

As he focused on the page, she observed his ability to put his thoughts down in written form, not the writing itself, but the brain-to-fingers interaction. Slow, methodical and intensely thought-out.

Calling Simon Ruhl crossed her mind again. Not yet. She wasn't completely sure there was reason to call at this point. What would she say? *I'm sitting in the apartment of a man splattered in blood. His roommate is dead. The police consider him a suspect but I don't think he did it.*

She would definitely wait about that call.

Minutes ticked by. Three...five...then ten. Finally his fingers flattened the pen against the paper and his attention returned to her. "Done."

Now for the real test. The classic symptoms were

undeniable. But Brandon Thomas had to be around thirty years old. No question. Her assessment was not in keeping with his age. He was at least half a decade beyond the usual age guidelines. "Would you read what you've written to me, please?"

He blinked. Stared at her as if she'd asked him to light himself on fire, then he extended the notebook in her direction. "You read it."

"I need you to read it," she pressed. "Stand up and read it." She hated to add the "stand up" part but if he stood, she would be able to read his lips most of the time from her position below him.

The hesitation lasted at least half a minute. She had almost decided he wasn't going to comply. Finally he stood. As he stumbled through the passage he'd written, he glanced up at her periodically. It wasn't imperative that she catch every word, only that she could see the pacing and flow of how he formed the sentences.

Slow. Halting. As if he had a difficult time reading his own words aloud.

When he'd finished, she held out her hand for the notebook. He placed it in her outstretched palm, his expression full of guilt. He was embarrassed that he couldn't read smoothly. She glanced over what he'd written. His handwriting was bold and neat. But one thing was glaringly apparent. He'd misspelled five words. Two of those words were not only simple but used several times throughout the passage. In each instance, the two words were misspelled differently.

Merri pulled the pages, as well as the three clean ones after the last one, from the notebook, folded and placed them in her purse. She understood Brandon's situation now. As she pushed to her feet, she glanced around the compact living room once more. She would ask him about it… eventually, but not now.

"Why don't you shower and change," she suggested, "and we'll go have coffee some place neutral and try to figure out what Kick was telling you with these seemingly disconnected phrases."

Brandon tugged at the T-shirt he wore, then stood. "You'll…"

He turned away from her as he spoke. But the slumped shoulders told her exactly what he was worried about. "Don't worry. I'll do all I can to help you figure this out, Brandon."

He turned back to her then. "You're sure you're not going to slip out while I'm in the shower?"

What she'd missed was him asking if she would still be here. Made sense in light of the desperation choking his reason and logic. "I won't be going anywhere until we determine how to move forward with proving your innocence. That's a guarantee."

He held her gaze a moment longer. The heavy defeat that had weighed down his shoulders had given way to glittering fear in those dark eyes. Something shifted deep in her chest. She'd only met this guy and already she wanted desperately to help him. There was more here than met the eye, so to speak. Brandon Thomas wouldn't have a chance with the police. If they couldn't find any-one else to hang this one on, they would railroad Brandon or push the case aside.

That he trusted her enough to shower, leaving her to do as she pleased, surprised her and was likely indicative of his desperation. She under-stood it far better than she wanted to admit.

When the water was going in the bathroom, she carefully went over the apartment once more. Using a pen from her purse, she flipped through files and the desk Rolodex. A framed photograph of Brandon and his roommate showed that the two were about the same age. Both good-looking. Kick's framed degree in journalism decorated the otherwise stark wall above the desk. If Brandon had a degree, he wasn't sporting any indication of the accomplishment. The drawing desk appeared to be where he did his work. After snooping around she decided he was an architect of some sort.

In the deceased's bedroom, she found several family snapshots in the top drawer of the night-stand. Golf clubs on the bed amid the rest of the items that had been taken from the closet. Kick was not only proud of his accomplishments, he had pricey taste in attire, as well. Designer labels were stamped on virtually all of his sizable wardrobe.

Brandon's bedroom revealed quite the opposite. No family connections that she found. Not a single photo. His closet had apparently been as sparsely furnished as the rest of the apartment. He defined the phrase *living simply*.

It wasn't until she went through the kitchen a second time that she found the shared bulletin board. On the back side of an upper cabinet door was a makeshift bulletin board with numerous handwritten telephone numbers, most belonging to women. Not Brandon's writing. Something else Kick appeared to have plenty of—female atten-tion. Or, at least, their numbers.

Only three names were male, also evidently in

Kick's handwriting. Merri made a note of the male names and numbers on one of the sheets she'd tucked into her purse. Though she doubted he would keep the name of the contact Brandon had seen posted in such a way.

The cupboards were bare, as she'd expected. Mismatched dishware and flatware. The dishwasher held nothing but a cup and one small plate; the rest of the soiled eating utensils were in the sink. Microwave and oven were empty. Nothing beneath the stovetop burners. The range in Kick's puzzle definitely wasn't the one in their apartment. Not that she'd expected it would be, but she'd given it a look just the same. She had to cover all bases.

A window above the sink stared directly at another window some twenty feet across a side alley. The neighboring apartment was dark. She wondered briefly if Brandon ever came face-to-face with his neighbor via this window. A woman would have a shade over that window. She shook her head and leaned down to check the lower-level cabinets.

The cabinet beneath the sink held a few cleaning supplies but nothing else of interest.

The final place she inspected was what at first appeared to be a pantry-type closet but was, in fact, a laundry closet complete with a stackable appliances set. A white button-down shirt had dried in the washer. She wondered why the techs hadn't taken it. As difficult as it had been to see in the white laundry tub, if she'd noticed it, the techs should have. She lifted the stiff material to her face and sniffed. The pungent smell of bleach had permeated the fabric. She shook out the shirt and looked it over, couldn't see any trace of stains.

Merri dropped the shirt back into the washer and leaned forward to see if she could spot anything on either side of the stacked appliances. Nothing but dust bunnies and an old newspaper.

Closing the door, she turned back to the kitchen at large. Her breath trapped in her lungs. Clean shaven, Brandon stood in the doorway. He wore a blue sweater over a white T-shirt, well-worn jeans and the only pair of sneakers she had seen in his room.

"Are you okay?" he asked.

The realization that he'd likely spoken to her once or twice without her reacting was no doubt the reason for the question.

"Is that your shirt?" If she skirted the question smoothly enough he might leave it alone. "The one in the washer?"

He shook his head. "Kick's."

Maybe Kick just liked his whites extra white. That would certainly explain the bleach.

"You ready?" she encouraged, manufacturing a smile of assurance.

"Sure." He glanced around the kitchen as if he'd just now considered that she had likely looked at everything, hoping to find clues.

Would he worry that she'd found some secret he'd kept? If he was innocent, he had no need to worry. She had already made a preliminary judgment: innocent. That assessment remained subject to change, but she read people fairly well. She picked up no vibes whatsoever that Brandon was the type to hurt another human in this manner. Still, he was guarded.

The hint of suspicion that lingered in his eyes didn't bother her that much. She figured it was as much to do with her lack of a response when he'd entered the room as anything.

"Don't forget your coat." She walked past him and made her way to the front door. There was a coffee shop a few blocks away that would work well for her purposes. She was acquainted with lots and lots of restaurants all over town since she rarely dined at home. The place she had in mind stayed open until eleven, so there was plenty of time. At that point she would decide the best course of action for delving into this case.

After ducking under the tape once more, she waited while Brandon locked the door. His pale blue coat looked lightweight but she knew from the brand, one skiers preferred, that it would keep him warm despite the chilly Chicago weather.

He stood back, allowing her to descend the stairs first. A few steps down, she glanced back to see if he had said anything. That he watched her so closely warned her that he was suspicious to some degree. She would have to share the truth with him—soon.

It was only fair.

She had already made an assessment about his challenges. Approaching the subject would be touchy and would have to wait. Her own challenge, however, would not wait. Yet she put off the inevitable. Selfishly clung to any reprieve. Her previous superior had called her on that strategy many times.

The stairwell abruptly shook as if an earthquake had rocked the entire building or block. Brandon had stopped his downward momentum and now whirled back toward his apartment. With her attention over her shoulder, Merri lost her balance and barely caught the railing before plunging forward.

When the building had stopped shaking, she turned back to check on Brandon and to better assess the situation. The door of his apartment had blown open, and now hung precariously on its hinges. Even as she stared at the unexpected sight, debris drifted downward to settle on the scarred tile floor.

Fear brushed against Merri's skin.

Not an earthquake or any other natural disaster.

An *explosion*.

They had just exited the apartment. Fifteen, twenty seconds ago! Her sense of smell was keen. She'd noticed no gas…nothing.

Instinct railed at her.

Get out of the building!

Now!

Chapter Three

"Brandon!"

He couldn't look away from the landing outside his door.

"That was an explosion!"

Something had blown up in his apartment! He blinked, stared at the door barely hanging on its hinges.

What the hell had just happened?

"Brandon!"

He turned to the woman waiting a few steps below him. The questions reeling through his mind would be the same as hers. Should they call the police? What the hell would they say? *Your crime scene just blew up.* But this wasn't just a crime scene, this was his home.

"We have to get out of here," Merri urged.

His feet were taking him down the stairs before his brain analyzed her warning. They were in danger. Imminent danger. If they hadn't walked out that door when they had…damn! It was a miracle they weren't dead.

Like Kick.

When Brandon hit the step where she waited, she grabbed his hand and rushed downward. They moved past the second floor and onto the first in record time. He moved toward the front entrance.

She held him back, her face a study in worry. "Is there a rear exit? There could be trouble waiting for us out there."

"A side exit. To the alley."

"We'll try that way."

Once more she urged him forward. He took the lead, showing the way. She stayed close behind him, weaving through the narrow corridor that ended at the only other exit on the ground floor.

Brandon hit the release on the door, bursting out into the alley between his building and the next. The cold air slapped him in the face, making him immensely thankful for the coat and sneakers. He'd half frozen this morning. The cops hadn't cared, probably could care less that there had been an explosion in his apartment, except that there might have been more evidence to collect. This was insane!

Why would anyone do that?

The tug on his hand slowed his rush toward the street. He turned back to the woman who'd stopped shy of his destination.

"We should call the police."

He tried to catch his breath and slow his racing heart. She was right. He patted his pockets for his cell phone. Tried to remember if the police had given the phone back to him. No, he decided, they hadn't, hadn't given him back his wallet, either.

Didn't matter. She had her phone in her hand before he could explain the absence of his own.

Headlights fanned across the dim alley. The vehicle had come from the narrow cross street at the back of the alley. Only the city's garbage collection truck or a delivery truck usually drove through the area. The lights bobbed as the vehicle cut around Dumpsters and trashcans, coming closer. Too close.

What the hell?

She was pulling on his hand again, moving toward the street at the front of the alley.

Hadn't she said they shouldn't go out toward the front?

But the vehicle was bearing down on them now.

After them.

Damn! What the hell?

He surged forward, letting her drag him toward the street.

Tires squealed.

Brandon ran faster in an effort to keep up with the woman one step in front of him.

"Stop!"

The male voice was close behind them. Too close.

Merri Walters kept running for the street that seemed so far away. Brandon slowed but didn't stop as ordered. She kept moving…shouldn't he?

"Stop or I'll shoot!"

Brandon dared to glance back. The blinding headlights on either side of the man made Brandon squint. But there was no mistaking the black ski mask he wore, his fire-ready stance…or the gun in his hand.

Brandon stopped. Merri's forward momentum jerked on his hand. He tightened his grip, halting her movement. He didn't have to wonder if she looked back and saw what he'd seen. She was suddenly standing next to him, staring at the man with the gun.

"Put your hands up," the man warned. "Now!"

Brandon heard the sirens in the distance. Help

was on its way, but it wouldn't get here in time to stop this man from shooting one or both of them if they failed to obey his command. Brandon's hands lifted in surrender. Merri looked at him, then did the same. He didn't know if she carried a weapon, but Brandon definitely didn't. This was bad.

"This way," the gunman ordered as he gestured with his weapon toward the van behind him.

Brandon glanced toward the woman at his side. She didn't move. Should he?

"Now!" the man shouted. "Or you're both dead."

Brandon didn't wait for Merri to make the first move. Keeping his hands up, he started toward the van. Merri followed him. Was she playing the part of reluctant victim? Trying to seem the noncompliant of the two? Sort of good cop-bad cop?

The van's side door glided open. Another dark figure popped out. Another weapon. Another mask. What the hell was this? Brandon climbed into what he now recognized as a cargo van. The interior lights were dim, but those from the dash allowed him to see that a network of canvas straps were fashioned like mesh separating the front seats from the open space where Brandon found himself. No seats. The low height of the interior forced him to lower his head and shoulders. His hands remained up as he watched Merri climb into the vehicle.

The gunman behind her shouted, "Sit. Keep your hands on your head." When she didn't readily comply, the man snatched the bag from her shoulder. She glared at him but still did not obey his order. Fear for her safety rammed into Brandon's chest.

The van was moving in reverse before the side door slammed shut. Brandon had scarcely hit the floor, his hands positioned on his head as he'd been told, before the backward momentum had him struggling to stay sitting upright. He resisted the urge to use his hands to keep his balance.

Merri practically fell on top of him as the gunman pushed her to the floor. The first man, the one who'd shouted at them in the alley, was behind the steering wheel. He continued backing the van until he wheeled out onto the cross street at the back of the alley. Brandon got a glimpse of blue lights pulsing from the street at the front of the alley.

The police had arrived…too late for them.

His attention settled on Merrilee Walters. Brandon didn't have to wonder if this had anything to do with Kick's death and his story. Brandon understood that both he and the woman he'd gone to for help were in serious trouble.

The police should have listened to him.

Now they would both likely end up like Kick.

Dead.

MERRI CLOSED HER EYES and ordered them to adjust to the darkness. She had to be able to see the faces and read the lips of anyone speaking. The mask the second gunman wore, like the first, pretty much prevented her from reading his lips. The near non-existent lighting kept her from seeing Brandon's lips well enough to understand anything he might say.

Brandon leaned slightly closer and whispered something against her ear.

She didn't understand!

She should have told him right up front. That was one of the points Ian Michaels had attempted to get across to her. She could not pretend she was like everyone else. The need to ensure her potential clients understood her lack of hearing was essential.

Ian had been right, it seemed. Simon would be immensely disappointed in her. She'd not only screwed up a case, her actions would likely get both her and the client killed.

Damn it!

Brandon stared at her, his confusion evident in his rigid posture. He had no idea why she chose not to respond to whatever he'd said.

She had messed up.

Maybe her family and Metro's top brass had been right about her. She was handicapped and didn't want to admit her shortcoming. The inability to own her boundaries was a danger to herself and anyone else. The line came up frequently on her performance evaluations.

For years she had fought that issue. Had proven time and again that she could do what any individual who could hear could do.

But she had been wrong. *This* was proof positive.

She watched the gunman standing above them, his fingers locked on an overhead strap to maintain his balance in the moving vehicle.

Brandon elbowed her. She turned toward him. He leaned in, whispered something against her ear yet again. She shuddered, drew away. She didn't dare make eye contact with him until they could speak privately. At this point he would be even more frustrated and confused.

The gunman watching over them released the strap and walked crookedly up to the back of the driver's seat. He glanced at Merri and Brandon before leaning his face closer to the webbing and speaking to the driver.

Brandon was whispering to her again. Damn it! She turned her face to his and whispered, "What?" He attempted to lean close to her ear but she grabbed him by the chin and pointed his face at hers. "Look at me when you speak," she murmured.

Another of those near constant frowns lined his brow. "What do we do now?" he asked, his nose only a few inches from hers.

Her gaze glued to his lips, she got it. "We remain calm," she whispered, "until we learn what this is about." She fixed her eyes directly on his. "No sudden moves. Do exactly as they tell you."

The muzzle of the weapon was suddenly against her head.

Judging by the way Brandon stared up at the gunman, their captor had said something, but Merri hadn't heard his approach or his words.

She looked up at the gunman. Part of her wanted to tell him she was deaf and hope that news would somehow influence his actions. But giving him any usable information would be a mistake.

"Go to hell," she said instead.

The need to grab the overhead strapping to keep his balance prevented the gunman from slapping her but as soon as he had a hold on the strap, he kicked her in the side. The air rushed out of Merri's lungs. She wrapped her arms around her middle, struggled to suck in a breath. Brandon reached for the guy, but she stopped him. Shook her head.

Brandon looked from Merri to the gunman and back. She wished she could see his eyes better. He had to be confused as hell. She'd told Brandon to do whatever they said and she had lashed out.

Dumb move, Merri. But her goal had been accomplished. Whatever the gunman had said to her, she'd covered for her inability to respond appropriately.

Brandon scooted closer, wrapped his arm around her shoulders and pulled her against his chest. The gunman aimed the muzzle at Brandon's face. He stared at it, but didn't make a comment or a move to release his hold on her. The gunman made no further attempt to separate them. She was grateful for that. Somehow she felt safer in Brandon's arms. All this time she'd fought the idea of a protector and here she was…being protected.

Though the gunman grabbed Merri's purse, he

hadn't bothered to pat either of them down. Armed or not, the weapon in the bad guy's hand kept them from attempting any escape. The man with the gun was banking on their fear.

Two more times Brandon whispered something to her. Merri turned to him, hoping he would repeat his comments, but he didn't. His continued hold on her gave her an unexpected feeling of strength. She hadn't looked at him that way. But now, with his arm around her shoulders and her upper body supported by his chest, she realized that though he was lean he was well-muscled. Funny, she realized, how first impressions were so many times way off the mark. She told herself that was why she didn't like to explain her hearing challenge when she first met a person. Her short-sightedness regarding Brandon's physical prowess was evidence of that theory. Yet their current situation was serious evidence of the opposite…of hiding her own challenge.

With no windows other than those around the driver's and front passenger's seats, she couldn't assess where they were headed. They'd gone south out of the alley. Since no hard turns had been made she had to assume they were still traveling south. She might not be able to see where they were going but she felt every slowdown and turn. So far they hadn't turned.

As if she'd spoken the observation out loud, the driver slowed and took a hard left. Brandon held her more tightly against him. He smelled good, she realized. No cologne, just the subtle scent of what was likely his soap or his antiperspirant. The urge to close her eyes and enjoy the secure feeling unexpectedly overwhelmed her. She mentally shook it off. What was wrong with her? Yes, it had been a while since she'd let herself feel anything in a man's arms. But it hadn't been that long, had it? Not to mention this was a stranger. She didn't often have reactions so strong to strangers.

Another deceleration for a turn sent her senses on alert. The van didn't speed up once the turn was made. Merri concluded that they had reached their destination. A hard stop and the change in the posture of the gunman hovering above them confirmed her assessment.

The gunman waved his weapon. Merri understood that he had issued an instruction but it was totally lost on her. Brandon released her and scrambled to his feet. He offered Merri a hand and she did the same.

The door slid open and the gunman hustled them out. Merri immediately took stock of her surroundings. She blinked to adjust to the bright fluorescent lighting. Large warehouse. The van had driven directly into the warehouse, and the drive-through door had immediately closed. A couple of unopened wooden crates sat against one wall. Another van similar to the one in which they had arrived and a generic four-door black sedan were parked inside. She counted six men, all wearing black from boots to masks. They milled about as if the abducting folks were an everyday affair. To them, it seemed, loading something into the back of the van was paramount. They paid no real attention to the arrival of the hostages. And that was what they were—hostages.

Stop, she ordered herself. *Pay attention to the details.* There was a second floor at the back of the building. Beneath that were several doors leading to what appeared to be offices.

The two masked gunmen who had picked them up led Merri and Brandon to one of the rooms or offices. The room was empty. Once they were shoved inside the door was closed and, Merri presumed, locked. Just in case, she rushed over to the closed door and attempted to open it. Locked. Definitely.

She turned back to Brandon who stood in the middle of the well-lit room staring at her.

"They're going to kill us."

She couldn't argue with his reasoning. "They're going to try." That was a given. Sometime during the run or struggle that followed she had dropped her cell phone. The fact that the 911 dispatcher had been on the line might or might not prove useful. But, as soon as the Colby Agency was contacted, and they would be contacted, that would be a step in the right direction. The agency would pull out all the stops to find her.

"We have to…"

Merri waved to him. "What?" That he'd turned around in a circle and thrust his arms up when he spoke had prevented her from getting all that he said.

He shifted to face her more fully. "Don't you get it? These guys have guns. Do you have a gun?"

"No." She had a weapon at home. But unless she was on assignment, she wasn't supposed to carry it. She wasn't supposed to be on assignment. She wasn't supposed to have a client. She wasn't supposed to allow a client, if she had one, to believe she had no physical challenge. She was batting a thousand on all counts.

"I came to your agency for help." He turned to pace. "And I got…"

Okay, time to tell him.

Merri swallowed back the lump rising in her throat. She hated this part. "Brandon."

He just kept pacing and rambling about something. She could see his lips moving but not from a view that allowed her to understand every word. She could imagine, however, that whatever he was saying about her wasn't particularly flattering.

"Brandon!"

He turned, glared at her.

"There's something I should have told you." The blood pounded in her skull. If she hadn't lost her hearing, the whooshing sound inside her right now would be overwhelming. She braced herself, looked him in the eye and prepared to confess her disability.

Disability.

The word. She hated that word.

"What?" He motioned for her to spit it out.

Just do it, Merrilee.

"Brandon, I—"

That he was staring beyond her now and his eyes had widened with worry warned that someone had walked into the room. She turned around.

A man, his mask shielding his face, slammed the door behind him.

Merri focused her gaze on his lips, or what she could see of them. The mask was a little close around his mouth but the bright light helped her to distinguish between the two.

"Against the wall," the man ordered. The pistol in his right hand was leveled on them.

Merri backed across the room, never taking her eyes off the man with the weapon.

When her back hit the wall, she demanded, "What do you want?"

The man glanced at Brandon. "He knows what I want."

Merri assessed the size of the man with the gun. Too tall and heavy to be the one Brandon had seen meeting with his roommate. It appeared to be their original abductor, the one in the alley. Merri turned her face toward Brandon. He was shaking his head and saying something. The best she could tell it was that he didn't know what the man was talking about.

The muzzle of the weapon suddenly bored into the soft underside of Merri's chin. The man's face was close to hers but she didn't miss all that he said to Brandon. "You'll cooperate or…"

She didn't have to see the movement of his lips to know he'd threatened her life. If she'd had any doubts about what had been said, the terror on Brandon's face told her all she needed to know.

"What is it you think I can help you with?" Brandon asked.

Merri shifted her gaze to the man in front of her. Her heart threatened to burst from her chest. She blocked out the pain caused by the muzzle.

"I want the video."

Video? Had Brandon's roommate actually had an incriminating video? Brandon had mentioned a video. Merri supposed it was related to the story somehow.

"I don't know what you're talking about," Brandon said at last.

Strangely, Merri felt relieved that he hadn't lied to her. Not even by omission. He evidently knew nothing of any video. Other than the bizarre clues he'd shared with her.

"By the time I get through with your girlfriend here," the masked man warned, "you'll remember everything I need to know."

With her head immobile, Merri had to strain her eyeballs to see Brandon's response in her peripheral vision.

"She's not my girlfriend."

Please don't tell them I'm with the Colby Agency. Merri prayed he would keep that info to himself for the moment. They would know who she was from her ID in her purse. But there was a difference between being a friend or girlfriend than being an investigator on official business.

"If this is about my friend…my roommate," Brandon told the man, "I don't know anything about his work or his murder. I've already told the police that trying to get information from me is a waste of time. There's nothing to get."

Merri swung her gaze to the man poking her with the gun. "We're not the police, Thomas," the bastard warned, his lips twisting slightly with smugness. "We don't care what you've told anyone else. You will tell us what you know before you die." He shifted his attention to Merri. "That's a promise to both of you."

He drew the muzzle away from her and backed up a step. "You have one hour. Think long and hard about your answer before I come back. If you don't have what I'm looking for, then you'll both die."

When the door had closed behind the gunman, Merri turned to Brandon. "You okay?" She struggled to slow her breathing. Damn, that was close.

Brandon closed in on her. "Am I okay?" He looked her over. "You're the one who had the gun in your face. Are *you* okay?"

"I'm okay." She dragged in another deep breath, told herself to remain calm. She'd been in similar circumstances before. It wasn't as if this was the first time she'd faced the threat of death.

"You were going to tell me something," he said, suspicion in those dark eyes again. "Something you said you should have told me already."

"First," she offered, she was rationalizing, using excuses to avoid the inevitable, "we have to find a way to get out of here."

He glanced around the room. No windows. One locked door. "You can't be serious."

Merri summoned the fire that she refused to let die. "You came to me for help. Trust me. We will get out of here before that bastard comes back."

She had no idea how, but somehow.

As for her deafness, no need to worry her client about that right now.

She could tell him later...when staying alive wasn't an issue.

Chapter Four

9:20 p.m.

She had to think.

Fifty-five minutes and they could very well be dead.

"These men…to kill us."

Merri stared up at Brandon. Struggled a moment to fill in the parts she had missed. Clearly he had never been in this situation before and he was scared. As he should be.

"Unless you give them what they want," she countered, an idea coming to her.

Her suggestion wasn't exactly a palatable option, but it might buy them a little much-needed time. Unless she came up with something better, that might very well be their only option.

He stared at her as if she'd lost her mind.

Maybe she had.

"Just let me do the talking," she said, in case anyone was listening. "Neither of us wants to die just because your roommate was into something he shouldn't have been." When he would have interrupted, she held up a hand to silence him. "These guys don't want us at all. They want the video Kick had. This isn't really about us. I know you want to clear yourself with the police, but this is about saving our lives. We can deal with the police later."

The confusion marring his brow told her that he didn't get it. Thankfully, however, he did as she'd asked and kept his mouth shut.

Heart thudding, Merri turned and strode to the door. She had to do this right the first time. If she missed anything their captor said, she could screw this up. There wouldn't likely be any second chances. She tightened her fingers into a fist and pounded on the door.

She swallowed, prayed that whoever was on the other side of that steel door hadn't responded verbally to her banging. When five trauma-filled seconds had passed, she reached up to beat on the door once more. It swung inward, she scarcely backed up in time to prevent the damned thing from smacking her in the face.

"Eight minutes," proclaimed the same man who had pushed them into the room. "Didn't take too long to decide that staying alive was more appealing than being dead. Aren't we proud of ourselves?"

Oh, yes, proud beyond words. And he had been listening. "Look." Merri braced her hands on her hips and stood toe-to-toe with the man. He was a good half foot taller than her and his age was showing. What she could see of his hair was gray, and he had a bit of a thick middle. No doubt the guy in charge at field level. "All we're trying to do is stay out of trouble," she allowed. "Brandon didn't kill his roommate. The guy was a total jerk but he didn't deserve to die." She shrugged. "As far as I'm concerned, he got what he deserved. I didn't know him that well. The only thing we're trying to do is stay out of trouble with the police. Problem is, we don't have a clue what Kick was up to, but we do have some idea of where he may have hidden what you're looking for."

The corners of those watchful eyes crinkled as he narrowed them in suspicion. "If you don't know what he was up to, why would you think you know where he'd hidden what we're looking for?"

Fair question. "Because he told us he was in

trouble." That was the truth as far as Merri knew. "He gave Brandon a package in case something happened to him." Since she'd made up that part of the story, she glanced briefly at her client to judge his reaction to where she was going. His brown eyes were wide with worry. "We can take you to the package. My guess is that's what you're looking for."

"How 'bout you give me the location and I'll check it out. If the package contains what we're looking for, I'll tell my men to let you go."

Though she couldn't hear the nuances of his tone, she didn't miss the haughty expression, the certainty in his eyes. He wanted the information, then he wanted both her and Brandon out of the way. There would be no letting them go.

"We could," she offered, "but that scenario wouldn't be in our best interests. Neither of us presents a threat to you. We take you to the package, you get what you want and we get our freedom. Seems like the perfect compromise to me."

He studied her eyes a moment. Assessing. "I checked out your ID, Ms. Walters. You work for a private investigations agency."

She lifted her chin in defiance of the fear that niggled at her determination. "That's right. I'm a researcher. That's why Brandon thought of me when he followed Kick's bizarre order."

The gray-haired man looked from Merri to Brandon and back. "How do I know you're not an investigator? Maybe he—" he hitched his thumb toward Brandon "—hired you to find the video for his own purposes."

She didn't have to ask for a clarification of what he meant by that last statement. Clearly the video contained some sort of evidence valuable enough to merit a blackmail situation for someone prestigious enough to be nervous. She laughed. "Do I look like an investigator to you?" At a couple inches over five feet and a lean one hundred pounds, she didn't exactly possess the stature to physically intimidate.

"I run background searches all day," she went on. "I dig up info. That's it. Brandon is my boyfriend. He didn't tell you that because he was afraid you'd do just what you did—try hurting me to get him to cooperate. I'm trying to help him. The only reason he didn't tell the police about the package was because I was afraid of him doing anything until we figured out if doing so was in his best interests."

Brandon was suddenly at her side. "…person I

can trust to help me with this. We can give you what you want. We don't care about whatever Kick was working on. We just want to be left alone."

Merri caught the latter part of his disclaimer before swinging her attention back to the man standing between them and freedom.

"Tell me where the package is—" the man withdrew his weapon "—or I'll finish this now."

The business end of the gun bored into Merri's chest. Her heart bumped her sternum in protest. He was doing it again. Jerk.

Brandon started to push between her and the weapon. He said something but Merri didn't get it. What she did get was that he shouldn't take risks like that when a weapon was drawn and leveled.

"Back off, lover boy," the man warned.

Merri placed a hand on Brandon's arm. His gaze swung to her. She shook her head at him, then promptly returned her attention to the man with the gun.

"Give me the location."

Fine. "At my agency." She held her breath. Brandon stared at her as if she'd lost her mind—again.

The tension ramped higher as the bastard stared at her. Then his lips moved. "You can't be serious."

It was the perfect setup for her and Brandon. But it sucked big-time for the man with the weapon in his hand. "I locked the package in my desk. I knew it would be safe there." Damn straight. The only thing locked in her desk that was important to her at the moment was her weapon. Not to mention, she'd just given this dirtbag a no-win situation. Now the ball was in his court.

"I'll need the key." He thrust out his free hand.

She moved her head side to side and heaved a heavy breath. "I'm afraid it's not that simple. The building is locked down for the weekend. Security is the best available. On-site personnel as well as high-tech surveillance. You won't get in after business hours without risking alerting security and the authorities." The Colby Agency had survived that kind of intrusion. Anyone getting in after lockdown would have had to do some major planning or gotten lucky about rounds the way Brandon had. Even the best security personnel went a little lax on a holiday weekend.

There were more of those pulse-pounding moments of no reaction.

Finally the man with the gun made his decision. "No problem. We'll take the two of you there. You go in and get the package. The cops show up or you don't come back, your boyfriend dies. You come back without what we want, you both die."

Simple enough.

10:55 p.m.

"REMEMBER."

Merri focused hard on the man's lips. He'd turned to stare at her from the front seat. The dim light of the van's dash was all that allowed her to see the movement as he spoke. She couldn't afford to miss a word, though she felt confident she knew what he had to say.

"You go in, get the package and come straight back to the van." He hitched his head toward where Brandon sat in the back, an accomplice holding a gun to his head. "You don't come back, you call the police, you make a single move we don't like and he dies."

"I understand." Merri reached for the handle of the sliding door. She didn't dare turn her back until she was absolutely certain the man in charge had nothing else to say. "Anything else?"

He shoved her purse at her. "Go." His lips tightened into a firm line, indicating his lack of patience and no small amount of fury.

Merri hung the bag's strap on her shoulder, opened the sliding door and hopped out. She sent Brandon one last reassuring look, hoped he understood that she would figure something out. Then she turned and walked steadily toward the building's front entrance. Her mind spun with a multitude of scenarios. It didn't matter if she produced what the man wanted; he intended to kill both her and Brandon.

She had to come up with a plan.

At the door, she reached into her purse and dug for her badge. Her cell was missing, of course—she'd seen it on the dash of the van. The bastard had obviously picked it up back in the alley. Pepper spray was missing, too. She slid the badge through the reader and the lock mechanism released immediately.

With a deep breath she opened the door and stepped into the lobby. The security guard, Raymond Shooke, was watching her from his position behind the reception desk. He smiled and said, "What brings you back here this late the night before Christmas Eve, Ms. Walters?"

She manufactured a smile. "Left something in my office. I won't be long."

Raymond moved his head side to side. "Bless

your heart. You've had a busy night. Least you won't be alone."

Merri hesitated. She had to be careful here. The man in the van would be watching her with binoculars. The massive glass front allowed a clear view into the lobby. No missteps.

"Someone else from the Colby Agency is here?"

Raymond nodded. "Simon Ruhl."

Why would he be here? Before she could voice the question, the guard went on, "I'm sorry, Ms. Walters. I know it's none of my business but when you left with that gentleman…" He shrugged. "I was worried. Since I wasn't at the desk when that gentleman came in and he looked a little strange, I felt I should let Mr. Ruhl know what had gone down on my watch."

Equal measures of relief and fear rushed through Merri's veins. "I'm sorry I worried you, Raymond. The gentleman I left with is a new client. He really is okay, as I told you." She'd assured the guard when she left with Brandon to go to his apartment that all was well. Evidently because she was Merrilee Walters, the new deaf investigator, he'd felt compelled to call in any suspicious activity.

That's unfair, Merri. Simon probably instructed security to watch out for her. Not Raymond's fault.

Raymond smiled. "The nature of the business draws some strange folks, ma'am. It's my job to double-check anything I feel uncertain about."

"Of course." She gestured toward the bank of elevators. "I'll just go up and explain things to Simon."

Raymond nodded. "Yes, ma'am."

Merri headed for the elevators, her pulse rate racing. Simon had likely attempted to call her cell. She hadn't thought to check it while she was at Brandon's apartment. Then the bad guys had shown up and everything had gone crazy.

Simon would not be happy. It was a miracle he hadn't already called in backup from Ian and/or some of the others. It wouldn't be pretty.

Problem was, she had no idea how she was going to explain this to him and have him understand.

Brandon's life depended on the next few minutes, which would play out based on her every move.

No pressure there.

She rode to the agency's floor and stepped into the reception lobby. No sign of Simon. With a deep breath, she headed for his office. They ran into each other as she turned into the door.

Before he spoke, he looked her up and down.

"You okay? I've been trying to reach you on your cell for the last hour. Ian is on his way."

Damn it. That was what she hadn't wanted to happen. "Get him on the phone now," Merri urged. Simon's gaze narrowed. Before he could voice his concern, she said, "Hurry. Tell him to park near the rear exit. He cannot come into the front parking area or the building's lower level garage. Brandon will die if he does."

Simon pulled out his phone and entered Ian's speed dial number. Thankfully, he didn't ask any questions. Merri watched his lips closely as he related her instructions to Ian. Then he added, "I don't know what's going on, but I'll call you back in a few minutes with an update." He closed the phone and slid it back into his jacket pocket. "All right, what's going on?"

She gave him a condensed version. She didn't have time to spell out every detail. "Two men are in that van in the front lot. One has a gun to Brandon's head. They're going to kill him." Either way, she didn't have to add. Simon knew moreso than she what was on the agenda of the men holding Brandon hostage.

Simon hesitated only a moment. "Let's give him what he wants."

Relief flooded Merri. "We need a video storage device. One that isn't common."

Simon grabbed her by the elbow and rushed toward the research department. Every imaginable storage device could be found in the supply closet there.

Once in the massive room with its half a dozen desks, Simon turned to her. "Get a padded envelope and put your client's name on it."

Merri rushed to the drawers of the common storage cabinet near the shared printer, found what she needed and went to a desk to get a marker for labeling the envelope. She called to mind what Kick's handwriting looked like and wrote Brandon Thomas on the envelope.

Simon had moved to a computer at one of the desks. She moved up behind him and watched as he downloaded a video from a research file that included some covert surveillance of a former client. He cut the file before the face of the man being monitored came into view. A full three minutes of footage. He removed the device and passed it to her. She placed it in the envelope and sealed the flap.

"You know you can't go back out there," Simon said when her gaze landed on his face once more.

She nodded. That would be a death sentence for both her and Brandon.

"He has your cell phone?"

She nodded. "It's on the dash of the van." She'd noticed it there as she'd gotten out.

"Good." Simon stood. "Let's go to your office."

Merri had an idea where this was going. She just hoped it would work. When they reached her office, Simon indicated the phone on her desk, the one designed for the hearing impaired. "Call your cell and tell your captor that you'll meet him at the front entrance. You'll trade the package for Brandon, then he can drive away."

"He warned that if I made one misstep he would kill Brandon."

Simon's gaze locked with hers. "He'll kill both of you if you go back out there."

No question. "So I tell him to come to the door with Brandon. I give him the package. He lets Brandon come inside. The door locks. The glass is bulletproof."

"I'll contact the police and have them head this way so they can surround the van in the parking lot before the bastards get away. It only takes a couple of minutes. I know the captain of one of the teams who specialize in just this sort of situation.

I'll tell him not to move in until I give the word. I'll monitor the situation from Victoria's office. When you give Raymond the word, he'll buzz Victoria's office and I'll tell the team to move in."

Victoria Colby-Camp's office overlooked the street as well as the small visitor parking area in front. As the head of the Colby Agency, there was an alarm wired directly from the security desk to her office.

"I'll let Raymond know what's going on. He can appear to step away from his desk and monitor you and the entrance from nearby."

Merri kept picturing Brandon's face. He was depending solely on her to make sure he got out of this alive. But Simon was right. This was their best shot at survival. "Okay."

As Simon stepped out of her office to put through his call, Merri made *the* call. She had to call twice before the bastard answered her phone. Though her cell was equipped for the hearing impaired, it operated as a regular cell phone unless that particular software was enabled with the push of a button on the side of the phone.

"You're running out of time," the man said. Merri read his words on the screen on her desk phone.

"I have the package," she said flatly. "If you

want it, bring Brandon to the front entrance and I'll exchange the package for him."

Silence. When no words appeared on the screen her heart surged into her throat. She wasn't sure her phone could relay the sound of a gunshot in words.

"No way. Get down here now or he dies."

Merri bit her lip. What if this was a mistake? What if Simon was wrong? What if… This was the only option. "Look," she said, "I really like my boyfriend, but I'm not ready to die for him. If I come out there, you'll kill us both. I don't care about you or whoever is paying you or anything else. Just bring him to the door and we'll exchange. You drive away with what you came for and we get to stay alive. It's very simple."

"Just so you know," he boasted, "I'm monitoring the police bands as we speak. If you've called the police, your boyfriend will pay the price."

Fear pounded in her brain. "You said I shouldn't call the police," she said, hopefully loud enough for Simon to hear. "Why would I do that? I don't care about that. I only care about keeping myself and my boyfriend alive through this."

Simon came into the room as she spoke. He stepped around her desk and viewed the screen. He shook his head and gave her that look that said she had nothing to worry about on that score.

More breath-stealing silence elapsed.

"Okay. I will meet you at the door for the exchange. But just because you don't see a gun doesn't mean one isn't zeroed in right on your pretty head. So watch your step."

"I understand."

The line went dead.

Merri placed the handset back in the cradle. She turned to Simon. "Your captain friend is bringing in his team dark?"

"Absolutely. And Ian is waiting in his car west of the rear entrance. Whatever we need him to do, he's prepared to act."

"I don't know who is behind this threat," Merri explained. "But I'm not sure it will be over just because we take down these guys. Unless they talk, it's doubtful that we'll get to the bottom of Brandon's problem." Not to mention that the police consider him a suspect—the *only* suspect—in Kick Randolph's murder.

"We'll deal with that when the time comes," her superior assured her. "For now, stick with the plan and whatever happens do *not* step outside the door. Stay behind the bulletproof glass."

Enough said. Simon's instincts were right on target. She hadn't expected any less from this experienced man. She had to trust that he knew what he was doing.

"Okay." Merri's fingers tightened on the package. "Let's do this, then."

The ride down in the elevator seemed to vanquish the last of the air in her lungs. Simon had moved to Victoria's office to monitor the situation in the parking lot from her massive window. Ian waited in the rear as requested.

There was every reason to believe that this would end well for all involved, except the bad guys.

But there was so much she still didn't know… that Brandon didn't know.

That he might not live to know.

Merri understood his special circumstances; she wanted to help him. If what she suspected was true, he might end up behind bars for a crime he hadn't committed.

He needed her help.

But they had to survive this night first.

Raymond had already left his post as per Simon's instructions by the time she arrived in the lobby. Exactly as planned.

Think positively, Merri.

This had to work.

Simon knew what he was doing even if she hesitated or had a misstep. He would have a Plan B.

At the door, she peered through the protective glass at the nondescript white van that waited in the lot.

Stay calm. Do what you have to do. Show this guy that sheer desperation and determination are your motives. Not that the police was standing by or that Ian and Simon were now on the case.

She waved the envelope. Waited. Nothing or no one moved. She waved it again. "Come on. I'm not coming to you."

Please, God, don't let Brandon get killed.

The front passenger door as well as the sliding door behind it opened simultaneously.

Merri held her breath.

The man who appeared to be in charge of this operation left his door open and stepped toward the opening where Brandon waited. He grabbed Brandon by the arm and started toward the building, hauling his captive at his side.

The streetlights beamed their glow across the dark lot. No other vehicles waited. Nothing moved except the man with the gun.

And Brandon.

As they neared the building, Merri fortified her defenses. She was unarmed, but that was necessary. She resurrected the proper emotions for him to see.

The two men stopped in front of the door. Merri pushed the inside release with her free hand and held the door open just far enough for Brandon to come inside.

"Send him inside and I'll toss you the envelope." She stared directly at the man in charge. His partner no doubt had a bead on her or Brandon from his position inside the dark interior of the van.

"No way. Toss me the envelope, let me confirm that it contains what I need and then I'll release him."

Thankfully Brandon continued to keep quiet. He couldn't possibly have any idea that help was all around them. Merri would have to show her appreciation for his trust later.

She tossed the envelope to the man. Simon had told her not to step outside the door. She wasn't about to disobey his order.

The man passed the envelope to Brandon. "Open it."

Hands shaking, Brandon picked at the tab until it slid across the length of the envelope. He passed it back to the man next to him.

The bastard pulled the compact storage device from inside. He frowned, then looked at Merri. "If what we're looking for is not on here, we'll be back." His gaze narrowed. "Trust me. There won't be any place you can hide from us." He glanced at Brandon, then turned his attention back to Merri. "No place on Earth. You understand me?"

She nodded, amping up the fear on her face.

He pushed Brandon toward her and turned to hustle back to the van. Merri got a glimpse of the man inside, his weapon trained on her even as the jerk walked away. She yanked Brandon inside, then pulled the door closed.

Relief flooded her, making her legs weak.

"What…the hell did…give him?"

"Let's go." She didn't have time to ask him to repeat what he'd said. Instead, she started backing across the lobby, Brandon in tow. Before they reached the halfway mark, two dark vans barreled into the small lot and SWAT personnel spilled from the open doors.

A satisfied smile tickled her lips. "That's how

the game is played," she muttered to herself. Chalk one up for the Colby Agency.

A burst of light and flame split the darkness.

The floor shook beneath her feet.

The official personnel in black charging forward were tossed about and thrown to the ground.

Merri stared in disbelief at what was left of the white van. Mangled metal and fierce flames shooting toward the night sky were all that remained.

The van had exploded with the two would-be killers inside.

How was that possible? Would the two men have pushed some sort of self-destruct button just to protect the person in charge?

That didn't seem possible. Yet it had happened.

And she still had no proof that Brandon was innocent. Their one lead had just gone up in flames.

Chapter Five

Christmas Eve, 2:15 a.m.

Brandon felt as if he were sitting in a corner after being caught cutting class. The investigator who'd willingly took his case, Merri Walters, and her associates were squaring off in the conference room of the Colby Agency.

The one named Simon Ruhl agreed with Merri's conclusion that whoever had sent those men, possibly some of the ones Brandon and Merri had glimpsed at the warehouse, were more than prepared to finish the job. The authorities had confirmed that two bodies were discovered amid the remains of the van.

Brandon swallowed back the lump of anxiety clogging his throat. He would be dead right now if not for Merri's quick thinking.

She had saved his life. The risk she had chosen to take was the only one that would have worked. Period. It had been a shot in the dark but the only one they'd had. Her associate, Ruhl, had played his hand with the SWAT folks perfectly. Yet the end result had backfired.

Brandon had to come clean with Merri soon. She'd risked a hell of a lot to help him and the job wasn't finished yet. He owed her an explanation. He'd watched how she analyzed him. How she rephrased questions to help him respond rationally. She suspected there was a problem in how he processed information.

She deserved the whole truth.

"This is a mistake," Ian Michaels announced. He was totally against Merri continuing to handle Brandon's case alone. The aloof man had scarcely spared Brandon a glance. Not that Brandon could blame him. Not really. He'd rushed into the agency's offices without checking in with security. Then he'd been the cause of one investigator being abducted along with him. And if that wasn't enough, he'd generated havoc in the agency's parking lot. Two more people were dead. Good or bad, dead was dead.

Talk about getting off on the wrong foot.

"We have the clues," Merri argued. "All we

have to do at this point is see where they lead us. We have to know what we're up against before taking measures to protect our client."

"Not exactly a stellar starting place," Michaels argued. "Our *client* is a homicide suspect with killers right on his heels. In case you haven't noticed, we're dealing with professionals here. Not some fired-up bad guys who want to interfere with whatever this Randolph fellow was up to. This is no mere grudge, Ms. Walters. This is serious. Very serious.

"As we've deducted," he continued before Merri could react verbally, "there will be more. Friends or associates of the dead men, perhaps. Whoever comes after Mr. Thomas next time won't take any chances. They will learn from this mistake and shoot first, then ask questions later."

"I would agree with you," Merri countered quickly, "but if the goal is to gain access to the evidence, taking us alive will be the ultimate objective in any scenario. Don't you agree?"

"I agree," Ruhl offered, his posture and tone far more amiable than his colleague's. "Our only option, as I see it, is that you and Mr. Thomas plunge into your search for the video and/or written evidence while we run interference from this end. The police will be all over this."

Michaels pushed out of his chair and walked to the window. He thrust his hands into his pockets and leaned a hip on the window ledge.

Brandon couldn't help holding his breath. Though Mr. Ruhl appeared to want to allow Merri to help Brandon, Michaels seemed to be the one with the power to make the ultimate decision. Not good for Brandon.

"That could work," Michaels agreed, "except we have no evidence of who these men were. We don't know who hired them. We don't even know what they're after." He sent a pointed look at Brandon. "We don't actually know anything except that three men are dead."

"Finding the answers to those questions," Merri insisted, drawing her superior's intense scrutiny once more, "is the only way to clear Brandon of the murder as well as keep him alive."

"You're certain that's what you want to do?" Michaels asked Merri, his tone less stern. His expression was almost compassionate. "Despite the stumbling block that could prove detrimental to your survival as well as his?"

They stared at each other for a full ten seconds. "Yes." Merri stood her ground. "I am fully capable of conducting this investigation."

Brandon couldn't help wondering if that last exchange had been about him and his personal *situation*. It sure as hell sounded as if that was the case.

"Well, then," Michaels pushed off the ledge, looked directly at Merri, "I suppose you should get started. I'm certain whoever hired those men is fully aware what has occurred and likely has this building under surveillance as we speak."

Brandon blocked the worry that accompanied those very true words. Maybe he should just try to find Kick's stuff alone. This nightmare had put Merri in serious danger already. He shouldn't be dragging anyone else into this, not after all that had happened. His mind kept playing the apartment and van explosions over and over in his head.

But could he do this alone?

The answer was easy—no. Obviously Merri had already warned her associates as to the severity of Brandon's personal challenge. That pointed exchange between her and Michaels left no question. She'd figured it out on her own. Brandon should have just told her from the start. But he hadn't.

He'd learned the hard way that discovering his challenge changed people's perspective about him. They saw nothing else after that. He already had enough black marks against him, considering he was the only suspect in his roommate's murder and he had no real idea what this whole thing was really about. Anything more, and he was sure Merri wouldn't want his case at all. It was a miracle that she did at this point.

"First," Ruhl suggested, "we have to get the two of you out the door under the radar of anyone who might be watching."

Despite the decision to take his case, the two men continued to speak directly to Merri. Brandon supposed he should be thankful he wasn't on his own with this. He wasn't sure what he would have done if he'd been forced to walk out the door with no support from the Colby Agency. He could deal with them acting as if he weren't in the room and speaking directly to Merri.

The agency's reputation was what had brought him here. He'd heard Kick talk about the best private investigators in the nation and the Colby Agency had ranked right up there at the top. Chances were he would never have remembered the remark, except that when he left the precinct after being interrogated for hours he'd noticed a business card on the ground while waiting at the bus stop.

The Most Private Of Investigations: The Colby Agency.

Brandon had known what he had to do.

"Let's go," Merri said to him.

He hadn't realized she had walked up to where he sat. He blinked, pushed to his feet. "What happens now?" He'd heard the decision, but he couldn't recall the sequence of events as outlined by Mr. Ruhl.

"Two more cars are on the way to the rear entrance. Slade Convoy and Ted Tallant will pull up behind Ian's car at the rear entrance. You'll exchange coats with Ian, then you, Ian and I will load into the three different vehicles, taking different directions. We'll rendezvous when it's safe to do so."

Brandon hesitated, giving Michaels and Ruhl time to leave the room since they were on their way out anyway. He searched Merri's face then. "Are you sure you want to do this?" There was something about her…the way she ignored him when she chose. As if she hadn't heard whatever he'd said or noticed something that had happened. But then, he had been in a full-blown panic most of the evening. It was possible that he was reading between lines that weren't there.

Merri placed a hand on his arm. She'd done that

a couple of times tonight. Brandon couldn't remember when a mere touch had given him so much confidence. It was as if she understood him thoroughly—which wasn't possible. She didn't know the truth, didn't know his awful secret. With each passing moment, sharing that awful part of who he was became more difficult.

"Don't worry," she assured him when he definitely didn't deserve her assurance, "we'll figure this out. The Colby Agency is the best. We'll find the truth and see that the person responsible for Kick's murder pays."

Fear nagged at Brandon. When she discovered a certain truth about him, would she still want to be a part of this?

He nodded. "All right."

She flashed him one last smile and headed for the door.

Why the hell didn't he just tell her?

"Merri!"

She kept walking, disappearing into the corridor.

He shook his head and went after her. Maybe the fact that she hadn't heard him was a sign for him to keep his mouth shut for now. Too bad he didn't believe in those kinds of signs.

Images from his apartment…finding his roommate dead on the floor...all the blood. He'd tried to help Kick but it had been too late. Then the explosion. Two explosions, no less.

He was friendless...homeless.

Damn. His feet slowed, allowing Merri to get even farther ahead of him. Kick was dead. And he had no place to go when this was over.

Assuming he was still alive when it was over.

MERRI CHECKED HER PURSE once more to see that she'd gotten everything she needed. Cell phone— she kept a backup in her desk. Weapon. Her fingers glided over the smooth steel. She'd thought those days were over. The Colby Agency had an outstanding record when it came to solving cases without excessive force. Just her luck to get the case that was the exception. She had cash. And a few other toys Simon had ensured she took with her. GPS, couple of communication devices, and two tracking devices—all miniscule in size. Except for the GPS, it was about the size of her cell phone.

She was good to go.

Simon tapped her on the arm. She met his expectant gaze. "Ian finally lost his tail," he explained.

"Excellent."

Ian had insisted on being Brandon's driver. Ted Tallant had ridden with him in case he needed backup in the way of firepower. Slade Convoy had driven his own vehicle.

Apparently whoever had been watching the agency had decided that Ian was Brandon, since he'd been wearing Brandon's coat and he had dark hair, a little long like the other man's. Ted had used Merri's coat to cover his head and the upper part of his body. Since the guy was seriously taller than Merri, she was surprised those conducting the surveillance had been fooled. Then again, Brandon was the target. More likely they had decided to follow him whether Merri was with him or not.

The three vehicles would rendezvous at Lincoln Park. Merri and Brandon would take Simon's car and go to the Colby safe house.

Off the beaten path and near the water, the place was a palace. Built when Victoria's son was a child, the house had stood empty for many, many years. It was only the last few years that Victoria and her family had started to use it again for weekend getaways. There were a lot of bad memories there. Jim, Victoria's son, had gone missing from that yard.

Just went to show that beauty and elegance couldn't protect a person when evil lurked nearby.

The house was a state-of-the-art fortress now. Merri and Brandon would be safe there, for sure. The time and space they needed for getting to the bottom of this puzzle would be available. Bridget Turner, a research analyst at the agency, had been assigned to work on putting the few lines together or sorting out possible meanings. Merri didn't hold out much hope for any real results. She was certain the answers lay one place only—Brandon Thomas's head. She had to find a way to draw out the meanings behind those phrases. Randolph wouldn't have used those phrases if they hadn't meant something to Brandon.

All she had to do was figure out how those pieces fit into the puzzle of his life.

That thought dragged her back to the idea that something wasn't quite right with Brandon. She had her suspicions but she couldn't be sure. Not one hundred percent. Pushing him for an answer would only make him question her. He'd noticed something was off with her, but the situation hadn't allowed for follow-up.

It was coming.

She understood that with complete certainty.

Simon braked to a stop along the sidewalk on a deserted stretch of street. Ian's sedan was already parked up the block. Slade's sedan eased to a stop some thirty or so feet behind Simon's.

Simon turned to Merri. "Do not hesitate to call upon me if you need anything at all. Research will be in touch regarding what they turn up."

Merri nodded. "Thank you for backing me up."

The man she felt closer to than anyone else at the agency smiled. "Don't make me regret it."

With that he emerged from the car and walked toward where Ian had parked. Merri got out and went around to the driver's side. She didn't miss the look Ian sent her way. The streetlight didn't allow her to overlook the worry on his face. He didn't like this one bit.

Wearing his own coat once more, Brandon joined her. "Can you tell me where we're going? Mr. Michaels didn't have much to say on the way here."

Merri nodded to the car. "Let's get going. I'll explain on the way."

As she drove away from the rendezvous point, she didn't look back. She didn't need to. Ian and Simon would still be debating this decision. She had to do this right so Ian would at last fully trust her. More important, she couldn't let Simon down.

Any more than she could Brandon.

Merri tried her best to fill every second of the

trip with dialogue. If she gave Brandon an opportunity to speak he would notice that she didn't hear him. Only when she stopped at an intersection did she pause and look his way, inviting his comments.

"I suppose you're right," he allowed, "Michaels was a little busy evading that tail. It probably wasn't personal."

"Exactly." When she'd run out of anything else to tell him about the safe house, she'd explained that Ian likely hadn't been slighting him en route, but had focused on the task at hand.

"Here we are," she announced as she made the final turn to the safe house address. She'd only been here once. She entered the code for the gate, then glanced at her passenger as the gates slid open.

"Wow…"

"I had the same reaction the first time I came here." Though she didn't catch all that he'd said, judging by what she could see of his expression, he was impressed. She had already explained about Victoria's family, including the harrowing years her son was missing.

"Housekeeping came while we were en route and stocked the kitchen and anything else we might need. Like clothes and toiletries." She was thankful for that since she could definitely use a shower and clean clothes.

As she rounded the hood to meet Brandon in front of the parked car, he said, "The Colby Agency thinks of everything."

"We try."

At the front entrance she entered the security code that she had memorized, then pressed her thumb to the scanner for final identification. No key was required. Only the code and an authenticated fingerprint. Simple, yet nearly impossible to breach.

Inside she closed the door and reset the alarm. She turned in time to see Brandon's lips moving. "…Colby must be rich."

"Victoria has worked a lot of years to reach this point of financial comfort." Merri had a great deal of respect for the woman. She hadn't been born into this level of wealth. She and both her husbands had worked hard to reach this pinnacle. "Come on, I'll show you to your room."

The house had a number of bedrooms. Clients were usually housed in the far room upstairs, leaving the others—closer to the staircase—for their protectors, in this case for Merri.

The light was on in the last bedroom down the long hall on the second floor. Two changes of clothes, in addition to toiletries and sleepwear, were carefully laid out on the bed.

Merri didn't have to look to know that the clothes would be the correct size. She'd estimated Brandon's sizes and passed them along to Simon.

Brandon was talking again, his attention still focused on the items spread across the luxurious bed.

"What?" She stepped closer, waiting for him to turn his face toward her.

He shrugged. "I was just saying that this is incredible." He searched her eyes. "You know, I didn't even ask." His mouth worked a moment before readable words were formed. "I'm not sure I can afford your fee. I should have asked before—" he gestured to the room at large "—all this." His arms dropped to his sides. "Before you risked your life." The regret in his expression dug at her heart.

"We take a few pro bono cases." She didn't want to make him feel bad about his inability to pay. "Sometimes," she went on, "justice doesn't have a price. We do what needs to be done."

He thought about that for a moment. Those dark eyes remained filled with uncertainty even as he spoke. "So what do we do now?"

Truth was, they had had quite a night. "We get

some sleep." Personally, she was going to take a long hot bath and then sleep like the dead for at least a few hours. At his crestfallen expression, she added, "Then we'll dig in and figure out where those phrases lead us."

When she was about to turn away, he stopped her. "How is it that no one knows about this place?"

Translation: are you sure we're safe here?

"Victoria built this house a very long time ago, more than two decades ago. She didn't use it for a very long time. Most of her friends and associates believe she sold it. You have nothing to worry about here." She lifted her shoulders, then let them fall. "There's nothing to be afraid of, you have my word. Even if somehow those yahoos followed us, there's an alarm system that is what all other state-of-the-art systems aspire to be. We're hooked directly into the agency. And—" she patted her purse "—I'm armed."

He stared at her purse a moment. "Do you know how to use it?"

One corner of her mouth lifted in a knowing half smile. God, she was tired. "I definitely know how to use it. I worked as a homicide detective in Nashville for several years before coming to the Colby Agency."

"Was there trouble in your past career?" He watched her closely in an attempt to read what her words wouldn't tell him. "Is that why you moved here? Or why Mr. Michaels sounded as if he would prefer some other investigator work my case?"

Ah, so he'd noticed Ian's innuendo in the conference room. "No. No trouble. I just decided I wanted to do something different. And Ian didn't want me to take your case because I'm fairly new at the agency. He would have preferred a more experienced investigator." That was true, in part.

Brandon's brow furrowed. "If you used to be a homicide detective in your former job, it makes sense to me that Michaels would consider you the best person for the job."

Good point. She wasn't going there. "Get some sleep, Brandon. You're going to need it just as much as I do. We'll talk about the case later when we're rested and our heads are clear."

She exited the room before he could ask another question. A long hot bath was on her agenda. In her room, the one next to Brandon's, there was a comfy nightgown and two changes of clothes. Not colors she would have picked—she liked bright colors—but she could live with it. The selections had been made with blending in mind. Beiges, tans and browns.

The bed looked so inviting, she scarcely worked up the wherewithal to go for that bath.

But her aching muscles would thank her when she awakened a few hours from now.

She turned on the faucet in the big, jetted tub, and adjusted the temperature of the water. She stripped off her clothes and stepped into the ankle-deep water. Waiting until it had filled was out of the question. A variety of bath salts and bubbly, scented oil lined the tiled edge. She picked one, poured it into the water and watched the scented bubbles build. Smelled good.

The water had reached her torso and she leaned back, letting her skin adjust to the cool feel of the tub, and closed her eyes. That wouldn't last long. Soon the water and the tub would be nice and hot all around her.

The bubbles tickled her breasts as the water level rose.

Heaven.

Her mind drifted, then floated away. God, she'd needed this.

Cool fingers touched her shoulder.

Her lids fluttered open and she sat up, crossing her arms over her breasts.

Brandon Thomas stood next to the tub, his eyes wide with something like frustration. But it was his bare chest that captured the better part of her attention. Wide shoulders, lean waist and lots of muscled terrain in between. The jeans hung low on his hips, giving just a glimpse of the dark, silky hair that veered down to off-limits territory.

"Is something wrong?" She really didn't know what else to say.

"The house phone is ringing off the hook." He planted his long-fingered hands on those lean hips. "Didn't you hear it?"

Of course she didn't. She was deaf. But he didn't know that. She twisted the faucet knobs to the Off position then flashed him a proper glare. "I guess not." Her chin shot up a little higher as defiance arrowed through her. "The water was running and the door was closed." She wasn't sure about that last part, but maybe she'd closed it.

"What do you want me to do?"

Climb in here with me, she thought with a start. She blinked the idea away. She was tired. Not thinking straight. "I'll check the voice mail. If it's urgent," she said, nodding to her cell on the closed toilet lid, "whoever is calling will use my cell."

"Okay." He shrugged those incredibly wide shoulders. "Sorry." He glanced at the bubbles shielding her naked body. "I guess I'll go back to my room."

"I'll let you know if the call was news."

His dark, dark eyes meshed with hers and what she saw startled her all over again.

Approval. He liked what he saw.

She was the one wowed now.

But this was definitely not the time, much less the place.

He stalled at the door, turned back to her. The idea that her pulse rate had climbed significantly annoyed the heck out of her.

"It's Christmas Eve, you know."

"Yeah." A slight nod accompanied her response. She hadn't forgotten, but it was just another day to her this year. "Is that a problem for you?"

He gave that good-looking head a shake. Something else she shouldn't have noticed.

Depending upon how long it took them to figure this out, maybe she would take a break and look around for an artificial tree and decorations. There were lots of places around here to store stuff.

"Good night," she offered.

"'Night."

The door closed behind him.

Merri leaned back, tried to relax again. Maybe she was in over her head.

She hadn't heard the house phone and she damn sure hadn't heard him come into the room.

First thing after they'd had breakfast, she would tell him the truth.

It wasn't as if he could decide he wanted another investigator at this point.

She chewed her lower lip.

Could he?

Chapter Six

Christmas Eve, 1:52 p.m.

On the range. Nothing can change. My space and no place. Invisible.

Merri stared at the phrases she'd written on her notepad. She pursed her lips and took a moment to consider her thoughts before she spoke. "This has to mean the place where he grew up." They had gone over every other possibility. There were no other reasonable alternatives.

"Seems logical."

Brandon's noncommittal attitude was beginning to get on her nerves. They had awoken about ten. She'd prepared breakfast with his help. He'd wanted to know what the call was about last night. She hadn't mentioned it until he'd asked because the call was nothing important, just property security wanting to ensure that all was as it should be as they settled in for the remainder of the night. Routine call.

The staff at the agency knew to call her on her cell phone. The specially designed phone would blink, allowing her to see that a call was coming in.

For more than two hours after dragging themselves out of bed and having breakfast, they had been brainstorming the phrases Kick had given Brandon a while back. He couldn't recall exactly when he'd been given this information. Sometime during the past month. For a man barely thirty, he had a heck of a time remembering the little things. But then, she suspected there was a reason for that. One he didn't want to talk about any more than she wanted to discuss being deaf.

Turner from Research had called. She'd come up with nothing more than what they had surmised on their own. Kick's selection of phrases wasn't related to any former headline or book or even a movie—at least not according to the elaborate software system employed by the Colby computers.

Kick had apparently been very careful not to connect his message to anything that would allow for easy access or misinterpretation. In doing so, he'd left Merri, who knew nothing about him other than what Google and Brandon had told her, to attempt to piece together a revealing message with little or no foundation in reasoning or logic.

"Where did Kick grow up?" she asked.

Brandon dropped back onto the sofa. Like Merri, he was still exhausted. "Blue Island. Maybe forty-five minutes from our old apartment."

The deceased's childhood home remained the only reasonable conclusion. "Home doesn't usually change." Unless there's a death or a divorce. "Home would certainly be his space and yet no place. Particularly if he didn't have any fond memories of growing up or if he hadn't been able to wait to get away."

Brandon sat up straight. "Wait. There was something he always said." His forehead furrowed in concentration. "That he was nobody growing up—invisible. He always dreamed of making it big in the city. That's why this story was so important to him. He wanted to prove they were wrong—the kids he grew up with, I mean."

"Invisible." That certainly covered the final part of the puzzle and fell in line with the rest of Merri's conclusions.

Brandon braced his forearms on his knees and

searched Merri's eyes. A little shiver tangoed up her spine. *Stop,* she ordered. Not allowed. She'd spent way too much time in the past getting personally involved with one aspect or another of a case. Wasn't going to happen this time. The Colby Agency was a new beginning for her, professionally and personally.

"Since our apartment is history," Brandon continued, "and the bad guys no doubt still want to locate the video, we have to assume, I suppose, that they're probably watching any other place we might show up. They're expecting us to lead them to the evidence."

"Like the precinct where the investigation is assigned. The *Trib.* His girlfriend's place—if he had one." That was a question she should have already asked, but then the last twenty-four hours had been a little crazy. The last couple of hours had been the only time available for thinking.

"He didn't have a steady girlfriend," Brandon assured her. "Kick liked playing the field. No permanent attachments whatsoever, on or off the job. He liked his space."

"And the homes of any close family," Merri offered. "They'll be watching those, too."

"But we have to go to Blue Island."

She nodded. "We do." There was no better place to begin this search. "With the apartment gone and no girlfriend to check out, that leaves work and where he grew up."

Brandon's head was moving side to side before she finished her deductions. "No way would he leave anything important at the *Trib,* much less share even a hint of what he was working on with any of his colleagues. He claimed this was his big chance. He wasn't about to risk having anyone steal his glory."

"Blue Island it is, then." Merri reached for her phone to send Simon a text as to their plans. "I'll let the office know our strategy."

Brandon stood. She looked up at him.

"…to eat."

"Sure," she acknowledged though she hadn't gotten the entire sentence. She'd evolved into quite the expert at estimating what had likely been said. He was hungry. He wanted to eat. "I'll get something in a minute."

No sooner had she sent the text than the screen on her cell flashed, indicating that she had an incoming text.

Walters.

What's in Blue Island?

Simon.

We're relatively certain the puzzle or riddle or whatever the hell it is points to where he grew up. Kick, aka Kevin Randolph, grew up in Blue Island so that's where we'll go first.

Makes sense. Turner indicated his parents still live there and he has one sister, Bethany Stover, in the area, as well.

We'll be checking out both in addition to any neighbors or childhood friends we discover along the way.

Be careful, Merri.

Definitely.

A Detective Whitehall is in charge of the Randolph case. He's nosing around. I told him we're looking into the situation and that we'll keep him apprised.

Text his cell number to me and I'll touch base with him as soon as we determine if there's anything to know in Blue Island.

The Colby Agency had an outstanding reputation of cooperating with the local police. Keeping it that way was part of her job.

Is he aware that we're working with Brandon?

She typed the letters quickly across the screen.
In light of the two explosions, perhaps the police were having second thoughts about Brandon's suspected guilt.

Whitehall still considers Brandon a person of interest, but under the circumstances they're looking into his story about someone else being involved a bit more seriously.

At least the loss of Brandon's home was proving worthwhile on some level. Not to mention the two dead men in the mangled van. Simon reminded her once more to watch her back, then the exchange ended.

Merri had checked Randolph's two social network pages. Photos of his parents and sister were posted for public viewing. The men after Brandon would definitely be watching the homes of Randolph's immediate family. That meant going to those locations was risky business, but there was no way around it. Particular care would need to be taken on this field trip to Blue Island.

A hand waved in front of her face. She jumped, looked up to find Brandon hovering over her.

"You want a sandwich?"

She'd been so lost in thought she hadn't noticed that he'd walked back into the room. That had to stop. But there was only one way to do that. "Sure." She got to her feet and headed for the kitchen.

Brandon kept time with her pace. She glanced at him to see if he was speaking. He wasn't. Just watching her from the corners of his eyes.

She couldn't put off telling him the rest of the story much longer. Trust was key here, and she was showing a lack of it.

When they'd reached the island in the massive kitchen, she saw that he'd spread all the sandwich fixings on the counter. She grabbed a couple of slices of bread. "Looks like there's a little of everything." Cheese, an array of sandwich meats, all the trimmings.

He picked up the thick sandwich he'd already prepared and tore off a bite. "Yep," he said between chews. "We wouldn't have to worry about going hungry any time soon around here."

Her gaze lingered on his lips when he licked them. She blinked, ordered herself to focus on preparing the sandwich. Focus on the case, Merri— not the man or his intensely dark eyes. With a soft drink from the fridge and her sandwich piled high, she headed back to the great room. She wanted to review her notes once more as she ate. And to avoid looking at him. Or his eyes.

Last night she hadn't really had much of a chance to analyze her new client. Now that she had the time, she recognized the too familiar mistake. On some level, whether her brain was ready to admit it or not, she was attracted to the guy. Maybe because he appeared to have a challenge of his own. The whole delay-confusion-memory sequence situation didn't sit right with her. Or maybe just because, to use a clichéd phrase, he was tall, dark and handsome.

Scanning her notes, she kept an eye on Brandon. He polished off his sandwich and went back for another. When the lunch clutter was cleaned up, they packed up their change of clothes and notes and headed for the car. So far, no more communication glitches.

She was thankful for the jeans, sweater and

sneakers. Dressing up was something she did for work, but in her off time she lived in jeans. Hugging her parka a little closer as Brandon piled their stuff into the trunk, she worked at ignoring how his jeans molded to his backside. The size was a perfect fit. The shirt and sweater combination looked good on him. He'd been wearing sneakers already. She imagined that he lived in those just as she did when classier duds weren't required.

"Maybe I'll bring the laptop," she said when he turned around and caught her checking him out.

Before he could respond she dashed back to the house, provided the necessary security info and went inside. She slid the laptop into its case and grabbed the AC adapter and cord. When she returned to the door, she hesitated and watched Brandon. He surveyed the yard and the water beyond. Did he know more than he was telling her? She didn't think so. He was afraid of getting killed, but he was determined to do the right thing.

Going to the Randolph family would be tricky. Innocent or not, the police considered him a person of interest in the investigation—a suspect, really. The family would be aware of his standing with the police. Kick's parents might not want Brandon coming around, even if they could get close to the parents without getting caught by the enemy.

BRANDON VOLUNTEERED to drive. Mostly he wanted to distract himself. Since they had arrived at the safe house, he'd had a hell of a time keeping his thoughts on the task at hand.

Dumb, seriously dumb.

He was a murder suspect. This woman might be his only hope of proving his innocence. And still he found himself looking at her as a *woman*.

Blond hair, pretty blue eyes. Petite, but with an athletic frame. He had been surprised to learn she had once worked as a homicide detective. She didn't seem like the type. He would have labeled her a teacher or a counselor. Maybe because of the way she questioned him. He'd had plenty of experience with teachers and counselors.

Merri Walters carried a gun. The teachers and counselors he'd been exposed to as a kid and then a teenager certainly hadn't carried lethal weapons. Unless he counted their ability to prevent his forward movement, academically or otherwise. That was why his folks had opted for homeschooling.

Still, outsiders had been involved and there were always difficulties.

He should call his mother and wish her a Merry Christmas, but that would only open the door for questions. He continued to work diligently toward his own goals. As much as he loved his mother, she was one powerfully controlling woman. His father hadn't had a problem with that, but Brandon had. Even as a kid, he'd given her a fit. He needed his freedom to make his own choices. At thirty that shouldn't be an issue. But his mother loved him and she'd been focused solely on him since his father's death three years ago.

Merri wasn't like that. She was smart. Determined and self-sacrificing. He liked her. Wanted to know more about her.

Mostly, he wanted this to be over.

But logic dictated that when the case was over, so would be his connection to her. Be that as it may, he would cross that bridge when he came to it.

Not now.

He eased into the flow of traffic on I-90. Another thirty minutes and they would arrive at their destination. Brandon had been invited to a holiday dinner or two at the Randolph home. Kick's parents liked him, or they had until their son had been murdered and Brandon had become the prime suspect.

They might not be happy to see him under the circumstances. But there was no way around this step. He wished there were. He'd searched his memory for every moment of conversation he and Kick had exchanged the past few months. Truth was, recently they had spent most of their time yelling. Kick was entirely focused on this story, while Brandon worked extended hours to keep a roof over their heads. Kick's failure to pay his share of the rent this month had pushed Brandon over the edge.

But not far enough over to kill the guy.

Next to him, Merri checked the screen of her cell phone. She made a face. "Not a call you care to take, eh?" Being nosey wasn't usually a part of his personality but she made him want to know more…about her.

She glanced at him, blinked. "Excuse me?"

"I was just saying that you apparently didn't want to take that call."

"No." Her lips flattened into a firm line. "That call was a part of my past I'd just as soon forget."

Could mean only one of two things—a former boss or an old lover. "Someone you broke up with?"

Her silence dragged his attention from the road once more. "Didn't mean to get too personal."

The frown that lined her forehead was all too familiar. She looked at him that way a lot. Was there something about him that annoyed her? Maybe she had a headache.

"Let's just say we came to a mutual decision that it was over."

"From your days as a cop?" He wanted to bite his tongue for asking. This was clearly none of his business. But the winter landscape did little to hold his attention. And traffic was sparse since it was Christmas Eve afternoon. Most folks had already arrived at their holiday destinations.

"What?"

He pointed his face in her direction. "The ex-boyfriend. Was he part of your life as a cop?"

"Yes."

Brandon couldn't decide if the frustration in her voice was directed at him or the question. Other than frustration, the pitch of her voice rarely changed. He wished he had that much control over his emotional reactions.

"Why does he still call you?" He should just let it go. But somehow he couldn't.

She'd been staring at him since he'd repeated his last question. Those tiny lines still etched her brow. Maybe she was trying to form a case strategy and just didn't want to talk.

"Because he thinks I'm a traitor."

He sent her a *Really?* look.

"He wanted to move to the next level and I didn't. I came here instead."

"Oh." Lots of baggage and history there. If her former lover was persistent, she could end up with him once more.

"What does *oh* mean?"

Now there was something different. Anger. Another emotion he knew well. "He still wants you." Might as well get to the point.

"Steven Barlow and I are done," she said, her tone simmering with frustration and anger. "He's a great guy, but I can't stand to be smothered. He smothers me."

Now he got it. Merri Walters liked being her own woman. She wasn't about to live or work under anyone else's thumb. Kind of like him.

"Never been married, huh?" He had. In his early twenties he'd fallen madly in love and married within weeks of meeting the girl. Big mistake. Though he liked everything about her, she had one plan: change everything about him. At first he'd tried to make her happy, but then he'd admitted defeat. He was who he was and nothing, except maybe time, was going to change that. She hadn't wanted to wait. According to Kick, Brandon had married his mother.

"I was engaged once," she confessed. "But I fell below the mark where his expectations were concerned and that was the end of that.

She glanced at the screen of her phone again. This time she opened it and said hello.

Brandon attempted to focus on the road. But he couldn't prevent his ears from listening to every word of the conversation.

"Merry Christmas Eve to you, too, Mom."

The quiet went on for several minutes while Merri repeatedly checked the screen on her phone in between listening to her caller. He could never talk and text at the same time. Good for her. Then she said, "Yes, I'm having a nice holiday. No, I'm not at home."

During the next few minutes, Brandon was relatively certain she spoke to each of her family members. When she finally ended the call, Brandon had surmised that Merri was either the youngest of her clan or she was the one everyone wanted to take care of. And she was fully capable of handling conversation and text simultaneously. She'd done that the entire time on the phone. Maybe she was keeping the agency updated since that Michaels guy had been so concerned for her well being.

Funny, he had the distinct impression that she could take care of herself quite well.

It was quarter past four and near dark as they reached the Blue Island city limits.

"There are a couple of modest motels that we could check out before going to the Randolph home," he suggested. Since he wasn't paying for her services, the least he could do was attempt to keep costs down.

Merri didn't respond. He glanced her way. She was staring at the evolving urban landscape. She never even glanced in his direction.

Maybe she was lost in thought.

He'd noticed that several times already. But it bothered him on some level. Keen senses would be critical to her job.

Rather than touching her, he repeated the question, "Are we planning to stay the night here?"

Merri leaned back in her seat, her gaze focused

beyond the front windshield now. Nothing about her posture indicated that she'd heard.

"Merri."

Maybe it was the way he leaned toward her. She jumped as her gaze collided with his. She had been completely zoned out.

"What?" she declared, clearly frustrated.

"You didn't hear me…did you?"

Chapter Seven

Randolph Home, 6:05 p.m.

Merri stepped onto the porch. A large, welcoming wreath decked in Christmas trimmings hung on the door. The electric candles burning in the windows sent a glow of light across the wide porch. Passing by, one would never know that the family inside had suffered a great tragedy. The holiday decor had likely been in place well before the heinous murder.

Brandon waited in the car, both to avoid facing Kick's family and to be able to escape the instant he spotted trouble. Merri could take care of herself. But if anything—anything at all—seemed fishy, she wanted him out of here. The street in front of the lovely old home had been quiet and clear of vehicles. Those belonging to the homeowners were apparently already secured in garages against the cold Illinois night.

Brandon had let her out on the street behind the Randolph home and he'd parked several houses away on that same back street. She needed him safe. If he hadn't refused to stay at the motel, life would have been much simpler.

WIDELY SPACED STREETLAMPS left all but the sidewalks in near total darkness. Folks in the neighborhood were apparently not concerned about the crime that festered only a few miles away in the big city. Additionally, the few streetlamps allowed the homeowners to observe the stars and prevented too much light from venturing into bedrooms at night.

Merri raised her fist and pounded on the painted wood door. Her purse dragged at her right shoulder. Her parka kept her warm but she would be glad to get inside. The risk that someone was watching remained great no matter how serene the street appeared. For all she knew, trouble could be waiting inside one of the homes. The men who had killed Kick Randolph wouldn't be put off by a little more collateral damage.

The moment she raised her first to knock again,

the door opened and the overhead porch light came on. Kick's father, Merri surmised. Tall, like his son, with the same blond hair that had long since turned gray. The pain in his eyes warned that he had no time for solicitors. Yet basic human compassion prevented him from showing any rude tendencies.

"May I help you?"

"Mr. Randolph, my name is Merrilee Walters and I'm from the Colby Agency in Chicago." She pulled out her credentials case and showed her identification. "If you don't mind, I'd like to come inside and speak to you about your son." She didn't add the words *murder* or *homicide.* Mr. Randolph knew full well what had happened to his son.

That aggrieved gaze narrowed with suspicion. "The what agency?"

"Sir, I know this is difficult, but if I could come inside, I'm certain you'll understand that I'm here to help."

He stepped back, pulling the door open wide. "I can't imagine how you believe you can help, but you can come in, I suppose."

Relief flowed along her limbs when the door was closed behind her. Having heard the sounds of a visitor, Mrs. Randolph had come to the entry hall.

"Les, what's going on?" She looked to her husband for explanation. Karen Randolph was tall, like her husband and son, but her blond hair remained so with the aid of chemicals, Merri could tell.

"This woman says she's from the Colby Agency in Chicago and she believes she can help somehow." The man's halfhearted gesture said far more than his words. They had been visited before.

Karen turned to Merri. "Why would you come here at a time like this? Haven't we answered enough questions? The men from that other agency were here for hours this morning. We just need to be left in peace." Tears brimmed on her lashes.

Merri felt horrible for bothering them, but this couldn't wait. Someone else had been here already. "Ma'am, are you referring to the detectives in charge of your son's case?" The woman had said *agency,* but Merri wanted to confirm she'd understood correctly.

Karen shook her head. "The…" she looked to her husband.

"Blackburn Agency," Mr. Randolph said to Merri. "Two men with identification like yours." He nodded at her credential case. "The paper where Kick worked hired them to look into…the case."

Merri couldn't be sure whether the *Trib* had hired someone or not, but Simon could check it out. "Do you mind if I call my superior and ask him to verify that the Blackburn Agency has been retained by the *Tribune?*"

The couple exchanged a look, then settled their collective attention on Merri once more. The husband said, "I can't see any harm in that, but, are you implying that the men who were here today weren't hired by the *Trib?*"

The fear that glinted in the mother's eyes tore at Merri's heart.

"Sir, I'm not suggesting anything at this point. What I am trying to do is to make sure that I'm not unnecessarily repeating another party's efforts." That should assuage their misgivings for the moment.

"Certainly then," Randolph agreed. "We would very much like confirmation."

"Why…" Karen took a steadying breath. "Why don't you come into the living room and sit down."

Merri was thankful for her hospitality. "That would be very nice."

As soon as she'd taken a seat directly across from the Randolphs' position on the sofa, she sent a text to Simon. He would call when he had an answer.

"…your agency?"

Merri's gaze zeroed in on Mr. Randolph's face. "I'm sorry, sir, you'll have to wait until I'm looking at you to speak." *Just say it!* "I read lips."

Why couldn't she just say that to Brandon? Vanity, pure and simple. She didn't want him to see her that way.

"Oh." Mr. Randolph glanced at his wife, then settled his full attention on Merri. "I was asking who retained your agency."

That was one answer she couldn't give him. "The Colby Agency is working with the official investigation." It wasn't exactly true, but it wasn't a lie, either. "We're trying to get to the bottom of exactly what happened."

The conversation turned to Brandon. Neither of Kick's parents could believe Brandon capable of such a thing, but their son's death was far too painful at the moment to truly rule out Brandon as a suspect. They needed the facts, for the peace of all concerned.

"Would you mind going over with me what the men who were here earlier wanted to know?"

Kick's mother spoke first. "They wanted to know about the story Kevin was working on. We knew it was something big, but he refused to discuss anything about it. So we couldn't help."

The exhaustion and misery had deepened and darkened around her eyes, giving her already pale complexion a deathly pallor.

"I know just how difficult this is," Merri qualified, "but it would help tremendously if you could tell me as much as possible about your son's life here at home. School. Friends."

The two exchanged another look. The father spoke this time. "The Blackburn investigators asked those same questions."

Not surprising. "Do you mind going over those painful elements once more?"

Merri's cell vibrated. "Excuse me one moment. This is my superior." She opened the phone. "Walters." She read the text her screen provided as Simon spoke, relating that the *Trib* insisted they were leaving the investigation up to the experts—Chicago PD. They insisted they had not hired anyone.

As she closed the phone, she considered the best way to relay this information. These folks had been hurt enough already. But they needed the truth.

"Ma'am, sir," she said to them, "the *Tribune*

insists they are leaving the investigation to Chicago PD."

She quickly wrote the name and number of the man Simon had contacted on one of her business cards and placed it on the table between them. "If you want to confirm that information, please call this gentleman. My number is there as well if you have any questions after I'm gone."

"You're saying those men were…" Mr. Randolph fell silent.

"Your son," Merri began, "was working on a big story that may have rattled some cages. Powerful cages. If that's the case, and I believe it is, you should protect yourselves. Check in with the detective in charge of the case whenever anyone shows up with questions."

"Then," Mrs. Randolph said, "you won't mind if we call Detective Whitehall and ask about you."

"Of course not." The Colby Agency maintained an outstanding relationship with Chicago PD. Simon had already discussed Merri's involvement with the detective. "We'll all feel more comfortable if you verify why I'm here and what I've told you."

Mr. Randolph stood. "I'll give the detective a call."

When he'd left the room, his wife turned to Merri. "Do you believe, based on what you know, that Brandon killed Kick?" The misery on her face spoke volumes about her fear that her son may have trusted a man capable of such heinousness.

"No, ma'am," Merri said honestly. "I don't believe that at all. There is a concerted effort to gain access to evidence related to the story your son was working on. I believe Brandon Thomas is a scapegoat, as well as the only connection whoever is doing this feels they have to the evidence."

Karen Randolph closed her eyes a moment, then opened them to Merri once more. "Thank you. I need to hang on to that. My son is dead, whoever killed him. But the idea that his roommate…his best friend…" She shook her head. "I can't get right with that."

Merri was glad to have confirmation that her instincts were right on target.

"What did you discuss with the other men?" Merri asked.

"They wanted to see his room. If he had any special secret places where he might hide something relevant to what he was working on."

Even his own family had no idea what he was up to. For their own protection, Merri presumed.

"We had no knowledge of his work, other than the articles that made it into the paper." Karen shrugged. "And if he ever had a secret place where he might hide things, we never knew about it."

"Did he have any friends in the neighborhood? Maybe someone he attended school with? Someone he was particularly close to?"

Again, Karen shook her head. "He wasn't the athletic type, so he never did sports. He didn't join any clubs. He had a couple of sort-of friends back in high school, but they've all moved away. I can't imagine that he would have contacted any of them. But I'll be glad to give you names if you'd like."

Merri wasn't sure she would need them, but better to err on the side of caution. "That could prove helpful as we go along."

"Would you like to see his room?" The hopeful expression in her eyes told Merri that Karen was looking for an excuse to talk about her son…to show off his things.

"Yes, please."

Karen rose and headed for the stairs in the entry hall. Merri did the same. Lester Randolph met them at the bottom of the stairs.

An alarm sounded deep inside Merri. If possible, the pain had deepened on the man's face.

"I spoke to Detective Whitehall," he said to Merri. Then turning to his wife, he continued, "The Colby Agency is looking into the case. They were retained by Brandon Thomas."

For one long trauma-filled moment Merri feared that would be the end of her visit.

Merri knew that Mrs. Randolph spoke but since her back was turned, she couldn't read the words on her lips.

"I know how you feel about that," Randolph said to his wife, "I didn't say I thought it was true. I just—" his gaze lit on Merri "—want the truth."

"Mr. Randolph—" Merri acknowledged him, then his wife when she turned back to her "—Mrs. Randolph, I wasn't trying to mislead you in any way. I certainly wouldn't have suggested you call the detective if I'd planned on deceiving you. I didn't mention that Brandon was involved with this investigation because I didn't want to add to your suffering in any way."

The two stared at her for a time. Mrs. Randolph broke the ice first. "I don't care who you're working for as long as it's the truth you're seeking."

Merri gave her a nod of assurance. "You have my word and my agency's word. Feel free to call me or the office any time. This is about the truth. Yes, I'd like nothing better than to prove my client's innocence, but the bottom line is the truth. Detective Whitehall will be appraised of all my findings."

"That's all we can ask for." Mr. Randolph led the way to his son's room.

Merri followed his wife.

The first door on the right led to Kick's room, which faced the street side of the property. The walls were white. The furnishings were oak. Beige carpet. No posters, no trophies. A few books on the shelves. No personality whatsoever.

Except for the ancient computer sitting atop a desk in the corner. Even then, this wasn't what she would have expected from an aspiring journalist.

"Is the room similar to the way he left it when he went away to college?" She wanted to ask were these the things that marked the room as Kick's, but she hadn't wanted to say it exactly that way.

"This is exactly the way it's always been. We've painted the walls a couple of times but he always wanted it white."

Unexpected.

Together they went through the drawers and the closet, which were mostly bare. The few CDs he'd left behind were without cases. Nothing in the pockets of the few items of clothing in the closet. Nothing under the bed or mattress. The only items that gave any indication that he'd ever lived here was the computer and his senior yearbook.

While Mr. Randolph powered up the computer, Mrs. Randolph covered the highlights of the yearbook. Nothing there, either. The guy hadn't belonged to anything. There were two pictures of him in the yearbook. His senior portrait and a class photo.

"There's nothing on the computer's hard drive," his father said. "It's as if when he finished with it he wiped it clean."

The father was correct. The computer held nothing but the original software installed.

"What about his sister?"

"Bethany is at home with her family," Mrs. Randolph put in quickly.

"It is Christmas Eve," Mr. Randolph added. "And she has small children."

Perfectly logical explanation. But Merri needed to speak to the sister.

"If you think of anything else or if anyone who makes you uncomfortable comes around," Merri urged, "call me. You have my number on that card."

Mr. Randolph moved toward the window. Mrs. Randolph turned that way, as well. The two had a brief exchange, but Merri only picked up bits and pieces.

"What's happening?" she asked, her instincts screaming a warning.

Mr. Randolph frowned. "Someone in the street is blowing the horn. Don't they know that it's late?"

Merri rushed to the window. Verified as the vehicle rolled beneath a streetlight that it was Simon's sedan moving slowly down the street. "Is that the car making the noise?"

"I believe so," Randolph said.

"I have to go." Merri thrust out her hand. "Thank you so much for your help." She started backing out of the room. "I'll call you."

She rushed down the stairs. Wasn't sure whether she dared go out the front. Instead, she rushed through the kitchen and out the back door. She couldn't hear the horn blowing, but Brandon wouldn't have known that.

She spotted a car moving slowly down the street in front of the house where he'd dropped her off.

Merri sprinted across the Randolphs' yard and then the one behind that. The streetlamp he passed under allowed her to once more identify Simon's car.

It was definitely Brandon.

She raced to the street.

The car squealed to a stop.

She'd jumped into the passenger seat before it completely stopped rocking. "What's going on?"

Brandon turned to her. "A dark sedan, four doors, three men. Drove past the Randolph house four times. Then they didn't come back."

Damn it. "They may have parked somewhere to come back on foot and check things out. They must have a spotter watching the house." She pressed him with her gaze. "They know we're here."

Headlights cut through the darkness behind them.

Brandon stomped the accelerator.

Merri was thankful he didn't need directions.

There was only one thing to do at this point…

Clear out.

Brandon skidded into a right turn, then a sharp left.

He'd been here before. Surely he knew the most efficient route for losing a tail.

Merri slid her safety belt across her torso and snapped it into place as the vehicle bolted forward.

Brandon slammed the brakes and took a hard left at the next intersection.

She twisted at the waist, tried to see what was behind them.

The rear windshield cracked right before her eyes. A web of lines split from the crack.

A gunshot!

Brandon flattened a palm against her head and pushed her down into the seat. The safety belt cut into her neck.

Merri grappled for the weapon in her purse. The way the car was fishtailing and skidding, she dropped the gun twice before she got a firm grip on it.

She raised her torso upward. He shoved her down again. She glared at him. His lips were moving but his face was turned away toward the street. What the hell was he saying?

Another high-velocity turn, then he rammed his foot against the accelerator and the vehicle charged forward. Every time she tried to rise up, he pushed her back down. She was a highly trained investigator, a former cop. What the hell was he doing?

A lunge to the right and then an abrupt stop.

Headlights went off. Brandon slammed the gearshift into Park and turned the key in the ignition to the off position as the car rocked one last time.

Total darkness.

Brandon didn't move.

Merri didn't dare move.

A long minute passed with no movement. No light. Nothing.

Then the pressure on her head and shoulder eased and he allowed her to sit upright.

It was dark as pitch.

She couldn't see enough of his face to read his lips but she understood the universal gesture to remain quiet. He held his finger to his lips, then to hers. Despite the circumstances, a spear of warmth shot through her body.

Another minute, maybe two passed with no movement, no light and utter stillness. Then he slid down in the seat until his head was lower than the back of it, ensuring no one could see him. Merri did the same. He took her cell phone and held it open so that the light from the screen would illuminate his face.

It wasn't until that moment that she considered that he didn't have his cell phone on him. The police had taken it along with his wallet and apparently not returned it. No wonder he hadn't been able to call her when she was in the Randolphs' house.

His lips moved and she peered intently to recognize the words.

"We're safe here. They won't see us."

She didn't know precisely where they were, but she had to trust him.

"Don't move. Don't talk," he warned, his expression unyielding. "If we're completely still, we'll be okay until the coast is clear."

Merri told herself to relax. They were safe.

For now.

Chapter Eight

Christmas Day, 4:48 a.m.

It was still dark.

And it was cold as hell.

They had waited quietly for hours last night. The winter chill had invaded the vehicle. But between their coats and, more important, the warmth of their bodies they had managed to stay warm. At some point they had both fallen asleep. Merri wasn't sure if she'd surrendered to the weariness first or if he had.

Whatever the case, she'd slept like the dead. Even better than she had at the lake house yesterday morning. Had to be the man holding her tightly against him…as if he were afraid she would suddenly disappear.

Brandon appeared to be asleep even now.

It was still too dark to see his face, but Merri confirmed her conclusion by the rise and fall of his muscled chest. After she'd fallen asleep, she'd somehow managed to make a pillow out of his torso. He felt strong, and warm. She'd snuggled deeper inside his coat, pressing her face to his sweater—the only thing separating her cheek from his chest. Her legs cramped in their curled-up position along the length of the front seat. Brandon's were stretched out in the floorboard all the way across to her side of the vehicle.

If she wasn't careful in moving up and away from the draw of his warmth, she would encounter the steering wheel. But she had to move. She couldn't let him wake up and find her sprawled across his body like this.

Any way she moved, there was no way to avoid a part of him stretched out that way.

She scooted her backside as close to the passenger door as possible as she pulled up, grasping the back of the seat for leverage. If she could just find the door handle, she didn't care if she fell out of the car. Right now, she had to remove herself from this compromising position before he woke up and noticed.

Her fingers wrapped around the handle and

yanked. The door moved. So did Merri. She scrambled, righting herself, until her feet were on the ground. She swayed upward. Careful not to make any more noise than she already had, she eased the door closed and tried to survey their surroundings.

Merri stumbled around the car. They were in a driveway of some sort. There was a house…as best she could see in the darkness. The canopy of trees didn't allow the meager light from the stars and the streetlamps to filter through.

Taking care, she moved toward the edge of the yard and peeked past the thick shrubs that towered well over her head. The street was deserted. The streetlamp on the corner provided sufficient light for her to see that the coast appeared to be clear.

Their tail had given up on the chase.

She breathed a sigh of relief. They could leave. Go back to the motel and…

A hand settled on her shoulder. She jumped. Barely bit back a squeak.

His scent told her it was Brandon before her eyes took in and registered his frame in the deep gloom.

He said something but she couldn't see well enough in the near darkness to comprehend the words.

Taking her hand in his, he led her back to the car. She shouldn't have noticed how the warm feel of his palm sent a shiver along her arm. Or that the smell of him had completely invaded her lungs and had her pulse thumping faster. She would have much preferred blaming the physical reaction on the scare he'd given her, but she understood that wasn't the problem.

That silly attraction she'd noted before was playing havoc with her ability to remain neutral toward the man who was her client. Her *first* client. Not a good thing at all. She had to get a handle on her professionalism.

He opened the passenger side door for her, she slid into the seat. Thankfully the interior light didn't come on when the door was opened. Obviously Simon or Brandon had recently set the interior lamp to the Off position, which was good because someone could be watching from a position she hadn't detected on the street.

Brandon moved around the hood and settled behind the steering wheel, then fiddled with the controls until the interior light came on.

Before she could protest, he turned to her and said, "We have to talk. This can't wait."

Several things flashed through her mind as he

said the words. Him pushing her down in the seat during the car chase. His holding her there until they were safely away from the threat. Then, him holding his finger to his lips then hers…and using the light from her cell phone to ensure she could see when he spoke to her.

He knew.

"You should have told me." Those dark eyes were impossible to read with any certainty. But she understood from the expression on his face that he was not happy.

"It's not something I find easy to admit right up front." She hadn't had any trouble explaining her situation to the Randolphs. But that was different. Brandon was her client. She wanted him to feel confident in her ability.

And he was a man to whom she felt some physical attraction, like it or not.

"You can't hear anything at all."

That the disappointment or whatever she'd seen turned into worry shouldn't have given her such a warm, fuzzy feeling just then, but it did. She shook her head. "Though I do remember what things sound like." When she wanted to take the time, she could conjure up the sounds in her mind related to any activity she'd done in the past. She didn't do that as much anymore. She'd gotten used to the silence. Operating in that mode felt normal, instinctive. Strange, she mused, how the human body adapted to whatever circumstances became necessary.

"You read lips extraordinarily well."

The teachers and experts she'd sought out at first had been amazed by her lipreading. She'd done some of that, she'd realized eventually, her entire life. Watching people had always been her favorite pastime. She hadn't meant to eavesdrop on anyone's conversation, but she had occasionally. Honing that skill had been part of the natural evolution after she'd lost her ability to hear. Ultimately she'd done what she had to do to survive. The same way a person who'd lost a limb learned to overcome that challenge. End of story.

"I didn't like the business of sign language," she admitted. Though it was a great communication method for some, she didn't go for it. Mainly, she supposed, because that was a blatant admission to any and all that she couldn't hear. She'd wrestled with the question as to whether she didn't want people to know because it indicated a physical weakness or because she wanted to prove she was just as capable as anyone who still possessed their hearing.

Bottom line: she'd been denying that her life was different for several years now.

"So there was a time when you could hear."

She nodded. "Until I was into my twenties."

"What happened?" He searched her eyes. "If you don't mind sharing that with me."

The answer to that question was still a little cloudy. "It was one of the bizarre infections the medical professionals couldn't find a way to treat. When I was finally well again, I couldn't hear. I tried a couple of surgical procedures but neither one worked. It seemed smarter to go on with my life and just attempt to live with the situation."

He reached out. She braced. His fingers traced her left ear. The anticipation of feeling those fingertips on her mouth had her catching her breath. As if he'd read her mind, he made a path with those long fingers along the line of her jaw to her mouth before he let his hand fall away. The intent expression on his face tightened her chest. She liked having him touch her.

"I noticed you'd missed a couple of things I said," he explained, "but it wasn't obvious until we were running from those men. I shouted for you to get down when the first shot rang out but you didn't hear me."

He'd pushed her down in the seat when she

didn't listen. He'd saved both their lives by losing that tail. He'd saved her by thinking quickly. "Thank you for getting us out of that situation."

"I need coffee."

There it was. She saw it even as he turned away and started the car.

He looked at her differently now.

No one ever saw her the same way after they found out.

Brandon would be no exception, even though she was pretty sure he struggled with a challenge of his own. One he'd managed to set aside quite well during that intense chase. She didn't understand that part.

Men…they were the worst at accepting flaws.

5:30 a.m.

"THEY'LL BE LOOKING for this car."

"If we're lucky," Merri said as they braked to a stop at an intersection near their destination, "they won't be out this early." She looked around the neighborhood. "We need to visit Kick's sister, but it's a little early for that, too."

Brandon sat at the intersection a moment, his foot on the brake so the car wouldn't move forward.

He needed to get his bearings, and it wasn't daylight. He turned to Merri. "Bethany lives a few streets over." But Merri was right; it was early and he needed coffee badly. "There's a church—"

"What?"

Damn. He'd momentarily forgotten that she needed to see his lips. He turned his face toward hers. "There's a church a couple of blocks from Bethany's house. We could wait it out there."

"Sounds workable."

Kick had taken Brandon to that church once or twice. The doors stayed open 24/7 so people could come in and pray whenever they wanted. Brandon hoped that hadn't changed since he'd been here last.

Keeping an eye out for other vehicles, he drove the short distance. The church parking lot was empty as he'd known it would be. Instead of pulling into the lot, he drove past it and parked on a side street. If the bastards after them spotted this car, they would surely descend upon the church. Brandon might not get so lucky the next time they gave chase. His ability to react hadn't been delayed...*that time.*

He tapped Merri on the shoulder so she would look at him and said, "We can walk to the church from here. Then when we're ready to go to Bethany's house, it's within walking distance also."

"They'll be watching her house."

True. He wasn't sure what the best course of action was to avoid that scenario. Maybe Merri would have some ideas. Right now he needed that coffee.

He took a route across several back lawns, finally approaching the church from the rear. The back door was locked. Worry inched up his spine. Thankfully, the front entrance opened without hesitation. A church bulletin stuck on one door announced that Christmas mass would be from eight until eleven a.m. that day.

Inside, he led the way through the vestibule to the main sanctuary. Dim lights highlighted the altar area where a kneeling bar waited for those who sought to bow down before the massive cross.

Instead of going to the altar, he weaved his way around it and to the rooms in the rear.

Merri tugged on his hand, and he turned to face her.

"Where are we going?"

He hitched his head toward the narrow hall beyond the door to his right. "Bathrooms and a kitchen are back this way."

Her expression brightened. "Great."

In the hall, she disappeared into the ladies'

room while he headed for the kitchen. He went through the cabinets until he found what he'd hoped for: coffee and filters. When he had a pot brewing, he made a path for the men's room. He passed Merri en route. "The coffee's brewing," he said to her.

She'd washed her face and finger-combed her hair, but she still looked rumpled and as sexy as hell. He resisted the urge to smile. Merri Walters looked damn good in the mornings. No matter under what conditions she had spent the night.

When he'd taken care of personal business he hesitated at the sink. How could his life have gone downhill so far so quickly? He stared at his reflection and wondered how anyone could believe him to be a murderer. As angry as he often got at Kick, he would never have done anything like that. The knucklehead was like a brother to him. Otherwise, Brandon would have gotten a new roommate years ago. This was all way too insane.

He threaded his fingers through his hair, didn't care if it looked tousled. Brandon had never tried to be the spit-and-polish type. He couldn't care less.

Until now. Somehow it was important on a level he didn't fully understand that Merri thought the best of him. That she liked him.

"Dumb, Brandon."

When he joined her in the kitchen she'd located two mugs and poured warm brew into each.

"I couldn't find any cream."

He didn't care. "Thanks." He downed a gulp of the hot liquid. Warm, tasty. Felt good just knowing that the caffeine would soon infuse his veins. He needed a jolt this morning. Sleeping with her practically on top of him, the uncomfortable circumstances not withstanding, had been seriously difficult. His body had tightened and rushed toward arousal with no way to slow it down. She'd felt good against him. Her weight…her warmth. And, God, her shape. He'd wanted to run his hands over every part of her body, but he hadn't dared cross that line.

The woman was armed, after all.

As they sipped a second cup of coffee more slowly, Merri broached the subject he had dreaded. "How old were you when your dyslexia was diagnosed?"

Like her, he didn't exactly go around broadcasting the fact that he was dyslexic. He'd expected her to figure it out. "Ten."

"Your teachers didn't notice before then?"

"My mother was my teacher," he explained. "I was homeschooled."

Merri nodded, the expression on her face showing her disapproval.

"Public schools can be problematic."

She set her cup on the counter. "Tell me about it. I taught elementary school for a couple of years. Problematic is putting it mildly."

He'd known it! "I thought you'd been a teacher at some point."

Her eyebrows formed a vee, creating the cutest image of surprise. "How did you know that? I told you I used to be a cop."

"The way you rephrased your questions when you quizzed me back at the apartment." He poured himself a third cup, then realized the pot was empty. He motioned to her cup. She shook her head so he set the carafe back on the warmer and turned the machine off. "You recognized that you weren't getting through to me so you rephrased the question until I caught on."

She smiled. He liked when she smiled. She looked soft and sweet…and womanly. "I saw the clues but I couldn't be sure. Usually by the mid-twenties, it's not an obvious problem."

It generally wasn't. "I seem to fall back into my old patterns when I'm stressed." And he'd definitely been stressed the past forty-eight hours.

"Understandable." She inclined her head and studied him. "That's probably typical. I just haven't had that much experience with the adult side of the problem. You can't recall events in proper sequence. Things get jumbled up. There's a delayed reaction in physical and mental responses."

He nodded. Like all the things he should remember that Kick had said to him, he didn't. But the murder and everything since had churned things up. He couldn't retrieve the information in any kind of decent order. Some things he couldn't seem to pull from his brain at all.

The clock on the wall indicated that it was close to seven. "Since it's Christmas morning, Bethany's likely up by now." Her kids would never allow her to sleep late on this day. "We could head that way." According to what Merri had told him last night she hadn't learned much from Kick's parents— except that two men pretending to represent another P.I. agency had questioned the couple. Merri had warned them to beware. Their ignorance had likely been the reason they had survived the encounter without being tortured or killed.

"Since Kick's parents don't consider you a real suspect," Merri offered, "we can assume the sister might not. That could prove to our advantage."

"She won't." Brandon knew Bethany would never believe he was a suspect.

Merri pulled her coat closer around her and shifted the purse strap on her shoulder. "Lead the way. I'll follow."

Brandon cleaned up the mess they'd made first, then led the way outside. He chose his route carefully. Through more yards. Most were decorated for Christmas with snowmen and Santas. Sleighs and reindeer. Lots of twinkling lights that had come on since they'd taken refuge in the church. Beyond some of the windows he saw families gathered around the trees opening presents. Not one suspected the trouble right outside their home.

Life had once been like that for Brandon. Before he'd decided his mother was hampering his life. She worried so about him. She sheltered him entirely too much. He'd dated, had a few girlfriends. Even married at a really young age. But none of those women had connected with him.

None ever understood his challenge. He couldn't always react the way he should. And every time he screwed up, he paid the price.

A private college had given him the skills he needed to survive in the world of architectural engineering. He'd learned that he worked better alone and on his own. Private contracting had served him well. He worked from home more often than not. By the time this was over, he would be behind, but a few all-nighters and he would be caught up.

If this was ever over.

He still refused to believe that the justice system would put him behind bars for a murder he hadn't committed. To hedge his bets he'd gone to the Colby Agency. He glanced at the woman at his side. He'd made the right choice on more levels than one.

At Bethany Stover's kitchen door, Brandon approached with caution. The lights were on, and he could smell breakfast. Brandon's stomach rumbled as he peered through the window of the door.

He could imagine Bethany, her husband and two kids gathered around the Christmas tree in the family room. He and Merri might be forced to wait a while longer before interrupting that wondrous event but—

Bethany, flannel gown flowing to the floor, entered the kitchen. She, at least, was up and about and not already too deeply entrenched in the Christmas tradition.

Merri knocked on the door before Brandon had a chance to properly brace for the reunion.

Startled, Bethany turned toward the door. Since it was dark on the stoop beyond the door, she shuffled across the room and flipped the switch. Brandon waved to her and she blinked, startled all over again.

The hesitation lasted only a few seconds, but her reaction to seeing him was mixed. Still, she unlocked and opened the door.

"Brandon?" She glanced at Merri. "What're you doing here?"

"Hey, Bethany." Brandon didn't move to step inside. Not until he was invited…or more certain of her feelings. "I know it's not a good time, considering what's happened and the fact that it's Christmas morning, but we need to talk."

Another second's hesitation and Bethany stepped back far enough to allow them in. "I guess it's okay. The kids and Larry are still asleep."

As Brandon and Merri moved past her, she added, "We haven't gotten a lot of sleep the past couple of nights."

She didn't have to explain. Her brother was dead. Brandon was supposed to be his best friend. Instead he was a person of interest in his murder.

"I'm really sorry about what happened," Brandon said.

"My parents told me about what you'd done. I

understand you're trying to help." She looked to Merri. "Have you learned anything yet?"

"Considering," Merri said carefully, "what I've experienced since taking Brandon as a client, I'd have to say he's telling the truth—if you're asking me whether or not I believe he's innocent."

Bethany gestured to the table. "Have a seat."

When they'd settled around the table, Kick's sister added, "I never considered you a suspect." This she said to Brandon. "I knew something was wrong. I just didn't know what. I couldn't understand why I hadn't been able to contact you." She studied his face. "Are you all right? The police called and told us about the apartment. It's all just horrible and doesn't seem to end." Her eyes glistened with emotion.

He still had trouble accepting that Kick was dead and that he had no home. "I'm okay. I just want to stop these guys. I want whoever's responsible for Kick's murder brought to justice."

Bethany nodded. "I'm hoping that happens, too, but I don't want you caught up in this. Why don't you let the police handle it? You could go into hiding if the men who hurt Kick are after you, too." She meant what she said. Her eyes told him that they'd come from the heart.

Merri shook her head, drawing the woman's attention back to her. "It won't be that easy. Whoever hired these men wants the evidence your brother had in his possession. They're not going to stop until they find it or the man who hired them is revealed so the police can deal with him. It may get even uglier."

Bethany shook her head. "If you came here because you think I know something." She gave her head another shake. "I don't know anything. Kick talked about working on a big story the last time he was here." Tears glimmered in her already puffy eyes. "He wouldn't say a word. Not a word. Except that it was big and someone was going down. Someone important to the city of Chicago."

"You think," Brandon suggested, "this person might have been a politician? A high-level member of law enforcement? Something like that?"

"I wish I could help you, but I just don't know." She glanced longingly at the coffeemaker. "Why don't I make us some coffee?"

Brandon didn't mention that they'd already had coffee. He imagined it made Bethany feel somewhat more in control to do something.

When she'd poured the coffee, she brought a

tray to the table and passed out the mugs. "Would you like pancakes? They're hot off the griddle?"

Merri shook her head, then offered, "There is one way you could help us."

Bethany settled in her chair and cradled her mug. "Name it."

"Kick gave Brandon some random clues to finding where he'd hidden the evidence these men are looking for. But we haven't been able to make a lot of sense of the phrases yet."

Bethany stopped mid-sip of her coffee and looked at Brandon.

"It may be nothing," Brandon said, not wanting her to get her hopes up. "But we do believe the phrases indicate that he left something here, in his hometown. But that's as far as we've gotten."

"The part we haven't figured out," Merri put in before Bethany could ask questions, "is the final clue: *Invisible.*"

Bethany's face went pale. "Invisible?"

Merri nodded. "Does that mean something to you?"

Brandon had considered the word a dozen ways and other than that the item was well hidden, he couldn't fathom what Kick meant by the term.

"Back in high school," Bethany clarified, "Kick

wasn't the guy he is—was—more recently." To Brandon, she said, "By the time you met him, he'd become Kick Randolph, the man with a plan to make it all the way to the top of his field." She sighed, stared into her cup. "But back in high school he was a total introvert. No friends to speak of. He didn't play any sports, wasn't in the band. He was nobody. That's what the kids who liked to make fun of him called him. It was awful for him." A tear slid down her cheek, she swiped at it with the back of her hand. "His senior year he was given a trophy by those snotty cheerleaders he'd gone to school with for four years."

"A trophy?" Merri repeated.

Bethany nodded as she swiped away more of those tears. "Mr. Invisible. That's what they dubbed him. The guy in their graduating class most likely to spend the rest of his life being *unseen*."

Invisible. That had to be it. "That explains the term." Brandon clenched his fists beneath the table. Now he understood why Kick would always boast about the fact that he understood how Brandon felt about his dyslexia. He'd suffered, too. Why the hell hadn't he ever told Brandon the whole story?

Didn't matter now. What mattered was finding

the truth. "The evidence he had hidden would be on some sort of storage device," Brandon described. "Does the word *invisible* give you any idea where he might have hidden a video or some kind of electronic storage device?"

Bethany started to shake her head no, but then she stopped. "Wait. There was a trophy." She frowned in concentration. "At the high school." Insight replaced some of the emotion still glistening in her eyes. "They gave him a trophy on Awards Day. The principal was so appalled at what his classmates did, he stuck it away in some storage room." A slight smile tilted her lips. "But when Kick started making a name for himself in Chicago, the principal pulled out that old trophy and put it in the display case with all the other ones. You know, all the state championship ones. Kind of an in-your-face move since a lot of my brother's old classmates still live around here."

"You believe it's possible the trophy may provide some insight into where he hid the evidence," Merri suggested, her face hopeful.

Bethany nodded. "That has to be it. That's the only thing that comes to mind. Kick was pretty proud of what the principal had done."

"How does a guy so invisible during school get a nickname like Kick?" Merri asked.

Brandon could understand how she would wonder. Now that he knew the whole story, he wondered, as well.

Bethany made another of those exasperated sounds. "He used to hate the nickname since it was about him being the guy everyone could *kick* around. But after he moved to Chicago and started garnering a few kudos in his career, he liked the sort of inside distinction."

"There's one more thing," Merri said, breaking the silence that had fallen over Brandon and Bethany. "The men who questioned your parents will come to you next, most likely. You cannot share any of this with them. They can't know we've been here. If they press you by saying they know we were here, tell them that you kicked us out because you're angry with Brandon."

"I understand." Another frown marred Bethany's brow. "What're you going to do?"

Merri got to her feet and pushed in her chair. "We're going to find that evidence and ensure justice is done for Kick and for Brandon."

It took some persuading to get Bethany to go along with the idea that they had to go back out there and do this alone. But she insisted Merri and Brandon use her minivan. Brandon didn't argue. The car they had been in was damaged and would be recognizable by the bad guys. They needed to keep as low a profile as possible.

Equally helpful, Bethany had given them the key to the school. Her husband was a math teacher at the high school as well as a coach. If they were lucky, her husband would never know he'd facilitated an illegal entry of school property.

Again Brandon drove, since he knew the neighborhood.

Bethany had also insisted they wear different clothes. The fit wasn't so great, but it would work. The ski hats and change of coats provided the best disguises.

Now all they had to do was break into the high school without getting caught.

On Christmas.

Chapter Nine

Chicago, Home of Victoria Colby-Camp, 8:30 a.m.

Victoria Colby-Camp slipped her arms into her coat and smiled as her husband smoothed the heavy wool over her shoulders. She and Lucas were nearing their sixth anniversary, and life could not be better.

Their granddaughter was safely at home with her parents enjoying Christmas after the harrowing scare by the thugs who would have kidnapped her this past summer had Victoria and the entire Colby agency not intervened. Jim, Victoria's son, and his wife Tasha were happier than ever with a second child on the way. The scare of the last ill-fated pregnancy was well behind them as this pregnancy moved into the second trimester.

Things at the Colby Agency were running more smoothly than ever.

Life was good.

The Colby family had fought evil and triumphed once more.

The telephone rang and Victoria paused at the door.

"We're going to be late," Lucas suggested, knowing his wife couldn't resist answering the call.

"It could be Jim," she allowed by way of an excuse, even though Jim would call her cell phone if he needed to reach her.

"That's not entirely impossible," Lucas offered with a knowing smile.

Victoria laughed as she made her way to where the phone sat on the side table next to the door. She answered, expecting to hear Simon's or Ian's voice. Either one could be calling to be the first to wish her a good Christmas morning.

"Victoria," the unfamiliar voice said, "this is Clive Mathias. I apologize for calling you so early on this auspicious day, but I have an urgent matter to discuss that involves both of us."

A frown spread its way across Victoria's brow as the identity of the caller nudged its way through her distraction. "Good morning, Clive. How can I help you?" She shrugged in question at her husband who looked equally confounded.

"I've become aware that an investigator of yours is hindering a homicide investigation."

Now Victoria was really confused. "I'm afraid you have me at a loss." Of course, she was aware that the investigation of which he spoke was no doubt the Randolph case. What she could not fathom was why Clive Mathias, the head of Chicago's Crime Commission, would feel compelled to call and discuss the investigation.

"You're aware," Mathias went on, "that your investigator, Merrilee Walters, is looking into the Randolph homicide."

"Well aware," Victoria returned. "Is there a problem with how the investigation is being handled? It was my impression that Ms. Walters intends to cooperate with Detective Whitehall in the event she learns anything of significance to the case."

"The problem appears to be your investigator's inability to maintain any manner of control over her actions and their repercussions. I'm afraid she's making us both look rather bad."

The suggestion riled Victoria. "Again, I have no idea what you mean, Clive." To Victoria's knowledge, Merri hadn't called in last night or this morning, but she was well within her twenty-four-hour period of being incommunicado. There was absolutely no reason to be concerned yet.

"Ms. Walters has taken a person of interest out of our jurisdiction where he continues to be out of reach. It's my understanding that after visiting the family of the deceased there was some disruption of the peace in a nearby neighborhood."

This was all news to Victoria. "I can assure you, Clive, that I will look into the situation. If Ms. Walters has overstepped the bounds of her position as an investigator on my staff, appropriate measures will be taken." Victoria knew without question that the suggestion was ludicrous.

"Mr. Thomas should be returned to this jurisdiction immediately, Victoria. He should not be causing distress for the family of a murder victim. I'm certain you understand how difficult things could become if this gets out of hand."

Victoria assured the man that she would attend to the matter straight away. When she had replaced the handset in the charger stand, she turned to her husband. "Something's happened with Merri."

Lucas nodded. "Then you need to deal with the issue."

As they drove to her son's house, Victoria discussed the strange communication with Ian and

Simon via a three-way call. Neither of her seconds-in-command had heard from Merri since the afternoon before.

"I'll keep trying to get through to Merri's cell," Simon suggested. "If I don't connect with her in the next two hours, I will personally look into the situation in Blue Island."

As much as Victoria hated to disrupt Simon's holiday, verifying Merri's well-being was essential.

"My question," Ian chimed in, "is what does Mathias have to do with this?"

Victoria agreed wholeheartedly. Clive Mathias rarely got involved with day-to-day operations. Particularly with a fairly low-level investigation—not that any murder was actually low-level. But Kevin Randolph was no one important to Chicago politics or society. Mathias rarely delved into anything less than a "high-profile" case. He had underlings for the "regular" work.

"I would like to know the answer to that one myself, Ian." Victoria was thankful Ian didn't proclaim this instance as a perfect example of Merri's inability to handle an investigation alone.

"We'll take care of this, Victoria," Simon urged. "Enjoy your holiday with the family. If there's anything you need to know, we'll pass it along."

For more than two decades, Victoria had maintained the helm at the Colby Agency. Now, she was more than happy to have her two most trusted associates take care of business for her.

She deserved this time with her family.

Merri Walters knew what she was doing. If she needed backup, Ian and Simon would see that she got exactly that. Clive Mathis had no reason to worry.

Merri wouldn't let the Colby Agency or Chicago PD down.

Chapter Ten

Chicago, 9:00 a.m.

"I don't care what you have to do," Clive Mathias told his detective, "you get this situation under control."

The silence that emanated from the other end of the line warned Clive that Detective Whitehall was out of his league.

Finally the other man said, "Sir, I'm doing my best but this *situation* is totally out of control. I can't—"

"Just take care of it," Clive almost shouted. "It's Christmas, for God's sake, man. You know what to do. Just do it."

Clive disconnected. He had nothing more to say. Whitehall would regain control or else.

This was totally unacceptable. No one as pointless as Kevin Randolph, much less his inept friend, was going to ruin everything for Clive.

He slid his phone back into the pocket of his suit jacket and smiled at his wife as she entered the foyer. They were due at church in fifteen minutes. His children were presenting a short Christmas production.

Murder wasn't going to get in the way of Clive's enjoyment.

Chapter Eleven

The Christmas tree in the corner next to the trophy display case mocked Merri. It was Christmas and she had facilitated a break-in at a high school.

How unorthodox was that?

Her parents would be mortified.

Like many of the actions she had taken in the name of getting the job done, they didn't have to know. They were far better off not knowing. Or maybe she was the one who was better off.

The key had gotten them into the building. Fortunately the trophy display case was not locked. All they had to do now was determine how Kick had hidden a clue in or around the trophy.

As his sister had explained, the trophy, along with newspaper clippings regarding his success and a recent photo, held a position of prominence in the display case. No wonder Kick was so proud. Everyone who visited the school's office would see that Mr. Invisible was no longer invisible in the least.

In fact, in some ways he had been too visible.

Brandon touched her on the shoulder. As usual, heat simmered in her belly. Holding her breath, she turned to him.

"There's nothing on the bottom." Brandon tapped the trophy's marble base, then turned it upright. "I'll see if it's possible to take it apart."

Merri had already checked the entire shelf, as well as the one above it, and the newspaper clippings and photo. Nothing had been written, underlined or circled. If Kick had been trying to send them a message, it wasn't in the memorabilia related to the trophy.

Merri nodded her agreement. Like Brandon, she was certain the clues led to this collection. It was only a matter of determining what it meant.

If Kick had been trying to guide them to another location, they hadn't understood.

Brandon sat down on the tiled floor with the

trophy. Merri eased down into a cross-legged position next to him. The only place the trophy appeared to give was where it was screwed to the base. Her pulse began that rapid rat-a-tat-tat as Brandon removed the base.

As soon as the marble square was pulled away from the faux metal trophy, a mini storage device, a jump drive, fell to the tiled floor.

Brandon waited until Merri was looking at him and smiled. His lips formed the word, *"violà."*

Could this really be the evidence that had cost Kick his life?

"I should call Simon," Merri said.

"Let's see what's on it first," Brandon suggested.

Wouldn't hurt. Her cell phone was dead anyway. The battery had given out sometime during the night, and her stuff was at the motel. No doubt there were working phones in the school, but Brandon was right. The call could be made after they had verified the contents of the storage device.

Brandon handed her the jump drive, then carefully replaced the base on the trophy. He got to his feet and returned the trophy to its place in the display case.

Merri levered herself upward with his help. "Where can we look at this?" A high school would likely have computers.

"Come on."

She liked that he held on to her hand as they hurried down the dimly lit hall. With few windows in the long corridor, the route was very nearly dark. They didn't dare turn on any lights for fear that someone would notice they were inside. Merri doubted that anyone else was on the premises, but neither she nor Brandon could be certain. Why take the risk?

He led her to the math department and then into the computer lab. Signs of the holiday dotted the room. A wreath on the bulletin board and relevant items in the window. Brandon pulled an extra chair in front of the monitor he'd chosen.

While he booted up the computer, Merri took the opportunity to study his profile. She wondered if there was someone special in his life. A woman who would question where he was.

It shouldn't have bothered her that a significant other was a possibility, but it did. Somehow she liked it that he was all alone except for her. That he needed her. And she needed him.

Pathetic, Merri.

Just because she felt alone didn't mean everyone else had to.

Not everyone else, she acknowledged. Him. Brandon. She liked being his saving grace.

She liked being close to him.

Maybe because he understood what it was like to be different. None of the men in her life before had understood that. Not really. Lord knew, her fiancé hadn't cared, much less understood. She and her mentor, Steven Barlow, had attempted a relationship of sorts. But he was so busy playing protector that she couldn't deal with his smothering ways.

Mason Conrad didn't really count. He'd been a distraction for Merri. A dangerous distraction. He'd turned state's evidence and gotten the charges against him dropped. He still called her from time to time, but she wasn't going down that road.

He was into the protector gig, too. He wanted her safe. She reminded him of his sister. He'd said that to her. Merri wanted to be treated like an equal. Respected. Was that too much to ask for?

She shook off the thoughts. "What?" Brandon had spoken, but he hadn't been looking at her.

He faced her. "Sorry." He gestured to the computer screen. "Here we go."

A box opened on the screen. Brandon selected the only icon contained inside it. A larger box expanded on the screen and a video flickered into view.

Kevin Randolph's image cleared. "What you're about to see," he said, "is the statement of a man who is now dead. I copied the video to this storage device and hid it in a place only my best friend and roommate could possibly find."

Merri glanced at Brandon's profile. The hard, pained lines made her gut clench. This was more than a little difficult for him. He and Kick had been close despite their screaming matches over the rent.

Another image appeared, then cleared. This one an older man. He identified himself as a thug whose name Merri recognized from the obituaries a couple of weeks back.

She and Brandon sat, stunned, while the older gentleman cited all the infractions of those connected to Chicago's prestigious Crime Commission—including the leader, Clive Mathias. He listed case by case, infraction by infraction before closing.

When the man had completed his dissertation, Kick faded back into view.

"I've been a pain in the ass," Kick said. "But do this one thing for me, buddy. Make sure Clive

Mathias doesn't get away with keeping the funds rolling to his machine with continued Mob connections."

Randolph paused a moment, then added, "Tell my family I love them. That I don't regret what I chose to do."

The screen went to black.

Brandon removed the storage device from the hard drive and tucked it into his pocket. "What now?"

Merri blinked back the tears that had brimmed in her eyes. She didn't know Kevin Randolph, but he'd worked hard to prove he was as good as anyone else. He had a family. And now he was dead.

He deserved justice. It wouldn't bring him back, but it would be a big step toward finishing what he'd started. Mathias was not going to get away with this any longer.

"We call Simon." Merri pushed to her feet. "He'll see that this evidence gets into the hands of the proper authorities. Considering this—" she gestured to the storage device "—I'm certain we'll have no trouble proving you had nothing to do with his death."

"We can use the phone in the office." Brandon

was out of his seat before he'd completed the statement.

They ran to the office.

This couldn't wait.

The men tracking them could have gone to Kick's sister's house by now and figured out where they were. Merri needed Simon on this.

This part she and Brandon couldn't do alone.

"Damn it!"

The office was locked.

"Try the key," Merri urged.

The key that had allowed them access to the building wouldn't open the door to the office.

"There has to be another phone."

Brandon glanced around the corridor, then shifted his attention to her. "The cafeteria and library will be locked, as well."

Each would likely have an individual key.

"We'll have to drive to a pay phone." Merri didn't like the idea of allowing one more minute to pass without calling Simon but they had little choice.

"Wait." Brandon crossed the corridor, picked up a random chair and rushed toward the office.

Merri's jaw sagged when she realized what he planned to do. He slammed the wood chair into the glass wall of the office. It took a few tries, but the glass finally cracked, forming hundreds of veins before caving down onto itself in a pile on the floor. He tossed the damaged chair aside and grabbed her hand before treading cautiously across the broken safety glass.

"The alarm is going off," he told her. "Make the call before the police arrive."

Explaining to the authorities would steal precious time. The call had to be made before there were any interruptions.

Merri grabbed the handset from the cradle of the phone on the counter and began entering the numbers for Simon's cell phone. He wouldn't be caught without it wherever he was on this holiday.

She held her breath and counted to ten slowly, time enough for Simon to answer since she couldn't hear the rings.

Brandon's hand was suddenly on her shoulder. She glanced at him. "Put the phone down."

What the hell was he talking about? He nodded toward the door behind her. Merri turned around.

Two police officers stood in the middle of the broken glass, weapons drawn. "Hands up," one of them said.

Merri slowly placed the handset back in the cradle and did as the officer had asked.

Her heart thumped high in her chest. "Call Simon Ruhl at the Colby Agency," she demanded. "It's imperative that he come as quickly as possible."

"The chief gave orders that the two of you were to come with us," the second of the two officers commanded. "I don't know what the hell is going on, but we're to take you to Larry Stover's house."

Merri's attention flew to Brandon. What was going on here? Bethany had helped them.

"What's happened?" he demanded, fury and fear tightening his jaw.

"Bethany Stover's missing." The second officer's eyes narrowed. "And the two of you have her vehicle."

Merri's gaze met Brandon's once more.

"They've got her," he said, pain replacing the fury and fear.

Merri could think of nothing to say to reassure him.

Bethany Stover would end up as dead as her brother unless the criminals got what they wanted.

The evidence that would clear Brandon…that would ensure justice.

Chapter Twelve

Chicago, Home of Jim Colby, 10:30 a.m.

Jamie, Victoria's granddaughter, had opened the last of her Christmas presents and the family was enjoying spiced cider when the doorbell rang.

Victoria's gaze sought and found Lucas's. This would not be good news.

"I'll get it." Jim was up and moving toward the front door before Victoria could voice her worries.

She prayed nothing had happened to Merri.

Victoria attempted to hold a smile in place for her sweet grandchild. It didn't help that Tasha kept sending concerned looks Victoria's way. Lucas's stoic profile was equally troubling.

No one had been more certain than Victoria that Merri was fully capable of being a Colby Agency investigator and pursuing a case alone.

What if she had been wrong?

"Victoria."

She turned at the sound of her son's voice.

"Would you and Lucas come into the kitchen for a moment?"

"Of course."

Tasha busied her daughter with installing her new digital game player while Victoria and Lucas silently followed Jim to the kitchen.

Simon waited, his dire expression confirming Victoria's worst fears.

"Kevin Randolph's sister has been taken hostage," Simon explained, "for reasons that are still unclear. Merri and her client are at the Stover home along with the local police. Ian has already headed there. I wanted to inform you in person before I join him."

Victoria shook her head. "Good Lord, on Christmas, of all days. Doesn't this woman have small children?"

"Yes," Simon confirmed. "The local authorities won't allow any communication with Merri at this time. I'm certain when Ian arrives that will change. At this point, we can only assume that this is yet another attempt to gain access to this evidence that appears to be tied to Randolph's murder."

"Perhaps I should go," Victoria offered.

Simon shook his head. "There's no need for your involvement on that level as yet. Ian and I will handle the situation. I'll keep you informed."

"Very well. I'll expect to hear from you soon."

"Absolutely."

Jim showed Simon to the door.

Lucas put his arm around Victoria's shoulders. "Don't worry, my dear. Merri knows what she's doing. She'll have a plan in place. With Ian's and Simon's help, she can't possibly go wrong."

"If something happens to her or this missing woman," Victoria said, "the responsibility will be mine. It was my decision to move Merri forward into the field. No one else's."

"First of all," Lucas reminded her, "we both know that isn't true. Simon and numerous others, including myself, were on that same bandwagon. Secondly, I've never known you to read a potential investigator wrong. Merri's got what it takes. You made the right decision."

Victoria searched her loving husband's eyes for the confidence and determination she needed. But the truth was simple and all too straightforward.

"She's deaf, Lucas. If she goes after those men alone, she might not survive."

"Ian and Simon will never allow her to go off half-cocked like that."

"Unless she's pulled the trigger already," Victoria countered.

Merri wasn't one to waste time. If she believed the situation merited going in, she would go in.

With or without backup.

Chapter Thirteen

Chicago, 10:40 a.m.

"We have the woman."

The idea aggrieved Clive. He hated involving civilians like this. But Kick Randolph had left him no choice.

"Does the husband understand what's at stake?" Clear instructions had been given to his men; one foul-up could ruin everything.

"Yes, sir," his henchman guaranteed. "We told the husband that if he said a word beyond the script we had given him that his wife would die and his little boy would be next."

"Excellent." That would be sufficient motivation for the lowly schoolteacher to do the right thing. He wouldn't want to raise his two children alone or to risk losing one of them.

"We're waiting now for Thomas to follow through with his end."

Clive wondered how the fool intended to get past the police. But then, that wasn't his worry. Brandon Thomas would have to find a way unless he wanted to be responsible for Bethany Stover's death. He sure as hell wouldn't be welcomed into the Randolph home then.

Idiots. All of them. Kevin Randolph should have stayed out of this.

It was annoying enough that Randolph had had to be killed. This additional effort was beyond ridiculous.

"Do what you have to do," Clive instructed. "I don't want any loose ends left on this."

"I understand, sir."

Clive pressed the End Call button. In the future, he would ensure that loyalty was not an issue.

In this day, a man should be grateful for his job. That lesson needed to be driven home.

Clive had better things to do than to worry about whether his people were toeing the line. Perhaps the whole crew needed a humbling experience.

One that would remind them of what they had to lose. Of who was the boss.

Perhaps one dead reporter wasn't lesson enough.

Chapter Fourteen

"How many times do we have to go over this?" Brandon asked, disgusted with the cops.

The encounter had turned into a fiasco. Thank God the children weren't here to witness it. Larry's parents had come for them when this all began. The Randolphs were too distraught to be of any assistance under the circumstances.

The two men who had brought him and Merri to Bethany's house were posted outside. The chief had asked the same questions over and over.

Brandon had already passed off the storage device to Merri. He'd been right to do so. The chief had searched him the instant he'd set foot in the house. His search of Merri had been cursory at best. Wherever she'd hidden the jump drive, the chief hadn't found it. Until Brandon understood how he could help Bethany, he didn't want the evidence passed off to the police.

The front door opened and one of the officers stuck his head inside. "Chief, you've got a call I think you're going to want to take out here."

The chief grumbled but didn't argue. "I'll be right back." He glared at Brandon. "Don't either of you move."

When the chief was out the door, Larry rushed over to where Brandon stood. "I don't know what's going on," he whispered fiercely, "but they gave me this." He thrust a cell phone at Brandon. "As soon as you can get away, you're to call the one number programmed into this phone. They'll take whatever it is that you have in exchange for my Bethy." The misery in the man's eyes tore at Brandon's insides. "I don't care what you have to do, but get her back. Do you hear me?"

Brandon took the phone and nodded. "We know what they want."

Larry stepped back as the chief reentered the house.

"Any word, Chief?" Larry asked.

While the chief was distracted by Larry's

question, Brandon passed the phone to Merri just in case the chief decided to search him again.

"All right." The chief turned back to Brandon. "Let's go over this one more time."

Brandon wanted to shake the man. "Chief, you don't understand—"

"I'm sorry," Merri cut in, "but I have to go to the bathroom."

The chief held up his hands. "No way is anyone leaving this room until I know what the hell is going on."

Merri bit her bottom lip and made a pained face. "I really, really have to go."

"This isn't about her," Brandon interjected, "it's me they want."

The chief relaxed marginally. "We're finally getting somewhere." He glared at Merri. "Go. But you come right back here."

She nodded and rushed from the room.

Brandon watched her go. He had a bad feeling.

"Start at the beginning," the chief barked. "This time, don't leave anything out."

MERRI WATCHED from the hall. She waited until she was certain the men were fully involved in the conversation and then slipped into the kitchen. A

laptop sat on a section of the kitchen counter obviously designated the mail and/or bill-paying
station. The computer was up and running, the
screen saver flashing one photo after the other of
the Stover children. She pressed the Mute button
and went onto the Internet server. She quickly
inserted the storage device and downloaded a copy
onto the desktop. When she'd finished, she sent an
e-mail to Simon Ruhl's Colby Agency e-mail
address with the downloaded item attached.

She stuffed the storage device into the pocket of
her baggy, borrowed jeans and did the only thing she
could. She sneaked out the back door and lunged
across the yard in a full run. When she'd reached the
back of the church where Brandon had taken her,
she paused long enough to send a text message to
the number programmed into the cell phone.

Ready for pickup. Hurry!

She included the location of the church. Thankfully the backdoor was no longer locked, allowing
her to slip into the kitchen unnoticed by those
gathered in the sanctuary for mass. She did what
she knew she had to do, then she returned to the
parking lot.

Undoubtedly someone had been watching the Stover home since a sedan pulled into the already crowded lot scarcely three minutes later. Christmas mass was still ongoing, but thankfully there were no parishioners in the lot. Merri strode straight to the passenger side and got in.

"Where's Thomas?" the man behind the wheel demanded.

"He's a little tied up right now," Merri explained. "I'll be taking care of this part for him."

"You got the evidence?"

"I do."

The driver wasn't pleased, but he didn't argue. He pointed the car toward the street and gave it the gas.

He glanced at Merri. "I hope you know what you're getting into."

She did.

She was about to trade herself for Bethany Stover.

"WHERE IS your friend?" the chief demanded. He walked to the hall and shouted Merri's name toward the bathroom door.

Brandon didn't wait for a response. He hurried around the chief and banged on the door. "Merri!"

Then he stopped himself. She couldn't hear him

banging or calling. He twisted the knob and pushed the door inward.

The bathroom was empty.

They searched the house, the chief blubbering threats every step of the way.

Merri was gone.

In the living room once more, Brandon and Larry exchanged a look. Merri had the phone and the evidence. She had gone to do what neither of them could.

And it would likely get her killed.

Fear twisted into knots of agony in Brandon's gut.

The front door opened again.

This time the officer was accompanied by another man, this one in a dark suit and trench coat that Brandon recognized all too well.

"My name is Ian Michaels." He flashed his identification for the chief as he surveyed the room, then turned to Brandon. "Where is Merri?"

Chapter Fifteen

Blue Island Pie Factory, 12:05 p.m.

Merri raised her head up. A groan escaped her lips. She couldn't hear it, but she remembered what it sounded like. What it felt like, vibrating across her lips.

"...for yourself."

She blinked, tried to focus on the guy's lips. "What?" She'd missed part of what the bastard said.

"Just tell us where the evidence is and we'll release both you and the Stover woman."

Merri shook her head. Pain radiated through her skull. She'd been punched. Her hair had been pulled and her head banged against the wall a couple of times. All while poor Bethany Stover watched.

"Let her go," Merri repeated, "and I'll tell you where I hid the evidence." She cringed when her swollen lip burned with the movement of her lips.

She'd hidden the jump drive at the church. They would never in a million years find it. Not that it mattered. As soon as Simon saw the video, these bastards were finished, as was their boss.

The factory they'd brought her to had been closed for years. With the car hidden behind the old loading dock, she doubted anyone searching for her and Bethany would have any luck.

Not a good thing since Merri was reasonably sure that releasing Bethany had never been on the agenda.

The assault started once more. The fiercer the tactics, the louder Bethany wailed as if she were the one absorbing the blows.

Merri's vision dimmed. She was close to passing out. She couldn't let that happen or they both would end up dead. She had to make a move. She'd endured as much for as long as possible in order to buy time.

"Okay, okay," Merri said, halting the next blow, "I'll show you where I hid it." She peered through swollen lids at the woman on the other side of the room. "But we all go together."

She held her breath while the man considered her proposal. Her heart wouldn't let her breathe again until he'd nodded and said, "Let's go."

Merri and Bethany were shoved into the back-seat. Merri had approximately a dozen seconds to whisper to the woman next to her, "First chance you get, run like hell. Don't look back."

The man who appeared to be in charge slid behind the wheel while his cohort sat in the front passenger seat, carefully keeping his weapon trained on Bethany.

There were few options, so Merri went with the flow.

"At the church near the Stover home," she told the driver. "I hid it there after I escaped from the house."

The driver's eyes narrowed at her via the rear-view mirror. He threw her a glance over the seat. "You better not be lying if you want to stay alive."

"You'll see," she said as he turned back to the wheel.

And he would. He would see lots of things. One

more important than all the others: Merri Walters wasn't going down without a fight.

AT THE CHURCH, she instructed him to pull around back. When she'd gone inside and hidden the jump drive, the backdoor had been unlocked. She hoped like hell it still was. Mass had been over for a while and folks had gone home to enjoy the holiday with their loved ones.

The driver got out of the car and came around to her door. He opened it, and she staggered to her feet. Her entire body ached, felt like a punching bag. With good reason—it *had* been a punching bag.

She led the way through the back door. The church was empty as she hoped. Thankfully no one had hung around after the Christmas service. The last thing she wanted was more innocent victims involved in this.

In the kitchen, she nodded to the coffeemaker. "It's in a sandwich Baggie where the coffee filter goes."

Still suspicious but ever hopeful, the gunman snatched the filter basket from the machine and grabbed the plastic bag from inside. A smile spread across his lips when he saw that it was a computer storage device capable of holding the evidentiary video.

While he removed the jump drive from the bag, Merri made her move. She seized the carafe from the warming plate and slammed it against the side of his head with all her strength before he could block her move.

She kicked him hard in the shin. The weapon in his hand fell to the floor and slid across the well-worn vinyl. Blood running down his face, he grabbed for her when she made a run for it. She barely escaped the clutch of his cruel fingers.

Another weapon! She needed another weapon. First she had to run. As soon as he had gotten the gun palmed once more, he would be after her.

She darted into the sanctuary and dove between two rows of benches. Wood splintered in the back of the bench behind her.

She blinked, understood that it was a bullet hole. He had his gun. Was after her. If she was lucky, the other guy would hear the gunshots and come inside to see what was going on. Maybe Bethany would have a chance to run.

Merri rolled beneath the bench he'd fired at, then she kept rolling, moving toward the front door by way of the floor beneath the rows of pews.

More of those splintered holes appeared in the backs of the pews. Merri kept going, couldn't let herself be distracted. By the time she reached the final pew, the front door burst open.

The trouser legs and shoes weren't familiar to her. Not Brandon or the police—the other bad guy.

Run, Bethany, she urged with all her mental might.

Run!

"You're certain that besides the motel, this is the only place you took her?" Ian Michaels asked again.

He was as bad as the chief. "Yes," Brandon repeated.

Wait. He frowned. That wasn't entirely true. They'd spent the night in that old driveway by the abandoned house. Simon's car was still hidden there.

Would she go there?

They were almost at the church. Might as well check there first. It was well within walking distance of Bethany's home.

As if the thought had somehow summoned her, Bethany ran into the street screaming at the top of her lungs.

The car skidded to a stop, barely a foot from where she stood in shock.

The chief, Michaels, Ruhl and Brandon bailed out.

"Bethany." Brandon was the first to reach her. "Where's Merri?"

"She's—"

Before she could finish her statement shots rang out from the church.

Brandon lunged in that direction. He didn't care that he didn't have a weapon, much less a plan.

He only cared that Merri was in there and shots were being fired.

A bullet hit the door just as he reached it. He dropped on all fours onto the stoop.

With his peripheral vision, he could see that Ruhl and Michaels had fanned out around the building. The chief appeared to be calling for backup.

When the silence dragged on, Brandon reached up and grabbed the door handle. He hoisted himself up and flung the doors open.

One man was on the floor, down for the count.

The other sat astride Merri's waist, her back pinned to the floor. His weapon was bored into her forehead.

"Now you die!" the bastard roared.

"What she gave you was a fake," Brandon shouted.

The man suddenly looked up at him, the weapon still drilling a hole between Merri's eyes. "You're a little too late," he mused.

"Do you want the evidence or not?"

Brandon reached into his pocket. The man's preoccupation with whether Brandon would draw a weapon from his pocket was just the distraction Merri needed. She propelled the heel of her hand into the lower part of the gunman's chin. His head snapped back. The weapon fired, hitting the floor right next to her head.

Brandon rushed forward, kicked the guy in the skull.

The gunman tumbled off Merri.

She rolled away and grabbed a weapon lying a few feet away. Apparently, it was the other man's gun.

When she'd gotten to her feet, gun held expertly in her hands, she snarled, "Merry Christmas!" She kicked the gunman in the head again before he could get up.

The chief, Michaels and Ruhl rushed into the sanctuary.

Brandon pulled Merri into his arms and held her tight against his chest.

He was so glad she was safe.

He'd realized a few hours ago that his life would be immensely sad without her.

All he had to do was convince her that he was worth the trouble of getting to know.

Maybe that would take a while.

But he had plenty of time.

Chapter Sixteen

Chicago Police Department, 4:00 p.m.

Brandon had been here for two hours.

The police had taken both men from the church into custody.

The district attorney was reviewing the evidence Brandon had given him.

All good. Except that Merri was in the hospital and this crap was keeping Brandon from going to see her.

He wanted out of here.

"Mr. Thomas." Detective Morales, Whitehall's replacement on the case, entered the room. "You may go home now. You're a free man."

Brandon didn't remind him that he didn't actually have a home at the moment.

"Thank you." He hesitated before walking out the door of the interview room. "Does the D.A. have enough evidence to take down Mathias?"

That was what mattered to Brandon. The guy responsible for Kick's death should pay.

Morales smiled. "That and more."

Brandon was satisfied. He walked out of the interrogation room, down the long corridor and out of the building.

He had no idea where he'd left his car last. A taxi would do just fine. Anything to get to Merri.

A dark sedan rolled up in front of him. "You need a lift, Mr. Thomas?"

Ian Michaels.

"I want to see Merri," he said, making no bones about it. Brandon wasn't so sure this guy liked him, but right now he didn't care. He just wanted to get to Merri.

"Headed that way," Michaels agreed.

From the precinct, it took ten minutes to reach Mercy General.

When Brandon got out, he was surprised that Michaels didn't do the same.

"I've already checked in on her," Michaels told him. "She wants to see you." Michaels allowed the corners of his mouth to tilt into a smile. "That says a hell of a lot about you, Thomas. I hope you won't make her regret her faith in you."

Ian Michaels drove away then. It was just as well, because Brandon had no idea how to respond to the man.

Of course he wouldn't make Merri regret wanting to see him. Would he?

He was willing to take the risk. As long as she was.

As Brandon rode the elevator up to her floor, he considered that the D.A. had agreed to allow one of Kick's friends to have an exclusive on the breaking Mathias story as long as Kick got the byline. The *Trib* was willing to do whatever necessary to get the story of the decade.

Chicago's Crime Commissioner Goes Down for Dirty Deeds.

Merri's door was closed. Brandon started to knock but remembered that she wouldn't hear him so he pushed the door inward one slow inch at a time.

When she didn't object, he came into the room and sat down beside her bed. She was sleeping, he realized, and he let her be. He got comfortable in the chair next to her bed and closed his eyes. He couldn't remember when he'd slept more than a couple of hours. Before Kick's murder, he supposed.

Cool fingers touched his face, traced a path along his jaw.

His eyes fluttered open and he smiled. "You're awake. How do you feel?"

"Like hell."

He stood next to her bed so he could look at her and hold her hand. "You look like hell."

"Thanks. You really know how to sweet-talk a girl." She tried to smile, but then touched her bruised and broken lips. "They won't let me go home."

"When the tests are finished you can go," he promised. She didn't have any head injuries, contusions or concussions. But there were possibly a couple of cracked ribs and other bumps and bruises. She would be checked thoroughly before being released. "You may even have to stay the night." Michaels had mentioned that on the way over here.

"No way am I spending Christmas night in here," she argued. "I'd rather be home."

He inspected her fingers one by one. "I'll stay with you. That is, if you want me to."

"It'll be boring."

"I don't care."

"I'm pretty cranky."

"What's new?" he teased.

"Here you are asking me to stay the night," she said softly, "and you haven't even kissed me."

"I think I can remedy that." Brandon leaned down and gently brushed his lips across her cheek. That was the most he dared with her all banged up.

She arched an eyebrow at him. "If that's the best you can do, we've got trouble."

He stared at her lips, wanted nothing more than to taste those sweet, bruised lips. "If you're sure."

She grabbed him by the shirt front and pulled him down to her. "Kiss me, damn it."

He kissed her, softly, on the lips. She made a sound that sent an ache through him. The taste of her was addictive.

When he pulled his lips from hers, he swept the hair from her cheek with his fingertips. "We make quite the pair."

She took his hand in hers and kissed his palm, then winced.

He grimaced.

"We're two of a kind," she agreed. "I think tonight will be the first night of many."

"But I don't have a Christmas gift for you." He'd scarcely had time to think about the holiday.

Another of those wicked grins tugged at her battered lips. "Yes you do and I can't wait to open it."

"We'll open it together," he murmured before brushing a kiss to the tip of her nose, about the only part of her face that wasn't bruised and battered.

"Merry Christmas, Brandon." She stared deeply into his eyes. "This is the best Christmas ever."

"Ditto."

He sealed their sweet words with more kisses. He lightly touched his lips to every place that bastard had damaged. But mostly, he just wanted to touch her with his fingers…his mouth…and too many other parts to mention.

She was right. This was the best Christmas ever.

Chapter Seventeen

Colby Agency, Jan. 1, 8:00 p.m.

"A toast." Victoria held her glass high. When her entire staff had reciprocated, she said, "To all of us. May our New Year be filled with beauty and wonder and, most of all, peace."

The clinking of glasses and the murmurs of agreement went around the room.

Merri didn't have to hear the words and cheers; she remembered what they sounded like. She drank deeply of her champagne, then stared into the dark eyes of the man at her side. Her bruises were clearing up. The swelling was gone and she wasn't sore anymore.

Kick Randolph's story had seized attention all across the nation. His family was so proud. The mayor of Blue Island had even named a day in his honor.

Work at the Colby Agency was as steady as always. The prospects for the New Year were all favorable.

Merri was considering asking Brandon to move into her place with her. He'd been living in a hotel for the past week. They'd spent every possible moment together. They might as well live together.

Maybe in a couple of months she would take him down to Nashville to meet her parents. They would love him.

She, though she'd scarcely known him more than a week, was pretty sure she was in love with him.

Time would tell.

And between now and then, they would live life to the fullest. Not regretting, not looking back. Only forward.

Her cell phone vibrated in the glittery little purse hanging from her wrist.

She couldn't imagine who it was. Her family had already called and wished her a happy New Year. Steven had sent her a text, to which she did not respond. She wasn't giving him reason to hang on. They were over. He needed to get on with his life just as she had.

Tugging the phone from the small bag, she slid it open and viewed the incoming call.

Mason Conrad.

A shock rattled her.

Hadn't she made herself clear yet?

She couldn't hear herself think out here, so she ducked into the nearest office and answered the call.

"Walters."

She read the words he uttered as they filled the screen on her cell. "Merri. It's good to hear your voice."

She frowned. "Happy New Year, Mason, but I'm right in the middle of a party. I should let you go."

She watched as more of his words spilled across the screen. "Wait. We never talk anymore. Why don't I come up there and we'll spend some quality time together."

Oh, no. She'd fallen for that one before.

"The truth is," she said frankly, "I've found someone, Mason. I don't want you to call me anymore."

She stared at the blank screen in anticipation of his words.

"For real this time?"

He was referring to the doomed relationship she'd had with Steven.

"Yes, Mason. For real this time. I love this guy. As a matter of fact—" she screwed up her courage "—I think I'm going to marry this one. I've known since the first night we met that he was special."

"Great," he finally said, the word appearing on the screen with all the flatness she felt certain he'd said it.

"Yes, it is great. I love my job. I love my life. And I love the man. So just back off." The phone was abruptly lifted from her fingers. She looked up to find Brandon standing close behind her.

"You should listen to her, dude," Brandon warned. "We're together now and nothing else matters." Brandon pushed the End Call button and set her phone on the nearest surface. "Now—" he pulled her into his arms "—that's the first time I've heard you say you love me."

"I guess I was just a little afraid that it might be like a fleeting spell or something. You know, like Christmas magic."

"And what did you conclude?"

"That this is real." She kissed his chin. "And that we complete each other somehow."

"And," he said rubbing of his nose against hers, "that this is not only a new year, but a new beginning for us."

Forever.

The word echoed in her mind as his lips closed over hers.

This was the real thing.

And it was finally Merri's.

CHRISTMAS GUARDIAN

BY
DELORES FOSSEN

All the characters in this book have no existence outside the imagination of
the author, and have no relation whatsoever to anyone bearing the same name
or names. They are not even distantly inspired by any individual known or
unknown to the author, and all the incidents are pure invention.

First published in Great Britain 2010
Harlequin Mills & Boon Limited,
Eton House, 18-24 Paradise Road, Richmond, Surrey TW9 1SR

© Delores Fossen 2009

ISBN: 978 0 263 88278 0

46-1210

Harlequin Mills & Boon policy is to use papers that are natural, renewable
and recyclable products and made from wood grown in sustainable forests.
The logging and manufacturing processes conform to the legal environmental
regulations of the country of origin.

Printed and bound in Spain
by Litografía Rosés S.A., Barcelona

Imagine a family tree that includes Texas cowboys, Choctaw and Cherokee Indians, a Louisiana pirate and a Scottish rebel who battled side by side with William Wallace. With ancestors like that, it's easy to understand why Texas author and former air force captain **Delores Fossen** feels as if she were genetically predisposed to writing romances. Along the way to fulfilling her DNA destiny, Delores married an air force top gun who just happens to be of Viking descent. With all those romantic bases covered, she doesn't have to look too far for inspiration.

To Dakota and Danielle

Prologue

San Antonio, Texas

Jordan Taylor heard the pounding, but it took him a moment to realize it wasn't part of the nightmare he'd been having. Someone was banging on his door.

He checked the clock on the nightstand. Three in the morning. He cursed, threw back the covers and grabbed his Sig Sauer, because visits at this time of morning were never good.

"Jordan, open up!" a woman said. Not a shout, exactly, but close.

He recognized that voice and cursed again. Shelly Mackey, his ex, both as a business associate and a girl-friend. He wouldn't need the Sig Sauer. Well, probably not. Since he hadn't seen or heard from Shelly in months and since her voice sounded a couple of steps beyond frantic, Jordan decided to bring the gun with him anyway.

"You have to help me!" Shelly insisted. She continued to pound on the door. "Please. Hurry."

That got him moving faster. Shelly wasn't the drama queen type. Jordan didn't bother to dress. He pulled on only his boxers and raced out of his bedroom.

Her voice wasn't coming from the front of the house, he realized, but from the door off his kitchen. Jordan sprinted that way.

But the pounding stopped.

He stopped, too, just short of the door. He waited a moment. Listened.

And heard nothing.

"Shelly?" he called out.

Still nothing. That gave him another jolt of adrenaline. Shelly was likely in big trouble.

Jordan lifted his gun as he reached for the doorknob. Then, he heard it. The sound of a car engine.

Someone was driving away. Not fast. More like easing away, the tires barely whispering on the brick driveway that encircled his house. Jordan unlocked the door, jerked it open, but he caught only a flash of the bloodred taillights before the car disappeared into the darkness.

With his gun aimed, he shot glances around his heavily landscaped yard. He didn't see anyone, but the soft grunt he heard had him aiming his attention lower. To the porch.

There was a basket with a blanket draped over it.

"What the hell?" he mumbled.

Jordan kept his attention on the yard, just in case the someone or something that had caused Shelly to run was still out there. He stooped down and lifted the corner of the blanket.

A baby stared back at him.

Jordan had never remembered being speechless before, but he sure was now. He looked beneath the blanket again, certain he was mistaken.

No mistake.

The tiny baby was still there. Still staring at him with eyes that seemed to ask who are you and why am I here?

Jordan wanted to know the same thing.

He grabbed the basket, brought it inside so he could set it on the floor and shut the door. He also reached for his phone and jabbed in Shelly's number. Each ring felt like a week-long wait.

"Jordan," she finally answered. He didn't know who sounded more frantic—him or her.

"Talk to me," he snarled.

"Someone's trying to kill me."

Despite the baby-in-the-basket bombshell, he wasn't immune to the fear he heard in her voice. "Where are you? I'll send help, and then you can come back for the little delivery you left on my porch."

"I'm sorry. I didn't want to do things this way, but I had no choice. They're after me, because of the baby. He's in danger, Jordan. The worst kind. And I need you to protect him."

Him. A boy.

Then it hit Jordan. He threw back the blanket and had a better look at that little face. Dark brown hair. Dark brown eyes. About two months old at the most. He quickly did the math. He'd last slept with Shelly nine or ten months ago. Break-up sex. And he hadn't seen her since.

Jordan groaned, and because he had no choice, he sank down on the floor next to the basket.

"I've sanitized my office," Shelly continued, her words rushing together. "Actually, I burned it to the ground. They won't find anything there, but I don't want them tracing the baby to you. Don't let anyone know you have him. Please. There can be no chain of custody when it comes to him, understand?"

No. He didn't. But he focused on Shelly and her safety. "Tell me where you are so I can help you."

"You can help me by taking care of the baby. There are no records and no paperwork to connect me to that child. It has to stay that way. I've created a phony trail for us, too. If anyone digs into our connection, they'll find proof you fired me because I was embezzling from your company. The documentation will imply that we're enemies and that you're the last person on earth that I'd ask for help."

This conversation was getting more and more confusing. "Is this baby mine?" Jordan demanded.

Silence. He knew she was still on the line because he could hear her breathing. "Just protect him, please," she said moments later. "A person might come looking for him. If she uses the code words, red ruby, then you can trust her."

"Red ruby? You gotta be kidding me. A code word? For what? Why?"

"I have to disappear for a while," Shelly said, obviously ignoring him. "But when I can, I'll explain everything."

With that, she hung up.

Jordan didn't waste a second, not even to curse. He redialed Shelly's number. But she didn't answer. The call went straight to voice mail.

Time for plan B. He phoned one of his agents, Cody Guillory, his right-hand man at Sentron, the private security agency that Jordan owned. Since Cody was pulling duty at headquarters, he answered on the first ring.

"I'm guessing whatever's wrong got you out of bed?" Cody greeted.

"Yeah, it did. I have a situation," Jordan replied. "Shelly could be in danger. She still has the same cell number and possibly the same phone she used when she worked for Sentron so try to track that. Discreetly. Let me know where she is."

"Will do. Give me a couple of minutes. Anything else?"

Jordan looked at the baby and debated what he should say. *Don't let anyone know you have him,* Shelly had warned. She'd even used another rare *please.* For now, he'd take the plea and warning to heart. "Just find her and send someone in case she needs help," Jordan said, and he ended the call.

The only illumination came from the moonlight seeping in through the windows, but it was enough for him to see the basket. Jordan stared at the baby, whose eyes were drifting down to sleep, and because he didn't know what else to do, he groaned and considered the most obvious scenario. Had Shelly given birth to his child without telling him? And if so, why wouldn't he have heard rumors that he was a daddy? There'd been no signs, no hints, nothing to indicate that this child was his.

Except for the dark brown hair, dark brown eyes.

Like Jordan's own.

Still, that didn't mean he'd fathered this baby.

He needed to talk with Shelly, and even though it was clear she was in the middle of a personal crisis, he tried her number again. Again, it went straight to voice mail. This time he decided to leave a message.

"Shelly, we need to talk." He wanted to say more, much more, but a cell conversation wasn't secure. His number wouldn't show up on her caller ID or phone records because all calls from his house and business were routed through a scrambler, but someone could get her phone and listen to any message he might leave.

Someone's trying to kill me, she'd said. Even with the

shock of finding the baby, Jordan hadn't forgotten that. Like him, Shelly now owned a security agency. Even though she'd been in business less than a year, her start-up agency provided services as bodyguards, personal protection, P.I.s.

And probably more.

That *more* had nearly gotten him killed a few times. *Was that what was happening to Shelly now? Had a case gone wrong, and was someone trying to use the baby to get to her?* Maybe she'd had no choice but to bring the child to him, but it damn well had been her choice not to tell him before now.

If the child was his, that is.

The phone rang, slicing through the silence and waking the baby. He started to fuss. Jordan had no idea how to deal with that, so he lightly rocked the basket. Thankfully, the little guy hushed, and Jordan took the call.

"It's Cody. I tracked Shelly's phone, no problem, but while I was doing that, I heard her name on the police scanner, and I zoomed in on the conversation with our equipment." He paused. "About five minutes ago, a traffic cop responded to a failed carjacking just about a half mile from your place. It's Shelly's car."

Oh, God. "How bad?"

"Bad." And that was all Cody said for several long moments. "Shelly's dead."

That hit Jordan like a punch to the gut. He squeezed his eyes shut. "You're sure it's her?"

"Yes, I've tapped into the camera at the traffic light, and I can see her face. It's Shelly, all right. Looks like a gunshot to the head."

Jordan forced away the grief and pain and grabbed the basket so he could take the baby with him to his home office. He turned on his secure laptop. "Send me the feed from that traffic camera. Audio, too. And get one of our agents over there."

"I've already dispatched Desmond—" Cody paused, and in the background Jordan could hear the chatter from the laser listening device that Cody was using to zoom in on the scene. "An eyewitness is talking to the traffic cop right now."

The images popped onto his computer screen. Jordan saw Shelly's car. The driver's door was wide open. Her body was sprawled out in the middle of the street, limp and lifeless. *Hell.* If he'd just gotten to the door sooner, if he could have stopped her from leaving his place, then maybe she'd still be alive.

Another patrol car arrived, but Jordan zoomed in on the conversation between the traffic cop and a twenty-something woman dressed in a fast-food restaurant uniform. An eyewitness. Her body language and nearly hysterical tone told Jordan she probably hadn't been involved in this as anything more than a spectator to a horrific crime.

"The man didn't want her car," Jordan heard the woman say, and he cranked up the volume.

"What do you mean?" the cop asked.

Tears streamed down the eyewitness's face. "That man dragged her from her car and tried to force her into his black SUV. He was trying to kidnap her or something."

Or something. Jordan was afraid he knew what that something was. This man wanted information about the baby. But why?

The eyewitness broke down, sobbing while she frantically shook her head. "The woman fought him," she finally said, her trembling fingers held close to her mouth. "She tried to get away. But he shot her and then drove off."

There it was. The brutal end of one nightmare and the start of another.

This wasn't a botched carjacking. Shelly had been murdered. And Jordan instinctively knew the man in the SUV wasn't finished.

The killer would come after the baby next.

Chapter One

Kinley Ford was after two things: Jordan Taylor and the truth. Tonight, she might finally get both.

If she didn't get killed first, that is.

Because if he did indeed know what was going on, he might take extreme measures to stop anyone from finding out.

Swallowing hard, she stepped inside the reception area of the Sentron Security Agency to find the Christmas party in full swing. The place sparkled, not just with some of the guests in their glittery dresses. There was also an angel ice sculpture on a center table, and it was flanked on each side with white roses in crystal vases and bottles of champagne angled into gleaming, silver ice buckets.

Kinley dismissed all of that and looked around. There he was, on the far side of the room next to the massive Christmas tree.

Jordan Taylor.

He looked lethal. And was. She'd studied every bit

of information she could learn about him. Over the years, he'd killed three people. All in the line of duty, of course. But that still gave him a dangerous edge that she would be a fool to dismiss.

Kinley hated to think of him as her last resort, but she had exhausted her list of persons of interest. She'd exhausted her bank account. And herself. She wouldn't give up if she failed tonight—she would never give up—but she literally had no idea where to go next.

Beside her, her "date," Cody Guillory, took her coat, then her arm and led her not in Jordan's direction but toward a tall blond-haired man by the ten-foot-long table filled from corner to corner with party food.

"Anna," Cody said using the alias she'd given him, "this is Burke Dennison." Cody checked his watch. "In about three hours, he'll be my new boss."

Burke flashed a thousand-watt smile. With that sun-blond hair, blue eyes and tan, he looked every bit the golden boy he was. At thirty-one he was a self-made millionaire and about to take the reins of one of the most successful security agencies in the state.

Burke used his champagne glass to make a sweeping motion around the reception area at Sentron headquarters. "I bought the place," Burke let her know. "Isn't that a hoot? I'm a ranch hand's son from Dime Box, Texas, for Christ's sake. Who would have thought it?"

Jordan Taylor obviously had, since he was the present owner and about to relinquish control a mere three days before Christmas.

Kinley wanted to know why.

For fourteen months, she'd examined the lives of more than a hundred people and had looked for any changes in their lifestyles. This was a major change for

Jordan. But the question was, did it have anything to do with Shelly's murder?

"Well, if I'd had the cash, I certainly would have bought the place," Cody remarked. He, too, looked around. Almost lovingly. "My life is here." He shrugged, then smiled. "And usually my body. Burke, don't you expect me to give you eighty hours a week the way I gave Jordan."

Both men laughed, but she didn't think it was her imagination that there was some tension beneath. Maybe Cody wasn't thrilled with gaining a new owner, or losing the old one.

When a tuxed waiter moved closer, Cody snagged two fluted glasses of champagne and handed her one so they could toast Burke. Kinley thanked him and pretended to have a sip while she pretended to be interested in the conversation Burke started about some changes he wanted to make.

She'd gotten good at pretending.

In fact, everything about her was a facade, starting with the red party dress she'd bought from a secondhand store. The symbolic necklace that she wore twenty-four/seven. Her dyed-blond hair. Her name. She was using the alias Anna Carlyle tonight, but she had three other IDs in her apartment. She'd lived a lie for so long. Too long.

"Excuse me a moment," Kinley said to Cody and Burke.

She stepped away and tried to be subtle. She mingled, introducing herself. She even sampled a spicy bacon-wrapped shrimp from the table, all the while making her way to Jordan.

There was an auburn-haired woman talking with him, but as if he'd known all along that Kinley was coming his way, he slid his gaze in her direction. He whispered something to the redhead and she stepped away, but not before giving Kinley a bit of the evil eye. Probably because she thought Kinley was her romantic competition. That couldn't be further from the truth.

"Nice party," she said, extending her hand. "I'm Anna Carlyle."

He kept his attention fastened to her face. Studying her with those intense brown eyes that were as dark and rich as espresso.

This was the first time she'd seen him up close, the first time she'd gotten a good look at him, and sadly, Kinley realized she wasn't immune to a hot guy. Funny, after what she'd been through she was surprised to feel any emotions other than grief and fear, but Jordan Taylor had an old-fashioned way of reminding her that beneath the facade, she was still a woman.

Simply put, he was the most physically attractive man she'd ever met.

He wasn't slick and golden like his Sentron successor, Burke. Jordan had a sinister edge that extended from his classically chiseled face to the casual way he wore his tux. The tie was loose. His left hand was crammed in his pocket. The other held not a glass of champagne but whiskey straight up.

It smelled as expensive and high-end as he did.

His hair was loose, a bit long, brushing against the bottom of his collar. It was also fashionably unstyled, as if he didn't have to spend much time to make it look as if he could have been posing on the cover of some rock magazine.

"Anna Carlyle, huh?" he asked. And it was definitely a question.

That pulled her from her female fantasy induced by his good looks and smell. "Yes. Cody was kind enough to invite me to the party. And you're…?"

The corner of his mouth lifted. Not a smile of humor though. It made Kinley want to take a step back. She didn't. She held her ground.

"Jordan Taylor," he finally said. "But you already know that, don't you?"

She was in the process of bringing the champagne glass to her mouth for a fake sip, but Kinley froze. Nearly panicked. Then he tamped down the fear that she was about to be exposed. She didn't mind being revealed as a liar, but exposure could be deadly.

"Yes, I did know you were Jordan Taylor," she admitted. "You're the host of this party. I must have seen your picture in the paper or something."

He eased his hand from his pocket. In his palm was a slim platinum-colored PDA. He held up the tiny screen for her to see.

She saw a picture of herself.

Specifically, a picture of her in the coffee shop across the street. Her worried eyes were fixed on the Sentron building. He flicked a button, and another photo appeared. Also of her. This time she was parked in a car on the street just up from his San Antonio estate.

Oh, God.

Kinley glanced over her shoulder, looking for the quickest way out. There wasn't one. To get to the doors, she'd have to make her way through at least three dozen people, including twenty or so security specialists who among other things were trained to apprehend suspects. But Jordan likely wouldn't even let her get that far, because he was the most qualified security specialist in the room and was only a few inches from her.

She couldn't read his expression. He didn't seem angry. Or even curious. He just stood there, calmly, while he apparently waited for her to make the next move.

"I was thinking about hiring a bodyguard," she lied. "I wanted to check out Sentron first."

He made a *hmm* sound, slipped the PDA into his pocket, set both their drinks aside and grabbed her arm. "Let's take a walk, have a little chat."

Once again she held her ground. Fear shot through her, but Kinley couldn't go with him. She had to get out of there. "I should get back to my date. Cody will be wondering where I am."

"No, he won't."

Because Jordan said it so confidently, Kinley glanced over her shoulder again. Cody and Jordan exchanged a subtle glance, and Jordan's grip tightened on her arm.

"When I realized you were following me, I sent Cody to the coffee shop. His orders were to strike up a conversation with you and then to invite you to tonight's party— an invitation I figured you'd jump at." He paused, met her gaze. "Cody's very good at his job, isn't he?"

He was. Kinley hadn't suspected a thing. Maybe because she'd been so excited about the possibility of learning the truth of what'd happened fourteen months ago?

"I'm leaving," Kinley insisted.

"Yes. After we have that chat." Jordan didn't give her a choice. He practically dragged her in the direction of a hall.

"I have a gun," she warned.

"No, you don't. Before you stepped foot in this

building, I scanned you—thoroughly." He tipped his head to a small camera-like device positioned over the front doors. "If you'd been carrying concealed, I would have already disarmed you."

That caused her heart to drop even further. What had she gotten herself into? And better yet, how could she get herself out of it?

He opened a door and maneuvered her inside. Even though she didn't stand a chance of overpowering him, Kinley got ready to fight back. She gripped her purse so she could use it to hit him.

But Jordan didn't attack her. He turned on the lights and shut the door. The room was filled with wall monitors, desks, computers and other equipment. No people though. She was very much alone with a man who might kill her.

"This is Sentron's command center," he explained. "Soundproof and secure. We won't be overheard here."

Which meant there'd be no one to hear her if she screamed.

He took out the PDA again and began to flick through more pictures. There was one from her college yearbook. Another of her in an airport terminal. Her passport photo. But the bulk was from newspaper articles when she'd been reported missing and presumed dead two years ago.

"There's about three million dollars' worth of equipment in this room, including facial recognition software. When I realized you had me under surveillance, I pulled up every image in every available databank." Jordan turned, aimed those eyes at her again. "I know who you are, Kinley Ford."

Since she didn't know how to respond to that, she didn't say anything.

"You're twenty-eight. Not a natural blonde. You have a Ph.D. in Chemical Engineering from University of Texas. Two years ago the research lab where you worked exploded, and everyone thought you were dead. You obviously weren't. You surfaced again fourteen months ago, only to disappear again. Now you're here." He outstretched his hands. "Why?"

Kinley chose her words carefully. "I knew Shelly."

He drew his arms back in, clicked off his PDA. "Did you have something to do with her murder?"

"No." But Kinley knew she didn't sound very convincing. "Did you?"

For the first time, she saw some emotion. For just a second, there was something in his eyes. Not pain, exactly. But some sentiment that he quickly reined in. "No." He didn't sound any more convincing than she had.

They stared at each other.

"You knew Shelly," Kinley accused.

He nodded. "She was a former business associate. I fired her because she was embezzling from me."

Yes. She'd read all about that. "And she was your lover. I saw a picture of you two in the newspaper." In the photo, Shelly hadn't been able to conceal the attraction she was feeling. It'd come through even in a grainy black-and-white image. Not for Jordan, though. In that photo, he was wearing the same poker face he had now.

"What do you want?" he asked.

"The truth. Among other things, I want to know who killed Shelly and why."

For just a second, his mouth froze around the syllable he'd been about to say. Then, he obviously rethought his response. "What other things?"

Kinley blinked, because that'd been a slip of the

tongue. "I was her client. And her friend." She had to pause and take a deep breath. "I left something important with her."

Mercy, had she stuttered on the word *important?*

Her nerves were so raw now that she didn't know. "I tried to retrieve the item," she continued, "but then I learned her office was destroyed and that she was dead."

She didn't think for a minute that Jordan was just going to accept her explanation. No. The question came immediately. "What kind of item?"

"That's personal." And she'd had more than enough of this intimidation. Kinley straightened her shoulders, tucked her purse beneath her arm and started for the door.

She didn't make it far.

Jordan stepped in front of her, blocking her path and sending her straight into him. He was solid. She learned that the hard way when her breasts landed against his chest. If he had any reaction to the contact, he didn't show it. He merely stepped back so that he was right in front of the door.

"Who sent you here?" he demanded.

"No one." That was the first real truth she'd told tonight. "And I'm leaving."

"Not now, you're not." He blocked her again when she tried to go around him. When Kinley tried again, he caught her, whirled her around and pinned her against the door. "Who knows you're here?"

It wasn't a question she'd anticipated, and now it was her turn to study his eyes to see what had prompted him to bring up one of her biggest concerns. "Obviously your people know."

"Just Cody. And he doesn't know your real name. He

thinks you came because I wanted to have sex with you. So, who knows you're here?"

"No one. I've been careful."

He gave a slight eye roll and tipped his head toward the PDA where he had pictures of her. "If I saw you, someone else could have, too."

True. And that terrified her. It had terrified her from day one, but even that wasn't enough to make her stop this search. She had to know if Jordan had the answers she needed.

Well, one answer in particular.

"What's this really all about?" she asked, hating that her voice was shaky. Heck, she was shaking. And the full-body contact he was giving her wasn't helping. She felt trapped. Threatened.

"I want to know the same thing," he countered. "What *item* did you leave with Shelly?"

She shook her head. "I can't say."

"You mean you won't."

"Can't," she insisted. She met his gaze. "What do you know about this?"

He stayed quiet a moment. "I figure if you take what I know and what you know, we'll have a complete picture. So, you show me yours, and I'll show you mine. You first."

Kinley considered that and then considered the alternative. She couldn't afford a stalemate. Nor could she afford the consequences of what would happen if she spilled all. So, she took it slowly. "I honestly don't know who killed Shelly."

"But you know who was after her and why," he snapped.

"Maybe." She groaned. "Look, I can't think like this. Just back up."

To her surprise, he did, and then made an impatient circular motion with his right index finger to signal her to keep talking.

Best to start at the beginning, she thought. That was the easy part. Too bad she didn't know if she could trust him with the ending.

"Shelly's death could be linked to what happened at the Bassfield Research Facility where I worked," Kinley explained. "Secrets went missing. Illegal deals were made. The authorities have caught some people responsible, but since there might have been others involved in the illegal activity, they thought it best that I be placed in witness protection in another state."

"Yet you're here," he pointed out. "Not in witness protection but at my company's Christmas party."

Kinley was certain she couldn't keep the emotion or the heartbreak out of her expression. "Finding the item I left with Shelly is critical. It's worth the risk of leaving witness protection."

"And you think I know where this…'item' is?"

She closed her eyes a moment, shook her head. "I don't know. But I made a list of all of Shelly's friends, family members and enemies. I've made it through that entire list—"

He put her right back against the wall. It happened so fast that it robbed her of her breath. "You asked these people questions?"

That urgency and his stark concern didn't help her breathing. "No. I didn't want to raise any suspicions so I followed them the way I followed you. I watched them, looking for any signs that they might know something."

His eyes turned even darker. "Because if someone

got this *item,* they'd be able to draw you out of hiding. Why? What do they want?"

"Information about the last project I was working on." It was a guess. But a good one, since she hadn't been able to think of another reason. She hadn't been privy to all top-secret data used in the project, however.

"You were working on antidotes for chemical weapons." Again, it wasn't a question.

She nodded, not surprised that he knew about the project that'd nearly gotten her killed and had cost her everything. "The formula for the primary antidote went missing. Someone may think I know where it is. I don't," she quickly added. "That's the truth."

"For a change." He turned on his PDA again, scrolled through some pages and stopped on one. Not a picture. This one had some kind of code in it. "That's your DNA. Day before yesterday, I had Cody collect your cup from the coffee shop, and I ran the test myself. No one but me has seen the results. Or compared it to anyone else's."

Oh, mercy.

Her breath shuttered, and there was no way to hold back the flood of emotion or what she had to say. She touched her fingers to her necklace and waited until Jordan's attention went to the stone. "It's a red ruby."

She saw it. The recognition in his eyes. Just a split second. It was all she needed to continue.

"My son would be sixteen months old by now. Brown hair. Brown eyes." Kinley swallowed hard. "You have him, don't you? Shelly left him with you?"

Jordan calmly placed the PDA back into his jacket pocket. "Yes." A muscle flickered in his jaw. "I have him. Your DNA matches his."

A helpless sound left her mouth. She lost it. Her legs

turned limp. Her breath vanished. And if it hadn't been for Jordan catching her, she would have fallen to the floor. "Thank God." And even though she knew she sounded hysterical, Kinley just kept repeating it.

"Don't thank God just yet. The child was safe. Now he's not. By coming here, you've placed him, you and me in grave danger."

She fought to regain her breath so she could speak. "I never meant to do that, I swear."

"The road to hell is paved with good intentions," he mumbled. Then cursed. "We have to sanitize this situation and do some damage control."

She shook her head. "How?"

But before he could answer, the doorknob turned. Kinley tried to brace herself for anyone and anything. It was almost second nature since she'd been living in fear for months.

"This is damage control," Jordan whispered to her.

He shoved his left hand around the back of her neck, dragged her to him and kissed her.

Chapter Two

While he kissed her, Jordan drew his gun and used their bodies to hide the Sig Sauer.

He wanted the gun ready in case the pretense didn't work. And in case they were about to be met by someone who'd followed Kinley.

The door opened and from the corner of his eye, Jordan saw their visitors.

Cody and Burke.

Despite his instant relief at seeing nonenemy faces, Jordan didn't break the kiss. In fact, he took it up a notch and made it look as if he was groping Kinley's breasts when he reholstered his gun.

"Sorry for the interruption," Cody drawled.

Only then did Jordan jerk away from her. He tried to look surprised, which wasn't very difficult since that damage-control kiss had sent a coil of blazing heat through his entire body.

Hell.

Nothing like reacting like a red-blooded male instead of a security specialist in the middle of a potentially dangerous situation.

"Something wrong?" Jordan asked the men. Beside

him, Kinley was breathing hard. Hopefully from the danger and not the blasted kiss.

Jordan made a mental note to figure a different form of damage control. Something that didn't involve her mouth or her breasts.

"Nothing's wrong," Burke assured him. He smiled. Cody didn't. He had a puzzled look on his face. "It's just that some folks have to leave to go to other parties, and I want to make a toast to celebrate your new semi-retired status."

"Of course." It couldn't have come at a better time, because a toast and then an exit was the fastest way to get Kinley out of there.

Kinley smiled and fixed her lipstick. Her mouth was trembling a bit, and she looked as if she'd been popped with a stun gun. Again, he hoped that was from the fear. He took her by the arm, and they followed Burke and Cody.

"I give you a week," Cody said, looking over his shoulder at Jordan. "And you'll be so bored you'll be begging Burke to sell you back the company."

"I doubt that." There wasn't a chance of boredom now that Kinley had arrived with her dangerous baggage. Not a chance, either, of his wanting to buy back Sentron. He didn't intend to go back to working an eighty-hour week.

Well, maybe not.

He'd made that plan when he thought he would have to devote more time to protecting the child that'd been left on his doorstep. Now that Kinley was here, though, his life was in major limbo.

And so were his emotions.

Jordan slowed his pace and hated that ache in the pit

of his stomach. But from the moment he'd run that first DNA test, he had known the child wasn't his. Biologically, anyway. He'd also known that perhaps one day someone would show up and want the baby back.

He just hadn't counted on it being tonight.

Part of him had hoped it would never happen. He wasn't one to wish a person harm, but after fourteen months, he had adjusted to the idea that the baby's biological parents weren't coming for him. Or that they were dead, killed by the same people who'd murdered Shelly. And then he'd seen Kinley Ford's DNA he'd pulled from the coffee cup.

She was the biological mother, all right.

Now the question was, what was he going to do about it?

All eyes shifted in their direction when the four returned to the party. To speed things up, Jordan grabbed two glasses of champagne from the waiter, handed one to Kinley and then slid his arm back around her waist. He even gave her a lusty, long look that he figured everyone could interpret.

Burke lifted his glass into the air. "Ten years ago Jordan Taylor created this company from scratch. He trained every agent in this room. Now Jordan's company and mine, Burke Securities, will be merged to form not just the best, but the biggest personal security agency in the state. I only hope I'll earn the same loyalty and support that you've shown him over the years." The glass went higher. "To Jordan. Thanks for creating the benchmark of security services. And thanks even more for selling it all to me."

That brought a few chuckles, and the room echoed with "Hear! Hear!" and applause as others joined the toast.

Jordan took one last look around the room. "I'll miss this place and all of you." He shrugged. "Well, maybe not when I'm tossing back shots of Glen Garioch on a private beach somewhere in the Pacific, but I'm sure there'll be moments when I'll miss you…a little."

Jordan forced a smile, took the master keycard from his jacket and handed it to Burke. A symbolic gesture, but one that tugged at his heart. "Don't run the place into the ground, all right?"

"I won't," Burke assured him.

They shook hands, embraced briefly, while some photos were snapped. But Jordan had no intentions of lingering. He'd already said goodbye to his key agents, including Cody, Desmond Parisi and Alonzo Mateo, and he nodded farewell to two of his newer employees, Chris Sutton and Wally Arceneaux. Then, he took a final sip of the champagne, and he set Kinley's and his glasses aside so they could head for the door.

Cody stepped out of the gathering to hand Kinley her coat. "You might need this," he added. Still no smile, not even a phony one. He was obviously riled that Jordan had sold the company. One day Jordan might be able to explain to him why he'd done it. "Enjoy your evening."

Jordan seriously doubted there'd be anything enjoyable about it. He only hoped it didn't turn deadly.

He helped Kinley with her coat and tried not to rush to the door. Jordan got them out of there and headed to the adjacent parking lot. It was cold, near freezing, and the wind barreled out of the north right at them. He kept her close, snuggled intimately into the crook of his arm, and he kissed her. This time it was on the corner of her mouth in the hopes that it wouldn't carry the punch of a full-mouth kiss.

It did anyway.

She was attractive. There was no denying that. But he reminded himself that everything about her was a facade. Well, except for the fear. She was trembling, but he was almost certain it wasn't from the cold.

Kinley looked up at him. "Where's my—"

Jordan pressed his lips to hers so she couldn't finish the question. Still walking, he kept his mouth over hers a second and then drew back slightly. "Lip readers," he mumbled.

Her smoke-gray eyes widened, and she gave a shaky nod, understanding that if someone were filming them, a lip reader would be able to determine anything they said.

Including a question about the child.

They reached his silver Porsche and got inside, behind the bulletproof custom-tinted glass and into a space that would not only conceal them, but was also soundproof. They could see out, but no one could see in. And an alarm would beep if anyone tried to scan the vehicle with thermal or sound detectors. Since Jordan heard no beep, it was safe to talk.

But not necessarily smart to tell her everything he knew.

For now, he couldn't trust her. Yes, Kinley was the birth mother, and she also knew the code word, but that didn't mean her maternal instincts had been the reason she'd come to him. He needed more answers about her motives, and while he was finding those answers, he had to continue with more damage control.

"Now can I ask my question?" she wanted to know.

He settled for saying, "It's safe."

She didn't waste any time. "Where's my son?"

Jordan didn't waste time, either. "You had to have known the risks of coming to me. So why did you?"

She didn't get defensive. Thanks to the security lights in the parking lot, Jordan could see her clearly. The light bathed her troubled face and danced off the red crystals on her dress.

"I just needed to know he was alive," she whispered. "That he was okay. I couldn't live not knowing." She scraped her thumbnail over the red polish on her right index finger and flaked it off. "I knew there were risks, but I thought I'd minimized them."

"Obviously not, if I figured out who you were and what you wanted."

She shook her head. "I didn't think you had him. I only thought you'd have information. Or rather I hoped you would. I wasn't very optimistic because I'd read that Shelly and you were enemies, that she embezzled from you."

Jordan sighed. "That was Shelly's version of damage control. She didn't want anyone to be able to link me to the child."

Still, that hadn't stopped SAPD and even a federal investigator from questioning him. It also hadn't stopped three different P.I.s, who'd been hired by God knows who to find out what'd happened in the last minutes of Shelly's life. Jordan figured all three P.I.s had probably worked for the same person, but he'd never been able to dig through the layers of security and paperwork to come up with a name. Or a reason why the baby was so important.

But that was something Kinley could perhaps tell him.

He used the car's mirrors to glance around the parking lot. "You're a cautious woman," he remarked. "Would you know if someone had followed you?"

"I thought I would. But I was obviously wrong."

"Other than me, would you know if someone had

followed you?" He wasn't being cocky. He was just better than most at that sort of thing.

"People have followed me in the past, but after I left witness protection this last time, I haven't noticed anyone."

That didn't mean someone wasn't there. Jordan had another look at those mirrors.

"You gave up your company for my son," she said. Not a question, nor an accusation. Her voice was heavy with emotion.

He glanced at her and decided to change the subject. "I'm going with two possible theories here. First, that the child's father is behind all of this danger."

She was shaking her head before he even finished. "No. He's dead. He died trying to murder me and my brother."

Okay. That was a story he knew a little about but wanted to hear more of later. "Second theory. Someone wants the baby for leverage. The people after you want information, and they believe if they have your child, they'll be able to manipulate you into giving them what they want."

Kinley stared at him so long he wasn't sure she would jump on to this subject change, but she finally looked away and returned to chipping off her nail polish. "The research facility where I was employed was working on several projects. One was the chemical weapon antidote that I told you about. Several researchers were working on it, and occasionally, I assisted them."

"Assisted?" He latched right on to that and mentally cursed when he spotted something he didn't like in the mirror.

Hell.

"Usually I was just a consult for a particular facet of a project," she explained. "For instance, I only worked on a portion of the formula for the primary antidote. I never got to see the finished results. None of us did. That was the way the facility maintained security."

Jordan calmly started the car, put on his seat belt and kept his eyes on the mirror. "But even though you don't have the big picture, you have pieces. Others have pieces. And you have the names of those others."

"Yes." That was all she said for several moments. "Brenna Martel was one of the top lab assistants at the research facility. She's in a federal prison serving a life sentence. But there are others who disappeared after the facility was destroyed and the federal investigation started." Another pause. "I've written notes about the research, and I've gone over them a thousand times, but I just don't know why someone would still be after me."

"Notes?" he questioned.

"They're encrypted," she huffed, obviously noting his concern. "I wouldn't just leave information like that lying around for anyone to see."

But someone would look hard for info like that. "And these notes are where exactly?"

"Hidden in my apartment."

Jordan didn't even have to think about this. "I want to see them." In fact, he wanted to study them and then interrogate Kinley and put anyone in those notes under surveillance until all of this finally made some sense.

"I can show you what I have," she answered. "But I want to see Maddox."

He glanced at her, frowned. "Who the hell is Maddox?"

"My son," she said as if the answer were obvious. "That's what I named him. You didn't know?"

"No. Shelly didn't get around to that when she left him on my doorstep." Jordan had been calling him Gus.

"And I couldn't exactly go digging for his name or paternity, now could I?"

"No." Despite the fear and the seriousness of their situation, she smiled softly. "Do you have a picture of him?"

"Not a chance. And as for you seeing him, that's not gonna happen until you can convince me that you're here as a mother and not as someone who wants to use him as a pawn in some sick game."

The smile vanished, and her mouth opened in outrage. "I wouldn't do that. God, what do you think I am?"

"You're a woman who left her baby with a bodyguard because it was too dangerous to keep him with you. The danger's still there." He glanced in the mirror again.

"I know that," she snapped. "Shelly had been my friend since high school. I trusted her. And she died protecting my son. If I could change that I would. But I can't. And I've searched and searched, and I can't make the danger go away." The minitirade seemed to drain her, and she groaned and rested her head against the back of the seat.

Jordan huffed, glanced in the mirror again and tried not to let her emotion get to him. He didn't want sympathy or pity playing into this. "This isn't convincing me that you should be mother of the year."

That brought her head off the seat. "I don't want to be mother of the year. I simply want my son."

"And then what?" he challenged.

"I take him and I find someplace safe." Her voice grew softer. "If necessary, we'll live our lives in hiding, but we'll do that together."

Not anytime soon, she wouldn't. Maybe not ever. Jordan didn't intend to hand over Gus until he was damn sure that it was safe to do so, and Kinley hadn't done anything to convince him of that.

"So, what do we do now?" she asked.

"Soon, we'll go to your apartment and get those notes." However, he also had a more pressing problem. "But for now we'll just drive, and we'll see if that guy parked up the street plans to follow us."

She snapped toward the side mirror and stared into the glass. "What guy?"

"Black sedan near the intersection."

Her breath suddenly went uneven. "How long has he been there?"

"He arrived not long after we got in the car. It could be nothing," he admitted. But Jordan didn't believe that.

It was likely a huge *something*.

"Put on your seat belt," he instructed. As he eased out of the parking lot, Jordan kept his attention fastened to his rearview mirror so he could watch the other vehicle.

It pulled out just seconds after they did.

Hell.

Jordan drew his Sig Sauer and got ready for the worst.

Chapter Three

Kinley's heart dropped.

This couldn't be happening. She'd been so careful and so sure that no one had followed her. Yet, the black car was there and made the same turn Jordan did when he drove away from the Sentron building.

She felt sick to her stomach. And she was terrified. She had to do something to stop this.

But what?

What she couldn't do was call the police. That would likely alert the wrong people, and it'd be impossible to explain everything that had happened. That kind of explanation could get her son hurt.

"Let me out," she insisted. "Maybe he'll follow me and won't connect any of this to my son."

"Too late. We're already connected. I'm just hoping this person is curious, that's all, and we can convince him that we're together because we're would-be lovers."

Maybe. But she hated to risk that much on a *maybe*. She stared in the side mirror. The car stayed steady behind them. "Any idea who is back there?"

"Nope. But I hope to change that." Placing his gun

on his lap, Jordan took out his cell phone, and he pressed in some numbers.

"Cody," Jordan said when the man apparently answered. "I'm traveling north on San Pedro, and I have a shadow. Can you slip away from the party and run a visual?" A moment later, Jordan ended the call. "Cody will get back to me when he has something."

Kinley latched on to that hope but still had her doubts. "He'll be able to see the person following us? How?" she wanted to know.

"Traffic cameras. We might know soon who's after us. And knowing who might tell us why. We might get lucky. This could be someone from witness protection. It might not have anything to do with Gus."

"Gus?"

Jordan huffed. "That's what I call your son."

She repeated it under her breath. It was hard to pin that name to her baby. She'd always thought of him as Maddox. But then, she hadn't seen him in fourteen months. He wouldn't even know her.

But her son obviously knew Jordan.

Where had Jordan kept him all this time? What kind of a caregiver had he been? Kinley wanted to know every precious detail of what she'd missed, but first, they had to deal with the person in that black car.

She checked the mirror again, as did Jordan. The car was still there—at a distance but menacing. "Will you try to lose the guy?"

"Not just yet. I want to give Cody some time to get a photo so he can use the facial recognition program."

"Good," she mumbled.

"Well, maybe not good. Remember, I've identified others who've followed me, and I've never been able to link it back to the person who hired them." He glanced at her. "That's where you can help. Think hard. Who could have known that you left Gus with Shelly?"

She pulled in a long breath. "I've already thought hard, and I don't believe anyone knew. After all, Shelly had him for nearly a month before the trouble started."

"Okay. Then what started the trouble?"

Kinley had thought hard about this as well. "A lot of bad things happened around that time. I was drawn out of hiding because someone was trying to kill my brother, Lucky. He's a P.I., and he started looking for the head researcher, Dexter Sheppard, because Lucky believed Dexter had murdered me. He obviously hadn't, but Dexter *had* convinced me and his lab assistant, Brenna Martel, to fake our deaths and his in that explosion."

"Why do that?" Jordan wanted to know.

"Because Dexter said it was the only way for us to stay alive. He had taken money from the wrong people, and he'd promised to deliver a chemical weapon that we couldn't deliver. He convinced me that all of us would die if I went to the authorities."

"And you believed him?"

"Yes," she said with regret. "I guess Dexter did a good job faking my death because my brother thought I was indeed dead. But he didn't think the same of Dexter. He thought Dexter was in hiding but couldn't find him. So, Lucky followed Dexter's sister, Marin, to Fall Creek, a small town not too far from here. And when the attempts to kill both Marin and my brother started all over again, I knew I had to do something to try to save them."

"So you went to Fall Creek, too," Jordan commented.

"I did, and while I was trying to save my brother and

Marin, Brenna Martel showed up there. Someone had been trying to kill her, too, and Brenna was desperate. She mistakenly thought if she kidnapped me, then she could force my brother to tell her where Dexter was. But my brother didn't even have proof that Dexter was alive, much less where he might be hiding out. We soon got proof, of course…when Dexter tried to kill us. He died during that last attempt."

Jordan stayed quiet a moment, obviously processing all that. "Brenna Martel knew you'd had a baby?"

"Of course. But she didn't know where he was."

Jordan cursed under his breath. "This Brenna Martel could have figured out that you and Shelly were old friends. She could have sent someone to get Gus, and Shelly was murdered in the process."

"I doubt it. Brenna was on the run like me, and she didn't have the money to hire anyone." She checked the car behind them again. "I don't suppose the danger could have stemmed from Shelly? I mean, what if someone was after her for some reason, and they saw Maddox with her and decided to use him to get to her?"

He shook his head. "I dug deep for that connection. Didn't find it." Jordan didn't add more because his phone rang. The call was brief, just a couple of seconds. "Cody has a photo of our snoop in the black car and is looking for a match. Hold on."

That was the only warning she got before Jordan gunned the engine of the powerful sports car. They bolted forward, and then he took an immediate left turn. Even with her seat belt on, she went sliding against him. She righted herself, looked in the mirror.

The black car was still behind them.

"He's definitely following us," Kinley mumbled.

"Yeah." And that was all Jordan said for several moments. He kept his speed right at sixty, which wasn't too far over the limit. He also kept watch in the mirror and one hand on his gun when he made another turn.

Toward her apartment, she realized.

Of course, he knew where she lived. He'd probably learned that not long after figuring out who she was. "Is it wise to lead him straight to my place?"

"It is if we're aiming for more damage control. When we get there, we get out. We look like lovers who can't wait to hurry inside and have a go at each other. Get your key ready."

She huffed. "I hate to state the obvious here, but what if he shoots us when we get out?"

"If he'd wanted to shoot us, then he would have done it when we came out of the building. No, I suspect his orders are to follow us and hope that we lead him to whatever information you might have. Or to the baby."

Her heart dropped again. Because as long as someone was following them, she'd never get to see her son.

Kinley got her keys ready, and Jordan stopped his car directly in front of her apartment. It wasn't upscale by anyone's standards. A far cry from the lavish Sentron building and Jordan's palatial estate. But it'd been all she could afford.

"Stay put," he insisted. "I'll get out first and then open your car door."

She glanced back and saw the black car. It'd come to a stop just up the street. Away from the lights but still visible.

Tucking his gun into his holster, Jordan left the car, hurried to her side and helped her out.

He pulled her right into his arms.

And kissed her.

The kiss landed on the side of her mouth. Not a real kiss, of course. But it had a *real* impact, just as the other kiss had done. It made her wonder just what kind of impact a genuine kiss would have.

She didn't have the time or energy to find out, even if her body seemed more than willing to explore the idea.

"See?" he mumbled. "No one's shooting at us."

Yet. She hoped she didn't have to say I told you so.

Jordan kept her pressed to him, and he positioned his right hand next to her breast so he could get his gun. He didn't linger. He kept up the frenzied fake kiss while he maneuvered her to her apartment door. She reached behind her, unlocked it and they practically tumbled inside.

The security system started to beep, and she punched in the code to prevent it from going to a full alarm. Then, Kinley opened her mouth to tell him that she would get the notes, but Jordan put his fingers to her lips. He stayed close. Nose to nose with her.

"Don't say anything," he warned in a whisper.

That spiked her heart rate again. God, did he think someone had broken in? But if so, the person would have triggered the alarm. It was an inexpensive unit, one she'd bought at a discount store a couple of days after she moved in, but unless someone knew the code, she didn't think they could have easily disarmed it.

Jordan reholstered his gun and took out that strange little platinum PDA again. He pressed a few buttons, lifted it into the air.

"Make sex noises," he mouthed.

And with that, he added a manly sounding grunt and proceeded to walk around the room. After a few steps, he glanced over his shoulder at her and gave her a get-on-with-it bob of his head.

Kinley moaned.

Apparently, it was a good one because he nodded. Grunted. And he flapped his jacket as if mimicking the sound of clothing being removed. While she checked the bedroom and the small bath, Kinley tossed in some deep breathing, though she didn't think it was necessary. No one else was in the apartment.

Then she heard the whisper-soft beep.

She turned and spotted Jordan next to the sole lamp in the living room. It was on a scarred end table. Kinley went closer, and when he leaned down, he pointed to a small dime-size disk stuck to the base.

He made more of those sex noises. "A bug," he mouthed.

She pressed her hand to her lips to stop herself from repeating it, but she couldn't stop the little gasp. Hopefully, whoever was listening would think it was part of the sex that Jordan and she were faking.

He caught on to her arm, and with the PDA device lifted in the air, they made their way through the other rooms.

No more beeps.

But one was more than enough.

Jordan groaned loudly, hit his arm against the bedroom wall, and he maneuvered her into the bathroom. He slammed the door and turned on the shower.

"Any idea how the bug got there?" he whispered.

"No. But it probably happened before I bought the security system." And if so, that meant someone had been eavesdropping on her for over two months.

Anger soon replaced the shock. Kinley felt violated and wanted to catch the idiot who'd done this. But more than that, she wanted to know why.

Even though the water was running, and the door was

shut, Jordan put his mouth right against her ear. "While you've been here, have you talked about Gus?"

"No." Her answer was quick because she didn't even have to think about it. "I didn't have anyone to talk to."

He pulled back. Stared at her as if he wasn't sure if he could believe her. "You're positive?"

"Yes." Now it was her turn to put her mouth against his ear. "I did all my research on the Internet, and my laptop is password protected. Never once did I mention my son. When I did searches about the people connected to Shelly, I only used her name, not yours, not Maddox's. If anyone was checking, I wanted to make it look as if I were simply investigating the cold-case murder of an old friend."

During her entire explanation, she kept noticing the close contact.

Correction: she *felt* it.

Jordan was against her again. Body to body. He stared at her, and she stared back. Their breaths mingled, and she could smell the smooth whiskey and sip of champagne he'd had at the party.

They'd been doing a lot of touching for two people who were at odds. And they were at odds, no doubt about it. Kinley couldn't mistake the distrust she saw in him. Maybe other emotions, too.

He wasn't pleased with her arrival.

She wasn't pleased about it, either. If she'd known she would bring this kind of danger to her son, she would have stayed away.

"I'm really sorry," she said.

He continued to stare at her. There was a heat in his eyes. Maybe from the contact. Maybe from his anger. "You should be," he grumbled. He stepped away, turned off the water and threw open the door.

Jordan made a beeline for her kitchen and opened the only cabinet. "Hey, you don't have any scotch," he called out.

"No," Kinley answered tentatively, not sure if this was part of the game they were playing. "I can run out for some if you like."

"I have a better idea. Grab a change of clothes, and we'll go to my place. I have plenty of scotch there."

His place. Where they'd be able to talk without an eavesdropping device. But it would mean going back outside where that black car was likely still parked and waiting.

"What if he follows us?" she mouthed.

"That's what I'm hoping. You've opened Pandora's box, and now I'm going to see if I can close it."

Not understanding, Kinley shook her head. "What does that mean?"

He leaned in again. "I don't want him or anyone else to think I have something to hide." He glanced around. "And besides, this place isn't safe."

Even though he'd whispered that, it rang through her as if he'd shouted it. "But I don't want to lead him to Maddox."

"You won't." And with that, he motioned for her to pack. "Bring your laptop and your notes, but put them in an overnight bag so they can't be seen."

She didn't question him further. The only reassurance she'd needed was that this wouldn't put her son in any more danger than he already was. Besides, it might help if Jordan looked at her notes. He might find something she'd missed. And if they found it, they might also be able to figure out who was behind Shelly's murder.

Kinley grabbed a small suitcase and hurriedly

packed everything she might need for a short stay, including the notes, which she took from inside the lining of a coat she had hanging in the closet. When she came out of the bedroom, Jordan was by the door peeking out the side window.

"Is he still there?" she whispered.

Jordan nodded. He reached out and ran his hand through her hair, messing it up. He did the same to his. No doubt so it'd look as if they'd just had a quick round of sex.

They walked out, their arms hooked around each other, and got into the car. Jordan drove away quickly. So did the other car.

Just as Jordan had predicted, it followed them.

"You're sure this won't make things more dangerous for my son?" she asked.

"I'm sure."

So, that probably meant Maddox wasn't at his house. But then, there'd been no indication that he was. Jordan likely had him tucked away somewhere. But where? And who was caring for him? It broke her heart to think that her little boy might not get enough hugs and kisses.

Because she'd already driven to Jordan's house, she was familiar with the route. He lived in a subdivision within city limits but still secluded. It had pricy homes on massive lots, some of them several acres. Jordan's was one of the largest in the neighborhood. A true Texas-size estate for a Texas millionaire.

Shelly had certainly made a strange choice when she involved Jordan in this.

"Is it true what you said about Maddox—that Shelly left him on your porch the night she died?" Kinley asked. Right now, she wanted every little detail she could learn about her son and what he'd gone through.

Jordan didn't answer right away. He glanced at her first. "Yes."

It was hard for her to picture that in her mind. Her baby literally left on a doorstep. "God, what did you think when you opened the door and saw a baby?"

"I thought he was my son." He stared straight ahead and repeated that softly under his breath. "Then, with Shelly's murder, it took me a few days to get around to the DNA test. I had Shelly's DNA on file, since she was a former employee, and when I did the comparison, I learned he wasn't Shelly's. Nor mine."

Was it her imagination or did he sound disappointed? Hurt, even?

But she had to be wrong about that.

Jordan was a ruthless businessman, along with being a rich player who enjoyed the company of lots of women. He would have taken care of her son, but she seriously doubted he would ever think of himself as a father.

"Who's taking care of him?" Kinley asked.

She waited.

And waited.

He opened his mouth, and she thought she might finally learn an answer to one of her many questions, but before he could say anything, his phone rang.

Jordan didn't waste any time answering it. "Cody," he said after glancing at the screen. He took the turn toward his neighborhood. The street switched from four lanes to two, and though it was well lit with a line of streetlights, it felt isolated because the lots were so spacious.

She couldn't hear Cody's side of the conversation, but she could see Jordan's reaction. She noticed his grip tighten on the wheel. Saw the muscles flicker in his jaw.

"You're sure?" Jordan asked. Then he paused. "No.

I'll take it from here." Another pause. "I need to ask you to keep this between us."

A moment later, Jordan ended the call.

"What happened?" Kinley wanted to know when he didn't offer any information.

"Do you know a guy named Anderson Walker?"

Kinley thought a moment. "No. That name doesn't ring any bells. Why?"

"He's the one following us."

She glanced in the mirror. He was still following them. "What does he want?"

Jordan shrugged, but there was nothing casual about his body language. "He's a P.I. who works for Burke Securities."

Her mouth dropped open. "Burke Securities as in the Burke Dennison who bought your company?"

"The very one."

Kinley shook her head. "Why does Burke have someone following us?"

Another muscle went to work in his jaw. "I don't know, but I intend to find out."

"What do you mean?"

"I mean he's not being very subtle. And he knows we're on to him. If I just keep driving, it might send him the wrong message—that we have something to hide." Jordan took his foot off the accelerator. "Get down now."

Jordan spun the steering wheel around, causing his Porsche to do a hundred-and-eighty-degree turn. It was precise. As if he'd choreographed it, he bumped into the rear side of the black car and sent it into a spin.

Before Kinley could stop him, Jordan drew his gun and threw open the door.

Chapter Four

The black car screeched to a stop.

Jordan hadn't given the driver much of a choice, since he'd angled his Porsche so that the guy couldn't get around him. That was the plan, anyway.

It was time to confront this bozo.

Jordan didn't get out, but he aimed his gun. And he waited. Since this was Burke's man, Jordan was counting heavily on the fact that the P.I. didn't have orders to kill. His gut told him this was strictly surveillance. Too bad his gut didn't tell him why Burke had put a tail on him.

Thankfully, there were no other vehicles on the street. There probably wouldn't be, either. The street was private, leading only to his neighborhood, and this time of night, there weren't many residents out and about. Jordan wanted that privacy in case this took an ugly turn.

"Should I call the police?" Kinley asked. Her breath was jagged, and she had her purse in a white-knuckle grip.

"No." Not yet anyway. If he phoned anyone, it'd be Burke to find out what the devil was going on. That call would still happen, but first he wanted answers from the guy who'd tailed them.

"Anderson Walker!" Jordan called out, and he made sure it didn't sound like a question.

The man still didn't budge, and Jordan wondered if he'd made a mistake by jumping into this confrontation.

Especially with Kinley in the car.

Maybe he should have waited, but he really just wanted to end this here and now. He didn't want anyone following him, especially when he didn't know their intentions and when they were being so obvious about following Kinley and him.

"Walker!" Jordan shouted.

That did it. The door to the black car opened, and the sandy-haired guy stepped out. Anderson was what Jordan called a muscle man. Bulky shoulders. Young. He looked physically capable of pulverizing someone with his bare hands. Jordan had a few P.I.s like that on the Sentron staff because there were times when a strong arm was needed.

So, why had Burke or Anderson thought he needed some intimidation?

Anderson held his gun in his right hand. Not aimed. He had his index finger through the trigger loop, but the gun dangled upside down in a nonthreatening position.

Jordan went for the threat. He pointed his Sig Sauer right at the man.

"You plan to shoot me?" Anderson challenged. He had *cocky* written all over him.

"That depends on your answer to my question. Why are you following me?"

Anderson started to shift his gun, as if getting ready to aim. Jordan stepped forward and put his Sig Sauer at the guy's head. "Don't," Jordan warned.

Anderson froze. And Jordan said a silent prayer of

thanks. He didn't want to start a gunfight, and he didn't want to put Kinley in danger. She apparently had enough danger after her without his adding more.

"Toss your gun into your car," Jordan instructed.

Anderson looked at his gun. At Jordan's. Then at Jordan himself. Jordan put on his best scowl, which he didn't have to fake. There was plenty to scowl about. Anderson finally relented and put the gun inside his car. That didn't mean they were safe because Jordan figured the guy was carrying at least one other backup pistol. Heck, he might even have actual backup in the form of another P.I. or security agent.

"Why are you following me?" Jordan repeated.

"It's not personal."

Jordan arched his left eyebrow and gave him a flat look. "And that's not an answer."

"It's the only answer I can give you. My employer didn't say why he wanted you followed, only that I was to report where you went tonight and who went with you."

That was a lot of info crammed into that brief two-sentence report. "Why didn't Burke just ask me where I was going? I saw him at the party less than an hour ago."

The guy blinked. "Because Burke didn't hire me."

Jordan studied the guy's face, looking for any sign that he was lying, but he seemed darn smug about telling the truth. "Then who did?"

"Dunno. I was contracted freelance through a broker."

A broker. In other words, a middle man who acted as a go-between for P.I.s and clients who didn't want to be identified. That didn't mean the employer couldn't be traced. It just meant Jordan would have to dig through some layers to get to it. Judging from what Anderson had said, Kinley was the reason for this since his employer had wanted to know who went anywhere with Jordan.

"What did your broker-using employer tell you to do?" Jordan questioned.

"Wait outside Sentron." The man paused. "And when you left, I was to follow you and report back."

They were simple instructions, but they could have deadly implications.

Jordan stared at him. "I'm trying to figure out if you're a really lousy P.I. or if you wanted me to know I was being followed."

Anderson lifted his shoulder.

"Well?" Jordan pressed. "Which is it?"

It still took him several moments to answer. "I was told to be obvious."

So, this was for intimidation. "Why?"

"Wasn't told that," Anderson insisted.

Jordan was about to push for more details, but he spotted the headlights of another vehicle. He eased his gun to his side so as not to alarm any of his neighbors who might be coming home late.

But the car stopped.

It stayed idling just up the street. And the driver kept the high beams on so that the blinding light glared through the darkness.

Anderson glanced back at the car. "I'm leaving now. My advice—you do the same."

"Who's your friend in the car?" Jordan demanded.

"Don't have a clue." His cockiness and confidence vanished, and he turned.

Jordan considered stopping him, but it was too risky. If the guy with the high beams was an enemy, then Jordan would be outnumbered.

Maybe outgunned.

Normally, that wouldn't have bothered him, but he had Kinley in the car. And even though the car and glass were bulletproof, this whole situation was suddenly making him very uncomfortable. Jordan got that uneasy feeling in the pit of his stomach, and that feeling had saved him too many times to start ignoring it now.

"For the record," Jordan said to Anderson, "I'm taking my date to my house, and I'd prefer not to have any interruptions. Understand?"

Anderson held up his hands in mock surrender and looked over his shoulder again. "I'm not the one you should be worried about." And with that, he got into his vehicle, did a doughnut in the road and sped in the direction of the other waiting car. Anderson whipped past it and disappeared into the darkness.

The car didn't budge. It just sat there. Like a predator waiting to attack. Jordan kept his eye on it and walked backward to his Porsche.

"What just happened?" Kinley asked the moment he got inside. She swallowed hard.

"I'm not sure."

He worked fast so that they wouldn't have to sit there any longer than necessary. He opened his glove compartment and extracted a small pair of high-powered binoculars. Through his partially opened door, Jordan looked back at the car.

The high beams were a serious problem, but the binoculars were far from ordinary. His research team had designed them for all-weather, all-terrain surveillance. He made some adjustments and zoomed in on the Texas plates. The moment he had the number, he fed that into his PDA—which wasn't ordinary, either. He had been able to control most of Sentron, his estate and his training facility with that modified PDA.

Since it might take awhile for the data to be retrieved from the Department of Public Safety files, he put the Porsche in gear and started driving.

"What about that other car?" Kinley asked. She turned in the seat and kept watch.

"I'll know details soon." Maybe then he could figure out what was happening and fix the problem. But neither of those things were what troubled him most.

It was Gus.

Jordan prayed he was doing the right thing and wasn't putting the baby right in harm's way. He drove toward his estate.

And the other car followed.

KINLEY FOLLOWED JORDAN through the garage and into the three-story house.

When they'd first pulled into the circular driveway of the estate, Kinley had half expected a chauffeur, a butler or some other servant to come running out to assist Jordan. But no one had come, and with the other vehicle creeping along behind them, Jordan had pulled into the garage, waited for the door to shut and only then had he gotten her out of the car and into the estate.

They entered the house itself through a passageway that led to the kitchen. Massive was an understatement. Like the driveway, it too was circular with floor-to-ceiling windows on the back half of the room. Lights came on as they stepped inside and revealed all gleaming stainless-steel appliances and slick black granite countertops. Not exactly homey, but since there were dishes in the sink, it was obvious that Jordan used the place for mundane things like eating.

"Is it safe to talk?" she asked, looking around. But not at the kitchen decor. Kinley looked for any signs that a child lived here.

She saw none.

"It's safe," he assured her.

Jordan set her overnight bag on the counter, walked ahead of her and made his way through a butler's pantry, a formal dining room and finally into the foyer that was larger than her entire apartment. Again, lights flared on as they entered each new area.

No sign of a child here, either.

Just pristine slate floors, flawless dove-gray walls, a stately, double circular staircase and a twelve-foot-high Christmas tree decorated with silver foil ribbons and delicate Waterford crystal ornaments that seemed to catch every ray of the twinkling lights.

Jordan stopped at a landscape oil painting, one of the few pieces of artwork in the minimally decorated area, and he lifted it to reveal a panel of various buttons and even a small screen. He pressed some of those buttons, probably to activate a security system.

Which they might need.

After a few keystrokes, images popped onto the screen. He obviously had cameras all around the place, and he looked at each frame.

The car was no longer there.

"He must have left." Kinley let out a deep breath.

Jordan didn't respond to that. Instead, he took out his phone, scrolled through the numbers and pressed the call button. He put it on speaker.

Kinley could hear the ringing, but while Jordan waited

for someone to answer, he closed the painting and started down the hall that fed off the left side of the foyer.

"Burke, here," the man finally answered. "Jordan?" He obviously saw Jordan's name on his caller ID. "I didn't expect to hear from you tonight."

"Didn't you?" was all Jordan said.

Burke paused. "Hold on a minute and let me take this call in private."

"Yeah. Sure." Jordan zipped past the half dozen or so rooms, went to one at the far end of the hall and put his face close to a small device mounted on the wall. A red vertical thread of light moved over his eyes.

A retinal scan.

This was no ordinary security system.

The door opened, and he walked inside. It was his office, she realized. And as she'd expected, it was well equipped with laptops, various keyboards and plasma screens on the walls that completely encircled the room. With a flick of a switch, all the screens came on to show the different views of the security cameras.

Definitely not ordinary.

"Okay, I'm back," Burke said. "Am I supposed to know what you meant by your last remark? Why would you think I'd expected to hear from you tonight?" His voice was still friendly enough, as if he thought this might be the start of a joke.

Kinley wished it were a joke.

"Anderson Walker," Jordan countered. "Why was he following me?"

"Was he?"

"Yeah." More keystrokes and the largest screen on the center wall changed images. Not the estate any longer. But Sentron headquarters. The party was still going on, and Jordan zoomed in on Burke. The man was walking toward the far corner of the room, away from the others. Probably so this conversation wouldn't be overheard.

Burke's face looked almost the same as it had earlier, except for the slight tightness around his mouth. Hardly any emotion considering the terse discussion. The man certainly had a poker face.

"You think I'd send one of my men to follow you?" Burke questioned. "Why would I do that?"

"You tell me."

"Can't. Because there's nothing to tell. But trust me, I'll check into the matter. You're sure it was Walker?"

"Positive."

Burke walked even farther away from the others, until he was at the edge of the hall that led to the command center where Jordan had taken Kinley earlier. The man glanced around, his nerves showing slightly. "You confronted him?"

"I did. He said he was freelancing. But there was another car. Someone else. Any idea who that would be?"

"None." The assurance was fast and confident. "I'll get back to you when I find out what's going on." He paused. "Why do you distrust me?"

"I distrust everyone," Jordan answered. "And if you don't mind, I'd like to spend a quiet night with my date. No more P.I.s tailing me." And with that warning still hanging in the air, he hung up.

Jordan kept his attention fastened to Burke and zoomed in even closer when the man pulled back his phone and began to make another call.

But then Burke stopped.

Actually, he froze.

Burke's back was to them so Kinley could no longer

see his expression. He waited there just a few seconds before walking down the hall.

Jordan did more keystrokes, and the images on the screen changed. He'd picked up surveillance with Burke now in the command center.

While she knew this was important—they needed to find out why Anderson Walker had followed them—she couldn't get her mind off her son.

Was Maddox possibly at the estate?

It was certainly large enough for the child to be hidden away there. And he would indeed have to be hidden. After the events of the night, Kinley knew for a fact that her son was in danger.

Partly because of her.

And she silently cursed that she'd ever stepped foot in the Bassfield Research Facility. Of course, if she hadn't, she would have never met Maddox's father. It would take time to try to come to terms with that irony. The very man who had put her in such danger had also given her a child she loved more than life itself.

She glanced at Jordan, who had his attention fastened to the screen. Burke made that call, but she didn't think Jordan was able to see the numbers the man had pressed because Burke kept his back to them.

Kinley stepped into the doorway so she could have another look at the hall. She listened. There were no sounds of a child. No sounds except Jordan's keystrokes on one of the laptops. Her heart dropped a little. She'd wanted to see her child, but the evidence wasn't pointing to his being in the house. There were no servants visible and no nanny, either.

She walked up the hall. Still listening. Still hoping that she would get a glimpse of something that belonged to her son. But she didn't make it far. She heard Jordan mumble something, and she hurried back to see what'd caused that.

The center screen was blank.

"Burke just killed the camera feed," Jordan snarled.

Kinley was about to ask why, but the answer was obvious. "He doesn't want us to know what he's doing."

"Either that, or he's just trying to piss me off. Until midnight, I'm still the legal owner of Sentron." He sat down in the desk chair, took out his PDA and connected it to the computer. "I need to figure out who was in that second car, and it might take a while. If you want something to eat, help yourself to anything in the kitchen."

He was giving her free rein of the place. Her heart dropped even further. He likely wouldn't do that if her son was anywhere around.

New images popped onto the center screen. Frame by frame. It was still images of the other car that had followed them, and Jordan began to whittle away at the high-beam lights. He was trying to get a look at who was behind the wheel.

Kinley started to turn to do more snooping around the estate, but something caught her eye. Not the zipping-by images of the car. Or even Jordan's now-frantic keystrokes. But a screen six monitors to the right of the large center one.

She saw a room.

This time, she could indeed describe it as homey. There was a rocking chair. A sofa. But there was also something else in the corner.

She went closer and saw the chest.

Not some antique or high-end piece of furniture. It was white with bunnies painted on it.

A child's toy chest.

That thought had no sooner flashed in her mind when the image disappeared. In that exact moment, Jordan spared her a glance.

"That was a toy box," she said, pointing toward the screen. "Does that mean Maddox is here?"

But he didn't answer. There was a series of sharp beeps, and Jordan cursed.

Kinley frantically looked around at all the monitors, expecting to see some kind of security breach. Maybe the other vehicle had returned. But the screens showed no such threat.

"What's happening?" she asked.

He eased out of his chair and went to her. So close they were practically touching. Kinley stepped back, or rather she tried to, but he caught on to her arm, leaned in and put his mouth against her cheek.

"We have to do more damage control," Jordan told her.

Oh, God. Not again. "Someone's listening?" she whispered.

"No. Worse. Someone's watching."

Chapter Five

Jordan couldn't believe what was happening.

Someone was damn insistent, and to compound the problem, whoever was doing this had some high-tech resources. This wasn't an amateur intrusion. The equipment aimed at his estate was expensive, and judging from the signals that his security system had picked up, it was also powerful.

"Someone has a thermal scanner aimed at the house," Jordan explained.

And that meant the thermal scanner was recording their every move. They'd have to pretend to be lovers again, until he could neutralize the threat.

"Can you block the signals?" Kinley asked.

"Not this particular scanner. And not in this part of the estate. It'd possibly disrupt the security equipment. I can't risk that."

Because that might be the point. The scanner was perhaps a ploy to get him to disarm the system so there could be a break-in.

She pulled back, met his gaze and, judging from her expression, Kinley was aware of the dangers of a failed security system. "We need to figure out who's doing this. Is there a way to pinpoint the source?"

Good. She wasn't panicking. She was trying to think her way through this. Unfortunately, Jordan had already considered that option. "It's a remote signal. In other words, someone likely left a small device near the house, anywhere within a block radius, but it isn't being manned. So, we wouldn't easily be able to find it. Or trace it. The signals are being sent to some other location."

Probably a location at least a mile away. That's the way he would do it if he'd set up this operation.

And that was a big concern.

This person thought like him.

So who was doing this?

He hooked his arm around Kinley's waist and got her moving. First to the kitchen so he could retrieve her overnight bag, and then he started down the corridor on the opposite side of the house. He kept her close, pulled right against him, and hoped they were generating enough body heat to convince their intruder that sex was about to happen.

Jordan figured he would be convincing enough.

For reasons he didn't want to explore, just being near Kinley reminded him that he did indeed want to have sex with her.

"Where are we going?" she asked.

"My bedroom. Not for that," he added when her breath went still. "The thermal scan won't be able to penetrate the walls because I have them lined with thick metal."

Her breath didn't exactly even out. No doubt it was sinking in fast that he did not live a normal life.

On several levels.

He gave her a kiss, his lips landing on her cheek. It

was one last part of the show before he took her into his suite and shut the door.

"Sorry, but you'll have to sleep here tonight," Jordan informed her, his mind already a dozen steps ahead of what they had to do. "I can take the floor. You can take the bed."

She nodded, but her attention wasn't on him. It was on the room. He glanced around as well, trying to see it through her eyes. He wasn't much for decor—he'd left that to the experts—but this was indeed his space.

His sanctuary.

It wasn't palatial like some of the other rooms. It was homey despite the vaulted ceilings and wall of windows that overlooked the gardens. He'd kept the colors in shades of gray and white. Simple. Clean. And with the security features, it wasn't just homey, it was safe.

"Those windows," she questioned, pointing to them, "are they bulletproof?"

Jordan nodded. "And no one can see in."

She nodded as well. "That explains why there aren't any drapes."

"The glass can be darkened when I want to sleep in." Which wouldn't be anytime soon. Too much to do. He put her overnight bag on the corner desk. "I want to go over your notes."

"Of course." But she didn't move. Kinley took another moment to look around the room. Not just at the windows. But at the mantel over the slate fireplace, the custom carved nightstands, the desk.

"There aren't any," he informed her.

Her shoulders went back. "Any what?"

"Pictures of Gus."

"Yes. Because of the risk," she concluded. But there was still disappointment in her eyes.

Soon, very soon, he wouldn't be able to dodge her questions. Or her need to see her child.

But exactly how much and when should he tell her?

Jordan huffed and watched her reach into the dark gray bag and take out her notes. Kinley was literally the only spot of color in the room. Not that he needed her red sparkly dress to remind him that she was there. His body was certainly attentive to her presence.

"The notes are encrypted," she reminded him. "I'll have to interpret them for you."

"Then, start interpreting," he insisted. Jordan tipped his head toward the bed. "And get comfortable. It's going to be a long night."

She eyed the bed as if it were a coiled snake. Then she eyed him the same way.

Man, he hoped she couldn't read his very dirty mind.

"The bed's a lot more comfortable than the desk," Jordan assured her. Better to talk than think the thoughts he was having about stripping that dress off her. "Hit the switch on the side, and it'll adjust to a sitting position."

With the notes gripped in her hand, Kinley approached the bed with caution and sank down onto the mattress. "Oh," she mumbled.

Oh, as in she concurred with the comfortable part. Kinley gave the thick feather mattress a couple of test bounces, and she smiled.

It faded as quickly as it'd come.

Too bad. She was a knockout when she was scowling, but that smile was good enough to taste.

Something he wanted to do—bad.

Thankfully, one of them had the right mind-set because there were no more bounces. No more smiles. Her attention went straight to her notes. "Where should I start?"

He took a moment, focused and made a mental list. "I need names of everyone who might have had anything to do with the research facility." He went to the concealed bar, hit the button, and it opened. He offered her a drink by lifting a glass, but she shook her head, declining. Jordan fixed himself a double shot of his favorite scotch.

Kinley took a deep breath and looked at Jordan instead of her notes. "The lead researcher, Dexter Sheppard, is dead. He died over a year ago when he tried to set explosives that were meant to kill me. The blast killed him instead. Dexter had sold some of his research on the black market, and he didn't want me around because I could have testified against him and ultimately sent him to prison."

"Dexter Sheppard," he repeated. That was a name that'd popped up while he was checking Kinley's background. There had been no mention in her background about a personal relationship with Dexter, but there was something in Kinley's tone that made Jordan suspect that was the case. "He's Gus's father?"

She nodded. Hardly paused. "Grady Duran was his business partner. He's dead, too. Brenna Martel was an investor and Dexter's lab assistant. She's the one in prison. And then there's Howard Sheppard, Dexter's father who also was an investor. He's dead as well."

Yeah. Jordan had already learned that after discovering Kinley's identity. "What about living investors? Any left?"

"Just Martin Strahan," she answered, again without looking at the notes. The names were likely branded in her brain. God knew how many times she'd already gone over this. "He's a businessman from Houston, and he's the person I'm guessing was behind the initial attempts to kidnap me."

Yes, there had been multiple attempts. Attempts that had nearly killed her, too. That's why Kinley had been placed in the witness protection program.

Since Martin Strahan's name seemed uncomfortably familiar, Jordan went to his laptop on the desk, booted it up and ran a flash inquiry. Not using Sentron's equipment. After the stunt Burke had pulled with the surveillance shutdown, it was best if Jordan stuck with his own toys.

Within a couple of seconds, he had a photo and bio on this Martin Strahan.

It was bad news.

Martin was in his late twenties. Born filthy rich, he'd managed to lose nearly half of his trust fund, something that apparently didn't please his father, Martin Strahan, Sr.

"The guy's ruthless," Jordan concluded. "He operates just on the edge of the law." And he was exactly the kind of man who'd try to use Gus to get Kinley to cooperate.

"That's what I figured." Kinley took a deep breath. "He either wants me dead because he's upset about the money he lost on his investment or he wants me to tell him what he thinks I know."

"The latter would be a stronger motive. That way, he might think he can still recoup his money if he can get that missing formula from you." He tossed back some of the scotch and let it slide through him. It soothed a few muscles that needed relaxing. "Any other living investors and researchers?"

"I'm the last researcher," she mumbled. "And the final remaining investor was a silent partner that Dexter referred to only as Simon."

Jordan nearly choked on his scotch. "Simon? You're sure?"

Concern raced through her eyes. "Why? Do you know him?"

"Maybe." Jordan set his drink aside so he could use both hands on the keyboard. "Tell me everything you know about Simon."

"I never met him, but he must have been from the San Antonio area because Dexter would leave the lab about once a month to brief him. Dexter wouldn't be gone long. An hour tops."

Oh, yeah. This was not looking good. "How much did this Simon invest?"

She eased off the bed, walked closer and studied Martin Strahan's picture that was still on the screen. "Once when I was in Dexter's office, I saw a financial report. From what I remember, Simon invested about two million in phase one of the project. When that portion of the project sold, it made a huge profit. Something like two hundred and fifty million. As an investor, Simon would have gotten a nice chunk of that, at least a fourth, maybe more."

And it would have made Simon a very rich man.

"Was the project ever called Phoenix?" Jordan asked.

She sucked in her breath. "Yes. How did you know? That was supposed to be classified."

Jordan groaned. "It was classified. I found it when Burke Dennison approached me with an offer to buy Sentron. I had him thoroughly investigated."

"Burke?" she questioned.

"Yeah. He's Simon. That was the identity that was used on his investment account that was linked to profits from a classified project."

And because he needed it, Jordan finished off that drink. *Hell. Hell. Hell.* This was not a complication he wanted.

Kinley shook her head. "But what does it mean?"

"It means Burke and Strahan both got stinking rich off the phase-one deal. It also means they're the last investors standing. Judging from what I found in Burke's financials, he put about half his profits into phase two of the research."

"So, he'd be out thirty, maybe forty million dollars," she concluded. She no longer looked shocked. Kinley looked worried.

"That's a lot of reasons to find the missing formula, especially since he wouldn't just get back his investment, he'd stand to earn a big chunk of money when the formula finally sold." He looked at her. "How much would a chemical weapons antidote earn?"

She raked her hand through her hair to push it away from her face. "Dexter said the antidote would become a cornerstone for other antidotes and other research. He said it could end up being worth a quarter of a billion."

That's what he was afraid she'd say. And on the black market, it might go for double that.

People had killed, and kidnapped, for much, much less.

"It's my guess that the person who wants you is an investor," Jordan pointed.

"Or someone after the reward money," Kinley added. "The company that insured the project put up a ten-million-dollar reward."

Oh, hell. Yet another reason to come after Kinley. But ten million was a drop in the bucket compared to what a person could make if they got their hands on that formula.

"Okay, let's put aside any reward seekers for now and focus on the big guns in this. With only two living investors, that narrows it down. Added to that, Martin Strahan hasn't surfaced that we know of. Only Burke."

"Oh, God." Kinley repeated it, leaned against the wall and repeated it again. "Does this mean Burke knows you have my son?"

"Maybe. And maybe he's just on a fishing expedition." It might also explain why Burke was following them. And if so, that meant Burke perhaps knew who Kinley really was.

That was a huge problem that fake kissing or simple damage control couldn't fix.

"When did Burke make the offer to buy Sentron?" she asked.

He knew where this was going. "Three days ago."

"That's when I started following you."

Yeah. Did that mean Burke had been watching Kinley all this time? If so, it wouldn't have been hard to connect the dots when Kinley started spying on him.

And those dots led right to Gus.

Kinley groaned, squeezed her eyes shut and, with the wall supporting her back, slid to the floor and sat. Probably because her legs would not hold her. She stayed there a moment, eyes closed, and then she turned toward him. "Wait. If Burke is behind this, why not just kidnap me? If he knew I was following you, then he also could have taken me at any time."

There was so much hope in her eyes that Jordan hated to burst her bubble. "He might be waiting to see if you lead him to the missing formula."

"That I don't have," she reminded him.

"But if he thinks you do and that you'd be willing

to do anything to keep it for yourself or for someone else, he'd look for leverage." That's what Jordan would do anyway.

"Leverage," she said. Her breath shuddered. "You mean my son."

Jordan didn't verify the obvious.

She clumsily tried to get back to her feet, giving him a too-clear view of her thigh when her dress shimmied up. She staggered a bit in the high stilettos, and so that she wouldn't fall, Kinley grabbed on to his shoulder.

She stared at him. There were tears in her eyes, and they shimmered like the sparkles on her dress. "I have to know my son is okay."

"He's okay. Burke can't get to him."

She frantically shook her head. "But I might have led him to you. To Maddox."

"It doesn't matter. Even if he did follow you, that doesn't mean the baby's in danger." Not immediately anyway. And Jordan knew that reassurances weren't going to be nearly enough.

He was right.

"I need to see him," she begged. "Please. I need to see my son."

Hell. There it was again. That punch of empathy. Once, he would have been able to ignore her plea. Her pain. But that was before Gus. Before he realized that there was something more important in life than his precious company.

Hoping he didn't regret this but knowing he would, Jordan used a series of passwords to get into this portion of his security system. Finally, an image appeared on the screen. Not the room with the toy box. Nor any of the other rooms he'd encased with a cyber security shield.

This was the nursery.

Because of the late hour, it was dimly lit, but Jordan zoomed into the crib where Gus was sleeping.

Kinley made a helpless sound. The tears began to stream down her cheeks. And she touched the screen, gently putting her fingers on the image of Gus's face.

"He's so beautiful," she said, her voice broken by her raw breath.

Yes. He was.

"Who's taking care of him? Who's tucking him in at night?"

Jordan debated how much he should tell her. "He has two nannies, both of whom I trust completely." He'd not only handpicked them, Jordan had trained them himself. And he not only paid them extremely well, he did daily checks to make sure neither of them had betrayed him.

"And he's safe?" Kinley asked. "Where?"

He had another debate. One he lost. Because the truth was, Kinley needed to know. "He's here."

Her eyes widened. "Here?" All breath, no sound.

Jordan pointed to the door on the far side of the room. "There."

"So close," she muttered. Kinley smeared away the tears on her cheek and bolted right toward the nursery door.

Chapter Six

She would see her son.

Kinley wasn't about to compromise on that now. This had to happen.

She threw open the door where Jordan had pointed and came face-to-face with a massive walk-in closet. Certainly not the nursery she'd seen on the computer screen. She looked over her shoulder at Jordan. But instead of an explanation, he calmly closed down the laptop and walked toward her.

"You can't stop me from seeing him," she insisted, though he could. Jordan was in control here. That didn't prevent her from starting a frantic search of the closet. Maybe there was some secret entrance.

Kinley pushed aside some suits and checked the wall. No seams except for the corners. Jordan caught her hand when she reached to move more clothes aside. Maybe it was his touch that drew her back to reality, but it suddenly hit her.

She spun around toward him. "The thermal scanner—"

"Won't work in this area," he interrupted. "It's secured like the bedroom."

Kinley shook her head. "But won't the person scanning notice an entire area of the estate that's not accessible on the equipment?"

"No. The scanner only reads the heat and doesn't register depth. Besides, the estate is over fifteen thousand square feet. The rooms shielded by metal only make up about one sixth of that space, and they're not all clumped together. They feed through the house in a random pattern."

Maybe because her nerves were right at the surface and were making it hard to focus, Kinley had no idea what that meant. "I just want to see my son."

"I know." There was something in his voice. A sadness, maybe? Or maybe it was simply that he was concerned about revealing the hopefully safe haven he'd created.

Jordan reached out and opened the middle drawer of the built-in dresser. He reached to the back of the drawer, pressed in some numbers on a keypad, and a door opened. Not on the wall. But on the floor. She hadn't seen the seam because of the way the slate tiles fit together.

"Go first," Jordan instructed.

Kinley did. In the back of her mind, she considered the danger. That maybe Jordan was leading her here to silence her in some way. But she was surprised to realize that she trusted him.

Maybe that wouldn't turn out to be a fatal mistake.

She went down a flight of stairs that lit up with each step she took. Jordan closed the door behind them and followed her. They were in the basement, and when she reached the bottom, more lights came on. No nursery. No room with a toy box. It was cluttered with large wardrobe boxes. Jordan touched one of those boxes, and it slid to the side to reveal another set of stairs, these leading right back up.

"A security measure," he explained.

And Kinley was thankful for it.

She hurried up the steps to another door where Jordan used another keypad to press in some numbers. They came face-to-face with a gun. And the tall brunette pointing it at them seemed to know how to use the weapon.

"It's okay," Jordan said to the woman. Only then did she lower the gun.

The woman still eyed Kinley with suspicion. "You're sure everything's all right?"

Maybe she thought Kinley was coercing Jordan or something. Part of Kinley was thrilled with the security, and the other part of her hated that her son needed such measures to stay safe.

"Kinley, this is Elsa, one of Gus's nannies."

Kinley nodded a greeting. Elsa nodded back. But she kept that suspicion in her eyes as she stepped aside so they could enter.

"The nannies each have their own room," Jordan explained, pointing to the doors off what appeared to be a playroom. It was filled with toys and painted with bright primary colors, and in the corner was a Christmas tree. "When they need to leave the estate, they dress as maids, and on occasion they help me entertain houseguests. That way, no one will be suspicious if they see them around the place."

Good planning. God knew how long it'd taken him to find, and trust, these women.

Jordan walked to the door straight ahead, took a deep breath and opened it. It was the nursery, the room he'd shown her on the laptop.

And there was her baby.

Finally, she'd found him! The tears came in a flash, filling her eyes, but Kinley quickly blinked them away because she wanted to see her precious baby. She'd never doubted this moment would come because she would have never given up her search to find him. But now that he was here, so close, the emotion and the pain of the past fourteen months flooded through her. God, she had missed him so much.

Kinley couldn't stop herself. She rushed past Jordan and tried to keep her footsteps light so that she wouldn't wake him. He was sleeping so peacefully and was beautiful with his dark brown hair. Like hers. His face was like hers as well. So much of her was in him, and just looking at him broke her heart and filled it all at the same time.

She reached out and brushed her hand over his hair, then his cheek. He stirred, and for a moment she thought he might wake so she could get a better look at him, but his thumb went into his mouth, and he went back to sleep.

"He looks like a Gus," she whispered.

Jordan made a sound of agreement, and that drew her attention to him, so she could see how he was handling this. Even in the dimly lit room, she saw the emotion. Not the emotion of a mere caregiver.

Jordan Taylor loved her son.

"He gets up around seven each morning," Jordan said, checking his watch. "Elsa will call us so you can come and visit with him."

Visit. Yes. That said it all. She couldn't scoop him up and take him away. Not with all the danger and uncertainty lurking out there, but she could visit. For now, that would have to be enough, but it wouldn't be enough for long. One way or another, Kinley intended to reclaim her son.

But how?

Her life was a mess.

Jordan touched her arm, and she knew it was time to leave. She checked her watch as well. It was nearly 11:00 p.m., and that meant she still had eight hours before Gus woke. She'd be counting down the minutes.

She brushed a kiss on the baby's forehead and reluctantly followed Jordan. She had a dozen questions, and it was best if they had some privacy for that anyway. They retraced their steps through the main room, Jordan whispered something to Elsa, and the nanny locked the door behind them when they left.

"How long have you had Gus here?" Kinley asked as they made their way back through the basement. She surprised even herself that she called her son Gus.

"Since Shelly left him on my doorstep. I thought this would be the safest place for him. When I had the estate built, I added the area, thinking I might need it if I ever had to hide away witnesses and such."

In other words, short-term use. "But Gus has been there for fourteen months."

"Yes." That was all he said until they arrived back into the closet of his suite. Jordan closed the door on the floor and reset the security. "That's why I have to move. He needs room to play. He needs a life, and I couldn't give him that if we stayed here."

Jordan stopped and looked away. But Kinley caught on to his arm. "That's why you sold Sentron."

He didn't answer. He didn't have to. In that moment, she realized just how much he'd sacrificed for her son.

And just how much he loved him.

"This is going to be a problem, isn't it?" she heard herself say.

Now Jordan looked at her, with that warning in his eyes. She was getting too close to what he wanted to keep buried beneath.

He tore out of her grip and headed for the bedroom. Kinley went after him and managed to step in front of him before he made it to the desk, where he would no doubt start working so he could avoid this conversation.

But the conversation had to happen.

Their gazes met again. He tossed her another of those warnings, but Kinley didn't move. "You've been a father to him."

But that was as far as she got. Jordan latched on to her arm, pulled her closer.

He kissed her.

Kinley made a sound of surprise. She certainly hadn't seen this coming and she knew it was a ploy to stop the conversation, but much to her disgust, she didn't push him away. She stood there and let it happen.

His mouth moved over hers. Hard. Almost punishing. It was heavy with emotion, and even heartbreak. Maybe it was because Kinley understood those feelings. Heck, she was in the middle of them herself. And maybe she, too, needed to have physical contact with the one person on earth who understood exactly what she was going through.

At least, that's how it was in the beginning.

But then, the kiss softened. So did the grip he had on her arm. Jordan's mouth moved over hers with a clever touch that she hadn't expected. The heat moved from his mouth, generating little fires along the way to her belly. She felt that tug. That need. And Kinley melted, too, against him.

She fought to tear away from his grip, only so she

could slide her arms around him. The kiss deepened, and he used his tongue. The heat soared and turned those little fires to much larger ones.

He backed away from her, and the kiss ended just as abruptly as it'd begun. "You were supposed to stop me," he mumbled.

"Sorry." She ran her tongue over her bottom lip and tasted him there. "I was counting on you to do the stopping. And you did." Thank goodness. Because she'd gotten so consumed in the kiss that she'd forgotten the danger.

Amazing that a kiss could do that.

Which meant it was dangerous in its own right.

Jordan put his hands on his hips, and it seemed as if they were going to finish the conversation that the kiss had postponed. But before he could say anything, his cell phone rang. He jerked it from his pocket, glanced at the screen and groaned. When he showed her the screen, she saw the name of the caller.

Burke Dennison.

Jordan put it on speaker. "Burke, what do you want?" He wasn't friendly about it, either.

"I'm outside your place. We need to talk."

Jordan went to the laptop and pulled up the security screen. Yep, Burke was there, sitting in a high-end black car parked right in front of the estate.

"It's late," Jordan told him. "And I have company."

"Yes. The woman you left the party with. I'm sorry to interrupt, but after our last chat, I think you'll agree we need to sit down and straighten out some things."

Yes. They did. But Kinley wasn't sure they could trust Burke, and she didn't really want him in the house so close to her son.

Jordan glanced at the computer screen again. Then,

at her. Kinley shook her head, not knowing what they should do.

"We'll meet tomorrow morning at ten," Jordan countered, and he didn't wait for Burke to disagree. He hung up.

"You think it's safe to meet with him?" Kinley asked.

"No. But that's exactly why I have to." Jordan pointed to the bed. "Get some sleep because you'll need it."

Kinley mumbled an agreement, rummaged through her overnight bag and came up with a white cotton gown. Not provocative, but after that kiss, full armor might not be enough protection.

She started for the bathroom when she heard Jordan mumble something. She turned around and realized he had seen something on the laptop screen.

"Burke isn't still here, is he?" she asked.

"No. It's not that. I just got the identity of the person in that other car."

"The one who was behind Anderson Walker?" she clarified.

"Yes."

She walked closer when he didn't add anything. "Was it another of Burke's men?"

"No. One of mine. It was Cody Guillory."

Chapter Seven

Jordan checked his watch. Within minutes, he'd have to interrupt Kinley's visit with Gus. Judging from the little boy's and her expressions, neither would like it. Both were into the Lego tower they were building.

A skirt-clad Kinley was on the floor with Gus, who was wearing his usual jeans and a top. This one was a bright Christmas-red that one of the nannies had bought for him on their last secret shopping mission.

When Kinley had first come into the room that morning, Gus had looked at her with suspicion. Probably because his entire world had been Jordan and his nannies. Jordan had taken him to pediatric checkups, of course. But those had always happened in secret, with him driving the child to the small town of Fall Creek where Gus had been examined by Jordan's old friend, Dr. Finn McGrath. Finn was a man who knew how to keep secrets.

Gus had had few opportunities to be a normal kid. And that's why Jordan had decided to make some major changes in his life.

Now the question was, what would happen to all his plans?

Kinley's smiles and laughter said it all. She wouldn't just give up Gus. She was here to stay, and Jordan had to figure out how to deal with that while keeping Gus safe. Safety was his top priority.

But then, he rethought that.

It was a priority all right, but so was Gus himself. Watching the boy, Jordan knew he couldn't give him up, either. Even though he'd never allowed himself to say the words aloud, Gus was his son in every way that mattered. Jordan loved him.

He checked his watch again. "It's time," Jordan told Kinley.

Her smile faded, and she reluctantly gave Gus a kiss on the cheek before she got up from the floor. She brushed off her calf-length black skirt, straightened her top but didn't take her eyes off Gus. Gus watched her, too, and then looked at Jordan as if asking for some explanation as to what was going on.

Jordan stooped down to try to give that explanation but got a big hug instead. Gus launched himself at Jordan, and the little boy giggled.

"Jor-dad," Gus called him, and he laughed again because he knew that Jordan would, too. Jordan couldn't help it. He always laughed when Gus babbled the attempt to say Jordan, and it was a game they played nearly every day.

Jordan gave Gus a kiss on the cheek. "Be a good boy, okay?"

Gus babbled his version of "okay" and waved goodbye.

Jordan waited until the daytime nanny, Pamela, came back into the room. It wasn't necessary for him to remind the woman to lock up and stay vigilant. She would. And she'd keep Gus safe while Kinley and he went back into the main living quarters. Not that he wanted Kinley there for the meeting with Burke, but he didn't want Burke getting suspicious as to why she wasn't around.

"Gus is wonderful," Kinley said on their way out. "I had no idea he'd be able to say so many words."

"We all work with him, and Elsa's a former teacher."

"Teacher turned bodyguard," she mumbled.

Jordan heard the disapproval. Not that she disapproved of Gus's safety, but it was the need for safety that'd kept him shut away. That need had also kept Gus from her.

"He calls you dad," she pointed out.

"Jor-dad," he corrected. "He's trying to say Jordan." But he couldn't explain why he hadn't corrected the boy. He wanted to have that dad label.

It was time to change the subject.

"Burke should be here any minute," Jordan reminded her. "Make an appearance. Walk through the foyer when I open the door and then wait in the bedroom."

"But shouldn't I be there in case Burke says something about being Simon, the investor?"

"That's exactly why you shouldn't be there."

Once they worked their way back in through the closet and into his bedroom suite, he went to his laptop and made sure all the security cameras were registering their images on the split screen.

"But maybe I could guide the conversation in a direction where we could learn more info," she pointed out.

Jordan shook his head. "I don't trust Burke, and I'd rather you not be around him."

She blew out a long breath, obviously not happy that she wouldn't be part of this meeting. "What about Cody? Did you ever find out why he was following us last night?"

"Not yet. He hasn't returned my calls." Which didn't exactly please Jordan. He considered Cody more than a loyal former employee. Of course, it was possible that Cody was simply looking out for him since Jordan had told him that Kinley and he were being followed.

But then, why hadn't Cody let him know that?

It was definitely something he wanted to ask the man. But first, there was Burke to deal with.

Jordan pointed to an image on the top of the screen. "That's the pool house." It was glass encased and sat right in the middle of the garden. "That's where I'll be taking Burke for our chat."

She nodded. "Because you don't want him in the house near Gus."

"Right. Burke's a whiz with developing new equipment, and I can't take the risk that he might have some kind of scanner that can read signals through metal. I know it can't be done at long range, but the technology exits for it to happen at shorter distances."

"Oh," she said, obviously understanding the danger.

Jordan spotted Burke's car the moment it pulled into his driveway. "It's show time," he said to Kinley. And he looked at her to make sure she was steady.

She was.

Steady, and still gorgeous. The clothes didn't help. Her black skirt and silver-gray top clung to her in all the right places. Or the wrong ones, since he probably shouldn't have noticed all those interesting curves.

Jordan had hoped that this attraction would have cooled by now, that the kiss would have been enough for him to realize he couldn't have her. But the kiss had done the opposite. It had reminded him that kissing her wasn't nearly enough. He wanted her in his bed. And not just for sleeping as she'd done the night before when he'd slept on the floor.

He wanted her in his bed with him.

"What?" she said, searching his eyes.

"Nothing."

So that she wouldn't challenge that, Jordan headed toward the front door. "Remember, just make a quick appearance. If you want to listen in on the meeting, you can do that with the laptop."

Kinley agreed, hesitantly, and followed him to the front door. By the time they made it there, Burke had already rung the bell twice. Jordan made sure his gun was positioned for a quick draw in his concealed shoulder holster, and he opened the door to face the man.

"Jordan," Burke greeted, though it was far from friendly.

Jordan stepped aside so he could enter. Right on cue, Kinley made her appearance by walking past them and even managed to look a little mussed and embarrassed, as if she and Jordan had just finished a steamy tryst.

And in his mind, they had.

"This way," Jordan instructed. After he reset the security system, he led Burke past the Christmas tree and through the place. He didn't rush. Didn't want to make it too obvious that he wanted to get him out of the main house. However, he also didn't offer coffee or other refreshments.

"I've spent several hours looking for Anderson Walker," Burke let him know. "No sign of the man. Did he happen to say where he was going?"

"No." Jordan walked through the glass corridor that led to the pool house. "He wasn't exactly volunteering a lot of details. Did you find out who he was working for?"

"No. Did you?"

Jordan shook his head. Last night while Kinley had been sleeping in his bed, Jordan had tried, but the contract for Anderson's services was buried under layers of dummy corporations. Corporations that Burke could have easily created. It would take time and resources for Jordan to dig through them.

Later, that's exactly what he would do.

The pool house was made of prism glass, circular and with an open top. The outside temp was chilly, but the heated water and floor made the room comfortably warm. It was a room he rarely used anymore. Well, since Gus's arrival. He couldn't risk the boy being seen through the glass, and even though his security system ran the entire perimeter of his property, someone might still be able to see the child.

He and Burke sat across from each other in a pair of cushioned wicker chairs. Neither said anything, but a dozen thoughts passed between them. None good. Burke was now the owner of a company that Jordan had loved. And Jordan didn't trust him. The feeling was obviously mutual.

"You've been digging into my background," Burke tossed out. He didn't wait for Jordan to confirm it, either. "What exactly were you looking for?"

"The obvious. I wanted to know if you had your man following me, and why."

"And did you decide if I'm innocent or guilty?" Burke didn't seem overly alarmed at what the answer might be. Jordan knew the man was cocky, but he hadn't thought Burke would aim that cockiness at him. Of course, their positions were different now that Burke owned Sentron.

"Guilty," Jordan declared.

Still Burke offered no reaction. He calmly reached down and swirled his fingers through the lagoon-blue pool water. "Someone tapped into my investment accounts. Was that you?"

"Yes. And someone tried to tap into mine. The person failed."

They stared at each other again. Jordan decided to wait him out because Burke seemed to be on the verge of giving him some real information instead of just repeating things Jordan already knew.

"I've had some sensitive investments," Burke said as if carefully choosing his words. "You zoomed in on those that I made under the name Simon. Why?"

Ah. Now, this is where he'd lie. Except Jordan didn't get the chance. He saw the movement in the glass corridor that led from the main house, and he stood to draw his weapon.

But it was Kinley.

She stopped in the entryway and motioned for him to come to her. Jordan did. And he hurried. Because only an emergency would have caused her to interrupt this meeting.

"I was watching the security screen," she whispered. "Cody Guillory and another of your former agents just drove up in separate vehicles. They're sitting in their cars, looking at the estate."

Hell. This couldn't be good. Jordan glanced back at Burke. "Did you bring backup with you?"

Burke shrugged. "I don't know what you mean."

Jordan didn't believe him. That wasn't a cocky expression. It was a smug one. Burke was playing some kind of game, and Jordan wanted to know the rules.

And the stakes.

Jordan took out his phone and called Cody. The man answered on the first ring. "Looking for me?" Jordan asked.

"Desmond and I need to talk to you."

Desmond Parisi, Jordan's former communications guru. If a place needed to be bugged or put under surveillance, Desmond was the best at Sentron for that. It made Jordan extremely uncomfortable to have a man like that anywhere around the house. Ironic. Because twenty-four hours earlier he would have trusted these men with his life.

"Why do we need to talk?" Jordan questioned Cody.

"It's about Burke."

Jordan didn't know whether to be surprised or not. "He's here."

"Yes. I saw his car. What we need to say should be said in front of him. In front of both of you."

That was an interesting turn. Had Cody learned something about his new boss? And did it have anything to do with Cody following him the night before?

"We're in the pool house. Come in through the backyard," Jordan instructed. Of course, that left him with a huge problem. Two of them, actually. Kinley and Burke. He didn't trust Burke, and Jordan didn't want Kinley caught in the middle if there was any trouble.

He took out his PDA and routed the security surveillance to it so he could keep an eye on the place while this meeting was going on. Jordan also temporarily disengaged the side gate so the agents could enter.

"Go back inside," Jordan whispered to Kinley.

She nodded, took one step, but then Burke stood. "Kinley Ford."

That stopped her. It stopped Jordan's heart for a second as well. Both Kinley and Jordan turned to face the man who'd called her by her real name and not by the alias she'd used the night before when Cody had introduced them.

Jordan eased his hand over the butt of his weapon that he had concealed beneath his jacket.

Burke laughed and held up his hands. "You're going to shoot me, Jordan?"

"If necessary." Jordan made sure there was nothing joking about his tone or demeanor.

Burke chuckled again and sank back down into the chair. "After our conversation last night where you accused me of having you tailed, I decided to check through some surveillance footage taken at the Christmas party. I ran Ms. Ford's image through the facial-recognition software."

"And?" Jordan prompted when the man didn't say anything else. Because she seemed to be holding her breath, Jordan slipped his left arm around Kinley.

"There's no *and* to this," Burke insisted. "I wasn't pleased with your accusations, and I merely wanted to see what was going on that would make you have that kind of reaction." He paused. "But I have to wonder… why would a Ph.D. researcher want to worm her way into a party, only to leave mere minutes later with the host?"

"Because the host is extremely hot, and I wanted to be alone with him," Kinley answered before Jordan could tell Burke to mind his own business.

The tension got worse. A lot worse. And that's how Cody and Desmond found them when they crossed the backyard and came into the pool house. That brought

Burke to his feet again, and judging from his suddenly tight jaw, he didn't seem pleased with his employees' impromptu visit.

Both agents wore jeans and jackets. They also wore formidable expressions that matched their new boss's. Cody took the lead, walking in first. Tall and lean, his former agent looked like an all-American with his sandy blond hair and blue eyes. Desmond had more of an international look and had often done undercover assignments as someone from the Middle East.

"There's a problem," Cody announced. He tipped his head first to Burke and then to Jordan. "You two are in some kind of surveillance war, and you're putting us in the middle. Now, we want to know what this is all about."

Jordan wanted to know the same thing, and all eyes went to Burke.

Burke shrugged again. "I had Cody follow you last night."

"Yeah. I know. Why?" Jordan demanded.

"I thought there was something suspicious about you leaving with Kinley Ford."

Cody's attention snapped to Jordan, and even though he didn't ask the question, he probably wanted to know why Kinley had used an alias. Jordan didn't intend to give his former employee an explanation. The fewer people who knew about her, the better. Now maybe Cody wouldn't continue to dig when this meeting was over.

"I thought maybe Kinley's arrival at the party was connected to the sale of the company," Burke explained. "I was within hours of taking ownership, and I didn't want anything to go wrong. I also considered that maybe Kinley was blackmailing you, and that her actions would put the sale of Sentron at risk."

Jordan wanted to believe that Burke was telling the truth, but he couldn't. After all, Burke was connected to Kinley and the research facility. Depending on how much involvement he'd had with his investment, he might have recognized her the moment she stepped into the party.

Or even before.

Because if Jordan had noticed she was spying on him from the coffee shop, someone else like Burke could have noticed it as well.

Desmond stepped up to stand side by side with Cody, but he aimed his comment at Burke. "I know you're the owner now, but I don't want to do communications surveillance on my former boss."

"Neither do I," Cody agreed.

And the silence returned. Several snail-crawling moments later, Burke finally nodded. He looked at Jordan. "No more surveillance. Can I have the same assurance from you that you won't spy on me?"

"No." Jordan didn't even have to think about it.

There it was. For just a second. A flash of hot anger in Burke's otherwise cool eyes. Then he chuckled. "Go ahead. Keep me in your sight. Dig into my accounts. You won't find anything illegal."

No. But he might find a motive for Burke to go after Kinley, especially if Burke thought she could provide him with the missing formula for the antidote.

"I'll leave through the yard gate," Burke announced, and without lingering, he headed in the same direction from which Cody and Desmond had entered.

Jordan waited until Burke was out of earshot before he spoke to Cody and Desmond. "I'm sorry you two were put in the middle." But he wasn't sorry they'd ratted out Burke. Jordan intended to make full use of whatever loyalty to him the men had left. "Exactly how deep a surveillance did Burke put on me?"

Desmond tipped his head to Kinley. "It was aimed more at her. When Burke told Cody to follow you, he had me give him a comm pack."

A comm pack—a sensitive device that could be used for long-range eavesdropping. *Hell.* Jordan had developed the device himself and knew it was highly effective. Worse, it could bypass detection with nearly all security systems, including the one Jordan had in the Porsche.

"I only used the comm pack when I followed you in the car," Cody explained. "And I told Burke that I couldn't pick up your conversation."

Which meant he had.

It also meant Cody and Desmond had likely heard all about Gus. Of course, Jordan hadn't mentioned the child was at his estate, not until he was in his secure bedroom, but Cody and Desmond weren't fools. They could fill in the blanks.

"There's more," Cody continued, his voice practically a whisper. He stared at Jordan. Nope, make that a glare. Cody obviously wasn't happy about this meeting or with Jordan. "Consider this your retirement gift because after today, my allegiance will lie with Burke. Understand?"

"Yeah." Jordan also heard and understood Cody's resentment. It was there and was feeding the glare the man was still aiming at him.

"Desmond and I know who Kinley is," Cody explained. "Burke had us check on her most of last night."

Jordan's stomach tightened. "Did he say why?"

"He gave us the same spiel about being concerned that she could somehow hold up his taking ownership of Sentron," Desmond continued, keeping his voice low as well. "But after a while, Burke changed his tune and told us to dig into her background. It didn't take long for us to learn that she worked at the Bassfield Research Facility." Now it was Desmond's turn to pause. "We know about the research project and the missing formula. And we also know that this morning at six o'clock, Burke met with Martin Strahan."

The investor.

And the person with the most motive to find and hurt Kinley.

Jordan tried not to react. Hard to do, though, because he certainly hadn't expected Burke to do that. "Did you hear their conversation?"

Both Cody and Desmond shook their heads. "He met with him at the Sentron command center."

And that was the one place where Burke's conversation would indeed be private.

What the devil was going on? Since Burke and Strahan were the last remaining investors, maybe they'd teamed up to come after Kinley. If so, this wasn't good. Jordan didn't need the pair trying to sniff out Gus's whereabouts. And eventually that's what they would do.

Cody extended his hand for Jordan to shake. "Goodbye, Jordan. I wish things were different. I wish we could go back to the way things were." And he slipped a piece of paper into Jordan's palm.

Desmond echoed the sentiment, and the men left through the yard gate.

"My God," Kinley mumbled under her breath. "What do we do now?"

Because they both needed the contact, he tightened his grip around her waist. "We go back inside. I'll beef up security to make sure Burke doesn't have free rein of our privacy." He leaned in and put his mouth to her ear. "Don't say anything out here about Gus."

Her eyes widened, and she looked around. Yes, Burke could still be monitoring their conversation. So Jordan decided to play that to his advantage.

"If Burke is after the missing formula for the antidote, then he's going to be disappointed when he realizes you don't know anything about it."

"Yes," she said, obviously playing along. "Maybe he'll quit hounding us once he realizes that."

Jordan added a "yes" of his own. And he kissed her. It was supposed to be all for show, just in case Burke was somehow watching them. But for some reason his body missed the part about this being a pretense. Just like the other kisses, this one fired through him.

Oh, man.

Her mouth was foreplay, and he had to stop and get his mind back on business.

First, he checked his PDA to make sure the house was still safe. It was. Just as he'd expected. If someone had tried to break in, he would have been alerted. Unfortunately, that level of protection didn't extend to the pool house so he got Kinley moving.

He also discreetly looked at the note that Cody had handed him.

"What is it?" Kinley whispered.

"Martin Strahan's phone number." A real gift, since Jordan hadn't had any luck tracking down the man. "Cody must have gotten it when Burke arranged the meeting with Strahan in the command center."

"Will you call Strahan?"

Jordan hoped to do more than that. He hoped to meet

with the man to see if he could get to the bottom of this. Of course, he couldn't do that until he had Kinley tucked away in a safe place. He didn't want Martin Strahan within a hundred miles of Gus and her.

He hurried their pace so he could get Kinley out of the glass corridor and into the house. Jordan didn't breathe easier until they were inside and on their way to his suite, where they couldn't be monitored. But they'd barely made it to the corridor next to the kitchen when he heard the sound.

There was no warning. No time to react.

The explosion ripped through the house.

Chapter Eight

"Gus!" Kinley managed to shout a split second before Jordan shoved her to the floor.

She landed hard on the slate, and Jordan landed on top of her. Shielding her, she realized, from the blast.

The sound was deafening and shook the entire house. Crystal glasses from the open-faced cabinets crashed to the countertops and floor around them, and the stainless-steel pots on the rack overhead clanged and slammed against each other. Everywhere in the house, there were sounds of things falling and crashing.

Kinley fought to get up so she could race to check on Gus, but Jordan held her in place. She braced herself for the roof or walls to collapse, but other than the broken glasses, nothing else fell nearby.

The security system began to pulse through the house. Not nearly as loud as the blast, but it sent her adrenaline up another notch. If that was possible. Her body was already screaming for her to get to her son.

Jordan must have felt the same overwhelming need because he got up and hauled her to her feet. He began to run toward his suite, just as his cell phone rang.

"Pamela," he said, answering it. It was obviously the

nanny, and Kinley held her breath, waiting to hear what the woman had to say about Gus.

"They're okay," Jordan relayed a moment later. "She's calling the police and the fire department."

The relief nearly made her legs go limp, but Kinley kept running. She couldn't take the nanny's word that they were safe. She had to see for herself.

But Jordan didn't head toward the closet entrance. He stopped at the laptop on his bedroom desk and started viewing the security cameras. It was a smart thing to do. He could maybe pinpoint the origin of the blast. And, God forbid, maybe he could see if there was another one about to happen.

That thought sent her heart racing even more, but Kinley tried to force herself to stay calm.

Jordan touched the top right corner of the screen where she could see the cloud of gray smoke.

"A fire," she mumbled and tried again to run to the closet and the secret stairs.

Jordan held on to her. "Not a fire. That's just limestone and stucco debris from the blast."

That made her breathe a little easier, until she realized where the blast had occurred. On the very side of the house where Burke, Desmond and Cody had made their exit just minutes earlier.

Jordan continued to zoom in on all the areas around the house. The security alarm continued to wail. Her heartbeat continued to pound in her ears.

"The system's detected pieces of a detonator," Jordan informed her.

A detonator. In other words, this had not been an accident. Someone had just tried to kill them by blowing them to smithereens.

He typed in some codes, and the nursery area came onto the screen. Gus was playing with his rocking horse, and both nannies were in the room with him. Standing guard, though all appeared to be well. Thank God those inner rooms hadn't been damaged.

Jordan obviously felt the relief as well because he let out a long breath and pulled her into his arms for a quick hug. "We can't go in the nursery," he told her. Kinley shook her head, but he caught her chin to stop her. "We *can't*. The police will be here any minute. We'll be questioned, and they'll make sure there's not another explosive device, something that maybe my security system isn't picking up."

"What if there is another one?" Her words rushed out in an unbroken stream. "What if this monster tries to blow up the place again before the cops get here?"

"The house was built to withstand a heavy impact," he let her know. "And Gus's area is reinforced with steel."

That didn't eliminate her fears. "But what about a fire?"

"There's a sprinkler system through the place, even around the exterior." With his hands still gripping her face, Jordan stared at her. "We can't tell the police about Gus, understand?"

Her mind was racing, and it took her a moment to fight through the fear so she could nod. "Yes. I understand." It wouldn't be safe because all it would take was for one cop to say something, and Gus's whereabouts would be known.

"What's wrong?" she asked when she saw the renewed concern on Jordan's face.

"Normally, I'd call Cody at a time like this." He let go of her, took out his phone again and scrolled through the numbers. "But I need to stay away from him and anyone else at Sentron. I'll call a friend. Cal Rico. I know I can trust him."

Kinley hoped that was the case. They certainly needed someone on their side.

While Jordan made that call, he continued to check the surveillance cameras. There were no signs of Burke, Desmond or Cody. Just that billowing dust to indicate how close they'd come to being hurt.

She heard the sirens, and while Jordan finished up his call to his friend, they made their way toward the front of the house. The Christmas tree was still standing, but many of the expensive Waterford ornaments had shattered onto the floor.

"Stay back," Jordan warned her when he reached for the doorknob.

Oh, mercy. She hadn't even thought of an attack from something other than an explosive, but the culprit could be waiting outside. Waiting to kill them.

Still, Jordan put himself right in what could be the line of fire when he opened the door. The SAPD were there. Three cruisers and, in the distance, she could hear the sound of a fire engine.

One of the uniformed cops came up the steps and flashed his badge. "Any idea what caused the explosion?" he asked.

"My security system indicated fragments of a detonator," Jordan answered.

The cop motioned for them to move. "You need to evacuate."

"Evacuate?" Kinley challenged. "No—"

But Jordan cut off the rest of her protest by touching his fingers to her lips. "It'll be okay. We have to let the police do their job."

She shook her head and tried to tell Jordan that she wanted to stay in the house so she'd be near Gus, but that didn't stop Jordan from latching on to her arm and taking her down the steps. "We'll wait in the cruiser," he told the cop.

And then Jordan froze.

Kinley froze too and followed his gaze. She braced herself to see another explosive. Or something worse.

It was something worse.

Because across the street, standing on the sidewalk, was a man that she recognized from his photos.

The ruthless investor who was likely after her and her son.

Martin Strahan.

JORDAN CURSED. They certainly didn't need this now. But a confrontation was apparently about to happen because Martin Strahan stepped off the sidewalk and started toward them.

Jordan automatically moved in front of Kinley, and he opened his jacket so he could put his hand on the butt of his weapon.

Martin Strahan only held up his palms to indicate he wasn't carrying a weapon. That didn't mean, however, that he wasn't armed. He certainly looked the type to need a weapon. He was around six feet tall and had a solid enough build, but his pale blond hair and milk-white coloring made him look more like an anemic high school computer nerd than a high-stakes investor and businessman.

But he didn't need strength to set explosives.

Jordan figured that's exactly what he'd done. Well, maybe. It did seem stupid to hang around if Strahan had been the culprit. Still, he was there and had the means, motive and opportunity.

So did Burke.

And that meant Jordan had a mystery to solve. Fast. Because until he found the person responsible and put him behind bars, Kinley and Gus were in danger.

"Kinley Ford," Strahan greeted. He stopped right next to the police cruiser and didn't even glance at the chaos in the aftermath of the explosion. He kept his attention fastened to Kinley. "I've been looking for you for a long time. You're a hard person to find."

"I could say the same about you," Jordan countered. The sirens grew louder, and Jordan knew it was only a matter of seconds before the fire department arrived. "Are you responsible for the explosion?"

"Me? Of course not."

Jordan studied his expression but couldn't tell if the man was lying. "Then why are you here?"

"Bad timing on my part. I stepped from my car, and boom! I take it no one was hurt?"

"No one," Jordan assured him. The fire engine and a bomb squad van pulled to a stop in front of the house, and the men began to hurry toward the point of origin.

Now Strahan's ice-blue eyes turned toward Jordan. "I understand you're searching through my background. No need. I'll tell you everything you need to know."

Right. Everything that wouldn't land him in a jail cell. "I'd be very interested in having a conversation with you."

"Yes, I'll bet you would." Strahan turned back to Kinley. "And how about you? Are you finally ready to talk to me?"

"I'll talk to you," Kinley said, stepping out from

behind Jordan. "But I know nothing about the missing research information."

"Maybe. Sometimes people know more than they think they know." And with that cryptic response, he turned and walked toward one of the uniformed officers. "Jordan Taylor believes I had something to do with this. How soon can you exclude me as a suspect?"

The officer looked at Strahan as if he'd just sprouted a third eye. Then the cop looked at Jordan, obviously waiting for an explanation.

"I want him questioned," Jordan finally said.

"All right." The officer glanced around and motioned for another uniform to join them. "I'll have him taken down to headquarters."

Strahan started to walk away with the officer but then turned to face Jordan and Kinley. "I'll call you and set up a meeting. It'd be in all of our best interests if that meeting were to happen today."

Jordan wasn't so sure of that. He needed to get things under control here at the estate before he dove into new waters with the likes of Strahan. However, the man might be able to give them answers to put an end to all of this.

"You two need to move farther from the house," one of the firemen shouted to Jordan. "Just in case there's a secondary explosion."

Jordan heard the change in Kinley's breathing and knew she was thinking of Gus. He caught on to her arm and headed not for the cruiser but the guesthouse just inside the high wrought-iron fence that ran the entire perimeter of the backyard. He needed to find a private place where he could monitor security and make sure no one tried to get into the nursery area.

"We'll be in the guesthouse," he told the fireman, and Jordan headed there before anyone could object.

Later, of course, Kinley and he would have to give statements, but that could wait.

"We need to check on Gus," she whispered.

Jordan intended to do that ASAP. They hurried through the side gate and to the guesthouse. It had a keyless entry, and he punched in the code so they could enter the three-room cottage. He shut the door, locked it and immediately put another code into his PDA so he could rearm the estate's internal security system.

If someone went into the house, he'd know about it.

Then he clicked the screen to surveillance so he could take a look at the nursery. He turned the screen toward Kinley so that she could see Gus calmly watching a DVD with cartoon characters.

"Pamela and Elsa will guard Gus with their lives," Jordan reminded her.

She nodded and dropped back so that she was leaning against the door. She was pale. Shaking. And her breath was gusting to the point she was close to hyperventilation.

"I did this," Kinley said. "I brought this danger to Gus."

"No." Jordan couldn't believe he was on her side. But he was. "This has been brewing for a long time, and the only way it can end is for the person to be caught."

Jordan could see that now. He couldn't build a shelter strong enough or hire enough bodyguard-nannies to protect Gus. If they ever hoped to have a normal life, the danger had to stop.

Kinley shook her head. "If I leave—"

"It won't do any good. Burke and Strahan have both already connected you to me. That means they've connected us to Gus."

Tears sprang to her eyes. "God, I'm sorry. I'm so sorry."

Jordan hadn't intended to touch her, but he couldn't just stand there while she fell apart. He pulled her into his arms, and she relaxed as if she belonged there. Not exactly a comforting thought.

"Once we get the all clear," he explained, "I'll add more security measures, and if Strahan doesn't call back, I'll phone him to set up a meeting."

"What about Burke?"

Yeah. Burke had been on his mind, too. "Burke's a problem. Maybe Cody and Desmond as well."

She pulled back, blinked back more tears. "You think Cody or Desmond could be behind this?"

"I can't automatically rule them out. Both were upset that I sold Sentron." But he didn't want to believe his former employees would turn against him.

Of course, there was the issue of money. In addition to the substantial reward being offered by the insurance company, there was a lot of cash to be made if that antidote research resurfaced. Maybe this wasn't personal. But even then, Jordan couldn't quite wrap his mind around such a betrayal.

Since Kinley was staring at him and still looking very fragile, he showed her the image of Gus again. "See? He's fine, really."

"Why aren't you mad at me?" she asked. "You warned me this could happen. You told me I should have stayed away."

Yeah. He had. But if their situations had been reversed, he would have done the same thing. Nothing could have kept him from seeing Gus.

"We'll get through this," he promised, though he wasn't sure exactly how he could make that happen. He only knew that he had to. No case had ever been this important.

"You love Gus," she said, with those tears still shimmering in her eyes.

This was almost as uncomfortable a topic as the attraction between Kinley and him. "I don't talk about my feelings a lot," he answered. Which was an understatement.

"I understand."

He made a sound that could have meant anything and checked the PDA screen to make sure Gus was still okay. He was.

"I saw the newspaper articles when I was trying to figure out if you might have Gus," she added.

Then, she knew that his entire family—his parents, his brother and his sister—had all been kidnapped and then murdered.

"When you were eight years old, your father was an archeologist in the Middle East working on a sanctioned dig," Kinley continued. "All of you were taken hostage. Only you escaped."

"I didn't escape," he corrected. "The kidnappers released me so I could deliver a message to the American embassy that my family would be killed if other political prisoners were not released. Negotiations failed. My family died. End of story."

But not the end of the emotional baggage it'd created. He'd always have that particular dark passenger lurking in his memory.

She reached up and smoothed the worry lines on his bunched-up forehead. Until she did that, he had not even been aware of his tense expression. She came up on her toes and touched her lips lightly to his. "I'm sorry. I didn't mean to dredge up old memories."

She didn't have to dredge. They were always there. They drove him. They'd made him successful. Because no matter what he did in life, he'd always be trying to save them. An impossible task, and one that had gnawed away at him.

Until Gus came into his life.

Yeah. He loved the little boy. And that scared the hell out of him. Because the last time he'd loved someone, he hadn't been able to save them. They'd all died.

She took his hand, moved them closer to the screen and smiled when she saw Gus. "You've done an amazing job with him. He's happy, very well adjusted."

Kinley brushed her mouth over his again. No doubt a gesture meant to comfort, but his emotions were right there, right at the surface, and he didn't play fair the way she was doing.

He kissed her.

Why, he didn't know.

Yes, he did.

He always wanted to kiss her, and this was an excuse to do it. The sky-high levels of adrenaline. The fear. The strange union they'd been forced to form because of a child. All of that seemed like logical reasons even if they weren't.

The taste of her soothed him. It seemed to trickle through him, as if she'd touched him with those delicate fingers. And then she did touch him. She wound her hands around him and slid her fingers into his hair.

Everything stayed simple. Easy. Just a kiss. But just as quickly, it changed. Jordan moved closer the same moment she moved toward him.

Their bodies met.

And the fire blazed.

Oh, man. This was such a bad idea, but he didn't stop. In fact, he made things worse by sliding his left hand down her side and to the curve of her hip. Jordan gripped on to her and dragged her closer until his erection was right against a part of her that he wanted more of.

Kinley moaned. It was silky and rich. And she moved, too. Her sex against his caused a multitude of sensations. All good ones. Except for the dirty thoughts he had about what he wanted to do to her.

A groan rumbled deep within his chest.

"We can't do this now," Kinley mumbled against his mouth.

That made him curse. Because she was right. And because she'd added *now.* That left the door open for sex at a later time.

Jordan forced himself to pull back, and he met her gaze. He considered a lecture—meant more as a reminder for him than her—to reiterate that they shouldn't get involved. But he'd be wasting his breath. Sex would happen. It was inevitable. Now he just had to figure out how to handle the fallout.

The knock at the door caused Kinley to jump, and Jordan moved her to the side and got his weapon ready. However, he soon discovered their visitor was one of the men who'd arrived with the bomb squad.

"Sgt. Hernandez," the man said, identifying himself. "We've made a check of the house exterior, and we found the fragments of the detonator. It set off an I.E.D., an improvised explosive device. It was meant to do some damage, and if anyone had been walking near it at the time of detonation, they would have been seriously hurt or worse. You guys were real lucky."

Jordan had to take a deep breath. Now the question was, had the I.E.D. been left for Burke, or had Burke been the one to leave it?

"We need to know who'd do something like this," the sergeant continued.

"Yes. We want to cooperate, but is it possible to take our statements here at the estate?"

The sergeant stared at them. "Most people want to get away from something like this."

"I understand, but Ms. Ford is shaken up. It'd be easier on both of us if we could stay here."

And that way he'd be close to Gus.

"Okay." The sergeant nodded. "I'll send someone in to take your statements. Stay put, though, until we've finished cleaning up those bomb fragments."

"Will do." Jordan said goodbye, closed the door and relocked it. He looked at Kinley. "We'll have to tell them the truth about everything but Gus."

She didn't get a chance to concur because his cell phone rang. It was a call he'd been expecting from his friend, Agent Cal Rico. "Cal," Jordan answered, "please tell me you can help."

"Absolutely. I can have security measures in place within the next two hours. I can make your estate a fortress."

"Good. Because we're going to need it. One more thing. I need to arrange a meeting, and it can't be at the estate. I want to have it at my training warehouse. You know the location?"

"The one off Bulverde Road." He didn't wait for Jordan to confirm it. "Why there?"

"Because I can control the security while you keep a watch on things here at the house."

"But if you're going to be at the training facility, then why have me at the estate?"

For the biggest reason of all: Gus. "I'll explain that when you get here. Thanks, Cal."

Jordan ended the call. That was phase one. For phase two, he took out Strahan's number that Cody had given him, and he sent a secure text message to both Strahan and Burke.

Meet me at the training facility. Seven o'clock tonight. Come alone.

Kinley's eyes widened when she saw the message. "You think that's a safe thing to do?"

"No." It was far from safe. But one way or another, Jordan was going to get answers.

Chapter Nine

Kinley stared at the building in front of them.

The training facility was indeed a warehouse. A huge one with a dark gray metal exterior that looked exactly like the dozen or so other warehouses that surrounded it. This was not the part of the city that tourists normally saw. It was isolated and downright spooky with the winter mist in the air and lights streaming over the metal.

While he drove into the parking area in front of the building, Jordan entered a code on his PDA, and large doors slid open so he could drive right inside. Another code closed the doors, and while Kinley approved of them not having to walk across the parking lot, the inside of the warehouse was nearly as creepy as the exterior.

Even in the dim light, Kinley could see the center of the building was open from front to end. At least a five-hundred-foot stretch. But the sides were a different matter. Not exactly open space. There were ropes dangling from the ceiling, climbing webbing and what appeared to be bunkers and rooms painted in camouflage.

"I used to train agents here," Jordan explained.

He grabbed two thick legal-size manila envelopes, stepped out, entered something else on that PDA and more lights flared on. She didn't know what was in the envelopes, but Jordan had been working in his office for most of the afternoon while she spent time with Gus.

Even with the lights, the place still seemed just as intimidating. The place loomed over and around her, and Kinley wondered if this had been the safest place to meet Burke and Strahan. While she was wondering, she hoped that Agent Cal Rico was as good as Jordan claimed because the man was essentially responsible for keeping Gus safe. However, if this meeting went well, if she could convince Burke and Strahan that she knew nothing about the missing research, then the danger could possibly end here tonight.

And she'd have a safe Christmas with her son.

Kinley got out of Jordan's Porsche and walked toward where he was now standing. Her footsteps echoed on the concrete floor. "You said Agent Rico would call immediately if there was any sign of trouble back at the estate?" She already knew the answer, but Kinley needed one more reassurance that coming here wasn't the biggest mistake of her life.

"If there's a problem, Cal will call us," Jordan verified. "He has a daughter a little younger than Gus, and he knows what it's like to have a child in danger. Don't worry. He'll protect Gus."

Oh, she'd still worry. Nothing would stop that.

She rubbed her hands up and down her arms. She was wearing a jacket and wasn't especially cold, but she still felt a chill inside her. "Does Burke own this place now?"

"No. He has his own training facility. I decided to keep this for a while in case I ever started another agency."

She nodded, then checked her watch. It was still a

half hour until the meeting was supposed to start. That seemed a lot of time to kill, especially since she was already antsy to get started.

And to get back to the estate.

"Follow me," Jordan instructed. He led her to the right side, through a set of rooms that looked like something from a movie set. They had doors, windows and even some furniture.

There were bullet holes in the walls.

"I had a tunnel built beneath the place," he explained. "And there are all sorts of training tools. Rappelling gear. Rifles that shoot dummy bullets."

"There were real bullet holes in that wall back there," she pointed out.

He nodded. "Sometimes, we train with live ammo."

Good. She hoped his friend, Cal Rico, had as well. That way, if this turned into a worst-case scenario, he would know what to do.

They walked to the midway point of the warehouse where he dropped the two manila envelopes on the floor.

"Are you going to tell me what's in those?" she asked. "The last time I brought them up, you dodged the question."

"They're our freedom, I hope."

And with that cryptic response, he took her up a flight of stairs to a room that was half metal on the bottom and thick glass on top. "This is the observation deck and command center," Jordan explained. "It's bulletproof and has complete communication capabilities. I can control everything from here."

He pointed to the open space in the center below them. "That's where Burke and Strahan will be."

Kinley felt the instant relief and knew then the reason

he'd chosen this place. They couldn't have this kind of safety at the estate. This way, Burke and Strahan wouldn't be anywhere near her son, and Jordan and she would be tucked away in that observation area.

"And the envelopes?" she reminded him.

He sank down into one of the two chairs and clicked on some equipment mounted on a console that half circled the deck. "Among other things, I'm giving them copies of your encrypted notes."

Kinley's mouth dropped open. "What?"

"I'm hoping they'll find something to lead them to the person who stole the research. Since I know that wasn't you, it'll get them off your trail."

She tried to work through the logic of that and took the chair next to him. "But one of them might have stolen the info about the project from the lab. One of them could already have way too much information."

Jordan's gaze came to hers. "Good. I hope that's the case. Then, the two of them can fight it out."

Yes. That would be a godsend. Heck, they might even turn their attention to Brenna Martel in prison. Kinley didn't care as long as the men weren't around to endanger Gus. Finally, she could find a happy ending for all of this.

Well, maybe.

"And if they still believe I have the antidote?" she questioned.

"Then, I have a backup plan." He swiveled his chair in her direction. "Do you have any idea what I used to do for a living?"

It seemed an odd question, especially since she'd followed him for days. "Of course. You owned Sentron."

"I've killed people, Kinley," he flatly stated. "I've

been ruthless. Cutthroat. All within the parameters of the law. But barely," he added.

She certainly hadn't thought he was a boy scout, but that caused her a moment of uneasiness. Then she reminded herself that she trusted him.

"I can go head-to-head with Burke, Strahan or both, and I can win," Jordan continued. "But what I can't do is put Gus at risk. You understand what I'm saying?"

Afraid of the answer, she shook her head. "What do you mean?"

"If things don't go as planned tonight, if I can't get one hundred percent assurance that these men will back off, then I have to move Gus immediately. I have to send him out of the country."

I'll go with him, was her first thought.

Oh, God, was her second.

Because she couldn't go with Gus. The danger would just follow her, and her son. She'd already done that to him once and couldn't do it again.

"How long would he have to be gone?" But she waved off any response. She knew how this had to play out. As long as the research for the antidote was still missing, then she couldn't be with Gus.

"I'm sorry." Jordan slid his hand over hers. "I've gone over this all day, and I can't figure out another way."

Then, giving Burke and Strahan her encrypted notes would have to work. Because the idea of not seeing her son broke her heart. This had to end soon.

"Kinley?" Jordan said. He leaned over and slipped his arm around her. "I'm not going to let anything bad happen to Gus." And he hugged her.

The hug barely lasted a second because a buzzing sound came from the console. Jordan eased away from her, took a deep breath and pressed a button. On the screen she saw not one car but two approach the warehouse. A moment later, Jordan's cell phone rang.

"Burke," Jordan answered after glancing at the caller ID screen. He zoomed in on the vehicles. "Yes, that's Martin Strahan behind you. I thought it would be beneficial if we all talked face-to-face."

Kinley couldn't hear exactly what Burke was saying, but judging from Jordan's expression, the man wasn't pleased with the additional guest at this meeting. Tough. Kinley wasn't pleased with this entire situation. Well, except for the fact that she had Jordan by her side. As bad as all of this was, she couldn't imagine getting through this without him.

She froze.

Repeated that to herself.

And mentally groaned.

She was falling for him. Not good. The last man she'd gotten involved with had nearly gotten her killed. Besides, she needed to focus on her son and not a relationship. Even if a relationship was exactly what her heart and body thought she needed.

Jordan ended the call and pressed a button that opened the door where they'd driven in. The two cars pulled in and parked behind the Porsche.

"They're alone?" she asked, watching as both men exited their cars.

"They appear to be. I have an infrared monitor, and I'm not picking up any additional heat sources in either of their vehicles."

So, maybe they would play by Jordan's rules.

Burke had stepped from his car first. Then Strahan. Burke spared Strahan a glance—a frosty one—before he looked up at the observation desk. "Jordan," he greeted, obviously able to see them through the glass.

Jordan turned on the speaker function. "Thank you for coming."

Burke tipped his head to Strahan. "You didn't mention that you were inviting him."

"No? Must have slipped my mind. I didn't figure you'd care since you two are old friends."

"Former business associates," Strahan spoke up, his voice much higher pitched than Burke's drawl. "I don't trust him. Even more, I don't like him."

"The feeling's mutual," Burke snarled before he looked up at Jordan and Kinley again. "Do you plan to stay up there in your ivory tower or come down and join us?"

"The ivory tower suits me," Jordan commented. If he was distressed by this meeting, he certainly wasn't showing it. Kinley, on the other hand, was definitely distressed. Her heart was racing, and every muscle in her body had tightened to the point of being painful.

"Well?" Strahan prompted. He impatiently checked his watch. "Care to tell me why you called this meeting?"

"The envelopes on the floor are for you. Your names are on them."

Kinley glanced at Jordan to question why he would label them with their names, since the information inside was supposedly identical, but Jordan had his attention focused on the two men.

Strahan picked up his envelope and tore it open. Burke waited a moment before reaching down and retrieving his and doing the same. Both began to go through the pages.

"They're copies of Kinley's encrypted research notes. It shouldn't take either of you long to break the code, and when you do, I think you'll find something interesting—that Kinley doesn't know where the missing antidote is."

"So she says," Burke accused.

"No. It's the truth. She made those notes because she was trying to figure out what could have happened to the formula for the antidote before and after the research facility was destroyed in an explosion."

"And what did happen?" Strahan asked.

"I don't know," Kinley volunteered. "But I'm hoping you'll be able to figure it out when you go through those notes and compare them to what you two personally know about the situation."

"I've added copies of the federal investigation," Jordan continued. "There's also a log of everyone who entered the research facility the day it was blown up. Both your names are on the log, by the way."

That caused the men to toss each other a glare. Good. Kinley wanted them pitted against each other. Maybe that would take the focus off Gus, Jordan and her.

Strahan reached inside his jacket, causing Jordan to issue a warning. "The glass is bulletproof."

"And I'm not stupid. I wouldn't risk shooting the one woman who might be able to clear all of this up."

Maybe. Or maybe he wanted her dead for some other reason.

Strahan extracted a thick white envelope from his coat and tossed it on the floor where Jordan's had originally been. "Those are photocopies of Dexter Sheppard's final notes from the research project."

Kinley went still. Dexter's notes. She'd known they existed, of course, but she thought he had taken them with him when he faked their deaths.

She stared at the envelope.

Burke stared at it, too. "How did you get that information?" he demanded.

Strahan shrugged. "I stole Dexter's notes the night of the explosion. But before you accuse me of having the missing antidote formula, rethink that. They're just notes, and I've had men working on them for months, and they haven't been able to make heads or tails of them. I'm figuring that Kinley will be able to help. That's why I've been looking for her."

It made sense. Well, maybe. And maybe this was some kind of trick. "How did you find me?" she asked.

"Through Burke," Strahan calmly provided. "I've been watching him for months—just like he's been watching me—and lo and behold, you walk right into the Sentron Christmas party."

"You hired Anderson Walker to follow us?" Jordan demanded.

"No." Strahan seemed surprised, or something, with the question. "I used my own men. I wouldn't trust one of Burke's lackeys."

Which meant Burke had likely sent Anderson. But why? For intimidation, or was there something else behind that incident?

"Read Dexter's research notes," Strahan told her. "And get back to me. That antidote is worth more than all three of us have in our bank accounts. It's in your benefit to find it because frankly, I'm a bit desperate. I need the money back that I invested."

And desperate men did desperate things. Like trying to use her son to make her cooperate.

What other desperate things had Strahan done?

Kinley thought of Shelly Mackey and how the

woman had died to protect Gus. Strahan had been involved with this from the start—including fourteen months ago when Shelly had been killed.

"Are you the one who went after Shelly?" Kinley asked, staring straight at Strahan.

She watched his eyes and saw the flash of recognition. "Shelly who?" he asked.

He was lying. Strahan must have known every little detail about Kinley, and even if he hadn't figured out that Shelly had handed Gus over to Jordan, the man would have at least known that Kinley's P.I. friend had been murdered in the midst of all this. He would have had Shelly investigated to see if she was connected to the missing formula.

Burke tipped his head to the envelope that Strahan had put on the floor. "By giving Kinley and Jordan those, you have no guarantee that if she and Jordan find the truth, they'll tell you. I'm betting they go straight to the Feds."

Strahan smiled. "I think not. Kinley understands the need to have this resolved in such a way that all parties will be, well, content."

"Are you saying we share the profits from the antidote?" Burke questioned.

"I'm saying that when Kinley gives us what we want, she'll be free to go. And you and I can then work out an acceptable compromise that will compensate us for our initial investments and the time and trouble we've gone through since this dog and pony show started."

Burke didn't look like a man on the verge of a compromise, but he also didn't argue. He turned, headed for his car and, a moment later, Strahan did the same. After the men had backed out of the warehouse, Jordan closed the doors.

"I think Strahan hired the person who killed Shelly," Kinley let Jordan know.

"I think you're right." Since Jordan didn't hesitate, he'd likely already come to the same conclusion. "But we have to prove it. A traffic camera recorded Shelly's murder. I'll have someone go through it again and see if they can match Shelly's killer to anyone on Strahan's payroll."

That seemed a long shot, but it was better than no shot at all.

"You think those are really Dexter Sheppard's notes?" Jordan asked.

"If they are, I'll be able to tell. Dexter and I worked closely, and I can recognize his handwriting."

She swallowed hard, remembering her stormy relationship with Dexter. A relationship that had produced Gus. She was thankful for that, but Kinley would never be able to forgive the man for making her life a living hell. If it hadn't been for Dexter, there wouldn't have been a shady research project, and Gus and she wouldn't be in danger now.

Jordan adjusted some of the console instruments and stood so they could leave. Kinley hurried ahead of him on the stairs and reached for the envelope.

"Wait," Jordan practically shouted. He hurried in front of her, stooped down and examined it.

"You think it's some kind of booby trap?"

"With a man like Strahan, you just don't know."

Jordan was right. She'd been so anxious to find a resolution to all of this that she'd temporarily forgotten that she couldn't trust Burke or Strahan.

Jordan used the corner of his PDA to lift the envelope so he could further study it. He must have approved of what he saw, or didn't see, because he picked it up and opened it.

It was indeed notes, and it took Kinley just a glance to realize that was Dexter's handwriting. Or else it was a very good forgery.

Jordan handed them to her, then paused. "You were in love with him?"

The question threw her a moment, because it felt a little strange talking to Jordan about her former lover. "I thought I was." She shook her head. "I didn't really know him. And if he were alive, he'd be the one trying to use Gus to get to me. Dexter wouldn't have protected him the way you have."

A muscle flickered in Jordan's jaw, and he reached out and ran his hand down her arm. It seemed as if he were about to say something. Something personal about this attraction between them. But then he must have changed his mind because he started for the car.

"We have to move Gus tonight," he said from over his shoulder.

"What? Tonight? I thought this plan stood a chance of working?"

"A chance isn't good enough. I know now that neither Burke nor Strahan will back off, not even with a bribe. They're counting on hundreds of millions of dollars from this deal, and they won't stop until they have the antidote. Or until they kill each other." He opened the car door for her. His eyes met hers and in them she saw that he was right.

Still, this would break her heart.

"Then, maybe they'll kill each other," she mumbled, getting inside the Porsche.

"I doubt we'll get that lucky." Jordan got in the car

as well. "And even if we use Dexter's notes to learn the formula, we can't just give it to Strahan and Burke. We'll have to turn it over to the authorities."

"Of course." Though she had to admit, the idea of using it to get Burke and Strahan off their backs was tempting.

"They don't trust each other. That's obvious. So, maybe I can push that a little harder, give them a reason for the distrust to erupt." He started the car, opened the warehouse door and backed out. "It wouldn't have to be something to make them literally kill each other. Just enough to incriminate them so they land in jail."

"Jail," she repeated. "You think that would stop them from coming after us?"

Jordan took a deep breath and drove away. Fast. "No."

Kinley tried not to react to that. She'd known in her heart that it was true, that there was only one way this could end.

Someone would die.

The thought had no sooner formed in her head when she heard the sound. Not a blast. More like a swish. At first, Kinley thought it was the noise from the closing warehouse doors, but then the Porsche jerked violently to the right.

"Get down!" Jordan ordered. "Someone just shot out one of the tires."

Chapter Ten

Jordan latched on to the steering wheel and tried to keep the Porsche steady. It was next to impossible.

Especially after the second shot.

The bullet must have gone straight into the passenger's front tire because his car jerked violently in that direction. He had no control and certainly couldn't speed away from this attack.

"The glass is bulletproof," he reminded Kinley. But that wouldn't be nearly enough to keep her safe.

He had to slow to a crawl, and by doing so, they were sitting ducks.

Jordan grabbed Kinley's hand and put it on the steering wheel. Not that it would help much, but it freed him up to draw his gun and get ready to fire. He looked around, trying to pick through the dimly lit area, but he didn't see the shooter. Then he glanced up at the flat warehouse roof.

There was a man dressed all in black and wearing a dark ski mask. If it hadn't been for the glint of the security lights on the rifle, Jordan might never have seen him.

Jordan didn't want to risk lowering the window so he could return fire. That would create an even more dangerous situation. Instead, he drove forward, creeping along, so he could put some distance between them and the shooter.

There was another shot. The bullet smashed into the back of his car. The body had been modified to be bulletproof, as well, but sparks flew from the impact.

Another shot.

Then another.

"He's not trying to kill us," Jordan mumbled. But the words had no sooner left his mouth when he saw the headlights of another car. It was coming right at them.

Jordan tried to steer to the side of the narrow road, but he had almost no control. And besides, he needed his hands free in case this turned into a full-scale attack. It was a risk—anything he did would be a risk—but he stopped.

So did the other car.

Like the vehicle from the night before, the high beams were on, and they glared right into the Porsche and made it impossible for Jordan to see. He checked the rearview mirror to make sure the rooftop gunman wasn't about to join the fight.

But the man was no longer on the roof.

Hell.

Jordan reached over to the glove compartment and took out another gun and extra magazine clips. "Do you know how to shoot?" he asked Kinley, pressing the gun into her hand.

She shook her head. "But I'll try." Even in the milky light, he could see the terror on her face. "What about Gus?"

"Cal would have called if there'd been an attack." Jordan was sure of that. He was also sure that he couldn't count on Cal to back him up here. Cal needed to stay in place at the estate.

And that meant Kinley and he were on their own.

Well, almost.

"Call nine-one-one." Jordan passed her his phone and kept watch, looking all around them while he shoved the magazine clips into his jacket pocket.

He spotted yet another car. This one was parked on the side of the warehouse with its lights off. But Jordan could clearly see the front license plate, and he recognized it: SNTRN 06.

It was a Sentron vehicle.

He cursed again. This could be a three-prong attack, including one from a former employee who was likely now on Burke's side. Or else after that ten-million-dollar reward for the missing antidote formula. Was Cody or Desmond in that car?

Kinley made the call and told the 9-1-1 dispatcher that someone was shooting at them. She gave them the address and hung up. Jordan estimated it would be at least five minutes before the cops arrived.

During that time, anything could go down.

The adrenaline spiked through him, but he kept his breathing level. Kinley couldn't manage to do the same. Her breath sawed through the small space of the interior, and he knew she was terrified.

There was movement to his right. The rooftop gunman or someone dressed exactly like him was skulking his way across the parking lot toward the Sentron car. The driver's-side door of the car in front of them opened.

And Kinley and he were trapped in the middle.

A man stepped from the car in front of them. Anderson

Walker. He had a gun in his right hand and a cell phone in his left. He pressed something on the phone, and a moment later, Jordan's own cell phone rang.

"Jordan," Anderson greeted, when Jordan took the phone from Kinley and answered the call on speakerphone. "This is how this'll work. You give us Kinley Ford, and I call off the attack that I'm about to launch on your estate."

Kinley gasped.

"Stay put." Jordan grabbed her to stop her from getting out.

"Why would I care if you attack my house?" Jordan bluffed.

"Because it's my guess that the kid is there."

Jordan forced himself to stay calm. They knew about Gus, and it didn't matter if they weren't sure if he was there or not. Cal might not be able to stop a full-scale attack with explosives, and Gus could be hurt.

"Who are you working for?" Jordan asked the man. Not exactly a stall tactic. He wanted to know who'd orchestrated this. But he also wanted to buy some time for the police to arrive. Not that it would do any good, but he might be able to hurry out of this situation and get back to the estate so he could assist Cal. He'd need a car with undamaged tires for that, and a police cruiser would work.

"This isn't time for talking," Anderson answered. "I figure you've already called the cops or one of your G.I. Joe pals and that you're trying to figure out how to get out of this. Well, there's only one way. So, I'm giving you ten seconds to hand over Kinley."

"I have to do as he says." She reached for the door handle, but again Jordan stopped her.

"They'll torture you to get the antidote. Maybe kill you because you won't be able to give them what they want. And with all of that, there's still no guarantee that by sacrificing yourself, you'll be protecting Gus."

The color drained from her face, and her bottom lip trembled. He leaned over, gave her a quick kiss and got mentally ready for what he had to do. Jordan had no plans to die, but it was a distinct possibility.

"I'm getting out," he told her. When Kinley started to shake her head, he caught her chin and forced eye contact. "You stay put. I'll lead them away from the car, but if anyone tries to get in, you shoot them. Understand?"

She was still shaking her head, but he didn't have time to negotiate with her. He knew what he had to do, and that was make himself a decoy and hope that he could dodge enough bullets until the cops arrived.

Jordan opened the door, hit the lock switch and stepped out. He closed the door, locking her inside. She said something to him, something he couldn't understand. Something he shut out. Because right now the only thing he wanted on his mind was keeping them alive.

He crouched down, using his car as cover from the rifleman in black, but there could be others waiting to attack. Including the person in the Sentron vehicle.

"I said I wanted Kinley," Anderson yelled.

"Yeah, I know. You're not going to get her." Jordan turned, aimed his gun at Anderson. And he knew exactly what the man would do.

Anderson aimed back.

And fired.

Jordan ducked, letting the reinforced body of the

Porsche take the bullet. Then he returned fire. The shot slammed into Anderson's shoulder and sent the man staggering backward.

There was another shot. From a different weapon, a different angle. It took Jordan a moment to realize the point of origin.

Kinley.

She had her window partly down and had shot at the man with the rifle. *Hell*. That glass was her only protection.

"Kinley, no!" Jordan shouted.

But she fired again.

And missed.

The rifleman dove behind the concrete pylon that held the streetlight in place.

Jordan glanced at Anderson. The man dropped to the ground. Probably not because he was dead. He was merely injured and therefore still dangerous. Kinley and he could still be caught in cross fire.

He heard the siren from a police car. That didn't make Jordan breathe any easier. This was the deadly time, when Anderson and the other man would either try to escape or make a stand.

Jordan didn't have to wait long to find out which.

The rifleman started shooting at them. Not single shots, but a stream of deadly gunfire.

"Put up your window," Jordan told Kinley.

She did. Thank God. But then she reached over and opened his door. "Get in," she insisted.

Since the gaping opening from the door was a bad idea, Jordan fired off several shots at the gunman, added another round in Anderson's direction, and then he dove inside so he could slam the door shut behind him.

The shots continued pelting into Jordan's car. One slammed into the glass, webbing it, but it held in place.

Jordan spotted the flashing blue lights from the police cruiser as it turned onto the road that led to the row of warehouses. The shooter obviously saw it, too, because he stopped firing, and Jordan saw him start to run. He wanted to follow in pursuit, so he could learn the person's identity and apprehend him.

But Jordan couldn't do that.

It would leave Kinley vulnerable and in grave danger.

The Sentron car started to move as well. The driver didn't come in their direction but instead turned around and made an exit behind the warehouse.

Anderson, however, didn't budge.

Which meant the man might be dead after all. Jordan hadn't intended that. He needed answers from Anderson, and a dead man wouldn't be able to tell him who'd hired him to kidnap Kinley.

With the sirens wailing, the cruiser came to a stop just on the other side of Anderson's vehicle. The Hispanic officer who got out had his weapon drawn. So did his partner, a female uniformed cop who couldn't have been much older than twenty-one.

Anderson still didn't move.

Jordan reholstered his gun and handed Kinley his phone. "Call the estate. Speak to Cal and make sure everything is okay."

He got out, raising his hands so that the cops wouldn't think he was the bad guy. "I'm Jordan Taylor," he announced.

"From Sentron," one of the cops added with a confirming nod. "I'm Detective Sanchez." He looked at the man on the ground. "What happened here, Mr. Taylor?"

Jordan took a moment, debating how much he should say and how he should say it. "I'm not sure. When my friend and I came out of my warehouse, someone shot at us, and I returned fire. There's another gunman. Maybe two. They escaped that way." He pointed in the direction in which the Sentron car had gone. "What about the man I shot? Is he dead?"

The second officer stooped down while her partner kept watch. Not just of the area but of Jordan. "He's alive, for now," the woman announced, and Jordan heard her call for an ambulance and backup.

"What about you and your friend?" Sanchez asked, walking closer. But he barely looked at Jordan. He was still keeping an eye on their surroundings. "Are you hurt?"

Jordan looked in at Kinley. She had the cell phone pressed to her ear. She was shaken—and shaking—but they weren't injured. At least not physically. "We're okay."

Sanchez nodded, though he still seemed wary. With good reason. Jordan's Porsche was riddled with pockmarks from the impact of the bullets and a man was lying shot and bleeding on the ground. There'd be reports and an investigation, Jordan knew, but those were things that could wait. First, he had to know if Gus was all right.

"Cal," he finally heard Kinley say.

She didn't have the phone on speaker so he couldn't hear what Cal was saying.

There was a blur of movement from the corner of his eye, and Jordan automatically ducked down. With his gun aimed and ready, Sanchez turned in the direction of the sound. And Jordan got a glimpse of what was going on.

The gunman dressed all in black leaned out from the side of the warehouse and raised his rifle.

At Jordan.

Sanchez reacted quickly and fired. There was the sound of metal slicing through metal when the detective's bullet slammed into the warehouse. The gunman turned and started to run, following the path that the Sentron car had taken just moments earlier.

Sanchez went in pursuit and disappeared around the side of the building. Jordan was about to provide some assistance, but then he heard the voice. Not Kinley's.

Cal's.

She'd put the call on speaker and was holding it out so that Jordan could hear. Her hand was shaking.

"I was already on the phone to call you. Some men just arrived outside the estate," Cal said. "Three that I can see on the security monitors. They're all wearing ski masks."

Hell.

Jordan jumped back into the car. "What's your immediate status, Cal?"

"The men haven't broken in, and I've already called my brother at SAPD. But I'm in serious need of backup. Get here fast, Jordan."

Chapter Eleven

Kinley's heart was in her throat.

It seemed as if Detective Sanchez was crawling along in the cruiser, but she knew he was going as fast as he possibly could. No speed would have been fast enough.

At first the two cops on the scene at the warehouse hadn't exactly wanted to give Jordan and her permission to go, but as soon as backup and the ambulance had arrived, Jordan had convinced them that this was an emergency. So there was now another cruiser with blaring sirens behind them and others en route. Kinley didn't mind. She wanted every cop in the city at the estate so they could stop her son from being kidnapped.

When Sanchez turned the corner, she spotted the two cruisers already in front of the house. The blue strobe lights sliced through the semidark street, and there was a pair of uniformed officers on the front lawn.

No sign of any gunmen.

Thank God.

Jordan threw open the cruiser door before Sanchez brought his car to a full stop. Kinley was right behind them with Dexter's notes tucked beneath her arm, and they sprinted past the officers to get to the house.

"He's the owner," Sanchez verified to the other officers.

Jordan practically knocked down the front door, and they raced into the foyer. Cal was there, talking to a man in civilian clothes. "This is my brother, Lt. Joe Rico, SAPD."

"Is everything secure?" Kinley asked, choosing her words carefully. She had no idea how much Cal had revealed to his brother. Hopefully nothing about Gus.

"Everything's safe," Cal assured her. "The intruders left when the cops arrived. They didn't get in."

Kinley tried to catch her breath, but it was hard. The adrenaline had already soared through her, preparing her for a fight. She grabbed on to Jordan, and he pulled her into his arms. Gus was safe. The kidnapper hadn't managed to get to him.

Joe Rico studied them with eyes that were a genetic copy of his brother's but with a lot more suspicion. "I got a phone report of what went on at your warehouse. I'm guessing these incidents are related to the explosion that happened earlier?"

"Probably." Jordan eased away from her so he could face the officer. "This is Kinley Ford. She's in the federal witness protection program, and someone obviously wants to get to her."

The brothers exchanged glances. And concerned expressions. "Do you want SAPD to provide protection?" Joe asked.

Jordan seemed to have a debate with himself before he finally nodded. "Maybe they can patrol the immediate area just for tonight. Until I can make other arrangements."

Joe nodded too and gave a heavy sigh. "I'll contact the FBI and let them know what's going on. There'll be reports to do. And I'll need to get your statements."

"Of course," Jordan agreed. "I've already given Detective Sanchez the weapons we fired."

The lieutenant glanced at her and obviously noted the fear and weariness. "Your statements can wait until later. I'll send a uniform over to take them. Do either of you need to see a medic?"

"No," Jordan and Kinley said in unison, and the responses were loaded with impatience. Even though he was Cal's brother and a likely ally, Kinley wanted him out of there so she could check on Gus.

"Lock down the place," Joe said to his brother. "Call me when you decide what you need me to do. I'll wait out front." And he headed for the door.

None of them said anything until Joe was gone and the security system had been reset. "We have to move Gus immediately," Jordan instructed Cal.

"Yeah. That's what I figured. I have the vehicle and everything ready, just like we discussed. I'll use my brother for backup."

Kinley hadn't been part of that discussion, but she trusted these men, especially Jordan. However, she didn't trust their situation. Jordan had come close to dying tonight, and these arrangements seemed to be happening way too fast.

"Let's get this moving," Jordan insisted. He hurried down the hall to his office. But stopped when his PDA beeped. He cursed. "Someone's monitoring us, probably with a thermal scanner."

"Please, no," Kinley mumbled. It meant someone, maybe one of those gunmen, had gotten close enough to the house.

Kinley considered going to the basement to see Gus, but she knew this would be the faster way to see her son.

Jordan clicked on the surveillance, and on the screen, she saw the nannies waiting in the playroom. Pamela was holding a sleeping Gus in her arms. His head was resting on her shoulder, and she had a blanket draped around him.

"It's time to leave," Jordan said through the intercom that carried his voice into the playroom. "Go into the garage through the basement entrance."

Kinley started for the door. "I want to say goodbye to him."

But Jordan got up and caught on to her. "Sorry. You can't. They're monitoring us, and we can't risk it."

Oh, God. It felt as if someone had clamped a fist around her heart. But Jordan was right. She couldn't put Gus in any more danger.

"How will Cal get him out?" Kinley heard her voice trembling but couldn't stop it.

"We have a plan. The car in the garage is armored and with tinted windows and a thermal blocker for the back area where Gus and one of the nannies will be. It will appear that only Cal is leaving."

"But what if someone follows him?"

"His brother will monitor that. He'll trail behind Cal to a small private airport about twenty miles from here."

She choked back a gasp. "An airport?"

"It'll be safer if he's completely out of the area. Cal's taking him to a place near Houston. For now. If things heat up, we'll move him again."

Kinley had to sit down, but she refused to lose it. She couldn't cry because if she started, she might not stop.

"We need some distractions," Jordan told her. "Find the number to the prison where your research partner, Brenna Martel, is being held. Use the phone in the hall. It isn't secure. Someone will be able to monitor the call."

She shook her head. "Why would you want that?"

"I want them to hear. Burke, Strahan and anyone else involved in this will want to know what Brenna has to say, so ask to speak to her. If the guards won't let you, which they probably won't, then leave her a message asking her about any research notes she made. If they exist, you want a copy. If not, you want to set up a meeting to discuss everything she remembers."

She managed a nod and hoped she could remember all of that. Her head was far from clear, and the only thing she wanted to think about was her baby.

"While you're doing that, I'll find out who was in that Sentron car parked at the warehouse," Jordan continued. "I'll make waves while I'm doing it."

Kinley prayed the waves worked. Anything to give her son a head start.

She went several feet away to the phone on a hall table, and using directory assistance, she got the number of Claridge Prison. Kinley made her way through the automated answering system until she finally got to speak to a person at the guards' desk.

"I need to get an urgent message to an inmate, Brenna Martel." She glanced at Jordan, who was making his own call, while she listened to the man tell her why she wouldn't be able to speak to any of the prisoners tonight. However, he took her message about needing the notes and said he would relay it to Brenna and her attorney. Kinley didn't know when or if Brenna would get back to her, but it was a start and maybe the diversion they needed while moving Gus.

Jordan was still on the phone when she went back

into his office, but he had the images of the nursery rooms and basement on the screen. Pamela had Gus still cradled in her arms while she, Cal and Elsa were making their way through the basement. With some keystrokes on the security system, Jordan zoomed in on Gus's sleeping face.

Tears sprang to Kinley's eyes. It was so unfair. Here, she'd finally found her precious baby and had had mere hours with him, and now he was being whisked away. Heaven knew how long it would be before she'd see him again.

Jordan ended the call, stood and watched the images with her. Cal and others entered the garage through stairs that led up from the basement, and without wasting even a second, Cal got Pamela, Gus and himself into a black SUV. Pamela sat in the backseat with Gus. Elsa, however, went to another vehicle in the massive garage. A dark green van. She was obviously going to be a decoy. And from the front security camera, Kinley could see Cal's brother waiting to follow and back them up.

"What about the thermal scanner?" she asked. "Please tell me it couldn't detect them while they were getting into the vehicles."

"It couldn't. The stairs and the garage are protected, and that blanket around Gus will block the scanner. Pamela will keep it over him until they're on the airplane."

So many details, and yet Jordan had seemingly addressed them all despite the distraction of the warehouse attack and the earlier explosion.

"The vehicles will leave at the same time," Jordan let her know. "Once they get on the interstate, Elsa will take the first exit in the opposite direction, toward the San Antonio international airport. If it looks as if no one is following them, an unmarked police car will tail Elsa, to make it look as if Gus is in the van. Cal's brother, Joe, will continue to follow Cal's SUV."

It was a solid plan. As safe as Jordan could possibly make it. But that didn't stop her from being terrified. Because no plan was foolproof, and that meant her son was at risk no matter what they did.

"What about your call?" he asked.

Kinley didn't take her eyes off the screen. "I had to leave a message with the prison guard. What about you, any luck?"

"Not yet. But I'm running a computer search of Sentron's records to find out who was in that car at the warehouse."

Yes. Because that person might not have only had a part in this. He might even be the ringleader.

"Whoever was in that car knew we were in danger," Jordan verified. "He knew someone was either trying to kill us or kidnap us, and yet he sat there and watched it happen."

So, this person could have been Anderson's boss. Or someone else who wanted to use her to try to get that antidote. In other words, definitely not a friend.

Her money was on Burke.

He could have easily switched out vehicles, even though she couldn't imagine why he would do that. If he wanted to watch them, why hadn't he used a car that Jordan wouldn't have easily recognized? Maybe because Burke had wanted them to know he would use Sentron resources against Jordan and her.

Was this part of their game meant to intimidate her? If so, it was working.

She watched as Cal shut the back door of the SUV,

and she could no longer see Gus. A moment later, Cal was behind the wheel and backed out of the garage. He waited until Elsa was right behind him.

And they drove away.

Out of sight.

Kinley forced herself to hold her emotions together, and she was succeeding. Until Jordan slipped his arm around her waist and pulled her to him. Just like that, she shattered. And the tears came in spite of the fight she had put up to stop them.

"He'll be okay," Jordan said, comforting her, though from the slight tremble in his voice, it was obvious he needed some comforting as well.

Gus was his son in every way that mattered, and he'd raised the child even though he could have easily turned that duty over to someone else. But he hadn't. And that's why Kinley had to trust what he was doing now.

Jordan placed his PDA on the counter next to them and showed her the little blips. "That's the car Gus is in," he said, pointing to the green one. "The red blip belongs to Elsa. The blue, to Joe. The yellow one is the unmarked police car tailing Elsa."

Other blips appeared on the screen. Obviously other vehicles on the road. But none stayed close to Cal.

They stood there, watching. Praying. Kinley was saying a lot of prayers. The minutes ticked off with the blips making their way on the GPS-style map. Finally, after what seemed an eternity, Elsa's car and the unmarked police vehicle turned toward the San Antonio airport. Cal went in the other direction.

"No one's following them." The relief was all through Jordan's voice.

Still, they didn't take their attention from the PDA. She

wasn't sure how much time passed, but she watched the green blip make its way along the highway that led out of the city limits. The road must have been fairly isolated because the only blips belonged to Cal and his brother.

"They're at the private airport," Jordan finally said.

And they waited again. Kinley held her breath so long that her lungs began to ache.

Then, the phone rang, the sound slicing through the room.

Jordan snatched it up. "Cal," he answered obviously seeing the man's number on the screen.

Kinley couldn't hear the conversation. Nor could she move. She just stood there and said a dozen more prayers.

"They're on the plane," Jordan said, ending the call. "Gus is safe."

He caught her to stop her from staggering. It was in the nick of time. The relief was overwhelming. Jordan had succeeded. Her son was safe.

Kinley looked up at him. His expression was a mixture of joy and relief. But some sadness, too. She understood that completely. Gus was safe, but he wasn't with them.

Since she was already in Jordan's arms, Kinley let him support her. Yes, it was a risk. The white-hot attraction was always there, but there was something else. Some strange intimacy that perhaps only parents of a young child could have shared. For some reason, that made her emotions run even higher.

It made the attraction even stronger.

She wished for more. That it would consume her. Overwhelm her. That it would make her forget what was going on with Gus.

"Oh, hell," Jordan mumbled.

At first Kinley thought he was saying that in reaction

to something he saw on the screen, but he was looking at her. "This is an adrenaline reaction," he said.

A split second before he kissed her.

Yes. It probably *was* an adrenaline reaction. And a human one. Kinley didn't doubt that she needed him in this most basic human way.

This was what she'd asked for. Something to overwhelm her. Jordan was certainly capable of doing that and more.

"We're still being monitored with the thermal scan," he whispered against her mouth.

Kinley tried to think of the consequences of that. Burke, Strahan or someone else might be seeing the heated images of their bodies. The kiss would be easy to detect, even though they'd be just thermal blobs on the scan. This was still an invasion of a very intimate moment.

But Kinley didn't care.

She wasn't going to give this up because someone had them under thermal surveillance.

"Consider it a diversion," Kinley whispered back.

But this was as much a diversion for her as it was for anyone who might be watching. Still, it might be a good idea if it distracted the person responsible for the surveillance.

Soon, though, that thought slid right out of her mind.

That's because Jordan continued to kiss her.

Yes, she was definitely being overwhelmed, and it'd never felt so right.

He slid his hands into her hair, angling her head so he could deepen the kiss. Kinley went right along with it, and even though nothing could have made her forget her son, she needed this moment. She needed Jordan.

She felt her back press against his office door and

realized Jordan was leaning into her. Good. She wanted him against her, and Kinley hooked her arm around his waist to drag him even closer. Until closer was as close as two bodies could get. Almost.

His kiss was clever. Not too hard. Not too soft. It was as if he'd found the perfect tempo and pressure to coax every bit of the passion from her. But the kiss also did something else; it revved up the attraction. The need.

The kiss turned from clever to frantic, and he slid his hand down her waist. He found the back of her thigh and lifted her leg so that it was anchored against his. The new position created some interesting pressure, especially when his sex touched hers.

Kinley lost her breath.

And didn't care if she ever found it.

"I can stop," Jordan suggested.

Kinley didn't look at him. Didn't listen. She didn't want to hear the voice of reason. But what did she want?

Full-blown sex?

That certainly wouldn't be wise right now since Gus was on the way to the airport and Jordan was waiting on a computer scan. Oh, and there were cops outside the estate who could come knocking at any minute. They didn't have time for sex.

Or did they?

Jordan moved his mouth to her neck. To the V of her shirt. And he shoved it down so he could kiss the top of her right breast. There went her breath again, and Kinley had no choice but to hang on to him and enjoy this crazy, forbidden moment.

His hand was still gripping her leg, holding it in place, but he also caught the bottom of her skirt.

"Sorry," he said. "This will be way too fast."

She shook her head, not understanding. But then he pushed her skirt up to her waist and just like that his hand went into her panties. And his fingers went into her.

Kinley moaned. Nearly lost her balance. But Jordan hung on to her, anchoring her in place with his body. He worked magic with those fingers but behind his hand was what she really wanted.

She pushed his hand away so she could unzip his pants. But he caught her wrist. "I can't think if we do that."

"It'll be quick," she bargained.

Jordan's jaw muscles stirred. He grimaced. But he didn't stop her when she shook off his grip and reached for his zipper again. He was huge and hard, and that didn't make things easy, but she managed to lower his zipper and take him into her hand.

That was apparently the only foreplay they would have because he dragged off her panties and hoisted her up, sandwiching her between the door and him.

Since time seemed to matter, Kinley didn't waste any of it. Maybe because if they stopped to think, this wouldn't happen. And her body wanted desperately for it to happen.

She wrapped her legs around him, and he entered her. He didn't stay still, didn't give himself a moment to savor the sensation. He moved once. One long stroke that shot the pleasure straight through her.

But then he stopped.

Just like that, he stopped.

With a groan rumbling deep within his throat, Jordan ground his forehead against hers. "Bad timing," he grumbled. "Really bad."

She shook her head and tried to think of what she could say to make him continue. But before she could speak, he shoved his hand back between their bodies and used his fingers instead of his sex.

"I want you," she clarified.

"I want you. Too much. But I don't have a condom here. They're in the bedroom, and I need to stay here to keep an eye on the monitor. I promise, I'll do better later."

He didn't give her a chance to object. Didn't give her a chance to do anything but go mindless. He touched her in just the right place. With the right pressure. But what caused Kinley to soar was seeing his face. Kissing him.

It was Jordan who sent her over the edge.

Even as the sensations still rippled through her, she instantly regretted it. Not the act itself, not the intimacy, but because she'd been the one to get all the pleasure here. Jordan had remained in control.

He kissed her again. There was control there, too. And he eased her from him so she could stand. He fixed his pants and even located her panties so he could hand them to her.

And the awkwardness settled in around them.

"I'm—" But she didn't know how to finish that.

"Don't think for one minute that I didn't want to have sex with you. I do. I *really* do." He cursed. "I just need to have a clear head right now, understand?"

"Yes." But that didn't stop her from being embarrassed. "And I, uh, need to start going over Dexter's notes." Something she should have started instead of kissing Jordan.

Right.

Who was she kidding? She couldn't have stopped kissing him any more than she could stop worrying about Gus. Jordan had gotten under her skin, and she was afraid he was there to stay. Great. Just what she needed. Another broken heart.

There was a beeping sound, and Kinley forced herself to come back to earth. To focus. Jordan did the same and hurried to one of the many computers.

"Is it about Gus?" she asked, afraid to hear the answer.

"No. I just got back the results of that computer search for the Sentron car that was parked at the warehouse."

So he had the identity of the person who'd sat and watched as they'd nearly been killed. "Was it Burke in the car?"

"No." Jordan scrubbed his hand over his face and groaned. "It was Cody Guillory."

Chapter Twelve

Jordan took a gulp of the strong coffee and hoped the caffeine would kick in soon.

Eventually, Kinley and he would have to sleep. He wanted to keep going. He wanted to find the person creating the danger so he could stop him and bring Gus home. But he was exhausted. Kinley, too, though she wouldn't admit it. The caffeine had to buy them a little more time before they would no doubt collapse.

After an officer from SAPD had taken their statements about the attempted kidnapping and shooting, Kinley had taken a couple of catnaps in his office while still in the process of going over Dexter Sheppard's research notes. Jordan knew this because even though he'd spent most of the night in his bedroom coordinating the new living arrangements for Gus, he'd checked on her and twice he'd found her dozing with her face literally pressed against the notes. The other dozen or so times, she'd been hard at work staring at the pages.

He poured Kinley a cup of coffee as well—it'd be her sixth of the day—and he walked out of the kitchen and through the foyer. The Christmas lights were still on, and with the broken crystal ornaments littering the floor like diamonds, the place managed to look festive. Even if it wasn't.

It wasn't shaping up to be much of a peaceful Christmas Eve.

He'd wanted this to be a special holiday for Gus. For months, Jordan had bought presents and hidden them away. He'd planned on spending the day opening those presents and relaxing with the little boy. A prelude to the move.

A move that'd come early, of course, thanks to the danger.

Jordan had no idea when they'd get around to opening those presents now, and a relaxing day just wasn't in his immediate future.

Looking at the tree, he thought of Kinley. There'd be no real Christmas for her, either, and he wished he'd had the time to buy her some kind of gift. But maybe the best gift he could give her was to distance himself from her. He wasn't doing her any favors by having sex with her. She was an emotional wreck right now, and he needed to give her space so she could sort out her feelings and get the right mind-set for motherhood.

He drew in a weary breath and went to his office. Kinley was still there, seated at the long counter that held monitors, computers and security equipment. She looked up at him and offered a thin smile.

So much for his little pep talk about giving her some space.

Despite her sleep-starved eyes and the impossible situation they were in, he still wanted her.

"I thought you could use this," he said, and set the coffee next to the notes.

"Thanks." She made a sound of pleasure when she took the first sip. "What's the latest from Cal?"

"I called him about fifteen minutes ago. It's all good. Gus is settled in an estate near Houston. I've been there. With all the security modifications Cal has made, it's a safe place. Gus will be fine while we wrap up things here."

"Yes." Definitely not a sound of pleasure but of disappointment and frustration. God knew when they'd actually be able to wrap up things. "And the thermal scanner situation? Are we still being monitored?"

"No. It stopped several hours ago." Which could be a good or bad sign. Maybe the person had given up. Or maybe he was just lying in wait and trying to come up with a new plan as to the best way to kidnap Kinley.

"What about Anderson Walker?" she asked. "I don't suppose he's said anything yet about who his boss is so the police can make an arrest?"

Jordan shook his head. "He's in the hospital, recovering from the gunshot wound. And he lawyered up and isn't saying a word. But maybe if we figure who's behind this, Anderson might be willing to make a deal."

Might being the crucial word.

Anderson almost certainly wouldn't get through this without some serious jail time, but he might not get a good enough deal to force him to cooperate and do the right thing.

Strahan was another matter.

"Cal's brother, Lt. Rico from the San Antonio police, studied the disk of Shelly's murder. He thinks he might have an ID on her killer—a guy named Pete Mendenhall."

Kinley's eyes widened. "Does this guy work for Strahan?"

"We don't know yet. SAPD tried to do a facial recognition match right after Shelly died, but her killer wasn't in any of the databases."

"But he is now?" she clarified.

Jordan nodded. "Not a criminal database, though, but there are a lot more faces and names in the facial recognition system than there were fourteen months ago. Rico got a hit. When he brings in this Pete Mendenhall for questioning, he'll try to link him to Strahan."

And maybe Strahan could be arrested for murder.

"What about Dexter's notes?" Jordan asked.

Her look of frustration went up a notch. "Well, I've solved most of the code but only because I was familiar with it. It's something he used often during his research, even though there are a few entries that don't follow the normal pattern."

"But you're sure they're his notes and not a forgery?"

She nodded. "Oh, they're his. There are some summaries about failed experiments that happened only when Dexter and I were in the lab. No one else would have known about them. That makes them authentic."

That was a start. "Anything about the missing antidote yet?"

"Yes and no. His research for the antidote is here, but he didn't include just one formula but nearly a hundred. I've started to run them on the computer, but the first five took me over eight hours to do."

Jordan wasn't surprised. Dexter wouldn't have plainly stated something like that in notes that could be found. Or stolen.

"I'll keep working," she insisted.

"Maybe after a nap?"

She blinked. And he caught the gist of her surprise. She no doubt wondered if he was inviting her to his bed.

As good as that sounded—and it sounded damn good—it couldn't happen right now.

"This morning I called Burke, Cody, Desmond and Strahan. I have a two o'clock video conference set up with them." And that meant he could expect to hear from them any minute.

"Desmond?" she questioned. "I understand why you'd want to talk to the others, but why him?"

Jordan shrugged. "He was here minutes before the explosion."

She took a sip of coffee and peered at him over the rim of the cup. "And his motive?"

"Maybe the same as Cody's? Money that they think they could get from the antidote. Or the reward. Ten million is a lot of cash, and it has to be a serious temptation."

"But these are men you trained. You know them."

"Yeah, I do." That's why he had to at least consider they could do something like this. "There are parts of the job that require some, well, moral flexibility. That character trait that made them good agents might not keep them loyal to me."

She stared at him. Then sighed. "I was stunned when Dexter betrayed me so I understand."

The house phone rang before Jordan could say anything. He glanced at the caller ID. "Raymond Myers?"

Kinley sprang from her seat. "That's Brenna Martel's attorney." She grabbed the phone and answered it. Jordan put it on speaker.

"Ms. Ford, my client wanted me to contact you right away."

"Yes. Thank you. I left a message for her at the prison." Kinley stood soldier straight and stared at the phone.

"She got the message. And she does indeed have notes about the research project you both worked on. I have those notes, and several days ago, Brenna had instructed me to give a copy to Mr. Burke Dennison."

"Burke?" Kinley questioned.

Jordan silently cursed. Now, why hadn't Burke mentioned it? Jordan didn't have to guess why. Burke had likely been on this from the start.

Kinley scowled. "Mr. Myers, those notes are critical. You could say a matter of life and death."

"Yes. Brenna indicated that." He paused. "She instructed me to offer you a deal. She's authorized me to fax you copies if you'll agree to be a character witness at her upcoming trial."

The idea of that turned Jordan's stomach. Brenna had kidnapped Kinley, and he didn't want Kinley to have to endure something like vouching for the woman.

"I'll do it," Kinley told the attorney.

Jordan was certain he was scowling, too, but there was nothing he could do about it. He would have done the same thing because those notes could help them keep Gus safe.

"Good. The notes are in a safety deposit box. I'll leave now and fax them directly from there. You should have them within the hour."

"Thank you." Kinley reached down, clicked the end call button. "Once I have them, I can compare them to Dexter's and mine," she told Jordan.

Yes, and work hours and hours to try to figure out which formula was real and which were decoys. "Maybe I can help once this video conference is done."

She thanked him for the offer, sipped her coffee and looked a million miles away. Jordan understood that look. Despite all the other things they had to resolve, she was still thinking about Gus.

And that gave Jordan an idea of what he could get her for Christmas.

The phone on the communications console rang, and Jordan knew that was his cue. "Burke and the others are obviously ready."

He turned on the video feed, but he didn't make it two way just yet. He wanted a moment to study the scene. All four men were in the Sentron command center. None looked happy about having their Christmas interrupted like this. Tough. Jordan wanted answers, and he didn't care how much they were inconvenienced. Of course, one of them was no doubt there with the hopes of finding the missing antidote.

But which one?

Or was that the reason they were there?

"You should probably try to take a nap," Jordan suggested to her.

"Right. As if I'd miss this."

He was afraid she would say that. He certainly would have stayed put if she'd been the one telling him to take a nap. This conversation was critical, and Jordan decided it was a good time to place as many cards as he could on the table.

He hit the transmit-feed button so that the four men could see Kinley and him. "Now, which one of you tried to have Kinley kidnapped last night?" Jordan started.

Silence.

Not exactly the reaction he'd hoped for. He'd thought that Cody and Desmond would at least deny it.

"Well?" Jordan prompted.

"I'm insulted you'd ask that of me," Cody finally responded. Desmond echoed the same.

"I didn't," Strahan almost cheerfully volunteered. "I think Anderson Walker was acting alone. I believe he wanted all that reward money for himself. He got greedy."

Maybe. Jordan prayed that were true since it would mean none of these four was a danger. But he couldn't risk thinking that way.

"Burke," Jordan said, looking at the man. "Any reason you didn't tell us that Brenna Martel had given you her research notes?"

Burke shrugged. "That was a private business arrangement and not nearly as helpful as you might think. Without Dexter Sheppard's notes, I'm one-third in the dark." He tossed a stony glance at Strahan, who had those notes but had obviously chosen not to share them with Burke.

So, if Strahan didn't have Brenna's notes and Burke didn't have Dexter's, then that meant they each had two-thirds of the picture. Soon, within the hour maybe, Kinley and he would have all three sets. However, Jordan didn't intend to share that bit of information with anyone just yet.

"There's a lot of distrust in this room," Strahan continued. "I have a suggestion. You tell these two wannabe rich guys to take a hike." He tipped his head first to Cody, then to Desmond. "Burke and I are the wronged investors here."

"But anyone can collect the reward for finding the antidote," Desmond pointed out.

Which, of course, gave him motive.

"You'd risk Kinley's life for a reward?" Jordan asked.

Desmond shrugged. "Her life doesn't have to be risked to find the antidote."

"No, but it sure as hell has been." So had Gus's. "Plus, there's the matter of Shelly's death."

Desmond shrugged again. "I didn't even know about the antidote back then."

Cody still stayed silent.

"As I was saying," Strahan continued, "let's get Cody and Desmond out of here. Other than greed over that reward, they don't have anything to bring to this equation. Then, Burke, the two of you and I will pour through all three sets of notes together. We'll learn the truth, and none of us here are afraid of the truth, are we?"

That put a knot in Jordan's stomach. He turned a notepad so that Kinley could see it, and he wrote, "Did Dexter say anything in those notes about you being pregnant?"

She didn't have much of a reaction, other than a trembling hand when she wrote. "Maybe. I've been working on decrypting the formulas. I haven't tried to figure out the rest of it."

Hell. Jordan should have anticipated this.

"Burke, are you in on this offer?" Jordan asked.

Burke shoved his hands in the pockets of his perfectly tailored suit. "Yes. With one condition. Only Strahan and I will collect the profits from this. Cody and Desmond are nothing more than former employees to me. They've both been given their notice and won't be returning in the new year."

So, Burke had fired them, even though Burke had given his word that he'd keep on all the key staff when he assumed ownership of Sentron. That explained some of the tension he saw on Cody and Desmond's faces.

And maybe something else.

Maybe Burke hadn't fired them after all, and this was

merely a ploy to use whatever means necessary to find that antidote.

"You shouldn't have sold Sentron," Cody accused, staring right into the camera and therefore right at Jordan. "Early retirement? You're not the retiring kind, Jordan. And if you wanted a break, you could have temporarily put me in charge." He looked away, cursed. "Instead, you sold me—all of us—to the highest bidder. To a man who cares nothing about Sentron except for how much money it can make him. Now Desmond and I are out of a job."

He'd sold Sentron because of Gus. Because Jordan had wanted every penny in case they had to hide out indefinitely. But he couldn't say that to Cody or Desmond. He couldn't make them understand.

And by doing so, he'd made enemies of them.

"I'm sorry," Jordan said, hoping it conveyed his sincerity.

Judging from the agents' expressions, it didn't.

Later, after this was over, he could do more to make amends. Right now, though, he had enough to deal with, and saying anything could endanger Gus.

"Kinley and I will get back to you with our decision," Jordan announced.

He didn't give them time to object. He cut the feed so they couldn't see or hear Kinley and him. However, Jordan continued to observe the four. Nothing was said, probably because they knew he'd still be watching and listening. But the glances they gave each other were not ones of trust. One by one, the men filed out and Jordan cut the feed completely.

"So, Cody and Desmond do have motive," Kinley commented.

Yeah. All four did, and it came down to money. The worst motive because it was hard to reason with greed.

Still, Jordan couldn't totally surrender to the idea that Cody was pissed off enough at him to go after Kinley. Of course, Cody technically wasn't trying to hurt her if he only wanted to collect the reward.

However, that didn't mean he wasn't endangering her by trying to get to the truth. Desmond, too.

"I need to see about putting some pressure on Anderson Walker to reveal the identity of the person who hired him," Jordan said, more to himself than her. He reached for the phone, but he heard the beep from the fax machine. A moment later, a page started to feed through.

Kinley hurried to the machine. "Brenna's notes," she explained.

Good. So the lawyer and Brenna had come through after all. Now he prayed that Kinley would be able to use them to find out the formula to the antidote.

Kinley gathered the pages as the machine spit them out. "She used the same format as Dexter," she observed. "Different encryption, though."

Which would make things harder.

"I'm pretty sure this encryption is a list of formulas," Kinley continued. "But only about twenty. I can compare these to Dexter's and narrow down which formulas are strong possibilities."

With her attention riveted to the notes, she blindly made her way back to her chair, and rather than take her eyes off the pages, she groped for the seat and then dropped down into it.

He'd leave her to the formula, especially since he had more calls to make. First, about putting some pressure on Anderson to name his boss. Then he needed to do some digging into Cody's and Desmond's latest activities to see exactly how much of a threat they were.

Oh, and he still wanted that Christmas present for Kinley.

Jordan headed for his bedroom so he could get to work.

Chapter Thirteen

The correct formula had to be there, somewhere in the combined notes. Kinley was sure of it. But it seemed to be just out of her reach.

What was the problem?

Why couldn't she make any of the formulas work?

She grabbed her mug, because she needed another hit of caffeine, only to realize it was empty again. She'd lost count of how many times Jordan had filled it for her. Lost count of just how much coffee she'd consumed in the past twenty-four hours, but she knew it was enough to make her feel all raw and jittery.

She stood to go into the kitchen and fill it herself, but the phone on the console rang. She glanced at the caller ID screen.

It was Cal Rico.

Just like that, Kinley's heart jumped to her throat, and she grabbed the phone so she could answer it. "Cal, what's wrong?"

"Nothing," he answered just as quickly. "Jordan said I should call you at midnight."

Midnight? Her gaze flew to the clock on the bottom

of the laptop screen. It was indeed that late. She had no idea where the time had gone.

"I'm supposed to give you your Christmas present," Cal told her.

"What Christmas present?" But an answer wasn't necessary because the image popped onto one of the screens mounted on the wall.

Gus.

There he was, sleeping peacefully in a crib. Just seeing that precious face made her smile. And yes, her eyes misted up with tears. Her son was safe. He wasn't in the middle of a nightmare.

"This is a preview," Cal explained. "In about eight hours we're opening gifts, and you can watch every minute of it."

"Thank you," she managed to say.

"No. You need to thank Jordan. He's the one who set all of this up."

Of course. Who else?

Jordan knew how much she missed Gus. And that made her remember how much she cared for Jordan. He was indeed a special man to remember something like this with all the craziness going on in their lives.

"Eight hours," Cal reminded her. "All the cameras are already set up. Merry Christmas, Kinley."

She wished Cal the same, thanked him again and clicked off the feed and the call. The emotion hit her almost immediately. Maybe it was the fatigue, her gratitude for the perfect gift or the leftover emotion from her earlier encounter with Jordan. The reasons didn't seem to matter at the moment. She got up and made her way through the house.

And toward Jordan.

She walked through the house, and the corridor, and she stopped in the doorway, hoping this was a good idea. After all, she was here in Jordan's bedroom, and it was obvious why she was there. She intended to pick up where they'd left off in his office.

Jordan wasn't aware of her sanity check or doubt. He lay in bed. He was facedown, his arms outstretched, as if pure exhaustion had caused him to land that way. The pearl-colored sheet came up to his waist and outlined that lean, muscled body.

He was naked, his clothes discarded on the floor.

She understood the beauty of those massive windows then. The milky moonlight poured through the crystal-clear glass and onto him. He was a picture all right. And she understood something else in that moment.

That she'd never wanted a man the way she wanted him.

Kinley peeled off her skirt and top. She did the same with her underwear. She dropped the items on the floor, and before she could change her mind, she walked across the room toward him. She threw back the covers and slid in next to him.

He was warm. Solid. All man. And his scent went straight through her.

Jordan reached out, hauled her to him, shifting his body so that she was beneath him.

"What took you so long?" he drawled, sounding both sleepy and alert at the same time.

Doubts assaulted her. And fear. Kinley didn't think she could bear another broken heart. But that wasn't what she said to him. "I'm here now."

Jordan looked down at her. He then slipped his hand into her hair and leaned in. His mouth touched hers. So gently. Soft. Lingering. The slow, easy kiss surprised her. She expected him to take her with the same fury that he did everything else in life, but this was a different kind of lovemaking. Even when he deepened the kiss, and his tongue touched hers, everything was unhurried.

Her blood turned to fire.

He controlled the tempo. The angle of the kiss. Everything. And she didn't care. Kinley let herself be swept away.

He kissed his way down her body, his mouth lighting fires along the way. He didn't hurry. Definitely didn't shortchange her with those body kisses. He made his way back up to her face.

Kinley wrapped her legs around him, forced him closer. But Jordan still didn't give in to the crazy frenzy that he'd built inside her.

As if he had all the time in the world, he took a condom from his nightstand and put it on. He returned to her and gave her more of those steamy kisses.

He entered her slowly. Kinley felt every inch of him. And then he stopped. She saw it then. The need in his eyes. The intensity was simmering beneath the surface and ready to break free.

"I shouldn't need you this much," he mumbled.

"I know the feeling," she mumbled back.

He didn't give her a lingering look. Nor any more kisses.

He caught her hands, pinning them to the bed. He moved. Not gently now. He took her because he'd finally lost all control. Because he had to have her now.

Kinley wanted him like this. Wanted him a little crazy. But more than that, she just wanted him *now*.

She lifted her hips, matching those fierce thrusts. She took all of him and let those thrusts take her to the edge.

"Jordan," she said.

He said her name as well, repeating it with each of those frantic strokes.

Kinley came first, and even though the passion completely claimed her for those moments, she still managed to focus and see Jordan's face.

Like her, he lost control.

He gathered her into his arms, drew her close to him and went over the edge.

JORDAN EASED OUT of the bed, careful that he didn't wake Kinley.

It was only 4:00 a.m. Still hours away from the time Gus would be opening his presents. Then, he'd wake her so they could share the moment together.

She was obviously exhausted because she'd fallen asleep almost immediately after they'd had sex. Which meant they hadn't talked.

That was a good thing.

It would give Jordan some time to figure out what the hell he was going to do.

He'd known from the moment he first laid eyes on her that they'd eventually land in bed. He'd also known this couldn't be just casual sex. Kinley wasn't the casual-sex type. Plus, she had feelings for him. He wasn't stupid. He could see that.

And he had feelings for her.

On the surface that didn't seem like much of a problem, and it might not have been if it weren't for all their baggage. It'd been so long since he'd let anyone get close to him. So long since he'd shared himself with anyone. Gus had changed that. The little boy had made him see that love wasn't necessarily a painful commitment. That the good outweighed any of the bad.

But there was Kinley to consider.

Maybe—just maybe—what she felt for him wasn't love or a similar emotion but part of her gratitude for taking care of Gus.

Jordan groaned softly, pulled on a pair of black jeans, a black long-sleeved shirt and his boots. He shoved his PDA into his back pocket. The clothes weren't exactly festive wear for Christmas Day, but they suited his mood. He'd gotten himself personally involved at a time when it was imperative that he stay detached and objective.

Personal involvement meant a loss of focus.

It could mean making the situation more dangerous. And that's why he had to put some emotional distance between Kinley and himself. Yes, he'd had this pep talk before, but this time he had to listen.

Really.

He went to the kitchen and started a pot of coffee, something he'd been doing a lot of lately. Kinley's taste was still in his mouth. Her scent was on his skin.

Hell. He could still feel her.

And hear her. "Jordan." The way she'd said his name when he was still inside her.

"Jordan?"

That jerked him out of his daydream. Because her voice wasn't some great memory. It was real. Kinley had just walked into the kitchen.

She'd dressed. Thank goodness. Well, maybe not. He could remember what it was like to have her naked despite the dark brown pants and tan top that she wore now. Her hair was still tousled, and her face flushed with color that could only come from a great night of sex.

Okay, so maybe that was his imagination, too.

But it wasn't his imagination that he wanted her all over again. So much for his latest resolution to distance himself from her.

"You're up early," he commented, just so he wasn't standing there gawking at her.

"Yes." She sighed.

Uh-oh. That wasn't the sound of a satisfied woman. It was the sound of a troubled one, and Jordan thought he knew why. "You're having regrets?"

She blinked. "No. Absolutely not." And with that, she went to him and kissed him as if she were about to haul him off to bed. She smiled. "I didn't thank you for my Christmas present." She kissed him again. "Thank you."

Since he liked her way of showing thanks, he kissed her right back. "You're welcome." He eased away from her so he could see her face. "But you could have thanked me later. I was hoping you'd get a few more hours of sleep."

The sighing look returned. "I tried, but I kept thinking about the notes." She shook her head. "There's a problem, but I don't know what's wrong."

"What do you mean?"

She grabbed two cups and began to pour them both some of the fresh brew. "I've tested every single formula that Dexter and Brenna listed in common. None of them could have produced an antidote. Not even close. So, I guess I need to rerun everything—" Her head whipped up, and she looked at him.

Jordan knew what she was thinking. "Maybe that's

the point. Maybe none of the formulas could produce an antidote because Dexter never created one."

She set the coffeepot aside, probably because her hand was suddenly too shaky to hold it. "No antidote," Kinley repeated. Then, she groaned. "God, it makes sense. Every time I'd ask Dexter about how the formula was coming, he'd stall me. He locked up his research, and that's the only part of the project that he prevented me from seeing."

Jordan nodded. "And it explains why he wanted to destroy the lab and fake his own death. He'd already taken a fortune in research money, and he couldn't deliver." Unless… "You worked on the project. Could the antidote have even been made?"

"I didn't think so," she readily answered. "In fact, when Dexter took on the project, we argued about it because I knew it would take years just to come up with a workable formula, and by then the investors would already be screaming for results. But I think the idea of all that money was too tempting for him to pass up."

Oh, yeah. Because a man who'd endanger the mother of his child probably wasn't driven by his heart but rather by his wallet.

Kinley bracketed her hands on the granite counter and groaned. "Shelly and heaven knows who else died because of this. Gus, you and I were placed in danger. My son had to live in hiding since the moment he was born, and all of that was because of a lie that Dexter told."

And the worst thing—without an antidote, they didn't have anything to bargain with. Burke and Strahan likely wouldn't believe Kinley if she told them that Dexter had pulled off one big scam before faking his death and then being accidentally killed when he set explosives meant to eliminate her.

No.

As investors, they wanted only their profits.

"So where does this leave us?" she asked.

"First, I'll start with contacting the FBI. We'll give them copies of all the notes so they can run their own independent tests."

"That could take days or weeks," she pointed out. "The only reason I was able to do it so quickly is because I was familiar with the research."

True. It would take the FBI time, but there was no way around that. However, that was just one step. He had to do more, much more, to ensure Gus's and Kinley's safety.

"I have a friend who works at the *San Antonio Express-News*. I'll talk to him about doing some sort of investigative report so he can leak that the antidote was a fraud. Between that and an FBI report, we might be able to convince Burke, Strahan and anyone else that there's no reason to come after you."

He saw something else in her eyes. Something he hadn't seen before. Hope. "You really think that's possible?"

"I do. It might not happen today, or even next week, but it will happen." And that meant soon he'd be able to bring Gus home.

Of course, that posed a whole new set of problems. Kinley would want custody of her son. That was natural. But he wanted custody, too, and somehow, they'd have to work that out.

First, though, he needed to call the FBI.

He grabbed his coffee. Then he grabbed a kiss from Kinley. It made her smile, and he kissed her again just because he liked the way her smile lit her face.

"Work," he reminded himself when the third kiss turned hot and French.

Jordan forced himself away from her and headed for his office. However, he made it only a few steps before his PDA beeped. He took it out, looked at the screen and didn't like what he saw. It was a secure text message from Desmond.

Code Black, the message said.

Jordan stopped, set his coffee back on the counter and raced to his office.

"What's wrong?" Kinley asked, running behind him.

"We might have a problem." He dropped down into the chair and typed in some codes on the computer. The first was to verify that the message was indeed from Desmond.

It was.

Well, it'd come from his private secure line anyway. That didn't mean someone hadn't tapped into it and used it.

Jordan quickly called the man, and Desmond answered on the first ring. "What's happening?" Jordan asked. "Why the Code Black?"

"I came into Sentron to clear out my things and stopped by the command center," Desmond said, his words running together. "I ran a security check on your estate."

"Why?"

"Because I figured something would go wrong. I don't trust Burke, Cody or Strahan."

Then the feeling was mutual. But Jordan didn't trust Desmond, either. He punched in the code to run his own security check of the grounds and house. There were no flags, no indications that anything had been breached.

"I don't see anything," he told Desmond. "And none of the sensors have been triggered."

"Because the breach didn't exactly happen on your property. Jordan, you have to believe me. Look for it. It's just on the other side of the west fence in the greenbelt. If you look, there's no way you can miss it."

The greenbelt was a heavily treed area just about a hundred yards from his bedroom.

"I can't tell how much time you have left," Desmond warned.

Jordan ignored the man's increasingly frantic tone. For the moment, anyway.

With the phone sandwiched between his shoulder and his ear, Jordan gave the security cameras an adjustment. The first was useless. He couldn't see over the high stone privacy fence. But the second camera by the pool house was elevated enough to see down into the thick trees and underbrush. He'd designed it that way for just this type of security risk.

There it was.

A dull silver metal box with a timer on top.

Jordan zoomed in on that timer.

And cursed.

He got up and hit the buttons on the console to clear the codes so that no one could get access to and use the security feed to locate Gus. In the same motion, Jordan grabbed on to Kinley's arm. He started to run toward the garage. There wasn't time to get supplies or grab anything.

They had to get out of there now.

"What does Code Black mean?" Kinley asked, her voice a tangle of nerves and adrenaline.

"It means we have to get out of here. There's a bomb, and it's set to go off in two minutes."

Chapter Fourteen

Two minutes.

Kinley was afraid that wasn't enough time to escape, though Jordan was obviously going to try to do just that.

He plowed them through the house and into the garage and shoved her into a black Lexus. He made a quick check of his PDA, the screen showing the images from the various security cameras of the estate's surveillance system. Jordan no doubt did that to make sure no one was out there waiting, and he must have seen that it was safe because he pressed the remote control on the dashboard to open the garage door.

The moment the door raised, he barreled out of there.

"What about your neighbors?" Kinley asked, putting on her seat belt.

"They should be far enough away. This bomb was almost certainly set just to damage only my estate. I hope."

Yes, that was her hope as well. It was bad enough that they were in danger. No need to put anyone else smack in the middle of this nightmare that just wouldn't end.

"There's a gun and magazine clips in the glove compartment. Hand them to me," Jordan instructed. His gaze was darting all around, probably looking to see if they were about to be ambushed.

Kinley hadn't said that ambush fear aloud. There was no need. Both of them knew that this bomb could be just a ruse to draw them out. Maybe the person responsible thought Gus was still inside, and this would pull her baby out into the open, too.

And that infuriated her.

How dare this SOB risk endangering her child all to get a formula that didn't even exist.

She took the gun from the glove compartment and handed it to Jordan. He gripped it in his left hand while he sped away.

"Should I call nine-one-one?" Kinley asked. There were three magazine clips, and one by one, she handed those to him as well.

"No. Not at this point anyway. Besides, I didn't bring a cell with me. The GPS in them makes them easier to track. Don't worry, the neighbors will hear the explosion soon enough and report it."

No doubt. It wouldn't be a peaceful start to their Christmas morning.

It was dark, still several hours from sunrise, but the streetlights helped. What didn't help was the cold, thick pre-morning mist that cast an eerie blanket on the road.

Like Jordan, she looked around and didn't see anyone following them.

"The vehicle's behind us," Jordan told her.

That caused her heart to skip a couple of beats. "What? Where?" Kinley looked again and shook her head, and then she spotted the car. No headlights. That's why she had missed it. But it was there, all right.

Someone was following them.

"Stay low in the seat," Jordan insisted. "The glass is bulletproof, but I don't want to take any chances." And he hit the accelerator even harder.

There were no other cars out and about. That wasn't a surprise. It was, after all, the wee hours of Christmas morning. Still, with the roads slick with the condensation from the mist, it wasn't safe to be going eighty miles an hour on a residential street. But they had no choice. Which led Kinley to her next thought.

What did this person plan to do?

The bomb had perhaps been set to make them evacuate in a hurry. And they had done exactly that. Maybe the next step was to intercept them and kidnap her.

Or to break into the damaged estate and look for Gus.

She silently cursed. It all went back to that damn formula, and it wouldn't do any good to tell the person that it was a sham. No. That meant she and Jordan were both in grave danger all over again.

Kinley checked the clock on the dashboard. Judging from her calculations, two minutes had already passed, and she'd heard no explosion. Of course, they were far enough away that it still could have happened.

Or not.

"You think Desmond was telling the truth?" she asked, checking the mirror again. The car following them was still there, and the mist cloaked it so that she couldn't see who was in the driver's seat.

"Maybe." Jordan turned the steering wheel and took them into a sharp curve. The tires squealed in protest of the excessive speed. Behind them, the other car did the same.

"I know you said we can't call the police, but is

that where we're going—to police headquarters?" Kinley asked.

"No. If we do that, this person will back off. Then we'll have to go through this again and again. Until I stop him." Jordan glanced at her. "This morning, I'm going to stop him."

She shook her head, not understanding. "But how?"

He didn't answer right away, and that sent an icy chill through her. "This person wants you, and if I try to get in the way, there'll be an attempt to eliminate me."

"Oh, God. You're talking about going head-to-head with this person so you can sacrifice yourself? Jordan, you don't know who he is, or how many hired guns he has with him."

"It doesn't matter. This has to stop. We won't get Gus back until it does, and that's why it ends here. I'm sick and tired of playing games with this fool."

She couldn't exactly argue with the need for this to end, but the question was, how could Jordan make that happen? And better yet, where?

"Where are we going?" she asked.

"The training facility."

Of course. It was the place Jordan had built, and it had excellent security. That was the good news. On the downside, it was also in an isolated area where they might become trapped if things got worse.

She was afraid things would definitely get worse.

Kinley made another check of the rearview mirror. The other car was still there, following them, which meant it would also follow them to the warehouse. Then this head-to-head confrontation would happen.

"I have weapons at the training facility," he explained. "And I know the place like the back of my hand. I can have you stay in the command center, where you'll be safe, and I can put an end to this."

Yes, by putting himself in a position where he'd be far from safe. "I want to help you," she insisted. Kinley couldn't let him face this alone.

"Good. Because from the command center you'll be able to see what's going on. You can control the lights, the temperature, even the weather. There's an overhead sprinkler system to simulate a hard rain. You can watch what's going on with the monitors and can tell me where anyone is. And you can do all of that while you're safe behind the bulletproof glass."

She didn't approve of the idea of Jordan taking all the physical risks, but at least she could help him.

Maybe, just maybe, it would be enough.

Keeping the same high speed, Jordan ripped through the streets and drove toward the warehouse. With each mile ticking off the odometer, her heartbeat pounded even harder. The only thing that kept her from panicking was the thought of Gus. This would help him. This would make him safe.

It had to work.

Jordan made the final turn to the warehouse. He still didn't slow down, but he looked around. Not just in the rearview mirror but all around them. Probably checking to make sure they weren't about to be ambushed. If there were gunmen positioned nearby, she certainly didn't see them.

Of course, that didn't mean they weren't there.

Jordan used his PDA to open the massive doors to the warehouse. He still didn't slow down. He raced through the opening, and only then did he slam on the brakes. There were the sounds and the smells of the tires burning rubber onto the concrete, and he couldn't bring the vehicle to a full stop until he was about halfway into the training facility.

Kinley looked behind them and saw the other car coming. Oh, mercy. It was headed right into the warehouse as well. If the driver made it inside, there wouldn't be time for Jordan and her to get into place.

Jordan had obviously anticipated that. With his fingers moving fast, he coded in something on his PDA again, and the warehouse doors closed.

The other car slammed into the metal door.

The crash echoed through the warehouse, and with that deafening noise drumming through her head, they got out.

"Get to the command center now!" Jordan shouted.

Kinley hit the concrete running, but she also glanced over her shoulder. The car had indeed crashed into the warehouse, but the wrecked front end of the vehicle had prevented the doors from closing all the way. There was at least a two-foot gap of space.

Plenty of room for a gunman to get inside.

And maybe that was the point. After all, Jordan had wanted a showdown, and he was going to get it.

The cold winter air howled through the opening created by the crash, and coupled with the sound of their footsteps, it made it nearly impossible to hear if anyone was already following them. And she couldn't see much, either. The only illumination came from the headlights on Jordan's car.

"Don't look back," Jordan warned. "Just run." And to ensure that happened, he pushed her in front of him and guided her toward the stairs that led to the command center.

They only made it a third of the way up when Jordan

suddenly shoved her down. She landed hard on the steps. So hard that it temporarily knocked the breath out of her. Kinley tried to look around to see what had caused Jordan to do that.

"Someone's blocked off the command center," Jordan mumbled.

And he cursed.

Kinley looked up but couldn't see anything. "How do you know?"

"The access code to open the door doesn't work. Someone's jammed it so we can't get inside." He shoved his PDA into his pocket and got his gun ready.

That's when it hit her. They were perched on the stairs, literally out in the open. The exterior doors were jammed open with the wrecked car and could easily be breached. And someone had already shut off their access to the command center.

The one place of safety in the entire warehouse.

"We need to make it back to the car," Jordan whispered.

She looked down at the vehicle. Both doors were wide open, but the vehicle was sitting out in the middle of the warehouse with a lot of open space between it and them.

"We can't take the stairs," Jordan said. "We have to jump."

"Jump?"

"It's all right." He tipped his head to the floor. "It's padded below us, to break the fall."

Yes, but it was also a twenty-foot drop. Either of them could break a bone or two. Heck, even a twisted ankle at this point could turn out to be a fatal injury. Then, there was the whole problem of what might be waiting for them at ground level. The driver of that car could be waiting to shoot them. For that matter, so could the person who jammed the entrance of the command center.

Jordan and she could be attacked from both sides.

But that didn't stop Jordan. Probably because it was the only chance they had. "I'm going to slide over the railing and drop. Count to three and you do the same. Unless you hear shots being fired."

That speared the adrenaline through her. "And then what do I do?"

"Stay put. I'll get to you as soon as I can."

Yes, after he dodged bullets and risked getting himself killed. Still, it was obvious she wasn't going to talk him out of this. Besides, she certainly didn't have a better plan. She didn't have a plan at all, other than to do whatever was necessary to survive this.

Jordan brushed a kiss on her cheek and moved so quickly that he was almost a blur. He grabbed on to the metal railing, and with one deft move, he hoisted himself up and launched his body over the side. He'd been right. The floor had some kind of thick, feathery padding because it billowed up around him like a mattress and broke his fall. He bounced right up, aimed his gun and got ready for an attack.

"Now!" he told her.

Kinley got up off the steps. She didn't have the agility that Jordan did, but she still managed to get her leg over the railing. And she prayed. Because she was in a very vulnerable position.

She caught movement out of the corner of her eye and saw someone crawl through the space of the partially opened warehouse doors. Since the headlights weren't aimed in that direction, she couldn't see who it was. And there wasn't time to look farther. Kinley crawled over the railing. Said another prayer.

And dropped.

She landed on her butt and hands and didn't have a chance to get to her feet. That's because Jordan latched on to her arm and pulled her behind one of the wooden partitions draped with netting. The ceiling was low, barely an inch above her head, and Jordan pushed her to the back of the small enclosure. It was dark, cold and quiet.

But it didn't stay that way for long.

A shot rang out.

Chapter Fifteen

The shot slammed into the wall just inches from where Kinley and Jordan were standing.

So did the second bullet. The third tore through the partition and flew into the ceiling, scattering the acoustic tile into bits over them like little flakes of snow.

This was not how Jordan wanted things to go down. Bullets flying. God knew how many gunmen converging on them for an all-out attack. And with someone else in control. Soon, very soon, he needed to figure out who'd gotten into the warehouse ahead of him and jammed the command center entrance—which should have been next to impossible to do.

But first, he needed to get Kinley safely out of there.

That meant somehow getting her back into the car so he could drive out the back exit. Jordan only hoped his security codes still worked. It was possible they'd been altered as well. If so, Kinley and he were in deeper trouble than just having bullets fired at them.

They'd have no way out.

He could hear her breathing. It was way too hard and fast. And he knew her heart had to be racing out of control. He'd been in too many situations like this, but she didn't have his experience and training. She shouldn't have to be involved in this kind of danger, but she was.

And he could thank himself for that.

The moment she'd walked into the Sentron Christmas party, he should have put her in a safe house and kept her away from all of this. He shouldn't have tried to learn the truth until he had her out of harm's way. Jordan hoped he could undo that mistake and get her to safety.

"It'll be okay," he whispered to her, even though he had no idea if he could deliver on that promise.

Jordan pushed her deeper into the phase-one training room. It wasn't exactly bulletproof, but when he'd designed it, he'd added some metal insulation so a shot wasn't as likely to be deadly.

That didn't mean it couldn't be.

But for now, this was one of the best places for them to be. Soon, though, he'd need extra ammunition. Maybe even extra weapons. Those items were in the warehouse, but to get to them, he'd have to move, and that meant taking Kinley with him.

Perhaps the person who'd accessed the command center didn't know how to operate all the equipment. Jordan prayed that was true anyway. Because he'd personally designed some very realistic training obstacles, and he didn't want to have to go through those, especially with Kinley.

He didn't return fire. Best to save his ammunition for high-percentage shots, and for that to happen he needed to be able to see the target. Jordan used his PDA to enter some codes. And then he held his breath, hoping they hadn't been overridden by the person who'd accessed the command center.

The overhead lights flared on.

Since his eyes had already partly adjusted to the darkness, the lights were nearly blinding. But he forced himself to focus, and using the hole the bullet had made, he looked out to determine the position of the person firing those shots.

There was a ski-masked gunman near the back of his car. That was the only shooter he saw. The guy took aim again at the phase-one room where Kinley and Jordan were.

Jordan took aim, too.

And fired.

The guy dove away at the last second, and he used Jordan's car for cover. Not only was he out of the line of fire, it meant as long as the gunman was hiding there, Jordan couldn't get Kinley into the vehicle. Even more, Jordan didn't want to take too many more shots in that direction and risk shooting out one of the tires.

He needed a diversion.

Jordan used his PDA to see if he could get the overhead sprinklers to turn on, but before he could type in the codes, the place went dark.

Hell.

Someone definitely had tapped into the controls. But what else could the guy do?

Too much, he feared.

Using the backlight on his PDA, Jordan put in the codes to start the sprinkler system. They spewed on immediately, and it began to rain down on the place.

The gunman behind his car didn't move. Not good. Jordan needed the guy to budge, so he cranked up the speed on the sprinklers.

But the water stopped.

"Someone other than you is controlling things, isn't he?" Kinley asked, her voice barely audible.

Jordan considered lying, but a lie wasn't going to make her less afraid. "Yeah."

But the good news was that the person possibly didn't know what kind of power he had or else he would have already unleashed it.

Well, maybe.

Perhaps the culprit was saving those surprises for later. And that meant Jordan had to take some drastic action. If he couldn't immediately get to the vehicle, then he had to get to a phone and call the police. Yes, the officers would essentially be walking into a war zone, but that might be the only way he could get Kinley out of this alive. Still, his first choice was a getaway in the car, and he had to try to make that happen.

"Stay low and follow me," Jordan instructed.

He moved to her side and brushed against her arm. Every muscle was tight and knotted. Something he definitely understood. Every inch of him was primed for the fight, and the adrenaline was urging him on. They couldn't stay put. They needed to move now.

Jordan inched out of the phase-one room. There was only about four feet of space between it and the next area, but those four feet were in the shooter's kill zone. Not the place he wanted to linger.

Keeping himself in front of Kinley, he raced forward. She stayed right with him, and they practically dove into the other room.

The bullets started again.

Not single shots, either, but a barrage of gunfire, and it was all aimed at them.

Jordan pulled her to the floor, amid the dust and

straw that covered this particular section. The bullets had no problem eating their way through the partition, which meant the gunman had switched ammo. He was probably using some kind of Teflon-coated bullets.

And that meant they had to move again.

"Let's go," Jordan ordered. He caught her arm with his left hand. With his right, he got his own gun ready.

As he raced forward, he fired. And he just kept on firing until they were in the next room. He repeated the procedure again. And again. Until they were within ten yards of the car.

Moving so close to the gunman was probably scaring Kinley to death, but Jordan figured if he could just get closer, he could take the guy out.

"I'm going to try to draw out the gunman," Jordan whispered to her.

"How?"

She wouldn't like the plan, and he didn't have time to reassure her. "Stay right here, and when I tell you to run, get to the car as fast as you can. I'll be right behind you."

He hoped.

Jordan figured he had six shots left. He'd need them all and then would have to switch magazines. He put away his PDA, took a deep breath and launched himself out of the room. He caught the webbing that covered the adjacent training building, and he hoisted himself up so he could pinpoint the gunman hiding on the other side of his car.

Jordan fired.

The guy stayed down for the first two shots. Then Jordan went up another rung on the webbing, turned and fired again.

Two more shots.

These tore up chunks of the concrete and spewed the debris right in the man's face. Of course, the ski mask protected his skin, but not his eyes.

The man said something that Jordan couldn't distinguish, and he jumped back away from the flying bits of concrete.

Two more shots got the guy scrambling to the side, and he ducked behind one of the training partitions. Jordan changed his clip.

"Now," he told Kinley.

She was ready. She barreled out of the room and made a beeline for the car.

She didn't get far.

Jordan aimed his gun, but a gun was defenseless against this.

His car exploded in a fireball.

"OH MY GOD," KINLEY MUMBLED. And because she didn't know what else to say or do, she just kept repeating it.

Someone had blown up the car, their means of escape. Now what would they use to get out of there?

She forced herself to move, and she raced toward the cover of the training room. Something hit her hard in the back, and for a moment she thought she'd been shot. But it was just a piece of debris, she realized.

She didn't dare look back. Didn't dare pause to check her injuries. The fiery fragments of Jordan's car were literally raining down on them, and any of those fragments could be deadly.

So could the gunman.

He was no doubt still there on the other side of the warehouse, and if he could manage to see through the cloud of wreckage, he would shoot at them again.

She scrambled back into the room and yelled for Jordan to do the same. He jumped from the webbing and not a second too soon. A piece of the car's leather upholstery had flown against the webbing, setting it on fire.

The smoke was already thick from the explosion itself, but the new fire only added to it. Soon, they wouldn't be able to breathe, and that meant they had to move, maybe closer to the fresh air coming from the gap in the front warehouse door.

Of course, that meant going back through the maze of rooms, and that meant the gunman would once again have clean shots at them.

"Let's go," Jordan instructed.

He didn't waste another moment. With his gun ready and with him positioned at her side so he could shield her, they started to retrace their original path.

Kinley heard heavy footsteps on the concrete. Maybe the gunman was trying to escape, too. Unless he'd brought equipment with him, he wouldn't be able to breathe much longer, either. If he went in the same direction they did, there'd be another gun battle.

That caused her adrenaline to spike even more.

Jordan and Kinley made it through two of the training rooms. Then another. No shots came at them. No one attacked. They were about to race to the area nearest the front door, but the moment they reached it, overhead sprinklers came on again. Cold water began to pour down from the ceiling.

Jordan lowered his gun, putting it barrel down, no doubt to protect it from the water. However, there was nothing they could do to protect themselves. Within seconds, they were drenched. With the winter air rifling through the opening, she began to shiver, and her teeth began to chatter.

"Now," Jordan prompted.

They started to move again toward the front door. Heaven knew what they would do once they were outside. Maybe darkness would shield them long enough for them to take cover.

But then what?

With no cell phone and miles from anyone who might be able to help, getting out of the warehouse was only the first step to what would be a nightmare of obstacles.

They stopped in the first room. And waited. Jordan lifted his head, listening. But with the pounding downpour, they couldn't hear anything. Someone could be sneaking up on them, and they wouldn't know until it was too late.

"Let's move," Jordan finally said.

Just as the water stopped.

That caused him to stop, and she tried to listen again to see what was going on.

She heard a sound as if someone were dragging something heavy. That sound was followed by footsteps. Not one set this time. At least two. And the dragging sound and the footsteps were coming from the front door.

Mere feet away.

Kinley was almost certain someone was moving the wrecked car sandwiched beneath the warehouse door.

Jordan put his left index finger to his mouth in a keep-quiet gesture, and he aimed his gun at the opening to the room. But no one came inside. The footsteps moved quickly past them.

Without making a sound, Jordan leaned his head to the side and peered out the room's opening. Even though there was barely any light, Kinley could still see his expression. His jaw had turned to steel, and he mouthed some profanity.

"What's wrong?" Kinley put her mouth right against his ear so she wouldn't be heard.

Jordan didn't take his eyes off the opening, but he moved closer to her and whispered, "Two Sentron agents just arrived. Both armed."

"Not Cody and Desmond?" She held her breath, praying it wasn't.

He shook his head. "New recruits. I trained them both here just last month."

Now she understood the reason for his reaction. She doubted the men were on Jordan's side. No, they almost certainly had been sent here as hired guns. And they knew the warehouse. They were trained. By Jordan, no less.

The men would know how to kill.

When they joined up with their ski-masked comrade, Jordan and Kinley would be seriously outnumbered. They really had to get out of there now.

Jordan must have come to the same conclusion because he inched his way to the opening. "Stay as quiet as you can," he mouthed.

So, this wouldn't be a mad dash like before. They would need to sneak out without being seen or heard.

Jordan stopped at the room's door. He looked out again and then crouched down. Kinley did the same, and, following him, they crept toward the warehouse opening. It wasn't hard to find. It was the source of the wind and the only noise in the place.

Well, except for her heartbeat.

It was pounding like war drums in her ears, and she hoped that her breathing wasn't as audible as it sounded to her. She didn't want to give away their position.

Jordan eased out of the room, and, still crouched, he turned in the direction of the still-burning car and command center. He kept watch while they made their way out.

There was a crackle of sound, and Kinley braced herself for another explosion. Or for the overhead sprinklers to spew water onto them. But it wasn't a bomb or water.

The lights flared on.

Not just a few of them. Probably every light in the place. She spotted the still-blazing car.

And the men.

They were a lot closer than she'd anticipated. And both of them had assault rifles trained right on Jordan and her.

"Hold it right there," a heavily muscled, dark-haired man snarled.

Kinley looked at the opening. The wrecked car was indeed gone, giving them a clear path to escape. But the exit was at least ten feet away. Too far for her to even attempt it. The men would gun her down before she could make it another step.

Jordan lifted his hands, and he stood, positioning himself in front of her.

He was surrendering.

Behind them, there was a grinding sound of metal scraping against metal.

And the warehouse door dropped shut.

Jordan and Kinley were trapped.

Chapter Sixteen

Jordan hadn't thought things could get much worse.

But he'd obviously been wrong.

Here they were, being held at gunpoint by two of his former agents: Chris Sutton and Wally Arceneaux. Jordan had never worked an assignment with either of the men since they'd only been with Sentron a little over a month. But he knew what they were capable of doing.

And what they were capable of doing was killing.

All of his former agents had been trained to do that.

Now the question was, for whom were they willing to kill? Were they getting their orders from Burke, or had Strahan or someone else hired them? Or maybe they were working for Cody or Desmond.

Jordan made a quick check of the warehouse and spotted the ski-masked gunman. He didn't come closer, but he also had his rifle trained on Kinley and him.

Now they were facing three armed men, and with their escape route cut off, that meant he had to find another way to get her out of there.

"Drop your gun," Wally ordered.

Jordan held on to it, but he did ease it down to a

position that would hopefully not seem so threatening. "Is this a Sentron-directed mission?" he asked.

"Drop your gun," Wally repeated.

That was standard operating procedure. Don't engage the detainee in conversation. It could be a distraction. It could create an empathetic situation, not that Sentron agents were high on empathy. Jordan had hired them because they had ice water in their veins and weren't easily distracted.

Now that was coming back to haunt him.

"I want to speak to Burke," Jordan tried again. "He needs to know what Kinley found out about the formula for the antidote."

Jordan wouldn't tell them that the antidote didn't exist. That it was a fake. He had to let Burke or whoever believe that it was possible for him to get his hands on it. This way, it would buy Kinley some time and some safety. They wouldn't kill her as long as they believed she could give them what they'd been told to get.

"Drop your weapon," Wally said for the third time, and he lifted his gun, preparing to shoot.

Jordan recognized that look in the man's eyes. This wasn't a bluff. Wally had orders to kill him. And that meant he had to do something fast.

Kinley beat him to it.

She jumped in front of Jordan.

Hell. She was trying to protect him.

"I want to talk to Burke," she insisted. "And Martin Strahan. There are things they need to know."

Wally and Chris exchanged a brief glance. Then Wally nodded. "Come with me. I'll take you to the person you should be talking to."

Wally had chosen his words carefully and hadn't incriminated his boss. That meant Jordan wasn't any closer to learning the identity of the person behind this attack. But he pushed that aside for now because he had to do something to stop them from taking Kinley.

Even though the agents likely didn't have orders to kill her, they would no doubt torture her to get her to reveal secrets that she didn't even have.

Wally used his rifle to gesture for Kinley to move closer so she could no doubt go with him. She didn't budge, but Wally wouldn't put up with her stance for long. Soon, he'd try to grab her to get her moving. That's when Jordan would have to act, and he only hoped that neither Wally nor Chris would take shots at them.

The seconds crawled by. Each one ticked off in Jordan's head. Each one kicked his heartbeat up another notch. Finally, Wally took a step toward them. He kept his rifle aimed at them. So did Chris.

Wally took another step.

And that was Jordan's cue to spring into action.

Praying that Kinley wouldn't unintentionally do something to get in the way, Jordan threw his arm around her waist, and with her gripped to him, he dove toward the training room. They crashed to the floor, and his shoulder slammed into the concrete. The pain shot through him. Still, he did a quick check to make sure Kinley was okay. She seemed to be. She scrambled to get to her feet when he did.

Jordan fought off the pain and came up ready to fire. But Wally and Chris didn't shoot. What they did do was curse, which confirmed they had orders to keep her alive. Jordan would use those orders to his advantage.

"Move quietly," he mouthed and hitched his shoulder in the direction of the other room. They were going to backtrack, to make their way toward the center of the warehouse. Back to the command center stairs where he could get to the training tunnel he'd had installed.

With the lights on at full glare, Jordan had no trouble seeing Kinley's face. She was drenched from the simulated sprinkler rain, her hair had flecks of ash and debris from his car, and her bottom lip was trembling. Probably a combination of cold and fear. But despite what had to be a terrifying situation for her, she kept moving. When they reached the room exit, they bolted straight into the next area.

Jordan listened, to try to hear what Wally and Chris were doing. Not that he expected differently, but they moved too, following along the outside of the rooms. The men were no doubt waiting for Kinley and him to reach the last training area before the command center.

Then they would grab Kinley.

Or so they thought.

Jordan didn't want the duo to get suspicious and ambush them so he kept watch on the exit and worked as quickly and quietly as he could. He used his foot to kick back some of the soggy straw that covered this particular section of the training area. He grabbed the handle that the straw had concealed and lifted it.

There was a set of steps that led down to a tunnel. A tunnel that Chris and Wally didn't even know existed. This was a route used by the trainers to set up a simulated ambush for advanced training, something that neither of the men had received yet.

When she saw the tunnel, Kinley's eyes widened, and there was just a touch of relief in them. She didn't waste any time. She hurried down the steps and into the dark space. Jordan got in as well, and he pulled the door shut. It wouldn't stop Chris and Wally from finding the escape route, but all Jordan needed was a minute or two head start.

Since it was pitch black, Jordan handed Kinley his PDA so she could use the backlight to illuminate their way. Thankfully, there were no turns to take. They were literally on a direct path to another trapdoor exit near the command center. Too bad the tunnel didn't extend the entire length of the warehouse. That would have been a nice bonus about now, but he had to be satisfied with just making it to the halfway point.

One step at a time.

There was little or no chance for them to get into the command center now, but if they got very lucky, they could quietly make their way out of the tunnel and through the other training rooms at the far end of the warehouse. Then he'd need another dose of good luck that his PDA codes would still work so he could open the exit.

If not, well, he didn't want to go there.

Nor did he want to think of who or what might be waiting for them once they made it out.

This had to work.

Jordan moved ahead of her as they approached another set of stairs that led to the exit. He kept his gun ready in his right hand, and he used his left hand to ease open the hatch door. Just a fraction. Then he waited and listened.

No voices.

No footsteps.

Just the glare of the light bouncing off the water on the floor.

"I should go first," Kinley whispered. "They won't shoot me."

Not on purpose, anyway. But it was possible one of

them might have a quick trigger finger. Plus, they had to worry about the ski-masked guy. Jordan had no idea what his intentions were, but he doubted they were good.

"I'll go first," Jordan insisted. "There's about ten feet of space between the tunnel exit and the first training room. Get there as fast as you can."

She nodded, and as he'd done before, she brushed a kiss on his mouth. Jordan wished he had the time to tell her how sorry he was that she was in this predicament. He wished there was time to say a lot of things. But there wasn't. They had to make their move now.

Jordan inched the tunnel door to the side and looked out again. No one. He made his way up the steps, and while staying crouched down, he fired glances all around them. Wally and Chris still had their rifles trained on the room at the other end.

Good.

Two fewer guns to worry about.

Jordan motioned for Kinley to come up the steps as well, and he held his breath. Waiting and praying. She made it to the top, and he motioned for her to move. They needed to get to the cover of the nearest training room and then run like hell.

He reached for her hand and helped her to step out onto the concrete floor.

Just as the lights went out again.

Kinley gasped.

Jordan wanted to believe she'd made that sound because of the shock of the darkness, but he knew in his gut that it was much more than that.

There was some shuffling. Footsteps. Since his eyes hadn't adjusted to the darkness, Jordan had no idea what was happening. He couldn't fire and risk shooting

Kinley. He could only stand there in the pitchy blackness and wait for what he knew wouldn't be good news.

"Jordan," she said, her voice a tangle of nerves and concern.

"I'm here," Jordan answered and immediately moved to the side.

It wasn't a second too soon because the shot came right at him.

THE SOUND OF THE bullet blasted through the warehouse and echoed off the metal walls.

"Jordan!" Kinley called out.

That bullet could have hit him. He could be hurt, or worse. But there was nothing she could do to get to him because someone had grabbed her and put her in a fierce hold.

Worse, that someone had a gun pointed to her head.

"Move and Jordan dies," the person rasped in her ear.

Kinley couldn't recognize the voice, which was no doubt what he intended, but he obviously didn't intend to stay put. He began to move away from Jordan and to the stairs that led to the command center. If he got her there, Jordan wouldn't be able to get to her.

Even more frightening, Jordan would be a sitting duck.

She had to make a stand and stop this person from getting her up those stairs.

But how?

How could she do that without risking Jordan's life?

Kinley had his PDA still in her hand, and she'd seen him type in various codes to make things happen in the warehouse. She didn't know the codes, but maybe if she could randomly punch in some numbers, she might be able to create some kind of distraction.

Of course, it could be a deadly one.

God knew what kind of training exercises were in place. She hoped she didn't make something explode or cause shots to be fired. Still, she had to try. Her kidnapper was much stronger than she was, and he was using his muscle to get her up the stairs.

Trying not to draw attention to what she was doing, she used her thumb to push some buttons.

Nothing happened.

She pressed more. Then more when the darkness stayed, and still nothing changed. Maybe there was a special sequence of codes. Maybe even fingerprint recognition. If so, the PDA was useless.

The man dragged her up the first step, and when she struggled, he jammed the gun hard against her back. "Think of Jordan," he warned.

She couldn't think of anything else. Jordan was in danger because of her.

Kinley frantically stabbed more buttons.

Everything seemed to happen at once. The lights came back on. So did the overhead sprinklers, and netting dropped from the ceiling landing on the two agents who minutes earlier had held Jordan and her at gunpoint.

She didn't see Jordan.

God, where was he?

She didn't even know if he was alive since that shot could have been a direct hit.

Her kidnapper ripped something from his face. Night goggles, she realized. Now that the lights were on, they were useless. Still, she couldn't get a good look at him because beneath the goggles, he wore a ski mask. This was the man who'd taken cover behind Jordan's car.

But who was he?

He stopped on the stairs, yanked her against him so that her back was to his chest.

And he put the gun to her head.

"Call out Jordan's name," the man growled, his voice still unrecognizable.

She shook her head, but he only jammed the gun harder against her back. "Do it," he insisted. She realized then he was wearing some kind of device to alter his voice. "Or you die here."

"You won't kill me." She dug in her heels to keep him from moving her higher up the steps. "Because if you do, you'll never get the antidote."

"The antidote doesn't exist," he said. It sounded very much like a threat.

And it was.

Kinley didn't say anything. She just stood there, waiting for him to continue while she looked around the warehouse for Jordan. Still no sign of him. But the two agents on the floor were gradually making their way out of the netting. It wouldn't be long, a couple of minutes probably, before they could join forces with the man who had the gun jammed against her.

"I got copies of all the notes, too," he continued. "And I had people go through them. About two hours ago I was told the formula didn't exist. *Yet.*"

"Yet? What do you mean?"

"I mean you're going to create that antidote for me so I can sell it. I already have a buyer."

"Impossible. I can't make it."

"You'll find a way. If not, Jordan will die. And if that doesn't work, I'll track down your son and use him. One way or another, you'll cooperate."

Oh, God. He was talking about holding her hostage while he forced her to make something that probably couldn't even be done. This was just the beginning of the nightmare. Gus was still in danger. And he would stay in danger as long as this man believed she could create that formula.

She would have to die.

That was the only way.

If she were dead, it would stop. Gus wouldn't be in danger any longer and neither would Jordan because he would somehow escape this mess. There'd be no threat that could rear its ugly head years from now when some other person decided to get their hands on a potential gold mine.

A sudden calm came over her. She didn't want to die. She wanted to live and raise her son. Kinley wanted to see if she and Jordan could possibly have a future together, but her past had ruined any chances of that.

She took a deep breath. And got ready to jump. The padded floor would probably save her again, but her kidnapper might shoot. Either way, she'd be away from him.

There was a soft rattling sound that stopped her. It caused her kidnapper to freeze, too. She felt the muscles tighten in his chest and arms. His gaze flew up toward the ceiling.

But it was too late.

Jordan was there, hanging on to a pulley-type rope that was zooming down on them. Her kidnapper lifted his gun and aimed, just as Jordan crashed into him. The collision sent them all plummeting to the floor.

Kinley landed with a thud and quickly rolled to the side so that she wouldn't be crushed beneath them. Jordan's gun went flying, but that didn't stop him. He came up off the padded floor and launched himself at the kidnapper. He landed a quick punch and snatched the ski mask off the man's head.

Kinley got just a glimpse of the man's face before he fired a shot at Jordan.

"CODY," JORDAN SNARLED, and he dove out of the way of the shot.

After the way things had been happening in the warehouse, Jordan figured Kinley's would-be kidnapper was someone with insider knowledge of the training facility, but he'd hoped it wasn't Cody, the agent who'd once been his right-hand man.

Now that right-hand man was trying to kill him.

Jordan would have much preferred to be facing Strahan or Burke. Heck, even Desmond. Because none of them had as much training and experience as Cody.

"Don't!" Cody warned when Kinley went for the gun that had been dislodged from Jordan's hand during the fall. So had his PDA that Kinley had been holding. It was just a couple of inches from Jordan's feet.

Unfortunately, Cody had managed to hang on to his weapon and had it pointed at Kinley. When she continued to go after the fallen gun, Cody turned his weapon on Jordan.

That stopped her.

Kinley looked at Jordan, and he didn't see fear in her eyes. Just resolve. Which wasn't a good thing right now. He didn't want her taking any risks that could result in her getting hurt. Cody was obviously desperate and greedy enough to do just about anything.

"Cody wants me to create a formula," Kinley explained. She wiped the water from her face.

"I know she can do it," Cody insisted. "I read all about Kinley when I went through Burke's files."

"What were you doing in Burke's files?" Jordan asked. But he wasn't really interested in the answer. He was more interested in how he could get that gun away from Cody.

Cody shrugged. "I was checking up on my new boss. The boss you shoved down my throat when you sold Sentron. Bad move, Jordan. The company was as much mine as it was yours, and you had no right to sell it."

"I didn't have a choice."

"So you say." There was some movement to Cody's left. Chris and Wally were finally making their way out of the webbing that Kinley had dropped down onto them earlier. Once they were free and able to help Cody, Jordan didn't stand a chance of stopping them from taking Kinley.

"Get on the floor, Jordan," Cody demanded.

All in all, it wasn't a bad place to be. Jordan got to his knees, using his leg to hide the PDA. He scooped it into his hand.

"The formula is impossible to make," Jordan informed Cody. "The lab tried for months and couldn't do it." He didn't expect his former employee to believe that. Nor did he care if he did. Jordan needed the sound of his voice to cover the keystrokes he was making into his PDA, and once he was done, he eased the device back onto the floor.

Wally and Chris got to their feet and started to make their way toward Cody. Both turned, however, at the whirring sound. Neither knew what was coming.

"Kinley, get down!" Jordan shouted.

She did, thank God. Kinley dove toward him, just as the dummy bullets sprayed over them. Jordan had turned the training rifles toward them and had coded the signal for all to fire. It wasn't a training exercise he used often, but he was damn glad it was in place now.

The shock and the piercing pain from the rubber pellets caused Wally and Chris to run for cover. Cody automatically turned as well, to shelter his face.

Big mistake.

Jordan grabbed his gun from the floor.

Cody whirled back around and aimed his own weapon at Jordan and fired. But he was a split second too late. Jordan fired first, a double tap of the trigger.

Shots meant to kill.

And that's exactly what they did.

Jordan saw the startled look go through Cody's eyes. It was probably wishful thinking, but he thought he saw remorse and regret as well.

Then Cody dropped dead to the floor.

The rubber bullets continued to slam into them. Kinley yelped in pain. She was obviously getting hit. Jordan was, too, but he had something else to do before he could stop the training exercise.

He turned, pointing his hand in Wally and Chris's direction. "Drop your weapons and get on the floor," Jordan yelled.

There was hesitation, and for one sickening moment, Jordan thought he was going to have to kill again tonight. But both men finally complied. Their weapons fell, they kicked them toward Jordan, and they got to the ground.

"Code in six-seven-three on the PDA," Jordan instructed Kinley.

She did, and the assault from the dummy bullets stopped.

Jordan made his way to Cody and checked for a

pulse. He found none. He then rifled through Cody's pocket and located a cell phone. Without taking his eyes off Wally and Chris, Jordan tossed the phone to Kinley.

"Call nine-one-one," he told her.

He heard her press in the numbers, and because the warehouse was almost deadly silent, he heard the ring. And he also heard the emergency dispatcher say, "What's your emergency?"

What Jordan didn't hear was Kinley respond to that critical question.

He glanced at her to see what was wrong.

And his heart dropped to his knees.

She had the cell phone cradled next to her ear, but her eyes were closed. She was ash pale.

Lifeless.

And there was a pool of blood around her.

Chapter Seventeen

The sound of voices woke Kinley. Jordan's voice and several others that she didn't recognize.

She forced open her eyes. Everything was blurry and she was woozy, but she could tell she was in a hospital. Specifically, she was in a bed surrounded by white walls, white floors and white bedding.

Kinley started to get up but came to an abrupt halt when she felt the jab of pain in her shoulder. And then she remembered.

She'd been shot.

The bullet that Cody had fired had ricocheted off something in the warehouse and had slammed into her shoulder.

"You're awake," Jordan said. He practically ran across the room to get to her. Behind him, she saw the massive Christmas tree that several orderlies were decorating.

Jordan leaned down and kissed her. Not some lusty foreplay kiss. But one so soft that it barely touched her lips. He was gentle, and judging from those lines on his forehead he was worried about her.

"Where's Gus?" she asked.

"On the way. He should be here any minute."

Good. That would be the best medicine for her. She

put Jordan in that category, too. He could certainly cure a variety of ills, though he didn't seem certain of that. That's because he didn't know how she felt about him.

He didn't know that she loved him.

And that meant it was time to tell him.

Kinley tested her shoulder again. The pain was still there, but it was manageable so she tried to ease herself into a sitting position so they could talk.

Jordan stopped her.

With that same gentleness, he took hold of her arms and had her lie back down.

"I'm okay, really," Kinley assured him.

"No, you're not. You had to have surgery to remove a bullet lodged in your shoulder." He paused, put his hands on his hips. "Why didn't you tell me you'd been shot? Here I was ordering you to make calls, and I didn't even look at you to make sure you were okay."

Kinley knew where this was going.

Or rather where it'd already been.

While the doctors had been removing the bullet, Jordan had no doubt beaten himself up because he hadn't been able to stop her from being injured.

She reached out and pulled on his hand to draw him closer. Much closer. She dragged him down so that he was sitting on the bed next to her. "You saved my life a dozen times in that warehouse," she reminded him. "If it weren't for you, I'd be dead."

"But I didn't stop you from being shot."

She smiled. It was probably a weary one and God knew how bad she looked, but it was heartfelt. "Jordan, you have some amazing qualities, but even you can't stop a bullet from ricocheting and hitting my shoulder."

He shook his head. "I wasn't careful enough with you."

To stop him from continuing his guiltfest, she pulled him down to her for a real kiss. No whisper-soft one. Kinley kissed him as if he were the man she loved. Because he was.

"Women in hospital beds shouldn't kiss like that," he drawled with his mouth still hovering over hers.

She smiled. Though she wanted to continue this lighter banter, she heard a crash in the corner and automatically jumped and braced herself for the worst.

But there was no worst.

One of the orderlies who was decorating the tree had dropped an ornament, and it hadn't even broken. Amazingly, the delicate-looking glass had hit the floor and rolled a few feet away.

"The tree was no doubt your idea?" she asked.

He eased back just a bit. "Since you have to stay here for a day or two and since it is Christmas, I thought you and Gus would like the tree."

That brought tears to her eyes and reminded her that Jordan was a very thoughtful man. "Thank you. It's beautiful."

Her gaze left the tree and came back to Jordan at the same moment that he looked at her. "Cody's dead," he told her.

Yes. She remembered that. "You did what you had to do."

He shrugged. "Cody used his remote control to get into the facility. That's how he was able to set up those obstacles for us. If I'd figured out beforehand that he was responsible—"

Kinley grabbed him harder this time. Kissed him harder, too.

"I guess that means you don't want to talk about Cody," he remarked.

"Or maybe it means I just want to kiss you," she joked. But he was right. She didn't want to talk about the nightmare that had come to life in the warehouse. Unfortunately, though, she needed to know if it was safe for her son to come home.

"Is the danger over?" Kinley stilled, trying not to cry. But she was afraid she'd do just that if they had to go on the run again.

"It's over," Jordan assured her.

Because he said it so calmly, it took her a moment for that to sink in. "Really?"

"Really." He scrubbed his hand over his face and groaned softly in a where-do-I-start kind of way. "Martin Strahan has been arrested for Shelly's murder."

"How did that happen?" she asked, surprised.

"Lt. Rico brought in Pete Mendenhall, Shelly's killer, and the guy made a deal. He'll testify that Strahan hired him, and the D.A. will take the death penalty off the table. Don't worry, though. Pete will spend the rest of his life behind bars."

And Strahan wouldn't be able to terrorize them anymore. "What about Cody?"

"Anderson Walker, Chris and Wally have all confirmed that Cody put this plot together and hired them to help him. First, he wanted to get the formula just to collect the reward because he was riled with me for what he considered a betrayal for selling Sentron. But when he realized the formula didn't exist and that he could potentially earn a fortune if it did, he decided to kidnap you so you'd make it for him."

And now that Cody was dead, he could no longer threaten her. But someone else could.

Someone else who might believe she could create the formula.

Jordan reached out and smoothed his fingers over her bunched up forehead. "The FBI has put out the word that the formula was a sham, that it can't be developed."

The breath rushed out of her. "So, there'll be no more attacks, no more attempts to use Gus to make me cooperate?"

"No more," he promised.

She believed him. Besides, Jordan wouldn't be bringing Gus home unless he was positive that her son would be safe. After all, he'd devoted the last fourteen months of his life to the child.

"What about your company?" she asked. "Will you be able to buy Sentron back from Burke?"

"I don't want it back. To run it right, it would mean more eighty-hour workweeks. I'm thinking I'd like to create something smaller where I can hire some of the agents that Burke fired. Something more specialized. And less dangerous."

Well, that certainly sounded good to her. They'd had enough danger to last them several lifetimes.

"All done," one of the orderlies announced. The men gathered up the now empty boxes that'd held the decorations and went out the door.

Kinley spotted the gifts under the tree. At least a dozen beautifully wrapped boxes.

"For Gus," Jordan volunteered. "I had to do something while you were in surgery, so I ordered a few things and had them delivered. I also had some presents brought from the estate."

He'd done that so Gus would have a Christmas. Yes, Jordan was indeed thoughtful.

And much more.

She touched his face again so he would turn and make eye contact with her. "You gave up so much to keep Gus safe."

"Yeah. But I got a lot more in return. I wouldn't have you if it weren't for Gus." He paused and kissed her. "Do I have you, Kinley?"

Even with the pain meds making her a little woozy and the dizzying effects of that kiss, she didn't even have to think about her answer. "You have me, Jordan. Any way you want, you have me."

But then she stopped. Rethought that. And considered why he was asking. "Does this have anything to do with me getting shot?"

"In a way."

So this was a pity reaction? She didn't want his pity. She wanted *him*.

"When I came so close to losing you," he explained, "that's when I realized just how important you are to me."

Important? Well, he was more than important to her. "I'm in love with you, Jordan."

Yes, it was a risk. To a confirmed bachelor, an I'm-in-love-with-you confession might send him running, but Kinley didn't want to go through another minute without telling him. That nightmare in the warehouse had taught her that every minute was precious and that life was too short to hold anything back.

He took a deep breath. But didn't run. "You're in love with me," he flatly stated.

Kinley silently groaned and tried to brace herself for a rejection.

"Will you marry me?" Jordan asked.

Because she wasn't expecting to hear that, Kinley had to repeat his question. Several times. However, once the proposal sank in, she didn't have to think about the answer.

"Yes," she said.

Still no reaction from Jordan. But then, she wasn't reacting, either. They were both sitting there, holding their breaths.

Then he shouted, "Yes!" And he pumped his arm in a gesture of victory.

Kinley laughed, partly at seeing him so emotional and partly because she was overwhelmed with joy. "You really want to marry me?" she clarified.

He answered that with a kiss. It was long, hot and so Jordan. It was also the best way to answer because it left no doubt that he had marriage on his mind.

But what else did he have on his mind?

Maybe it was everything she'd recently been through that gave her doubts, but she had to wonder: Was this proposal for Gus's sake?

In part she loved Jordan for everything he'd done for her son, but she didn't want a marriage based on convenience for the sake of a child. She wanted a real marriage.

"Uh-oh," Jordan grumbled. "You're having doubts already."

Unfortunately, yes. But she didn't get a chance to voice them. That's because there was a knock at the door and a split second later, it opened. Kinley heard Gus before she even saw him in the doorway with Elsa.

Nothing would have stopped Kinley from sitting up then and there. She wanted to give Gus a huge Christmas hug.

Elsa stood the boy on the floor, and with a big grin

on his face, Gus began to toddle his way toward Jordan, who got off the bed and onto his feet.

"Jor-dad," Gus squealed. But the little boy stopped when he spotted the Christmas tree. His soft brown eyes lit up. "Tris-mas." And he clapped his hands, nearly throwing himself off-balance in the process.

Gus would have made it to those presents, too, if Jordan hadn't scooped him up in his arms. "Those are for later, buddy." And Jordan kissed him on the cheek. "For now, why don't you say hello to your mom."

"I'll give you guys some alone time," Elsa insisted. She stepped back into the hall and shut the door.

Jordan brought Gus to her, and even though those presents were still obviously distracting her son, Gus gave her a sloppy kiss on the forehead. But he got a concerned, curious look on his face when he saw the bandage on her shoulder.

"Boo-boo?" he asked.

"Just a little one," Kinley assured him, smiling.

"Boo-boo," Gus confirmed, and he leaned down and gently kissed the bandage.

Kinley's smile turned to a few tears of joy. Both Jordan and Gus had magical powers when it came to her pain and her mood. Just being there with them made her feel as if everything was right with the world.

Well, almost everything.

There was still that issue of why Jordan had proposed.

Apparently no longer concerned with her boo-boo, Gus pointed to the tree again, and Jordan walked with the boy in that direction. Jordan picked up one of the smaller boxes, carried it and Gus back to her.

"This one is for you," he told Kinley, and he placed the box on the bed beside her.

Surprised, she stared at him. "You found the time to get me a present?"

"I made the time." Jordan stared at her, too.

Gus, however, sprang into action. He yanked off the lid and looked inside. "Ohhhh," he said. "Pretty." He grabbed whatever was inside and brought it out for her to see.

It wasn't just *pretty*. It was beautiful.

Her son dropped the sparkly diamond engagement ring onto her lap and squirmed to get down, probably so he could head back toward the tree and the rest of the presents. Jordan let the child go, and while keeping an eye on him, he slipped the ring onto her finger.

"Well?" Jordan asked. "What about those doubts now?"

Kinley blinked back the tears, and not all of them were of the happy variety. "The ring is perfect," she started. "Gus is perfect. So are you." She shook her head and reached to take off the ring. "But I don't want a marriage of convenience—"

"Good." He caught her hand to stop her from removing the ring. "Because I wouldn't ask you to marry me for Gus's sake."

"You wouldn't?"

"No way. I have an even better reason. I asked you to marry me because I'm in love with you, and I want to spend the rest of my life with you."

Her breath caught, and she hadn't realized just how much she wanted to hear him say that. Kinley went into his arms and melted against them. "Then, everything is perfect because I want forever with you, too."

No broken breath for Jordan. But there was a sigh of relief, right before he kissed her blind.

The man definitely had a clever mouth.

Jordan was smiling when he finally eased away from her, and they both automatically checked on Gus. He was ripping the paper from one of the packages. When he got through all the ribbon and paper, he struggled and finally pulled out a red plastic fire engine that was large enough for him to sit on and ride. That's exactly what he did. With him in the driver's seat, he scooted it across the tile floor.

"I think he likes it," Kinley said, knowing that was an understatement. Gus was laughing and obviously enjoying his gift.

Kinley looked up at Jordan. "But I didn't get you anything. There aren't any presents under the tree for you."

He made a show of looking disappointed and then tapped his chin as if in deep thought. "Well, let's see. What can you get me? Not that," he joked and gave her a naughty grin. "Well, not at this moment. You have to heal first. Then we'll get married. And maybe next year, you can give me what I want for Christmas."

"And what would that be?" she asked, moving in for another kiss.

Jordan tightened the hold he had on her and tipped his head to Gus. "You can give me a baby. A brother or sister for Gus."

"A baby?" she questioned.

He nodded and seemed to hold his breath.

She nodded as well. "Jordan, I'd love to have your baby."

And that earned her the best kiss of all.

Kinley had thought the moment was perfect, but she realized it hadn't been. That had made it perfect.

Jordan and she weren't just in love and headed for the altar. They were a family—a soon to be growing one—and Kinley couldn't wait for them to begin their lives together.

* * * * *

INTRIGUE...

2-IN-1 ANTHOLOGY
COLBY LOCKDOWN
by Debra Webb

The Colby Agency is under siege! And Slade will do anything to save his team. Yet he didn't expect his illegal rescue mission with Mia to turn to sizzling attraction...

COLBY JUSTICE
by Debra Webb

Ben's worked in the most dangerous places on earth. If anyone can save the Colby Agency, he can. Guarding his heart from beautiful Penny, however, is another matter entirely...

•••

2-IN-1 ANTHOLOGY
THE SOCIALITE AND THE BODYGUARD
by Dana Marton

Nash is not happy about becoming bodyguard to a spoiled heiress and her precious lap dog. Soon, however, a real threat has him reconsidering his feelings for feisty Kayla.

CAVANAUGH REUNION
by Marie Ferrarella

Something about sexy cop Ethan spells "trouble." But when he kisses her, Kansas' defences melt, putting her in distinct danger of losing her heart...

On sale from 17th December 2010
Don't miss out!

Available at WHSmith, Tesco, ASDA, Eason
and all good bookshops

www.millsandboon.co.uk

1210/46a

INTRIGUE...

2-IN-1 ANTHOLOGY

COLD CASE AFFAIR
by Loreth Anne White

When pregnant Muirinn returns to her Alaska home town, she slams right into the past she's tried so hard to forget. But now rugged Jett could be her only hope of survival.

HER HERO IN HIDING
by Rachel Lee

After finding Kay injured and pregnant on a deserted country road, gorgeous rancher Clint swears to protect her—even if she is being hunted by a serial killer...

•••

SINGLE TITLE

SMOKIN' SIX-SHOOTER
by BJ Daniels

Although her new neighbour is all gorgeous cowboy, Dulcie isn't looking for love. She needs to solve a murder. But when she digs too deep Russell could be her saviour.

**On sale from 17th December 2010
Don't miss out!**

Available at WHSmith, Tesco, ASDA, Eason
and all good bookshops

www.millsandboon.co.uk

1210/46b

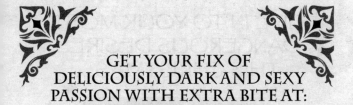

2 FREE BOOKS
AND A SURPRISE GIFT

We would like to take this opportunity to thank you for reading this Mills & Boon® book by offering you the chance to take TWO more specially selected books from the Intrigue series absolutely FREE! We're also making this offer to introduce you to the benefits of the Mills & Boon® Book Club™—

- **FREE home delivery**
- **FREE gifts and competitions**
- **FREE monthly Newsletter**
- **Exclusive Mills & Boon Book Club offers**
- **Books available before they're in the shops**

Accepting these FREE books and gift places you under no obligation to buy, you may cancel at any time, even after receiving your free books. Simply complete your details below and return the entire page to the address below. You don't even need a stamp!

YES Please send me 2 free Intrigue books and a surprise gift. I understand that unless you hear from me, I will receive 5 superb new stories every month, including two 2-in-1 books priced at £5.30 each and a single book priced at £3.30, postage and packing free. I am under no obligation to purchase any books and may cancel my subscription at any time. The free books and gift will be mine to keep in any case.

Ms/Mrs/Miss/Mr _____ Initials _____

_____

Surname _____

Address _____

_____

_____ Postcode _____

E-mail _____

Send this whole page to: Mills & Boon Book Club, Free Book Offer, FREEPOST NAT 10298, Richmond, TW9 1BR.